AT THE VANISHING POINT

The two astronauts continued their exploration of the derelict spaceship. Bulgakov shut off the laser and moved the cut-away metal disk, letting it drift past. Inside was a nightmare.

Back on the *Phoenix*, Harris saw bodies as they floated toward the camera's eye, clearly humanoid, but just as clearly *wrong*. He caught a glimpse of a misshapen, mummified face, and then the screen was suddenly washed clean with a rush of bright static.

"Oh, my god, *no*!" Coles's voice burst over the loudspeaker.

In the big display in the center of the bridge, the fist-size shape of the shuttle floated alone.

The alien ship was gone.

By John Blair
Published by Ballantine Books:

A LANDSCAPE OF DARKNESS

BRIGHT ANGEL

BRIGHT ANGEL

John Blair

DEL REY

A Del Rey Book

BALLANTINE BOOKS · NEW YORK

A Del Rey Book
Published by Ballantine Books

Library of Congress Catalog Card Number: 91-92190

ISBN 0-345-37058-9

Manufactured in the United States of America

First Edition: January 1992

Cover Art by Vincent Di Fate

For Sandy and James

Hath the rain a father? or who hath begotten
  the drops of dew?
Out of whose womb came the ice? and the hoary
  frost of heaven, who hath gendered it?
The waters are hid as with a stone, and the
  face of the deep is frozen.

JOB 38:28–30

TABLE OF CONTENTS

1

THE RETURN

CHAPTER ONE

The ice went on forever.

The wind gusted and howled around him, picking up snow and draping it like a curtain across the horizon. He surveyed his surroundings, trying to memorize the few features still distinctive under the mantle of white.

When the whiteout was complete, he knew, he would be lost unless he could freeze enough of the sparse details of the landscape in his mind. He glanced up at 61 Cygni B, the near sun, glowing faintly through the swirling clouds and snow. 61 Cygni A, dimmer and farther away, was already completely hidden. Behind him, the shallow tracks he had left were already being erased by the wind and blowing snow.

The snowshoes were heavy and clumsy and he was bone-achingly tired; he was shaking so steadily, as much from fatigue and despair as the cold, that it was difficult to keep his balance. He focused his eyes on his feet, willing one foot to lift and then the other. The snow matted and clung to the elkhide web of the snowshoes. It was endless, and useless.

He slogged on.

A spot of scarlet against the white caught his eye. He stopped, stared at it for a moment, then knelt painfully down. The blood was dark, clotted. Organ blood, he thought. It's dead by now, somewhere ahead.

A warm spark of hope flickered to life. He started to rise, then checked himself. He hesitated, then dug a hand gloved crudely with sewed animal skin into the snow beneath the clot of red and raised the fistful of bloody ice to his mouth. The blood was not quite frozen; the snow was tough and chewy, flat tasting. He swallowed convulsively.

He stood and continued on.

The blood spots came with more frequency, punctuating the white sheet. In the near distance the tangle of the forest loomed, dead and thick with drifts. He felt a twinge of panic. If the animal had made it into the maze of deadfalls and drifts under the few scattered trees that still stood, he would never find it.

Luck was with him. He found the reindeer lying against a snowdrift just outside the first snow-covered deadfall. Its hide was already covered and almost hidden beneath a powdering of snow. Another ten minutes, he thought, and the carcass would have disappeared under the perfect camouflage of the gathering white blanket. He kicked loose his snowshoes and fell to his knees beside the animal.

He felt for the knife tied with a leather thong around his neck and pulled it up from under the flight suit that was underneath his crazy-quilt robe of hides and furs. He tested its edge with his thumb: it was dull and clumsy—its original function had been to cut parachute cord and seat harnesses in emergencies, and so the cutting edge was placed inconveniently on the top of the blade—but it was serviceable. He cut a ragged gash across the animal's throat and let the blood drain out onto the snow. While he waited for the flow to stop, he ate handful after handful of the blood-soaked slush.

When the blood had drained, he cut a long slit down the reindeer's belly and let the rapidly cooling entrails slide out. He luxuriated for a moment in the stinking gust of warmth that rose up from the reindeer's insides. Then he set to work gutting the animal, cutting the windpipe and the rectum and pulling out the mass of organs. The heart and liver he set aside, wrapped in a strip of hide.

When he had finished, he cut small slits underneath the heel tendons on the forelegs, slipped a rawhide cord through the slits, and tied the forelegs together. He strapped the snowshoes to his feet once again, then lifted the front part of the reindeer up from the snow, grunting under the weight. The reindeer was small by Earth standards, about fifty kilos, but it took all the effort he could muster to get the bound forelegs up and over his head and onto his shoulders. He stood for a long minute before moving, breathing hard, fatigue weighing on him much more heavily than the animal's carcass.

The whiteout was complete around him, the horizon disappearing into the snow, the blank wall of the sky blending into the unbroken blanket of snow and ice. He forced his memory to work, and guessed at a direction. He stooped, picked up the bloody package that held the heart and liver, then leaned against the deadweight of his prey, dragging the body across the fresh powder.

He slogged wearily through the deepening snow for more than half an hour, looking for the familiar landmarks that would tell him he was approaching the dome where his wife and the forty-five other surviving members of the expeditionary party waited for his return. Almost all were near death. Sarah had been sick for months, slowly wasting away from malnutrition and the insipid effects of despair. The surviving team leaders, Keel and Jones, were barely alive, Keel suffering from a lingering pneumonia and Jones . . . He forced his mind away from Jones, from the slack face and empty eyes that the overdose of barbiturates had left instead of the easy, clean death he had tried for.

The food he was bringing back was their last hope. Without it they would all die. Somewhere in the back of his mind, a dark voice nagged, saying it was already too late.

The wind, which had dropped off, roared suddenly back to life and tried to knock him off his feet, very nearly succeeding. The reindeer's carcass had frozen and was stiff and clumsy, banging against his back and digging into the snow as he trudged on. The thought of Jones made him remember Jones's wife, Ann, and the rest of the crew of settlers who had come through sixteen years and nearly as many light-years to the planet they had named Comfort. The name wasn't even sad or funny anymore; he was beyond feeling a sensation as subtle as irony.

Ann had died the second month after planetfall, of exposure. She had been hysterical for most of the time they had been on Comfort. Jones had been scavenging for fuel when she had wandered away from the dome into the endless snow.

The others had followed her soon after; Parkinson and his wife—he searched his mind for her name, disturbed that he had forgotten; then he remembered, *June*—had overdosed, as Jones had tried to do. They had lost nearly a hundred that way. More than a dozen had never returned from hunting forays. Others had died of sickness. And so it went.

The wind gusted into his face and he stumbled and recovered; then another gust, loaded with sharp flakes of ice, shoved hard against him from the side and he fell to his knees. The thong with which he had tied the reindeer's forelegs together dug into his throat and he choked; panicking, he tried to twist his head out from between the animal's hocks. After a long moment he managed to control his panic and stopped, gasping desperately for breath. Forcing himself to be calm, to move slowly, he pried the reindeer's stiffened forelegs apart and lifted them above his head.

He rested on his knees before the frozen carcass and looked out into the empty, shifting whiteness. He slowly became conscious that he was shaking, the sweat from his efforts going cold under his hides. He forced himself to his feet and turned in a slow, swaying circle. He was lost. The temperature was falling rapidly without the meager warmth from Comfort's two suns, hidden by the strengthening storm.

He made a quick decision and moved toward a chest-high drift piled against an outcropping of stone. He dug down into the snow with his hands until he had hollowed out a space big enough for his body. He waited a moment before crawling in, hoping for inspiration, some miraculous revelation.

Then he slipped into the hole he had dug and pushed snow up above himself to seal it.

The storm raged over his head, muffled and distant. He imagined he could hear in its voice a note of sorrow.

Two hundred seventy-five people. Dead. One hundred twenty-four women. One hundred forty-six men. Almost sixty had died the first winter, the rest since. Cold, starvation, despair.

Summer had been a wan, brief time of thaw; too brief, they had discovered, for even the hardy, hybrid crops they had tried to grow. Some few of the animal species they had introduced had survived. The rest had died with the first of the snows that never seemed to end.

He thought of Sarah. He had married her two years before the Cygni expedition had left Earth's orbit. Their first bond had been one of adventure: colonists to the stars. He had married her because every heterosexual male colonist had to have a wife, and because she was on a list—as was he—that certified her as solid genetic stock. Later, he had discovered he loved her. And he had brought her to paradise.

Paradise. They had come to find Eden.

What they had found instead was Dante's lowest hell, an endless landscape of ice.

He prayed to the formless god of his ancestors. Fervently, he prayed for intercession, for salvation.

Soon he slept.

James Harris dreamed. Above him the storm moaned to itself, unheard. In his dreams he drifted through memory. He remembered how much he had hoped, how much Sarah had hoped. He dreamed of the terrible, bitter cold that held that hope in its frozen grip. He dreamed of Sarah dead, forever billions of miles from home. In his sleep, he wept.

Around him the packed snow acted as insulator and kept his body temperature up for hours. But slowly the warmth seeped away and his heart rate slowed. His dreams grew sluggish and surreal as the hypothermia spread through him. He became aware of a light, growing brighter. Something in it beckoned to him; he felt drawn.

He felt himself, somehow, moving toward it. With the surprising suddenness of an indrawn breath, he fell into the light, and it took him up.

Then darkness washed over him and he stopped dreaming.

CHAPTER TWO

Antarctica—March 16, 2063

The short summer had dissolved into the frenzied restlessness of the polar winds, which was the reason for the hurry of Specialist Five Jenkins. He scuttled across the narrow compound, head down against his chest to keep the biting flakes of ice from his face.

He was cursing under his breath as he walked. He had taken this assignment in the first place because of the adventure it entailed, the exotic climate and the nice piece of change he would pocket when his tour was up, what with the risk pay that would be added to his accumulated salary. He hadn't bargained for the necessity of venturing into the brutal cold to patch fuel bladders made brittle by the antarctic winter.

Across the flight line, two huge transports and a smaller reconnaissance VTOL stood like massive, awkward birds tied by the wings to anchors set deep in the permanent ice, ice more than five kilometers thick beneath the station. Or maybe the planes were more like the giant pterodactyls, he thought, frozen in place by the ice age that had killed them off.

Beyond the aircraft, reality disappeared into a white, opaque blur. When the wind picked up here, the horizon was the first thing to go. More than one pilot had died on the ice that surrounded the base for hundreds of square miles simply because the wind and blinding snow kept him from being able to distinguish ground from sky.

He lifted his head to orient himself toward the mechanic's shack where the tools he would need—patching material and a low-wattage hand laser—were stored. As he did so, something caught his eye. For a full minute or more he stood staring, heedless of the wind chafing his bare cheeks and forehead, trying to force his eyes to resolve the form he saw in the near distance, a moving flake of black against the blank wall of white. He squinted, barely able to make out arms and legs and a hooded head.

From out of the blasted wilderness of snow and ice that lay beyond the base there walked—or rather stumbled, swaying, falling to its knees and then recovering—the unmistakable figure of a man.

"Christ," Jenkins whispered. He brushed a gloved hand absently across his eyes.

Still two or three hundred meters away from the base's outer perimeter the figure collapsed. Jenkins moved toward it, broke into a trot and then a run. As he ran, he clawed at the stamp-size two-way radio sewn into the thick material of his parka's collar.

"Base Op, Base Op. Spec Five Jenkins. I'm outside. Send out a corpsman. *Quick.* North of the flight line."

A laconic voice came back. "Say again, Jenkins. Are you screwing around out there again? The major'll have your ass."

"Shove it, Bernie. Just get a doc out here, *now.*"

The man lay unmoving in the snow and at first Jenkins thought he was dead. He pulled aside the rank patchwork cape of hides and furs and found a pulse, shallow and fast, but there. He also found military dog tags, on a chain around his neck. He flipped them over and read, *Harris, James W, USAF.*

A hand grabbed him by the wrist and he jumped, dropping the tags. He stared down into a face wild with fear and disorientation. He tried to stand up, but the hand held him down.

"Who are you?" The man's voice was hoarse, strained.

"Jenkins, Ronald Jenkins," he answered. Then he added as an afterthought, "Spec Five. United Nations Coalition Forces."

The man seemed dazed. His eyes wandered from Jenkins for an instant, off into the white distance over his shoulder. Then they snapped back to Jenkins and focused.

"Where am I?"

"Amundsen-Scott Station, Antarctica. The South Pole. We're Americans."

"Earth?"

Jenkins stared at the man for a long moment, uncomprehending. "Yeah, Earth. Where the hell else?"

Florida—April 9, 2063

The sun broke across the waves like shards of bright glass, and Hugh Carney squinted through the Plexiglas window of the VTOL shuttle as it settled onto the concrete pad set into the grass a thousand meters or so from the glittering Atlantic.

A breath of hot, salty air blew back into the cabin as one of the stewards unsealed a door. He inhaled deeply the unfamiliar smell of tarmac and ocean. It had been eighteen years since he had been to the cape. It seemed a lifetime, another world.

As he stepped down from the plane onto the ramp, the heat and sunshine struck him like a damp, open palm. He felt the sweat pop out on his forehead and begin to soak the collar of his shirt. A man wearing dark glasses and a nondescript suit waited at the bottom of the ramp and took his briefcase from him.

"Welcome to the cape. Climate here must be a change for you."

"Yes. It's . . . sticky." Hot he was used to. For the last fifteen years he had lived in the arid heat of the Texas hill country. But he had forgotten what it felt like to *bathe* in the air you breathed. He hated Florida, had always hated it, from the plastic flamingoes to the never-ending filled-in-swamp acres of retirement villas that rolled away for miles under the plane's wing as it flew across the peninsula from the gulf side to the Atlantic. But most of all he hated the humidity and every Floridian's habit of making it the favored topic of conversation.

"A car is waiting, doctor. I know the sun is a little hard to take at first. We'll try to keep exposure to a minimum." The man's smile was pleasant but Carney found it irritating. He didn't like people who went out of their way to be pleasant, as a rule. They generally were either brainless or wanted something or both. He followed the man off the landing pad toward the small, cinder-block building that served as a terminal. Behind them the sound of the shuttle's engines began to build in pitch. He turned to watch as the plane lifted vertically off the tarmac, slowly rising to about thirty meters. Then the two engines tilted forward and the plane dipped and roared off across the beach and over the ocean.

His escort held open the door to a large, German-made sedan for him. The car was new and well appointed; Carney noted its make with a touch of displeasure. Almost every car on the road these days was produced somewhere in Asia by one of the partnerships that had formed half a century before between the United Republic of Germany and various Asian—primarily Japanese—companies. It was one of his pet peeves; generally, if he couldn't get a bus or a shuttle—both still American made—he generally didn't go. Nationalism was passé, and Carney knew even the few friends he still had—that is, those that were still alive—considered him a touch too eccentric. Personally, he didn't give a damn if that common-market nonsense about the near dissolution of partisan political identities that the politicians loved to go on about was a given fact or not; he had bought American for more than sixty years, since the first bat and ball he had purchased on his own when he was eight, and he wasn't about to change now. But sometimes, one had to put personal preferences aside.

Carney stepped into the cool luxury of the car and the door eased itself shut with a gasp. His escort walked around to the far side and slid into a seat that faced Carney at an angle; Carney had hoped the man would take the seat beside him and they could thereby avoid each other's eyes and the temptation toward conversation, but he realized with a mental sigh that it was not to be.

The fellow subvocalized an instruction to the car's computer and settled back. The car put itself into motion, the Chernetsky motor humming smoothly. "Must be a hell of change for you, this heat."

"We've already done weather," Carney answered shortly. The air-conditioning blew a musty coolness into his face. He turned his head gratefully, letting the air dry the perspiration under his collar.

The man didn't even change expression. "Most people find this weather quite a shock, for April. Cocoa is plenty hot this year. The beaches are covered with college students."

He nodded noncommittally. He was too tired to enjoy small talk, though normally he might appreciate the opportunity to be crusty to someone paid to be polite and take it. He had been in flight for more than twenty hours, first on a commercial jet from Gorky, where he had been involved in a genetic-longevity project sponsored by some international consortium or another—he often failed to pay attention to details outside his own work—then a military flight from a U.N. base in Germany, and finally the VTOL shuttle to Florida.

The man was quiet for a minute, and then he spoke again. "We'll be at the hospital in about five minutes."

"Good." He lay his head against the seat back and closed his eyes, signaling, he hoped, the end of conversation. He noticed for the first time how dry his eyes were and how much they burned. He watched the random patterns that etched themselves onto the backs of his eyelids and for a moment was back in San Antonio, where he had been born. He remembered a game he had played with his brother, late at night when they were supposed to be asleep. They would take turns pressing their closed eyelids with their thumbs and then announcing what colors and shapes they could see in the patterns. The point of the game was to guess what the other saw, to send each other silent messages in the dark. He seemed to remember that sometimes it had worked.

His brother had been dead for more than fifty years, killed by a genetically altered virus that had wiped out most of the population of Argentina, the country that had altered it for a reason lost in the chaos of its accidental release. Carl had been a member of the UN forces who had built the quarantine wall across Panama. The memory was a hard one; it was the reason he had become a physician.

The car eased to a gentle stop and chimed to let them know it had reached its programmed destination. The door sighed open and Carney pulled himself up and out with some effort, squinting against the harsh glare of the sunlight on concrete. His escort hurried around the car to offer a hand and Carney ignored it.

"Just show me where to go, son."

The driver led him to a door set into what seemed to be a very large, concrete pillbox, a windowless, squat structure set into the side of the larger base hospital building.

After the stunning glare of the hot parking lot, the inside of the building was soothingly dim and cool. A guard waited at a desk beyond the foyer; he checked his ID, then made him stare into a device that scanned the patterns on the back of his retina. He wondered for a fleeting instant if the machine could somehow see the same brilliant patterns that he and his brother had

traded in the dark so long ago, then brushed the fantasy aside
and forgot it.

"Welcome to the cape, doctor."

"Thanks. Someone want to take me to where I'm supposed
to go?"

"Yes, sir," the young guard answered. "Someone'll be down
shortly." He turned away and went back to the task he had been
at when Carney had walked in, shuffling papers between white-
gloved fingers.

His prison was carpeted and comfortable, but it was a prison,
nonetheless. He realized, without surprise, that that fact didn't
bother him. He was beyond caring about anything so incidental
as how he was treated. If there were a sure way to kill himself
available to him, he knew with a deadly certainty that he would
use it.

He rested his head in bandaged hands. The frostbite had been
bad, but they had saved his fingers and toes.

He had lost some flesh on one buttock, they had told him.
From the hours he had lain curled under the snow waiting to
die, three days before. On Comfort. Twelve light-years away.

Insanity. His or theirs, it didn't matter.

Three days. Without food, Sarah would be dead by now. Was
dead. He felt a strange emptiness where the grief should be.

Despair was all he felt; despair and a cold knot of guilt.

He had prayed for salvation and it had been granted him.
Something—God?—had taken him up and brought him home.
Alone.

He should have died. Instead, he had deserted Comfort, and
with it everything he had ever truly cared about.

"Time," he whispered to the room. A digital readout appeared in the air over the bed. *16:30:45* it read. The seconds
flashed by as he stared up at it. After a time it winked out but
he still continued to stare into the empty space where it had
been, his injured hands in his lap.

Because he hadn't told it *off*, the room sensed the motion
when he finally stirred and reinstated the readout: *17:28:30*. He
blinked, feeling a strange awareness drain away from him.

He stared at the numbers. Almost an hour.

"What is happening to me?" Even his own voice sounded
strange. Who am I asking? he wondered.

Myself.

But no answer was forthcoming. The room was empty and silent. He was alone.

Hugh Carney bit his lip irritably, waiting. It wasn't easy coming back; too many years, too much disappointment. When he had come here for the first time the International Space Administration had been a newborn bureaucracy, still small and open enough not to feel the need for a great deal of secrecy and security. There had certainly been a damn sight less formality about getting in and out of the place.

He had gotten involved in the Colonies Project himself more or less through the back door, friends pulling strings for the most part. Not the way he would have liked to have done things, but expedient nonetheless.

He had been a navy doctor during the Great Standoff of the thirties, when Russo-American forces had blockaded the coast of China after the last of their great purges had left militant extremists in charge of the country's ICBMs. A string of underwater launching platforms had been put in place in the narrow corridor between Taiwan and the mainland by the Joint Defense Command of the Soviet-American bloc.

The silos themselves were a very basic form of nuclear submarine. The subs were designed to very quietly, very slowly, move into an enemy's coastal waters. Then they sunk to the bottom and simply sat there, very quietly, the next thing to invisible, capable of launching missiles that were only seconds away from their targets, far too close to be countered. Carney's job had been to help select crews for these platforms, men and women who could bear the pressures of months of silence in quarters that allowed for only four square meters of space per crewman.

Before he had fallen victim to the reinstatement of selective service during the China crisis, he had been doing an internship in epidemiology at Johns Hopkins. During the last two years of the Great Standoff, the military, reasoning, he supposed, that an M.D. is an M.D., put him in charge of a group of physicians and psychologists who were responsible for weeding out those likely to be physically or psychologically unfit for duty aboard the sunken missile platforms.

The job was not easy; the candidates were selected from men

and women who had served more than a year each as sailors on submarines. That alone marked them as being more tolerant of close quarters and strict self-discipline than most. A platform tour was six months, sometimes longer, in duration. That meant six months of sponge baths—and no privacy for those—and the strictest noise discipline.

The installations' power plants were thickly shielded to prevent satellite detection of the reactors' thermal "footprints." The hulls were titanium, and therefore resisted identification by the minute disturbance an iron hull might create in Earth's magnetic field. The only reliable ways the platforms might be detected were either by direct echo sounding—and that was impractical, given the amount of ocean floor there was to search—or detection by passive sonar.

The crews could therefore never speak above a low whisper, had to consciously think through every motion before they made it to avoid creating sounds, had to, in effect, completely stifle any expression of emotion or anxiety. There was also very little opportunity for exercise or other physical relief. It was terribly demanding duty, and it required men and women with extremely resilient physical makeups and ego-structures.

Carney had become very good at his job. He had a natural aptitude for judging people, and only one of the dozens of missile platforms were ever compromised during the twelve years of the Great Standoff because of crew failure. The four members of that crew had killed each other before they could be extracted. Loudly. The Chinese had sonar buoys peppering the water's surface; they quickly found the installation and scuttled it soon after.

Only two other crews were lost during the Standoff, neither at the fault of the crew members. Both were found by Chinese patrol boats with echo sounders and both were victims of "accidents" of which the Chinese subsequently denied any involvement or knowledge.

It was a good record. Carney had made a strong reputation during those years; more important, perhaps, he had made strong friends.

When the Cygni probe's message had returned with its promise of a new Eden in the sky, he started making preparations. He knew he wouldn't be allowed to go—he was already almost ten years too old. But he was damned well going to be involved.

The stars. He had dreamed about them his entire life. Now, when they were within mankind's grasp, he was a few years— less than a heartbeat, an eyeblink in cosmic time—too old. But he had never let the awful irony keep him away. By the time the Cygni expedition was announced, he had already insinuated himself into its hierarchy.

When the ISA was formed, he was on its board of governors. When the project itself began, he was in charge of crew selection and training, as well as a consultant on the engineering aspects of the spacecraft itself; it was basically just a biospace—the drive and its strange physics were handled by people who knew what they were doing.

And then he had found a way to go. Almost. Vicariously. Just close enough that he felt, somehow, he would live on, billions of kilometers away, among the stars.

Carney stood fidgeting in front of the marine guard's desk. So far as he could tell from where he stood, the building was empty except for himself and the guard. Corridors led off to the left and right, gleaming in ivory tile and white acoustic paneling. There was no sound except the quiet rasp of paper and the distant sough of air-conditioning.

"Commander Carney."

"Commander? No one's called me commander in a cat's life."

"Sorry." The man was young, gleaming in navy whites. He strode up to Carney, his heels clicking rhythmically on the tile. Carney thought momentarily of arctic camouflage, white on white. The newcomer held out his hand and Carney took it.

"Dr. Carney, I'm Jake Riser. Lieutenant, Junior Grade. I'm to take you down to the director's office. They're waiting for you there. You're the last one to arrive."

"Then lead on, son. I'm not getting any younger."

"Yes, sir."

They walked for a distance through the cool, subterranean distances of the building.

"Last one to arrive for what?" Carney asked abruptly.

"I'm not free to say, sir. I'm sure they'll fill you in when we get there."

It was the answer he'd expected, but he still felt irked. They walked the remainder of the way in silence.

They arrived at a paneled door and the lieutenant knocked, then opened the door without waiting for an answer.

The room beyond was large and dark paneled. The blinds were drawn across the windows behind the large desk, but enough light filtered through that Carney could see four men seated in leather chairs arranged in a semicircle to one side of the desk. All four watched Carney.

"Gentlemen," the lieutenant said, and made his exit through the same door he and Carney had just come through.

"Gentlemen," Carney echoed. "What the hell are we doing here?" He recognized two of the seated men. He'd worked with both during the Cygni project. The other two were strangers. One looked as if he should be wearing a lab coat, probably an ISA staff scientist of some sort, Carney guessed. The other was a solid, well-dressed man who held a pipe in one hand. A thin curl of smoke rose from its bowl.

The man with the pipe gestured for him to sit. Carney did so, settling into one of the comfortable, overstuffed chairs. He nodded to his old comrades, waited for someone to speak.

"Dr. Carney," the pipe smoker began, "I'm Richard Moore, acting director of the International Space Project." He gestured with the pipe to the man who seemed to need a lab coat. "This is Dr. Douglas Arnault; he's head of our biomed section. You know David Spears and Dr. Cousins."

Carney leaned forward. "I do. And I know of you. I've heard you do a good job here." That *wasn't* what he'd heard, and the lie made his jaw ache. "So I repeat, why am I here? And what the hell is this about?"

"Dr. Cousins told me you tended to be direct."

Carney looked over at the older man seated to the director's right. Bill Cousins, Carney thought, was looking old. And tired. Cousins kept his glance lowered, refusing to meet Carney's eyes. Shame? Carney wondered. If so, why? Or was the man hiding something?

"Dr. Cousins is right," Carney said gruffly.

"I'll try to be just as direct then. The Cygni colony has failed."

"Jesus, Dick!" The fourth man, Spears, sat up in his chair. Carney remembered little about him, just that he had categorized him at the time in his mind under "family man." He had never liked to work past hours, preferring to spend his off time coaching Little League and serving on PTA committees. Carney suddenly remembered that Spears was a psychologist.

"I know, I *know*!" Moore waved a hand impatiently. He addressed Carney again. "Look, doctor, I don't know of a better way to do this—" He cast a meaningful glance at Spears. "—so against advice, I'm just going to lay all this on the line."

Carney cleared his throat. The antagonism he had felt was gone. It had been replaced by an emotion disturbingly like fear.

"They're dead? How do you know?"

"All dead except your son. He's come back."

Carney felt a dizzying sense of dislocation. *Come back?* "My *son*? What the hell are you talking about? How does someone come back from twelve light-years out in space?" He turned to Cousins. "Bill, what is this shit?"

Cousins looked up, finally met Carney's eye. "It's the truth, Hugh. He's back. Alive. And I'll be damned if we know how."

"Back?" Carney asked. He took a deep breath, tried to clear his head.

Spears stood up from his chair, making a soothing gesture with his hands. "Hugh, I know this is a lot to take in all at once—"

Carney ignored him. He stared at Cousins. "Tell me, slowly, what this is all about."

Cousins shrugged. "I'm just here for old times' sake, Hugh. At least, that's the impression I've been getting since they brought me here."

He turned to Moore.

The director blew out his breath between his teeth. "You now know just about everything we do. The Cygni expedition left Earth orbit approximately seventeen years ago, accelerating at one-and-one-half gravities for the Cygni star system. James Harris—your son—was on board, along with nearly three hundred others. Two days ago James Harris walked out of a snowstorm about a klick from the South Pole."

"The *South Pole*? *Our* South Pole?"

"None other. A crewman at the UN research station there found him, walking across the ice. Dressed in deer skins."

"Deer skins. What is this, a bad joke?"

"No, he's serious, Hugh. Jim is back. We don't know why, and we don't know how, but he's back." Spears had taken his seat again, but he still made patting motions with his hands as if he were trying to settle Hugh's fears by pushing them back down into him, from a distance.

Carney felt a sudden surge of wrath. He was being shoved hard in a direction he discovered he was unwilling to take. He turned on Spears. "What do you have to do with this? Are you here for *me*, you son of a bitch? You think I'm going to fly to pieces and you're going to try to patch me back up?"

Spears weathered the tirade and managed a smile; he was in familiar territory, dealing with a patient's anger. "Hugh, I'm part of the permanent staff here, now. I work for the ISA. I've seen Jim. I've talked to him. I'm just trying to keep things on an even keel."

"By things, you mean me? I don't need a shrink." He gestured to include Cousins and Moore. "I'm starting to think it's the bunch of you, you're the ones who need your goddamned heads examined."

"I'm not a shrink, Hugh. I'm not even a psychiatrist—"

Moore broke in impatiently. "Gentlemen, this is all beside the point. Dr. Carney, you asked me why you were here. The short answer is that we don't begin to understand this. We're hoping you could help, maybe elicit something from your son we haven't been able to uncover."

"Then you've dragged me out here for nothing. I don't know that boy any better than the rest of you. If you'd made the effort to check that dossier you've got on me, you'd know I didn't raise him, never really even saw him until he was in his midtwenties."

"We'd still like you to try."

Carney glared. "What is it you want me to ask him? Exactly?"

Moore didn't hesitate. "How he got back. It's essential we know the mechanism for his return. That man should be eleven-some-odd light-years from here. It's physically impossible that he isn't."

Carney gritted his teeth. He could never stand the phrase "physically impossible," particularly when the evidence that "it" clearly was possible very probably sat in a room somewhere in that very building.

"How certain are you that it's actually him?"

Arnault answered. "DNA match. That's either him or a clone of him."

"Could it be a clone? Could the Chinese or the United Arab Republics have done this to embarrass us?" Spears asked.

Arnault started to answer and Cousins broke in impatiently. "No, dammit, Spears. Don't be a fool if you can help it. The technology doesn't exist. Sure, we could make a clone. We could reproduce his body, from a skin cell, perhaps, but the Chinese or the Arabs can't, and even if they could, no one can make a clone *function*. No one can make it speak, or think, or react any more than the simplest organisms capable of sensation can react. This man thinks, feels, has memories. I've seen the transcripts from his debriefings. These are things no one could give a cloned body. Except maybe God, if he exists and if he cared to make us a miracle."

He sat back in his chair again. "Still, it would be interesting," he added, "to know whether the Arabs or the Chinese knew about this."

"Count on it," Moore said. "They are fully informed and wholly cognizant of our dilemma. Keeping things under wraps has always been a problem when the Antarctic Research Groups are involved. Scientists don't like to keep secrets, unfortunately. Especially not those fellows; hardship tours make for a tight community. It'll be on the evening news inside of a week—Tehran probably had it before we did."

Carney thought it oddly appropriate that this man would make rough commentary on the scientific community to three men who were, at least ostensibly, scientists themselves. Moore was a bureaucrat, an especially single-visioned beast.

"What are you going to do?" Carney asked quietly.

Moore looked at the pipe in his hand, turning it, watching the wisp of smoke rise. "Nothing. File it. Forget it. Deny the news reports. Ignore the questions. In a few weeks it'll blow over. Our investigation of the incident ended before it started. There's no physical evidence of what happened, and Harris isn't talking, at least not to us. If he doesn't talk to you, it's over. And I don't think he will."

"And what happens to my boy? Do you file him, too?"

Moore blew out his cheeks, glanced at Spears. "In a way of speaking, yes. Interstellar Settlement is still an ongoing program. We don't need the bad press. New identity, new job. Someplace without a lot of exposure.''

"Then why do you need me here?"

Spears answered. ''We don't, really. I thought you might want to be here, when he was released from observation. The director agreed. His wife is dead, and his friends. He's in pretty rough shape.'' Spears shrugged. ''You're his father.''

Carney sighed, rubbed his forehead with the palm of his hand.

"Yes," he said simply, "I'm his father."

''. . . whereas in normal space the speed of light is as fast as things can go, in adjacent realities—in what the physicists euphemistically call *imaginary* space—it is as *slow* as they can move. Using the same zero-point effect that provides us with power here on Earth, the Chernetsky drive creates an energy field that exists both in normal space and imaginary space. Through some process which we don't really understand, the field actually surrenders energy to the tachyon particles in imaginary space and this gives the drive, which still exists in normal space, its momentum. The cargo and passenger pods are pulled along several kilometers behind the drive itself, trailing the drive in order to take advantage of the zone directly behind it that is unaffected by the device's radiation. The Chernetsky drive creates waves of energy around itself; these waves of energy travel laterally out from the drive—the only protected areas are directly ahead and behind of the drive itself. As you know, when one of these engines is fired, spectacular auroral displays are seen across the entire northern hemisphere as the energy interacts with the Earth's atmosphere.

''An added bonus is that the drive acts as a shield for the ship itself; any particle which strikes the field, and all of the free hydrogen that permeates space, is converted instantly to energy, which is transferred to the tachyons in the alternate reality, slowing them down. It's all about twice as complicated as it sounds.''

The young man giving the lecture spoke confidently, his voice carrying without amplification to the group of eight or ten people who sat listening restlessly in the auditorium's first three rows. Carney sat alone in the sixth. The audience was composed of the sort of politicos and intelligence community sorts who tended to flock to interesting and secret happenings, getting their kicks out of flashing credentials and making themselves as visible as possible.

Even spies and politicians love a disaster, basking in the excitement and the tragedy, Carney thought. He'd pushed past the guard at the door to gain entrance to the auditorium, his ID badge, stamped VIP, keeping the young marine from pushing back.

Hell, he thought, especially spies and politicians.

He'd come in because he'd heard the speaker's voice and he couldn't bear the idea of the empty room in the VIP visitor's quarters he'd been assigned. He needed the solid comfort of people, the faceless community of a crowd.

The speaker droned on. "What's important is the effect this has, which is nearly unlimited acceleration. For reasons which have to do with the accretion of mass with momentum, a starship's maximum velocity is about .75 of the speed of light—fast enough to make the trip to 61 Cygni in about sixteen years, including the time it takes for acceleration and deceleration. Chernetsky probes were actually built and sent to five likely sunlike stars within twenty light-years of us. The first probe to send back what it had found was to Epsilon Eridani; it reported only gas giants orbiting the star. Two years later the 61 Cygni probe reported an Earth-like planet with the right mix of gases and a comfortable average temperature at the equatorial land mass of twenty-five degrees Celsius. Hence the Cygni expedition. The *Constellation*, built primarily by the Soviet Union and the United States but contributed to by all United Nations countries, left Earth orbit approximately sixteen years ago. The microwave transmission it sent upon landing should reach us in another nine years."

The speaker paused, seeming to anticipate questions. None were forthcoming. "Which still leaves unanswered the essential question . . ."

Carney squeezed his eyes shut, tried to block out the voice. It was all too much, all too tragic. He was riddled through with heartsickness. He felt old. A line from a poem he had read long ago, when he was a boy, flashed through his mind: *An aged man is but a paltry thing, a ragged coat upon a stick.*

He looked up, saw the young man on the stage spread his

hands, smile, make a point. He thought about another young man who had looked at him—looked *through* him—that morning and told him *go to hell, old man.*

I'm his father, Carney thought helplessly, I'm his father, and I'm the one who sent him out there.

He put his head in his hands and wept.

2

THE ICE

CHAPTER THREE

A cold wind blew ice and snow along the Avenue Changan Jie, making Song Lan pull her coat collar closer around her face. The motion was mostly unconscious; she walked with her eyes on the icy pavement, her mind preoccupied with her own frustrations.

It bothered her a great deal that her own work was going begging while she helped compile and sort through a century of observational data for what she—and the vast majority of her colleagues—considered to be a "wild-goose chase." The strange-sounding metaphor brought an even stranger image to her mind, herself in some clumsy outfit—hip boots maybe— chasing some large, wild bird she had no hope of catching. The phrase, an Americanism, was a popular one around the scientific community at Beijing University, and it had seemed particularly appropriate to the job they had given her. Still, even her own work seemed insignificant in light of the disaster that she had been told six months before was threatening, like the dragons of myth, to destroy the People's Republic of China.

Since then, anything she could do had seemed desperate and useless. Her work, especially, seemed irrelevant. Radio astronomy was one of the sciences barely tolerated by the committees—pure science of any kind was always slightly suspect, even the kinds as innocuous as her own.

The stars! It shamed her that she had never so much as seen them with her own eyes, that incredible cold wash of lights her adoptive mother had spoken of so often. In moving from her home in the Catacombs to the laboratories in the subbasements of the university, she only caught glimpses of the night sky,

27

obscured by the ambient light of the city. And the openness of the sky still terrified her; she shuddered even now to think of it.

Her work was done through computer linkups with giant radio telescopes built in craters on two of the large Trojan asteroids following Jupiter's orbit in that giant planet's Lagrangian points. Only occasionally was the university allowed access to this data, and then only parts of it, at the whim of the committees or of the United Nations, who owned the telescopes.

Still, she had adored the stars since she was a child, though she had adored them in the abstract. The idea of actually *being* in space sent agoraphobic chills up her spine.

Of late, though, she had come across her own theory about what was happening to the republic—and, she assumed, the rest of the world. That morning she had just finished a program to search the massive memory of the institute's mainframe computer to correlate certain data.

The meteorologists and geophysicists of the United Nations Global Atmospheric Research Program had all along seemed to be doing the most promising work, searching for terrestrial answers to a terrestrial problem—and they had been very open with their data, despite the tension that still existed between the People's Republic and the United Nations Governing Coalition. So she had dropped the series of computer analyses she had been doing for weeks as her official assignment—studying historic fluctuations of solar radiation and their relationship to changes in temperature averages—and had begun to look for other astronomical events in the Earth's neighborhood: planetary changes, comets and asteroids.

Her program might possibly suggest some anomaly no one had yet noticed, a correlation between a "near-miss" asteroid in a fly-by orbit, or maybe a comet's tail through which the planet had passed, with changes in average temperatures, the unusual severity of certain storm fronts, spring floods on rivers fed by mountain chains, the number of stripes on a specific hybrid of cantaloupe, fluctuations in the World Stock Exchange—anything out of the ordinary that might give her a starting point on the road to discovering what was causing what her colleagues referred to as the "climatic crisis." It was farfetched enough to be almost silly, she knew, but it was exiting simply because it was *new*, because she saw a possibility in the idea that all the work she had done to date had lacked.

She reached the streetcar line and hurried up the wooden steps, being careful to avoid the patchy ice that rimed the boards. Instead of joining the queue waiting for the next car, she walked in the gravel along the tracks the short distance to the broad, massive building that housed the Physical Sciences wing of Beijing University.

The building was a twentieth-century structure alive with stretches of opaque glass windows and flourishes of poured concrete; in a different way, it had the same overdone charm of the oldest buildings of Hong Kong. The excesses of the West had found a foothold here in the last century, though now those influences had been thoroughly and violently purged.

The main doors were huge, made of glass and tarnished brass that gave the impression of enormous solidity and weight. So far as she knew, they had been locked shut for decades. Everyone at the facility used the automatic doors set into the concrete of the front facade several meters to one side. The electronic sentry at the door recognized her vocal patterns when she spoke to it and let her in, the tinted Plexiglas sliding into its recess with a pneumatic gasp of air.

The building was quiet—it almost always was—yet still gave her the impression she had come to associate with it of intense and somehow hidden activity. An old-fashioned elevator opened noisily and took her to the third floor, where the small cubicle given over to her and her work was located.

As she had expected, there was an envelope waiting for her on her desk. She opened the envelope, took the data card from its sleeve, and fed it into the reader slot in her desktop. A display glowed to life, hovering over the translucent veneer of the desktop and she asked it to display what the mainframe had found.

"Event correlations?" she murmured.

The computer took a moment to answer, then spelled out in blocky letters that showed white against a projected background:

CORRELATIONS NOTED: 33,116. *"Display?"* a musical voice asked.

"No. How many correlations in the top one-fifth of one percent of probability?"

66. *"Display?"*

"Yes."

Information began to scroll across the dark square the computer had projected above itself. The first two possibilities the computer had found were disappointments, obvious coincidences that she dismissed out of hand.

The third entry made her hair stand on end.

Her first thought was to search out one of her colleagues to share her discovery. But she hesitated.

She read once again the information on the computer screen, her mind racing, considering the possible importance of what she had found.

She knew what she *should* do. Her colleagues would mouth commonplaces about her duty to the people, to the collective homeland; her superiors would take what she had found to their superiors—and what she had discovered would disappear forever in the maze of administrators and functionaries that was the bureaucracy of China's committees.

And what she had found was much too important to be lost in that maze.

The thoughts that crossed her mind, the actions she began to contemplate, were too frightening. She leapt to her feet and grabbed her coat. Before she left the room she pushed the space on the desk's surface that caused the data card to slide out of its reader and into her hand. She tucked it into a coat pocket.

The lift clanked its way down to the ground floor with excruciating slowness. She caught herself bouncing lightly on her heels, as if that motion could make the lift descend with more dispatch.

She would tell Zhang. Zhang Shan was her colleague at the university; he was only a few years older than she, an able and ambitious physicist. Song had fallen in love with him while she was still a student. Theirs had been a constant, slowly growing love. They had nurtured it platonically through the years of her schooling and her apprenticeship.

Then a year ago they had become lovers. Because she was single, she had lived with her adoptive mother in their small apartments in the Catacombs. So there had been rendezvous in her cramped office, and, later, in his tiny flat when they were sure no one would notice, and she had had to slip out every night to return home before curfew. She had almost been caught during curfew once, and she still trembled, thinking of how the soldiers had passed close by her while she hid in the shadows of a doorway.

Zhang would know what to do. There were people he would know, colleagues he had befriended during the years of his schooling who had traveled abroad, who had made contacts in the West. She had told him already of her research and of the disaster that threatened the republic. He had agreed it was important the people know of these things the government was keeping from them.

The lift's door slid open and she walked quickly out of the door, intent on the new sense of purpose she now felt.

They were waiting for her outside the building, three men in dark coats. When she stepped through the door, one took her wrist and the other two stepped in behind her.

They led her to a car. One opened a rear door while the others pushed her down into the vehicle.

The door closed behind her and locked itself.

Song Lan was too stunned to cry. *How?* How could they have known?

Then she knew. Zhang. She had told no one else.

She sat stiff and unmoving in the seat as the car jerked into motion, the new snow swirling out in a cloud from beneath its turbines.

Florida—October 16, 2069

They were still called "smudge pots," though the cylindrical heaters scattered throughout the grove were powered by the stored energies of a solar array that stood like a stainless-steel sentinel at the top of the rise that marked the right-hand boundary of the grove. The red and blue operating lights of the individual units looked festive shining among the dark shadows of the trees radiating the stored heat of the sun. But they weren't enough; the temperature had been too low for too long.

Frostproof, Florida, was named as it was because historically its low-lying, sandy citrus groves were immune to freezing weather, even when groves farther south were threatened. Jay McLaughlin had lived in the town of Frostproof his entire life. Now he sat alone in the heated cab of his truck and watched his trees die. The five-acre grove was a small part of the five hundred acres of groves his family now owned, but he had come to this one grove in the small hours of this morning because it had been the beginning, the grove his great-grandfather had put in eighty years before with juice-orange seedlings grafted to lemon rootstock.

In the truck's headlights he could see the foundations of the old house, which had burned down half a century before. His grandfather had rebuilt in town, but he had kept the grove because it had been his father's. Freezes were nothing new; every ten years or so a winter was harsh enough to take out a few groves in Ocala or Orlando. But not in Frostproof; very rarely had they lost a tree, never in October. Even when an early freeze took out trees and fruit in nearby Lake Wales or Bartow, his trees had survived.

But not this time. Even with the smudge pots going full blast, the trees were freezing. McLaughlin felt somehow betrayed; something he had grown up believing had been thrown back in his face. The town of Frostproof, Florida, was no longer frostproof.

He put the truck in gear and the fist-size Chernetsky motors whined, the backwash from the turbines throwing up loose sand and sandspurs into the cold morning air.

The Scotia Sea—March 3, 2070

The sea was fast disappearing under a broad sheet of ice. Dennis Calvin watched the pack grow toward him hour by hour, calming the rough seas and swallowing up the open water.

Calvin had been an operations chief on the krill platform Zulu Baker 252 for more than three years now—two years longer than a platform roughneck ordinarily lasted at this kind of duty. Zulutoo, he called her, and she was more to him than just an assignment. She was home.

Zulutoo was an anchored krill-harvesting platform operating in the frigid waters a couple of degrees south of the Antarctic Convergence, the point where the near-freezing antarctic waters met the warmer northern seas, in the middle of what the old mariners called the "howling fifties," the areas south of latitude fifty. And howl they did; every minute of every day the winds and seas lashed and pitched his "tub," a platform half a kilometer square, anchored to the sea bottom more than three kilometers below by dozens of long, thin—but very tough—composite cables. More than half the time the decks, three meters from the water's surface, were awash despite constant adjustments of cable length and ballast by the platform's computers.

That was the reason most personnel on the platforms were strictly short-timers. Few constitutions were up to the constant motion and noise and the abiding cold. Calvin thrived in it, relished the platform's bucking, the wind's omnipresent voice. His great-grandfather had been a whaler out of Grytviken on South Georgia Island in the Scotia Sea more than a century before and he had long believed that he was inheritor to his great-grandfather's blood, to his love for the storm-troubled emptiness of the southern seas.

The whaling station on Grytviken had been shut down in 1964, and whales were no longer hunted by any nation by the turn of the century, not even the recalcitrant Japanese. By then, though, it had been too late for the whales. The hugely majestic blue whales were now extinct; no one had spotted a fin whale in more than fifty years. A still-recovering population of minkes and seis were the only baleen-whale species still extant in the waters around the Antarctic continent. Where before the huge blues and fins had cruised through the frigid waters straining out the shrimplike krill with the laced, bony web of their baleen, harvesting platforms like Zulutoo now preyed on the world's largest single source of natural protein, the tiny *Euphausia superba*, the antarctic krill.

But Zulutoo's seines and pumps were still now. Two days before, Calvin had been forced to shut down the fifty-kilometer-wide funnel of magnetic energies that encouraged the swarms of krill to move into the platform's giant maw. The ice had begun to interfere with the harmonics of the magnetic fields that acted as a herder, then it had started taking the network apart. For two days he and the two other members of Zulutoo's working crew had sat about, in the operations room mostly, watching the ice bear down on them, at first with binoculars, when the ice was only a thin bright line on the dark horizon. Now the ice was no more than a half kilometer from the platform, looming white and gray and awesome. There was a good chance it was going to kill Zulutoo. The monitors that glowed red and blue across his control board told him that the ice pack had already crushed most of the anchored buoys that generated the funnel. As he watched another light flipped from blue to red.

"Son of a *bitch*," he muttered under his breath. In the distance he could hear the ice boom, the sound low-pitched and loud against the continuous general rumbling of the pack and the sharper howl of the westerlies.

The hatch out to the deck area opened and a gust of frigid air bellowed into the room.

"Secure that, damn it!"

A tall figure stooped through the low hatch, closed it and dogged it shut. The man's beard and eyebrows were caked thick with ice under the hood of his parka, making him look at once comical and oddly frightening. "Whoo-ee, boss, it's gettin' *nasty* out there."

"It's news to me, Perez," he said dryly. "The tender okay?" The tender was a crewboat moored in a hollow in the platform's northern end. It was used mostly as an equipment shuttle and for crew changes. It was a seaworthy little boat, thirty-five feet long, with a wide beam and high freeboard to withstand heavy seas, but it was no icebreaker. Calvin knew the time they had left on board the platform as limited to the time it would take the ice pack to reach them.

"Just checked her out, boss. Shipshape and ready to go. Man, it sounds just like a tornado out there, what with the wind and the rumble. Sounds like a goddamned freight train," Perez grumbled. "Wish to hell I'd stayed in Oklahoma. I think I'd *rather* tornadoes."

"Quit your bitching. It won't hurt you." But Calvin was not so sure. No krill platform had ever been caught up in pack ice before, so far as he knew. Hell, he thought sourly, so far as he knew the pack had never, even on the coldest years, made it out past the sixty-third parallel—and that was hundreds of kilometers farther south than the band of krill platforms which formed an arc far above the Antarctic continent between the Sandwich Islands and the vast emptiness of the south Atlantic. The platforms were built to take high seas, but not ice. No one ever dreamed they'd have to stand against the ice. The cables would go without a doubt; the pressure behind the building ice front was far more than they were designed for. The hull probably wouldn't stand the crushing force of the pack, and if it gave in more than a couple of places, the platform was doomed; she would sink wherever the ice left her when it started to break up. More likely, though, she would just be crumpled up on the spot like a beer can in the white, hard fist of the pack: her compacted weight would break the ice and it would let her go here, to sink to the bottom three kilometers below.

"Would you look at that!" Perez was bent over the screen of the high-frequency echo sounder that they used to spot krill swarms so that the funnel's field could be adjusted. Several large swarms were now within range of the funnel, making smeared, black streaks on the echo sounder's readout.

"Now there's a pretty penny that's going right down the tubes. Gonna be a blue Christmas in the Calvin household, I'll bet," Perez gibed. He knew Calvin, as crew chief, got a percentage of the catch profit as an efficiency incentive. Calvin growled under his breath.

"I saw a pod of minkes about a hundred meters northwest. They're eating well, anyhow."

Calvin raised an eyebrow. It was rare indeed to see whales anymore on the open—for the moment, he reflected wryly—water. There just weren't that many of them left.

"They still out there?"

Perez shrugged.

Calvin flipped a mental coin and decided to have a look. There was damned little else he could do until he got his orders from the company dispatcher. And he always got a charge out of watching the huge mammals on the infrequent occasions when they fed near the platforms, knowing that they were every bit as intelligent as he was and a damned sight more graceful.

"I'm going on deck. Watch the board. We're supposed to be getting a call sometime in the next hour telling us what the hell we're to do. Just send 'em a confirmation and come get me if it comes in before I get back."

"Aye, aye, boss."

As he had done a half-dozen times since sunrise—or, rather, what passed for sunrise since the long, dim twilight of winter had settled in—he pulled on his foul-weather gear. This time, for a change, he wasn't going out to check equipment or to fret over the approaching line of ice to the south. If Zulutoo was destined to go under, he wasn't going to miss the last opportunity he might get to watch a pod of whales feeding nearby. A blast of cold air greeted him as he opened the hatch. He stepped through onto the deck, closed the hatch behind him and dogged it shut.

The platform was surprisingly still. After three years on board with only two four-week furloughs a year, he had grown so accustomed to the pitching and rolling that he was distinctly uncomfortable walking on a surface that lay still under his feet. But the seas around the rig were quiet, the only movement long, low swells under the slush of the frazil ice that preceded the pack's front. The water itself looked oily, filmed.

It was dim but not pitch dark; more like the half hour before a normal northern dawn. The wide, flat deck was covered with frozen spray and snow, but there were paths marked with sand out across the glaze so that footing was not too bad so long as one remained aware of the gusting of the wind. Calvin shuffled, head down against the westerly wind, toward the northern edge of the platform. He could have made the same trip inside the platform, out of the weather, but it would have taken twice as long to make his way through the hatches that separated each of the watertight sections of the platform's structure, and he liked to feel the gusting power of the wind against his shoulder, anyway, relishing the bite of the blowing ice through the thick thermal insulation of his parka.

The northern edge was only a bit more than a hundred meters from the deckhouse and he made the waist-high railing in less than ten minutes. He fished around in one of the parka's deep pockets and drew out a compact set of binoculars. He brought them up to his eyes with his right hand, adjusted their brightness and focus with his left. He leaned against the narrow railing for balance: with the binoculars to his eyes, the subtle link between inner ear and vision was distorted and compensating for even the platform's now-gentle roll and pitch became a problem. The railing acted as an efficient brace against falling so long as he kept it jammed against his stomach. He dialed the glasses' light amplification up to maximum and scanned the open sea between himself and the horizon.

The minkes, he knew, would be hard to pick up in the general gray of sea and sky and whale. Lack of contrast camouflaged everything within sight and the light amplification in the binoculars tended to make contrast even worse, bleaching out the darker shades of gray while it made vision in general better. Fifteen minutes later he grunted in satisfaction as he picked up a puff of misty exhaled breath as one of the small, elusive shapes surfaced a few dozen meters out. He leaned forward, watching intently as the rest of the pod surfaced, a half-dozen clouds of mist erupting up to mark their path.

Then he was tumbling over the rail into the cold, black water of the Scotia Sea. The deck was three meters above the water's surface and he hit its cover of slush and pancake ice with enough force to knock him senseless for a few moments.

His parka, designed for just such an accident, inflated automatically across his chest and behind his head, and he bobbed quickly to the surface and floated, his legs down under the surface but his face and shoulders above the slush ice and freezing water.

In the near distance he could hear a scraping rumble, then the crash and screech of ice on metal. His mind was already going sluggish with hypothermia and it took him a long half minute to realize that an iceberg, one of the many that had been drifting near the platform for the last two days, vanguards for the ice pack, calved weeks before from the antarctic glaciers, must have glanced off the platform's hull. He wondered dully why there hadn't been an alarm from the proximity radar. He made a quick calculation of how much damage Zulutoo might have sustained and decided very little; the things only moved a few hundred meters an hour, and a berg with too little surface mass to set off the proximity alarms wouldn't have enough mass even under the surface to seriously damage the hull, as light as its plates were. Maybe flooded a processing section, he thought.

But none of that would matter soon to him. He knew he would be dead in minutes unless Perez or Dickson found him. He pushed against the slushy water with his hands to bring himself around so that he could look up at the platform's deck. The railing was deserted.

He fumbled around for the tiny signal beacon attached to the left shoulder of his parka, but he couldn't feel it through his gloves. He brought the shaking hand to his mouth, caught the tip of a glove finger in his teeth, and pulled his hand free. He touched the transmitter but couldn't feel it. His forced his stiff fingers to bend, grasped the device, and ripped it free from the cloth of the parka. The LED was flashing red; in the deckhouse an alarm would be sounding; somewhere on the control board a warning and a compass bearing would be printing across a display screen.

His breath grew shallower. He began to labor for each shud

dering gulp of air he drew in. He had spent the last three months on board with Perez: he knew that the moment the berg had struck the platform Perez had abandoned the control board and had run out to take a look. There was no one in the deckhouse to hear the alarm. They might miss him in another fifteen or twenty minutes; by then he would have frozen to death.

He shouted. The sound was lost in the roar of the wind.

He panicked, thrashing at the water until he bumped up against the platform's smooth sides. The long, oily smooth swells pushed him along slowly toward the eastern end of the platform. With one hand—he couldn't reach the other one around over the bulk of the parka's Mae West—he pawed for a grip on the wet metal. Suddenly, his numb fingers found purchase, a rung in an inspection ladder, a simple loop of steel welded onto the platform's steel skin.

Using the leverage the handle gave him, he pulled himself around so that he could reach it with his other hand. He strained to draw himself from the water, tried to force his frozen legs to work, to find the rungs he knew were beneath the surface of the water. He grunted and wept, pulling with every erg of strength to drag himself up.

After a few seconds he dropped away, exhausted.

He drifted at the edge of consciousness, the frazil ice hardening around him, making of his body a small satellite of the pack that still bellowed and howled its way closer on the far side of the platform. His easterly drift brought him by the opening inside of which the tender bumped in a steady rhythm against its moorings.

He stared into the darkness inside the dock and knew with an absolute certainty that he couldn't make even the smallest effort to drag himself through the thickening water toward the salvation it offered.

Just before his heart stopped he felt himself falling into an ocean of brilliant white light.

CHAPTER FOUR

Texas—October 16, 2070

Pete came into the house quickly, knocking the low door aside and shaking snow from his coat onto the Navajo carpet.

Carney scowled from his chair.

"You know better than that! That's why I put mats on the porch—you wipe your goddamned feet before coming in this house."

Pete stopped, staring up at Carney, his muzzle and throat convulsing as though he were trying to work something up from his throat.

"Hopper," he finally said, softly, the word low and guttural.

Carney set the book he had been reading on the cedar coffee table; his cigar he clenched between his teeth. "Somebody's coming, huh?"

The dog dipped his head in a nod, his permanent grin seemed to widen.

"Well, you and Tilly go give 'em a welcome. I'll be out presently."

Carney could hear the sound now himself, the gargling roar of a commuter helicopter coming in from the northeast. It came in low, swooping down on the house. Then it was past and he could hear banging from the stables, the horses kicking at the walls of their stalls, upset at the noise.

He took down his rifle from over the fireplace mantle and made sure of its load. Satisfied, he leaned the rifle against the doorjamb and pulled on his coat and gloves. He was in no hurry; he wanted his visitors to get a good chance to meet Tilly and Pete before he made his appearance.

A few years before he had bought a rural-residence beacon

and set the thing to broadcast on the local commuter frequencies. The devices were meant to be a welcome mat of sorts, confirming the owner's address and piping some innocuous message to visitors flying in. He broadcast a repeat message that would read out in bright red letters on a copter's dash display the words KEEP OUT. TRESPASSERS WILL BE SHOT. SURVIVORS WILL BE PROSECUTED. Very few folks were curious enough to come on in and see if he was serious.

He supposed these folks were.

He stepped outside onto the narrow porch and squinted at the glare of the light against the snow. The late afternoon sun was bright and cold. A wind blew down from the line of hills above the house. *Espinazo del Diablo*, the Devil's Backbone, the hills were called, each rise another vertebra in the arid juniper-and-cactus-covered spine. He turned slowly, surveying his dominion, as always invigorated—and slightly startled—by the vivid green on white and the dry crispness of the air.

It made him almost appreciative of the fact of his visitors. Occasionally he liked to share the harsh beauty of the Texas Hill Country.

That didn't mean, of course, that he intended to make whoever had arrived in the hopper feel that they were especially welcome. Whoever they were, they weren't invited, and therefore they weren't, by his definition, friends. In the last few years his privacy had become the one thing he guarded with absolute jealousy.

The house stood halfway up the slope of one of the Backbone's hills, and the closest spot where one could safely land a small helicopter was a half kilometer farther down, on a flat outcropping of limestone that jutted out from the slope, making a wide clearing in the cedar cover and therefore a fairly safe helipad.

He started down the path that led to the limestone shelf, the rifle cradled across his forearm.

He took his time, stepping slowly through the new snow that had settled onto the path during the night. The snow on the bare branches of the sycamore trees glistened in the sun with a crystalline intensity that bothered him a bit. It had been snowing a lot the last few years, and this year it had come earlier than he could ever remember. The hard, early frost had caught the sycamores unprepared, and he wondered if they'd recover again next year, or if the cold had finally killed them off.

It took about ten minutes to make the walk down to the waiting hopper. As he came through the last thicket of junipers he could see the smooth plastic of the machine's bubble glinting through the trees. Pete and Tilly lay together nearby, panting and watching the hopper, their breath steaming in the morning chill.

As Carney approached, one of the hopper's gull-wing doors started to rise open.

Tilly rose to her haunches and growled, the hair rising stiff on her shoulders. The hopper's door closed again.

"Dr. Carney!" The voice came from the hopper, amplified over the vehicle's loudspeaker. The words echoed back a moment later from the hills behind them, garbling somewhat the rest of the speaker's sentence. "Will you please call the dogs off? We'd like to talk to you."

Carney gestured for the dogs to stay put and walked up to within a few meters of the hopper. The passengers inside, he knew, were getting a pretty good view of the rifle he carried, and he hoped it made them more than a little nervous. He half expected the hopper's pilot to start the thing up again and take off. He was only a little disappointed when that didn't happen.

He stood staring at the blank opaqueness of the hopper's bubble. After a minute, the door started back up again. Tilly leapt to her feet, but Carney held up a restraining hand.

"Don't move too fast, friend. Pete over there's a pretty mellow guy, but Tilly's got a hankerin' to chew on you just a bit," he drawled.

As if to prove his point, Tilly bared her teeth and growled throatily. The big female Rottweiler looked perfectly capable of a good deal of mayhem, though Carney knew she'd have to be ordered to attack or be badly provoked to actually assault a human.

Of course, the people in the hopper didn't know that. And Carney had no qualms about taking advantage of their ignorance.

A woman stepped out from the hopper's door and faced him across the expanse of white limestone between them. She squinted against the snow-glare and shaded her eyes; she was

Oriental, he realized, probably Chinese. Her hair was blue-black and fell to the middle of her back.

"Dr. Carney?" she asked. Her voice was high and nervous, only slightly accented, and despite himself, Carney felt his rancor melt a degree.

"Who's asking?"

"My name is Song Lan. I came here to talk to you."

Carney shifted the rifle a bit, letting the barrel lift slightly. He saw the girl's eyes go wide and had to suppress a sudden urge to grin at her.

"Darlin', you're trespassing," he said, letting a little more Texas drawl come into his voice for effect. "This is private property and I haven't invited you to set foot on it. That's called trespassing here. It's illegal. I suggest you get back in that machine and take on off out of here."

She squirmed, but held her ground. "I can't do that, Doctor. I promise you, it will take very little of your time to talk to me. It's very important that you do."

Carney hesitated, tempted. Ordinarily, he would have insisted, and if that didn't work, he might even have fired a shot across their bows for effect. But living in the wilderness alone sometimes made him crave company. And he was curious.

"Who else is in the hopper?"

"Just the pilot."

"Come ahead, then," he said gruffly. "You've got an hour."

The house was warm and close after the brisk chill of the morning air. Hugh Carney walked up to a broad, stone fireplace and hung the rifle he had been carrying above the mantel on the wooden rests nailed there for it.

"Is that a real gun?" the girl asked.

"As real as they come." He lifted it again off the pegs and ran a thumb along the smooth maple of the weapon's stock. "Fires a slug about the size of your thumb from above the knuckle. Makes a hole about twice that big."

"Isn't that illegal?" This from the pilot, a man Carney judged to be about forty, lean and weathered brown. Song Lan had introduced him simply as Avery.

"Sounds like it oughta be, doesn't it? But, no, it's not. Every law has exceptions, loopholes. Our law against personal firearms makes exceptions for certain collector's pieces. For firearms that weren't made to fire cartridge ammunition, it even lets you keep them in working order. This darlin'—'' He hefted the rifle so that she could see it better. "—was made in 1854, in Springfield, Massachusetts. It fires a fifty-caliber soft lead slug propelled by a sulphur- and charcoal-based compound known as 'black powder.' It loads through the muzzle, is ignited by percussion caps, and at short ranges, it's deadly on a deer or a man. It also makes one hell of a lot of nicely scary noise and smoke. And, best of all, it's perfectly legal, so long as I fire it on my own property. And I own everything around here for about five miles square—it's all my property.''

The girl looked shocked, her jaw dropping a millimeter. He took in her expression and made an intuitive leap. "You're Chinese, aren't you? From the People's Republic.''

She nodded. "Yes, I am.''

"Thought so. Lot of people would fit into five miles there— that's what you were thinking, wasn't it?''

She nodded again.

He sighed, rubbed the back of his head. "Hell of a situation your people have gotten themselves into. Aren't so many people here in the States. Five square miles is still a lot of ground, though, even here. But the aquifer gave out in this part of Texas years and years ago. San Antonio, down south of here, drained it, and is still draining what's left of it. I catch rainwater here, but there's not enough falling to keep any kind of community going. Nobody minds much when you own a sizable chunk of something useless.''

"I see,'' she said quietly. She kept her eyes on the floor, and Carney found himself wishing that she would look up, just for a moment.

Avery reached out to touch the rifle's stock, sweat-dark and cracked with age. "Doesn't seem like a very civilized thing to carry around when you greet visitors.''

"No, it isn't. And if I'd invited you, I would've left her on the mantel.'' He replaced the rifle on its pegs.

Song Lan tried to explain. "We had no way of asking. You have no phone, no television communication circuit. Your mail isn't even transmitted to your home. You pick it up at a postal substation. And you haven't checked that in over two weeks, or we would have written you for permission. You are very . . .'' She hesitated, searching for the word.

"Antisocial?" Carney provided for her. "Yes, I'm that. I don't like most people. Most people don't like me. It works out pretty well, that way."

"Yes," she said, "I understand."

He looked at her. There was something oddly familiar about the girl, and oddly troubling. She was pretty, in a slightly plain, milk-and-butter way. But her eyes were flat, bitter—though occasionally, as at the moment, he saw a light in them that he found intriguing. "I think you actually might," he said after a moment. "You went to some trouble to find me out here."

"Yes. It was difficult."

"So? That's one of the reasons I live out here. I'm not interested in talking to anyone who doesn't have something at least that important to say to me."

"I understand. I work for the United Nations Council on Space Exploration and Research—" she began.

"COSEAR. What does COSEAR want with me?"

She looked distressed. "Doctor, there's so much to explain. Too much for an hour."

"Forty-five minutes, now. Give it a try, anyway."

She sighed. "All right."

He gestured them to chairs set on a large, brightly colored rug in the center of the house's main room. The girl sat, and Carney watched her trying to take in her surroundings. The first impression of the place tended to make people stare, he knew. That had been his intent in building it; in this age of preform and plastic sameness, he found the character of his home familiar and comforting.

The walls of the house were made of blocks and broken pieces of the same pale gray limestone that composed the hills surrounding it. Wooden beams spanned the ceiling, making the room look medieval and solid. The decorations were sparse: a few worn rugs, a stuffed deer's head crowned with an enormous rack of horns, and, on one wall, a device made of wool yarn and bird's feathers Carney had picked up years ago on one of the old Cherokee reservations in Oklahoma—a mandala. The furnishings were worn and comfortable, overstuffed and upholstered with a dry-smelling wool fabric.

"I'll get us something to drink," Carney said, and left the room. The kitchen was set off from the main room by a deceptively thick wall of glass brick. He could hear his guests talking as he poured iced tea from a jug into tumblers.

"Rustic," Avery commented.

"It is a little eccentric. I think I like it, though. It's a place for living; it is comfortable, textured. Real. It reminds me of home, in a way."

"Give me an apartment in the city any day. Besides, it's cold in here."

The girl laughed shortly. "Cold! Beijing is this cold and more." The laugh was cut short, as if she realized there was something wrong in what she had said. "Well, I like it here, anyway. Too much heat makes you slow and stupid."

Carney brought the tray of glasses into the main room. He handed a tumbler to Song and she sipped at it. Avery tasted his and made a face.

"What is this?"

"Tea. At one time the staple beverage of three-quarters of the world. Not supposed to be very healthy for you, though, lots of caffeine and tannic acid. People've pretty much stopped drinking it. Nothing like it if you're thirsty, though."

He set his own glass beside his chair and moved over to the fireplace. "If you'll excuse me, I'll make us a fire. Wouldn't be hospitable to leave my guests shivering in their boots, invited or not."

He piled split logs onto the fireplace's grate, spread a fistful of shavings and twigs under them and lit it all with a long match. After a minute, a cheery fire was crackling away behind the screen. Song edged her chair closer to the warmth and Avery followed suit.

"You don't have electric heat?"

"Have it. Don't use it. I only use power when I have to, though I've a good-size solar array on the far side of the hill if I need it. Right now, I just don't need it."

"But doesn't that pollute the air?" Avery gestured toward the fire that was warming his hands.

"Sure it does. Stupid question. But it makes damned little difference way out here. Nobody breathing the stuff but me, and I think it's worth it. It smells better and it feels better." He took a chair and sipped his tea. "Now, what can I do for you and COSEAR, Song Lan?"

Song hesitated, glanced at Avery. "Jack, some of what I have to tell Dr. Carney is, well, supposed to be kept secret. I mean, it's just—''

Avery waved a hand. ''Say no more. Nothing wrong with being hired help. I wouldn't mind taking a walk around the property, if Dr. Carney here'll put those dogs someplace where they'll let me be.''

''Pete and Tilly? Hell, they'll let you alone, son. They know you now. Just don't piss 'em off.''

''I'll trust you on that, Doctor. You hear me holler, though, you come and pick up my pieces.''

Song waited for a long minute after Avery had gone out before beginning. Carney sipped his tea and waited.

''Doctor—''

''Damn it, call me Hugh, or Carney. You make me feel even older than I am.''

''Okay. Hugh. I am an astrophysicist. I work for COSEAR. I am on loan to them from the Physical Institute of Beijing University.''

''Your accent is hardly noticeable.''

''Thank you. I worked very hard on my English.''

''I believe you. What brings a pretty China girl to the Texas Hill Country?''

She blushed slightly, but continued on. ''Doctor, what do you know about weather?''

Carney raised an eyebrow, shrugged. ''Not a whole lot. Is it important?''

''It could be,'' she said seriously. ''I know you're very isolated out here—''

''I keep up. Don't get the idea I've stuck my head in the sand out here. I know what's going on. I just don't choose to participate, for the most part.''

''It's been pretty cold out here?''

Carney nodded. ''Winters have been pretty bad the last few years. I haven't seen a hummingbird this year—I don't think they came this far north. This is the first year I ever remember it snowed in October. I thought it was odd . . . but, then, fifteen, twenty years ago we had two or three winters in a row where it didn't even get below freezing. Weather's a funny thing.''

''This is different.''

''Different how?''

''The planet is cooling.''

"Cooling? I don't follow."

"It's getting colder, on the average, across the surface of the Earth. The winters aren't just longer here; they're statistically longer everywhere in the world. The ice caps in Greenland and in Antarctica are growing at record rates. The rain forests are dying—slowly and piecemeal—but they're dying. Weather and precipitation patterns are changing on every continent."

"Including Asia?"

She nodded slowly.

"Hmm. I can see how that might cause some problems." He narrowed his eyes. "Things must be getting tough, with the mainland population what it is."

"I cannot say."

"State secrets, huh? You'd be surprised how much the rest of the world knows about what goes on in your fair country, darlin'. I suppose that's beside the point, though."

"Yes, sir."

"So. Glaciers in Michigan? Is that what you're telling me?"

"Yes. And no. Eventually, if trends continue, the Laurentide ice sheet will extend as far south on the American continent as St. Louis, Missouri. Michigan will someday be under a thousand feet of ice and your Detroit will be ground by the glaciers into rubble. But only in four or five thousand years. The immediate problem is habitat—our habitat. In a much shorter time the American breadbasket might become a desert and much of the Soviet Union and China could become tundra. There's no way to know the full effects until they happen; however, the effects we have observed are already becoming severe. Crops *are* dying, winters *are* becoming longer and harsher. And, yes, the glaciers are moving. Some in Alaska have been measured at a movement of more than thirty-five meters a day. And as the ice sheets grow, they lock up more water and the oceans shrink."

Carney shook his head impatiently. "That's all well and good, and if you're right, it's even fairly disturbing. But what does it have to do with me? And what does it have to do with the UN's committee on space? Actually, even more intriguing is why an astrophysicist would be working on weather problems."

" 'COSEAR is participating in an international, multidisciplinary effort to discover the causes of the present crisis.' That's from the letter that was given me when I arrived. The People's

Republic of China is only one of a score of nations that have contributed resources and people to the UN.''

"China doesn't belong to the UN anymore.''

"I know that. We are contributing as best we can to find a solution to a global problem, despite political differences. They are trying to centralize the research effort. COSEAR was responsible for coordinating research on Milankovitch cycles.''

"Which are?''

"They're not important. They're not the answer.''

"Humor me. I'm feeling particularly ignorant.''

She sighed, but explained. "One possible explanation for the substantial changes in the world's climatic condition that have occurred in the past—the ice ages—is that they are caused by astronomical irregularities, either variability in solar output or irregularities in the planet's orbit or in its axis of rotation. One of the most plausible ideas was one that a Yugoslavian geophysicist named Milankovitch posited in the 1920s to explain glaciation, that a combination of changes in the Earth's tilt on its axis, the direction of that tilt, and changes in the eccentricity of the planet's orbit could cause dramatic climatic change—could, in other words, cause the onset of an ice age. The theory had been largely accepted for more than a century, but the Milankovitch cycles were regular and predictable, and another period of cold isn't due for another twenty millennia by his theory. So it's wrong. As are the other theories dealing with things like the salinity of the seas and the depth of the ozone layer. But they were researching them all anyway, on the chance. I was doing some of the astronomical work on the computers at the institute. I found something. Maybe the real cause of what's happening.''

Carney raised an eyebrow. "Oh, yes? And why tell me about it?''

"I believe the coming catastrophe has a great deal to do with a man you know. A man named James Harris.'' Song hunched forward in her chair, eager to explain. "I believe something is changing our atmosphere and the way in which it absorbs and reflects sunlight, and I believe James Harris brought it here.''

Carney snorted. "If you knew how ridiculous that sounds—''

"I do know. But, please, let me finish. Listen to everything before you make a judgement.''

"James Harris is dead.''

"*Please*, Dr. Carney."

"All right," he said reluctantly. "But keep it brief. My patience has grown fairly short as I've gotten older." He was trying not to let himself be upset at the girl. He had been foolish to let her stay in the first place. One of the reasons he lived where he did was he had grown tired of dealing with people with pet theories. Now he had given in because of a pretty face, and he was regretting it mightily.

She seemed to guess at his thoughts and hurried ahead with her explanation. "You know how the Earth is heated. The sun, our sun, puts out an enormous amount of electromagnetic radiation, a fraction of which, about 175 billion megawatts, actually falls on the Earth. Maybe half of that actually reaches the Earth's surface and heats the planet. Some of the rest is absorbed in the thermosphere, about eighty klicks up; nitrous oxide and ozone absorb a great deal of the ultraviolet radiation in the stratosphere below that; carbon dioxide and water vapor take care of most of the infrared. And the remainder is absorbed by clouds or reflected back into space. It's really a very delicate balance, one the human race has upset more than once in the past—do you remember the global warming scare at the turn of the century? How it mobilized conservation efforts? Made us clean up our industries, here and in the Soviet Union, and even in China to an extent? Too much carbon dioxide in the atmosphere reduced the amount of radiation reflected from the Earth's surface back into space. The world overheated and things began to die. The same thing is happening now, I think, but in reverse."

She sipped her tea and took a breath. "Have you ever heard of the Tambora volcano?"

Carney shook his head.

"In 1815 the Tambora volcano exploded, throwing millions of tons of dust and debris into the upper atmosphere. They called 1815 'the year without a summer.' Snow fell in Beijing and in New England in August. Crops died, people starved. The same thing is happening now, but we don't know why. No more than normal volcanic activity. The sun's output hasn't changed. Astronomical variations can't explain it. That leaves the atmosphere; but we can't find anything abnormal, only a few odd trace compounds in the thermosphere, not enough to cause what's happening. If it were only in one region, or even one hemisphere, it could have been some sort of variation of the El Niño effect. But it's everywhere. We were at an impasse.''

"Sounds like that leaves us in a hell of a hole," Carney said quietly.

"Yes. A hole. To be buried in, maybe. Maybe not, though. We started to look for coincidences, for parallels. I found one, I think. You remember that your son's return caused a great deal of confusion in the scientific community?''

"My son's *return*? Foolishness! You're talking about rumors, undocumented stories that a member of the expedition had been returned, and that it happened to be my son." He heard the edge of sarcasm in his own voice, but let it stand.

She nodded. "I know. Your country's intelligence agencies did their best to obscure the facts. And then Harris simply disappeared—probably he's living somewhere in the U.S. now, with his name and his features altered. But there were too many witnesses and too much documentation from the Soviet and Argentinian scientists who interviewed him before he was taken from Amundsen-Scott Station. It happened. And it happened at the same time—I'd say at the same *moment*—that the changes in global temperatures began.''

"Let's just say you're right, just for argument. What makes you think these things coincide?''

"I asked the computer to follow back to the event source, to pinpoint the beginning of the climatic crisis and correlate any events of significance. The first evidences of climatic change were noted in the winter of the year 2064. Allowing for accumulation of effect the computer made the beginning of the cycle as March or April of 2063. James Harris was discovered at Amundsen-Scott Station, Antarctica, at 0930 hours local time on March 16th, 2063.''

"And you base a theory on *that*? That's pretty thin evidence, young lady, even for a working hypothesis. It's *damned* thin as an excuse to fly out here and impose on my hospitality.''

An anxious expression passed over her face. "I didn't mean—''

"Don't worry about it. Damage done. Besides, I've enjoyed your company.''

"You don't think it strange that the two most inexplicable events in our age occurred simultaneously? That's more than

coincidence, Doctor—Hugh—and if you thought about it carefully—''

''Darlin', I am thinking about it, and with plenty of care,
believe me. But what could my son's arrival on this planet—if it
happened—possibly have to do with the *weather*, of all things?
Use Occam's razor on this; the simplest explanation is that inexplicable events, everything from spontaneous combustion of
human beings to poltergeists, happen all the time. And coincidence does not cause prove.''

He stopped, looked at her sharply. ''And that is what you're
trying to get at here, isn't it, hon'? That the strange and unexplainable translation of a man across a dozen light-years *caused*
this global cooling that's got COSEAR and the UN in such a
heat?''

''Yes, but you don't understand!''

''How so? Seems to me I understand fine.''

She glared at him in pure frustration for the duration of a
breath, then closed her eyes and seemed to concentrate, whether
to think or to gather together more argumentative resources, he
didn't know.

''There is more to it than that.''

''So?''

She took a deep breath, let it out slowly. ''At the same *hour*
that James Harris was discovered on the polar ice, a small asteroid was observed by the automated optical telescopes at the
UN's Farside Base on the moon as making its closest approach
on a 'near-miss' flyby of the Earth, approximately eight hundred
thousand kilometers out. Very close by astronomical standards,
but not very unusual; there are dozens of such events a year for
asteroids under half a cubic kilometer in size. The event was
recorded and filed; there are far too many more interesting astronomical events to observe, and far too few personnel, to follow up on such a minor occurrence.

''But its closest approach occurred *simultaneously* with James
Harris's appearance. And the asteroid itself was very unusual:
its albedo was very high, almost wholly reflective, and its den-
sity was strangely low. I don't know who programmed the Farside computers . . .'' She hesitated, and he got the distinct
impression that she had just realized she was telling him too
much. He was tempted to press her, but he held his peace,
waiting for her to go on.

"Well, those things alone should have set off alarms, if some-one had done his job as it should have been done. But those weren't the only curious things about this asteroid. Its velocity was quite high; but more importantly, its trajectory would make it entirely possible that, had it somehow obviated gravitational influences, it could have originated somewhere near the 61 Cygni star system."

"Interesting," he said. Very interesting, he thought to him-self. She's hiding something, but for what reason?

"But you seem to have missed a rather obvious point, hon'." Carney was leaning forward in his chair; he was sure he knew what it was she was trying to keep from him, but he decided to play devil's advocate for the moment. "Even had that asteroid traveled here at the speed of light—and I assume it was moving past a hell of lot slower, or the Farside telescopes would never have even picked it up—it would have taken eleven-some-odd years to make the trip from Cygni, and that would've started it out eleven years before my boy got to Comfort. Not to mention that asteroids are intrasystem debris; they come from this neigh-borhood and get tossed around like marbles in a jar of planetary gravity."

"I know." She made the statement flatly, without inflection—without, he noted, any disappointment that his objections seemed to be unanswerable. He made a decision, stood up from his chair.

"So you want me to tell you where Jim is, then." It wasn't a question.

She nodded.

"You think it will do some good? You think you can find out how this started."

"Yes. Maybe."

"Your pilot, does he work for COSEAR, too?"

She stood then, too, her expression suddenly anxious. "No. I hired him in Austin, to bring me here."

"I'll call him in. Then you send him on back. You'll stay here the night in the spare room."

"All right," she agreed quietly.

"Tomorrow morning we'll go find my boy, then. Is that agreeable to you?"

She nodded again. The effort of revealing what she had told

him seemed to have drained her. Her shoulders sagged and her eyes were red.

"Sit," he said gently. "I'll be back shortly."

He took his coat from the rack by the door and went out on the porch, into the crisp, cold air. The sun had already begun to slide behind the hills behind the house and the wind had picked up, rattling the ice that sheathed the branches of the cedars and scrub oaks.

The pilot was nowhere in sight. Carney assumed he had walked back down to his hopper to wait. He whistled and, after a moment, Pete and Tilly came bounding up from underneath the porch.

"Go tell the man in the hopper to come back up," he commanded. "Quick, now."

The dogs ran off down the slope to carry out their commission.

Carney watched them until they were out of sight. Even then, he didn't go back in. The cold air helped him think. He dug in a coat pocket and found his cigar case. He took a cigar from it and bit off the end and lit it, absently drawing the soothing-sweet smoke into his mouth.

There were two things about the girl's story that disturbed him deeply, things that bothered him like an itch deep inside he couldn't scratch.

Rationally, he still couldn't quite believe what she had told him. At gut level, though, a fear gnawed, telling him that he should be very afraid, not just for himself, but for everyone who lived on the fragile ball of dirt they called home.

And, he wondered, why had she kept to herself the fact that that strange, atypical asteroid that the Farside observatory had picked up was an alien spaceship?

Carney sat in his chair before the fire and brooded, watching the girl sleep, slumped on the broad, overstuffed sofa.

She had been asleep when he had come in and he had let her be. She had probably, he guessed, traveled a good way even before hiring the hack that had brought her out to the Backbone. Besides, it gave him a chance to think.

He was convinced that the asteroid she had described was no asteroid at all. He was also convinced that she knew it as well as he did, and was counting on his ignorance.

What she hadn't seemed to have considered was that as much as he might look like an ignorant and rather aged country doctor, he had spent a half-dozen years working with the astronomers and physicists of the International Space Administration. He had in that time picked up enough savvy to know that what she had described was no asteroid. Brightly metallic, on a completely eccentric course heading through the Solar system, and it was *hollow*.

Which left him with some curious possibilities.

For one thing, she might not be working for COSEAR. This wasn't their style; they were a subbureaucracy of the world's largest and most complex bureaucratic entity. They wouldn't send a single young girl, alone, whatever her credentials, to ask him where his son was. They'd send a committee. Or two.

Or, he thought, they'd just do the obvious and bypass someone as low on the pole as Hugh Carney. As adamant about the secrecy of relocated persons as the Justice Department and the United States government might be, it was unlikely they'd refuse a direct request from the Secretary General of the United Nations, should that worthy choose to make it.

Which made her something else entirely. Probably. Carney rubbed his forehead with the heel of his hand. He should just toss her out on her ass and make her walk back to Austin.

But she intrigued him. What was the likelihood, he wondered, that she had kept what she knew from the political officers who, he had heard, were still running three to one to the scientists in the research facilities of the People's Republic? Slim.

And what were the possibilities she was working on her own, trying to find her own place in the history books, the Woman Who Saved The World? Again, slim.

Which meant she was probably an agent of some sort, working for the government of Red China.

So why was he seriously contemplating taking her to see James Harris, thereby compromising a persona under which his son had lived in safe anonymity for more than six years?

Because he was old. Because he was curious. Because despite her probable motives, he liked the girl.

Because maybe he had finally found the one thing that would make his son listen to him.

And because even after six years, he still knew what it was to be ashamed.

* * *

Song Lan woke with a disoriented start—she had been dreaming a dream that now drained away, leaving bitter dregs. She shuddered and pushed herself up on her elbows.

She saw Carney in his chair and remembered suddenly where she was. The older man was slumped down but not asleep, his hand palm-up over his eyes. The skin of the hand, Song noticed, was nut-brown with age, and she thought she could see the fingers tremble slightly, hovering in front of his face.

Carney stirred and dropped his hand. "Back among the living, I see."

"I apologize. I guess I was pretty tired."

"Apology noted and accepted. Why don't we go upstairs, and I'll show you your room. We can talk more in the morning."

She nodded. She *was* tired, very tired. The thought of a night's undisturbed sleep was almost more pleasant than she could bear. Even here, she was sure, she wouldn't be granted that; her dreaming mind was too certain to make her sleep a broken and restless business. But, still, she might get a few hours of much-needed rest.

She followed Carney up the narrow stairs to the house's second story. Carney gestured to one of the two rooms at the top.

"Everything you might need ought to be in there. Bed's made, and there's towels and such in the cupboard beside the sink in the john."

She smiled to show her thanks, and he waited until she was in the room before he spoke again.

"Sleep tight."

"I will."

He walked into the room across the short hall and shut the door. She entered her own room, considered a bath and decided on a shower. She stripped wearily out of her travel-stained clothes and stood in the tub, letting hot water pour in a comforting rush over her face and shoulders. Whatever else the years have changed, she thought, not very much felt as good as an ample supply of hot water applied liberally to the skin.

She reviewed the afternoon's conversation in her head, feeling both gratified and uneasy about its results. Though Carney had not told her where James Harris was, he had indicated he would take her to him in the morning.

She absently touched the almost undetectable rise under the skin of her cheek that marked the tiny transmitter anchored to the bone there. Her *masters*—she could think of them in no other terms—would soon know where Harris was, too. Then, perhaps, they would let her go home.

She felt an unbearable rush of shame. She squatted down on the warm porcelain of the tub's bottom and let the spray of water beat down on the back of her skull, the white noise of the rushing water almost enough to drown out the accusations her own conscience made against her.

The memory beat inside her head, counterpoint to her own pulse. After they had forced her into the car it had driven for what seemed hours, out into the cultivated countryside, the miles after miles of rice paddy and cabbage field. They had finally stopped at a small cluster of low buildings in the middle of a wide expanse of farmland.

The buildings were windowless and sere, she remembered, painted an ominous hospital white.

She touched her face again. There they had implanted the transmitter in the bone of her cheek.

She cringed and fought back the sudden impulse to weep.

There they had opened her skull and with their enzyme-scalpels and their microscopic tools they had changed her, made her *different*.

They had made certain neuroanatomical changes, manipulating the H-VI Purkinje cells in her cerebellar cortex. The Western scientists who had developed the technique—and were then promptly banned by their governments from using it—called it "hardwiring."

What it meant to Song was that without ever having fought another human being she had the martial skills to kill a man in a dozen different ways, all in the span of a heartbeat. They had made the parallel fibers and dendrites in her cerebellum "know" how to move her muscles in certain ways, to react precisely to certain stimuli.

They had made her a machine with abilities and memories that were not her own.

And then they had given her a mission.

To procure for them a man who had appeared from nowhere and then disappeared again. To find James Harris so that they could take him and pick his mind clean, using the fact that she was a scientist to get her a UN passport so that she could find him.

And she would do what they told her because though China publicly denied it, ten thousand people a day were dying of hunger in the People's Republic.

She would do it because the East still did not trust the West enough to share with it what she had found, because they feared the West would take the knowledge and find its own solution and leave China to die.

She would do it because also inside her head was a tiny explosive device that could be set off anytime by a simple signal to the transmitter/receiver buried in the flesh of her own face.

The skin of her face and shoulders was numb from the heat. Turning off the water, she stood and found a towel.

Carney had brought her bag up earlier, she found, and left it on the bed. She took out fresh underclothes and readied herself for sleep.

The sheets were cool and crisp as she slipped between them and she found herself shivering after the steam-warmth of the bathroom.

They had sent her to work for COSEAR. She had not lied to Carney about that. Her colleagues were still busy at what they believed was their contribution, sending up balloons to sample the upper atmosphere or studying the minute fluctuations in the Earth's relationships with the rest of the Solar system.

Her own expertise had been no more than a cover story. She had pretended to work long enough to establish herself. Then she had come here.

In some quirk of compassion—or as a warning to her that her own life was not the only life at stake should she fail—they had let her go home before shipping her off as part of Red China's contingent to the UN's emergency research effort.

She lay curled in the bed, waiting for the shivering to stop, remembering.

The sun, she remembered, had been high and bright in the sky over Tienanmen, but it had seemed somehow smaller, distant and cold. The central entrance to the Catacombs was west of the square, very near the National People's Congress Building. There was a low arch and underneath it the black maw that marked the beginning of the underground city.

The motor had hummed suddenly loud as the car maneuvered

down the wide ramp into the first level, the driver slowly forcing his way through the swarm of bicycles and people on foot that poured in and out in a constant river from the tunnels. She remembered what her colleagues had called the people of the Catacombs: *shu*—rats.

The soldiers who had brought her had been confident of her. They had let her go alone down the dozen levels to the place that had been her home.

She shuddered, remembering. She had come back, almost without knowing why. Certainly, she had not wanted to wish her ill luck on those who had cared for her.

Because we always come home, she told herself, no matter what home is. And because the only family she had ever had was still there. Because Jiang Qing was still there.

The one thing that was still of universal value, even in a totalitarian society, was intellect. Jiang Qing—Song had always called her Jiang-a-yi, or Auntie Jiang—had shown her her own worth, had helped her find a way out.

Song Lan had stayed in the orphan's crèche until she was thirteen. It had been a bare, frightening place. The matrons had been kind enough, but they had been overwhelmed by the sheer number of children under their care; and there had been little in the way of clothing or shoes, and less food.

At thirteen she had run away, though ''run'' was more euphemism than truth. No one had tried to stop her from leaving. No one had even noticed.

For two more years she had lived more or less by herself in the tunnels, running wild. There were sections of the tunnels that had been dug and then forgotten for reasons no one remembered. They were unlighted and cold, but she had lived there, along with other children who had left the crèche or their parents. They stole to keep alive, raiding the long, high-ceilinged tunnels where food was grown under the radiance of artificial lights.

For a while, they had been tolerated. Then, suddenly, they were not.

One night—it was night by convenience, night by the numbers on the clocks in the lighted, occupied tunnels—the troops came. Song had wakened to screams and bright lights and the sound of truncheons on flesh and bone. Someone struck her where she lay and she blacked out.

When she had come to, she found herself bound hand and foot. Above her, the lights of one of the main tunnels flashed by. She had been dumped into the cargo box of a tramcar with the others who had lived with her in the abandoned tunnel. The others were dead or unconscious, all bound as she herself was.

The plastic strap around her ankles had been carelessly fixed, and she had worked her feet free and jumped from the tram. She ran and was pursued. In one of the smaller, winding side tunnels, she had fallen. She lay there, waiting for the troops to catch up to her. She had felt hands reach under her arms then; she was lifted up, dragged from out of the public tunnel into someone's home.

That was how she had found Jiang; after that, her life changed.

She found out later that the others she had lived with had been taken above into the city. Some few were sent to work alongside the machines in the great farming cooperatives. Others were simply shot.

Song had been the fortunate one. Jiang had taken her in, fed her, taught her.

Jiang-a-yi had given her life: more, she had given her a reason to live.

She remembered Jiang's tiny apartment, the day they had let her come to visit. It was one sparsely furnished room. The lighting was dim, but she could remember letting her eyes travel hungrily over the floor-to-ceiling shelves of books that covered two of its walls. Not cards or spools, but books, solid, dull in their colored and mildewed covers. More real books than she had ever seen in one place anywhere else.

She could smell their musty, dry odor, even now, with Jiang thousands of miles and a lifetime away, a smell that she would forever associate with wisdom and learning. She felt her throat tighten and she fought back tears. The memory overwhelmed her with a sense of the familiarity and security that she had once had, and that she feared she would never have again.

She remembered that when she had opened the door to Jiang's home, a cat, one of a half dozen Jiang kept despite the laws, had shot out between her ankles and into the tunnels. She had watched it gallop away with a small sense of trepidation, though she knew it would likely find its way back.

Jiang's cats almost always did, though occasionally one would fail to return, caught late at night by the thumb-size predators that scuttled through the midnight tunnels in search of vermin.

Song shivered again, burrowed farther under the fragrant quilts. When she had lived as a tunnel-orphan, one of the group she had scavenged with had always stayed awake while the others slept, watching for the mechanical scorpions. The robots were attracted to floor-level body heat; when they found something appreciably warmer than the stone, they drew themselves close and very gently slipped a hair-fine needle under the skin and pumped in a strong nerve poison. Then they dug their sharp-pointed legs into the numbed flesh of the victim and settled in to wait.

The bugs were easily put out of commission; a sharp rap with a length of conduit was the preferred method. But you had to see one first. More than once one of her friends had failed to wake up with the rest and a quick search would turn up one of the little six-legged, cigar-shaped bugs stuck like a metal-and-plastic leech onto the child's cold body. She remembered finding one herself, dug into the skin of a girl's neck under her hair. She had pulled at it and it had hung on tenaciously; she had pulled harder and the girl's skin had started to tear. She had let go of it and gone off by herself to be sick.

That was its programming. To hang on like a bulldog to whatever it had killed. To never let go.

Always they'd have to drag the body into one of the occupied tunnels and leave it; the scorpions gave off a homing signal that would eventually bring sanitation around to pick up the corpse. It was better the garbage crews were kept away from the tunnels in which the orphans lived.

Jiang had known from the first instant that something was wrong. They had held each other without speaking, the older woman thin, gray, sixty years old or better; the younger woman thin, too, but taller, her hair long and black.

Jiang had comforted her with hands that were rough and knuckles that were swollen with arthritis and with the work she did at the reprocessing plant deep in the haunted bowels of the underground city. For thirty years she had spent ten hours a day with a scoop-shaped net separating larger waste from smaller in the cesspits below.

Before that, she had been a teacher. Physics, chemistry, astronomy. After the Great Standoff, paranoia and suspicion of intellectuals had been the rule of the day. Jiang had refused to teach every nuance of the new politics, the party line, in her classes, so, after a time, she was no longer a teacher. Until Song had come along.

Song had looked into the old face and felt grief. The inevitable cyclical swing in attitudes had returned to favor thinkers, and that fact had been Song's salvation. With Jiang's tutoring she had passed the aptitude tests and the entrance examinations. She had attended Beijing University, and for two years she had worked as an astrophysicist at the university's Physical Institute.

And Jiang-a-yi still shoveled dung.

She had cried for a long time, the older woman stroking her hair.

When she was able, she told her about Zhang Shan, the man she had loved. The man who had betrayed her.

She had been a virgin before Zhang; she had been naïve and trusting.

The entire time they had been together, Zhang had reported everything he came to know about her to the army's secret police. When she had found something Zhang had thought important, he had brought them down upon her.

She hadn't seen him since.

She never wanted to see him again.

What she had felt—what she still felt—had been horrible: betrayal, anger, despair . . . and love. She had still loved him, even when she knew beyond doubt that he had never loved her.

The one intractable rule she had learned, living as a child in the dark, empty tunnels below the city, was never to trust anyone. She had let herself forget that, had let herself become vulnerable to Zhang.

Never again. Only Jiang-a-yi could truly love her. She knew that now.

In the dark, she touched her cheek again, remembering the last touch of Jiang's knotted hand.

After a time, she slept.

CHAPTER FIVE

October 17, 2070

Song was wakened by the whine of an aircraft engine's turbines. She sat up suddenly, a little frightened, in the soft depth of the bed.

Her first thought was to wonder, again, where she was. The smell of the room she was in was very unfamiliar, the smell of cedar underlying a heavier smell of old wood and dust. Sunlight filtered brightly through a curtain.

The curtain brought it back to her; it was the same pale yellow as the curtains downstairs in Hugh Carney's living room.

Her second thought was tinged with wonder. She'd actually slept soundly, the entire night through. She took a deep breath of the cold morning air, feeling more refreshed than she had in months. Her head felt clear, free of the bitter residue of the dreams that haunted most of her nights.

She slipped out from beneath the thick quilts under which she'd slept and rushed shivering into the bathroom to grab the soft, thick robe that hung there from a hook behind the door. Then she went to the window.

Carney was nowhere in sight. She shielded her eyes with her hand against the sunlight that slanted through the trees on the nearby hillside. To the right of the porch was a large building that she had assumed was a barn of some kind. As she watched, its roof slowly folded back upon itself, the metal creaking and squealing as the hydraulics pulled the separate sections open from the middle.

From the vantage of the house's second story she could see the stubby wings of a VTOL airplane. As she watched, its second engine whined to life.

She dressed quickly, spent a moment on her hair and teeth, then rushed downstairs and out onto the porch.

Carney emerged from the barn's wide doors and waved to her, grinning. "Let's go," he shouted.

She joined him in the barn. He held the door to the passenger side of the plane's cockpit open for her and she climbed in. He closed the door behind her and the engine noise instantly fell off to a faint moan.

Carney pulled himself up through the pilot's door, grunting at the effort. He settled himself and buckled in.

"I told you I wasn't exactly cut off out here, didn't I?"

"I guess not." She looked around the cockpit and back into the cabin behind. "This is very large for a personal machine."

"It is indeed. Northrup Airvan. Comfortable, reliable, and almost infinite range. And we'll need that range. Where we're going there are damned few places for rest stops along the way."

He buckled himself in to his seat and she followed suit.

He worked the controls and the craft lifted smoothly through the roof of the building that had been its hanger.

"Where are we going?" Song asked, after Carney had put the plane into the state traffic net and let the computer take over his controls.

"You'll see."

She didn't press. In a very real way, she didn't want to know.

James Harris woke suddenly, the terror of a nightmare still intense enough to make his hands shake as he reached for the light beside the bed. The wind outside screamed at him, straining itself around and through the cracked bricks of the old house. Water pounded the roof as if thrown in buckets, clattering and roaring down the loose tin gutters.

The storm threw itself with a temperamental roar across the island, swept through the cobble and tarmac streets of Port-de-Paix and settled into a steady spatter of rain.

Harris took a deep breath and tried to calm himself. His heart beat loud in his ears and he tried to remember the relaxation exercises he'd been taught in basic training. He remembered suddenly an example the instructor had given him, how Chinese monks would meditate by concentrating on every sensation of taking a single step, the instant the toe touched a surface, the quality of feeling as the instep conformed itself to the ground.

It could take them all of a day to cross a courtyard, he remembered. He concentrated on the ticking of the raindrops as they struck the tin of the roof and fell from the eaves and soon he felt his heart stop racing, his pulse slow.

"Christ," he muttered irritably. He sat up, shaking his head gingerly. He felt washed out and weak. Hung over.

This was no way to live. The wind outside gusted again, battering the old house in which he rented a room, and he thought wryly of the recruitment brochures the company still put out touting Hispaniola as a "tropical paradise."

Tropical it was, with all the attendant heat and humidity, insects and rain. Paradise, he supposed, was a matter of attitude.

He had two days left of downtime before they shot him back up to the platforms, and he was spending it in the worst possible way, sleeping when he could and drinking the rest of the time. It was the way he spent all his days Earthside: numb, pickled to the gills.

The inside of his mouth tasted a good deal like the bottom of one of the drainage canals that crisscrossed the city outside, carrying away the storm water and with it the human waste of a place where too many people lived in too close a proximity.

He sat on the bed and listened to the rain until the storm died away. Daylight followed close on the heels of the storm, and as soon as the tick of raindrops thinned out, he pulled on his pants and boots.

He whistled sharply, one note high, one low. A head poked out from under the bed.

"Let's get some breakfast, boy."

The dog, a black-and-white terrier, pulled himself, front then rear, out from under the bed and followed him out the door into the street.

The house was close to the port and he walked, trying to keep out of the path of the little "shush" cars, as the native Creoles called them, that rushed up and down the narrow streets. The pilots of the little hovercars drove as much down the sidewalk as down the street; he knew from driving one that someone piloting the craft couldn't feel the road underneath. The cushion of air that supported it isolated pilot and passenger from curb and cobblestone alike. He preferred to walk.

Most of the buildings around the port were the concrete block and wattle of the old city. As decrepit and unsteady as they were,

Harris enjoyed their ambiance. It was one of the reasons that he preferred to live ''on the economy,'' as the platform roughnecks put it—living out among the Creoles rather than in the company-built, company-owned barracks just east of the city.

Down the block from his rooming house was a small open-air grocery. He passed through the bins of fruit and vegetables outside the store's open front and into the back where the proprietor, an elderly, wrinkled Creole man, sat on a stool behind a narrow wooden counter.

The old man acknowledged him with a nod. Harris nodded back and said, ''Morning, Jean.''

The old man handed him a small paper sack, accepted Harris's company chit, and touched it against the thumbnail-size reader set into the wood of the countertop. The machine soundlessly charged the amount to his company account.

He handed the chit back then reached under the counter, brought up a steak bone wrapped in paper. He unwrapped it and handed it down to the terrier, who took it, tail wagging.

''What do you say, Bim?''

The dog placed the bone carefully on the floor and sat. '' 'ank you,'' it croaked out with some effort.

''Welcome.''

''He loves you, Jean. Nobody else gives him bones without trying to pet him and talk to him cute.''

The old man just grinned and nodded, and Harris grinned back, took his sack, and made his way back out to the street. He hurried, not sure of the time. His watch was gone; sometime in the last three days he'd either lost it or had it stolen.

A stiff breeze, remnant of the night's storm, blew in from the sea, bringing with it the smell of salt and fish. He walked out onto a seawall, one of many that helped protect the harbor from the rougher waters of the open Caribbean. He sat down among the fishermen crowded onto the last rocks of the breakwater and spread out his breakfast, the boiled eggs and cheese that the shopkeeper Jean kept ready for him every morning when he was dirtside.

As he ate he looked out across the open water of the Caribbean to where he knew the island of Tortuga was, hidden in the still-hazy morning air, a few dozen kilometers off of the main island of Hispaniola. The view would be best there, he knew, in the concrete and glassteel tower that rose from the center of the square-mile field that acted as roof for the launch facilities buried a kilometer deep in the island's stone heart.

He felt it long before he could see or hear it. The rock under him vibrated just perceptibly, and tiny, standing ripples rose up from the water, giving it the appearance of gray-green corduroy. He twisted around on the flat slab of stone he'd chosen as his grandstand and leaned back on his elbows, watching the mountains that towered above Port-de-Paix.

Then he saw it, the narrow, needle-slim hull of the shuttle rocketing up above the haze into the sunlight, shining bright, a burning splinter, rising up and up out of the mountains' peaks. He craned his head to watch, following the ship up until he lost it in the distance of blue sky and all that was left was the ragged white line of its condensation trail.

By the time the winds had dispersed the shuttle's contrail, he had finished his meal. He tossed the scraps of bread out to the gulls who circled and dived around the breakwater, and headed back into the city.

The country of Haiti was a small, mostly ignored locus of poverty and corruption. In the decades before the end of the twentieth century, its old-growth forests had been stripped away, the tropical woods shipped out to first-world countries for furniture and boat decks. With the forest cover gone, the topsoil washed away with the rains and the land eroded to uselessness; since then, the people had suffered from hunger and ignorance and an endless string of violently amoral dictators.

Then the Company had come.

When the various governments that had participated in the expensive, nationalism-driven race to exploit space threw in the towel—except for a few dozen orbital military platforms—and turned their attentions elsewhere, private industry had rushed to fill the void. And private industry had lost its collective shirt.

Then the Shimizu Corporation had come in and bought aerospace companies by the dozen for next to nothing and used the resources drained from each to solve the one problem each company had been unable to overcome individually—an inexpensive way to put large amounts of mass into orbit. It had also, for all practical purposes, purchased the insolvent and starved island nation of Haiti.

Harris walked slowly through the city, savoring the morning.

The slight ache of hangover behind his eyes was a distraction, but not an important one.

As an entity there was little to love about the Company—it suffered from the same flaws inherent to any organization whose raison d'être was the pursuit of profit. But Shimizu's effect on Haiti, and on Tortuga and Port-de-Paix in particular, as much as it was a side effect of the Company's capital enterprise, had been inarguably good.

There were no unions in Haiti, though most of the Americans and Europeans were teamsters in their home countries. Shimizu didn't want them, so Haiti's president had made them illegal.

Which wasn't all that bad, Harris reflected. He was a teamster himself, belonging to the Chicago, Illinois, local, according to his union card. But the bad old days when companies indentured their workers through the abuse of the company store and hired enforcers, using the sap and the gun to keep the nonunion peace, were long gone.

As little as they might care for the individuals that made up the mass of its work force, the Company knew from long years of studying worker dynamics that there was little profit in oppressing the work force. Workers were more productive when they were happy, and labor disputes caused unpleasant dips in profit margins. So, within reason, Shimizu was openhanded and considerate toward not only the foreign workers but the Creole Haitians as well.

Port-de-Paix was still run-down and shabby, but that was more preference these days than unavoidable necessity. Haitians, the Company had found, liked the city in comfortable disrepair. There was no hunger in Haiti anymore, at least not in families that had a son or daughter on the payroll. And even those that didn't still benefited eventually from the trickle-down of Shimizu's rivers of yen.

The Haitians' insistence on keeping the *texture* of their poverty appealed to him. It meant that urgency tended to lack conviction here, that the people lived their lives instead of pursuing them.

James Harris was done with pursuit. Now he lived simply, for the day. When he was in space, he worked. When he was back dirtside he drank and slept and kept himself numb.

Right now, he thought, he needed a drink.

As much as the old quarter of Port-de-Paix resembled New Orleans, there was nothing alcoholic to be had, at least in public, so early in the morning. So he made his way back to his room, where he kept a liter of *clarin*, the raw Haitian rum that had been a large part of why the natives of the island had been so complacent in the face of penury and squalor for so many years.

There were children on the steps of the house as he walked up, three boys not yet teenagers, enjoying the cool of the morning and their freedom from classes. The Japanese had introduced universal education to the island, but their initial insistence that the Creole children attend as Japanese children did—six days a week, eight hours a day, with tutorials nights and Sundays—went by the wayside rather quickly. Haitian children now attended the Japanese schools three times a week, four hours at a time.

And this was still enough enforced learning to make the children relish the time that was their own. The three boys were sons of his landlord. All three were sprawled comfortably across the steps, throwing stones at the chickens that pecked and scratched in the dust of the narrow courtyard.

They reluctantly turned their attention to Harris and made room for him to climb the steps to the door.

"*Kouman ou ye?*" Harris asked the oldest boy, who took time to aim and throw an acorn-size pebble at the fat, white hen before answering.

"I'm just fine, Mr. Daniels."

"Your papa around?" The boy's father was his source for the *clarin*, one of the many native products that the Company had insisted the government make illegal. That, of course, hadn't stopped the Haitians from making it.

"No. He's traveling." Traveling meaning he hadn't come home after a binge, but was sleeping it off somewhere other than home. It was a code with which he was pretty familiar.

"Okay, I'll see you around."

"Hey, wait. There's an old man and a Company girl in your room, waiting for you."

Harris stopped with his hand on the door's weathered brass knob. "They say who they were?"

"Naw."

Harris stepped back from the door and considered. An old man and a "Company" girl. "Company" for the Haitians meant

Japanese. Which probably meant that his univited guests were
with Shimizu. Company cops, maybe. He didn't always remember what he did nights when he was tanked. So far as he knew,
he'd never hurt anyone.

He thought about it and decided there was nothing they could
tell him he would especially want to hear.

"Thanks, man," he said to the boy. He worked his way back
through the legs and arms, down and off the steps.

"See you," the boy replied. He threw another rock.

Carney paid off the cabbie and gave him extra to wait.

Four hours and an expensive series of bribes had brought them
back to a part of the city very close to where they had begun,
where James Harris, or James Daniels, kept a room.

Now they were going to look for him in a church.

Song hesitated before the wooden door of the chapel. It
seemed imposingly *solid*, not just in its physical substance, but
in the barrier of faith it represented.

To just barge in seemed faintly sacrilegious.

Carney had no such compunctions. He pushed the door open
and urged her inside.

The church was ill lighted, and it took a long second for her
eyes to adjust. When they did she saw that she was inside a
small, nearly empty room. The walls were bare, brown wattle,
the ceiling low and flat. At the back was an altar, above it a
crucifix with a graphic representation of Christ in his passion
nailed to it. The figure struck her as overtly ghoulish: the eyes
were dark shadows, the body emaciated, the ribs showing like
a boat's stringers; from the brow, the hands, and a gaping wound
in the figure's left side ran thick streams of very realistic, very
red blood. On the walls on either side were stylized representations of saints.

Under one of them, on a folding metal chair, sat a small,
dark-skinned man. He watched them quietly, his hands in his
lap.

Carney squinted at the man and cleared his throat. "We were
told someone here might know where we could find a platform
worker by the name of Daniels."

The man in the chair smiled suddenly, his teeth even and
white. He gestured for them to sit and they did so, taking

two of the folding chairs that were scattered around the room.

Song took a deep breath, smelling dust and wood.

"He's not here," the man announced when they were settled. "Is there something you should like me to tell him if I see him?" He spoke formally, his voice and accent pleasantly musical in Song's ear.

"You don't know where he might be?"

"No."

"Perhaps you could tell him that his father wants to speak to him."

"His father?" There was sudden interest in the man's voice. He peered at Carney. "Maybe so, maybe so. What do you want of him?"

"To talk."

The man shrugged. "If I see him . . ."

"You think he might come here, then?"

"I didn't say that, friend."

The two men talked on. Song could see that Carney was irritated and holding his temper only with great effort. His face was red and the lines in his forehead seemed deeper than before.

She was tired. Even with the sleep she had been blessed with the last two nights, in Carney's house and the night before in Port-de-Paix's one international hotel—glorious sleep, dreamless sleep—she was exhausted.

Consciously she knew the fatigue was as much in her spirit as in her body, but it weighed on her nonetheless.

She let her eyes wander again around the room. In the back, where the light was the lowest, she noticed a doorway she missed in her first survey of the little chapel. As she watched, her eyes seem to adjust one fine degree more and could see, faintly outlined against the darkness, the pale oval of a face.

Then the face was withdrawn into the deeper darkness of the room beyond. Or it was never there in the first place. She couldn't be certain.

She closed her eyes, looked again. Nothing.

Carney was standing up. She rose, too, for a moment disconcerted.

"If you see my son, tell him we have something important to talk to him about. Something he would want to hear."

The dark-skinned man—a priest? Song wondered—smiled again and nodded. He walked them to the door and back into the somewhat brighter light of the late afternoon.

There were storm clouds in the sky, rolling in from off the water, and the air smelled of coming rain.

They climbed into the waiting cab and the machine's turbines whined into a higher pitch and lifted it off the pavement. Song sat back in a seat that smelled of sweat and old plastic, her mind racing.

The fatigue that had seemed so heavy a moment before was gone. The face she had seen in the darkened doorway had been light skinned instead of the cocoa or deeper chocolate of the Haitians. She felt a growing certainty that it had been James Harris's.

Carney ordered the driver to return them to their hotel, his voice gruff with disappointment and fatigue. The old man, she realized, had a more personal stake in bringing her here than she had first thought. She wondered if her arguments to him had had anything at all to do with his decision to help her search out his son.

No matter. It was only important that he had led her to her quarry, whatever his motivations. Something deep inside her was troubled at Carney's unrest, but she suppressed it. Pity would only weaken her already shaky resolve.

She came to a sudden decision. She would return to the chapel tonight, after Carney was asleep.

She would come alone and she would find James Harris.

What she would do then—what she would have to do—she put from her mind.

She lay in her bed, nude, enjoying the subtle sensation of the cool night breeze flowing across her skin. The hotel, even by American standards, was modern and comfortable, and the environmental controls on the bedside table could have provided her with any combination of temperature, noise damping and humidity she preferred.

But she liked the punky smell of the island's night air, the movement of it against her body.

She could feel every nuance of the air's flow across her skin, many times better now than she had been able to before they had changed her. Now every nerve worked in an intense unison, reporting pressure and movement of the tiniest degree to the hard-wired parallel fibers and dendritic branches in her altered cerebellum.

She held her right hand up before her eyes, studied the short, masculine nails, the golden tone of the skin. The window whose curtains now billowed faintly in the light breeze had been bolted shut. No one in the West wanted fresh air anymore; they wanted it manufactured, manicured and polished in the way they liked their lives.

She had ripped the bolts from the sill almost without thinking, grasping the edge of the window between her thumb and forefinger and shoving it up. She closed the hand into a fist, studied the tendons and veins. It was a matter of leverage, her cerebellum had told those muscles, bypassing her conscious control of them. Push here, so; apply pressure on this precise line of force.

She had wished the window open, and suddenly, it was open.

It was like having a ghost living inside you, she thought. An ancestor, maybe, an ancient, brilliant warrior, turgid with martial wisdom and physical intuition.

She let her hand drop and a fingernail brushed against her bare breast. The sensation was like a lightning thrust of memory, bringing back images of too-brief moments of passion.

Passion betrayed, she remembered. Love denied.

The rush and hum of traffic on the street below the window had stopped, only the occasional distant rumble of thunder breaking the silence of the sleeping city.

She stood, dug in her bag and found a black body stocking that had been packed carefully inside a makeup case. She pulled it on, the material tight and clinging, sheer though not quite transparent. The material against her bare skin brought those thoughts back again but she refused to acknowledge them and concentrated on the business at hand.

She touched a thin strip of plastic set into the seam on her right thigh. The body stocking became mottled, the black crossed by strips and patches of various shades of gray. As she moved, the mottling moved, matching the light and dark in the colors around her.

Her room was on the third floor of the hotel. She slipped out the window onto the slim ledge that bordered it. Below her, the cobblestones of the pavement gleamed with rainwater.

She reached down a foot and found a seam of mortar between the lines of brick. That cut-off-but-controlling part of her mind—she thought of it now as the Mind, something wholly apart from her own thinking consciousness—told her toes how to find purchase in that small, narrow space and she began working her way down.

Once on the ground, that part of her mind went to work again, orienting her, telling her distance and direction.

She set out at a jog, heading east, staying in the shadows, where the stocking's camouflage worked best, moving, she imagined, like the warrior ghost who haunted her mind.

The little church was just short of three kilometers from the hotel. She covered the distance in ten unhurried minutes, flitting from shadow to shadow.

The street on which the chapel stood, like the house in which Harris lived, was in the oldest part of the city. Most of the buildings here were ancient and squat, made of sand-and-clay brick and of mud wattle. The church itself was one story with a shallow, slanting roof. Its front was plain and mud colored, only the crucifix on the door suggesting how the building was used.

She stood in the shadow of a doorway across the street from the church, watching that door, thinking through her next move.

The sound of voices approaching broke through her concentration.

She sank back into the shallow door frame as far as she was able, its latch pressing deep into the flesh of her back. A half-dozen men came into view, walking slowly together down the street beyond the church.

Boys, she corrected herself as they came closer. None were older than seventeen or eighteen, she guessed.

They were passing a bottle and a cigarette back and forth among themselves. She caught a whiff of the cigarette smoke and the Mind identified something besides tobacco in the smoke, a complex molecule that resembled any one of a dozen variations on a common synthetic hallucinogen.

They were laughing and shouting, preoccupied with their own somewhat-illegal good time. Song held herself very still in the door's shadow, waiting for them to pass.

They came close, but were preoccupied, and she knew that the body stocking and her black hair would make her very difficult to spot from their vantage in the middle of the lighted street.

Then one of the boys began to cough and retch. The others whistled and shouted, banging him on the back.

The afflicted boy stumbled and fell against Song.

Instantly she was out of the doorway, moving away from them. But the boy who had pressed against her grabbed at her in confusion and caught the body stocking she was wearing at the shoulder. She jerked away, but the tough material of the stocking held, stretching a little in the boy's grip.

The others pressed in close around her.

"Holy Mary, would you look at this."

Another hand grabbed a fistful of the stocking's fabric, near her waist. She felt herself pulled out into the light in the middle of the street.

"Great Jesus! A Company girl. And damned near naked!"

Someone dropped the bottle they'd been drinking from and it shattered loudly on the cobblestones. One of the boys blurted, "Shit!"

Song took advantage of the distraction and twisted free. She stood alone in a circle of boys who were nearly old enough to be men and who were obviously aroused, their eyes glazed with alcohol and with the drug they'd been smoking.

One of them reached out and touched the material that stretched taut across her breast. Faster than she could think her hand whipped out like a blade, the inside edge of her palm striking his arm just above the wrist.

The Mind told her that the bone broke under her hand, just as her right foot slipped a precise six inches forward and her left leg came up, using that momentum, into a snap-kick that would strike the boy's Adam's apple, crushing his windpipe and strangling him with his own collapsed larynx.

A fraction of an instant before she struck something took

her whole body away from her. It seemed to reach inside and, gripping her by everything vital, shake her like a dog might shake a rag doll. The boys, even the one with the broken forearm, jerked and shuddered around her in an insane, agonized dance.

Her mind—both her minds—gave way and she collapsed into blackness.

CHAPTER SIX

October 18, 2070

She woke with a throbbing headache.

The room she was in was pitch black and damp. Under her was a mattress of some kind, covered in rough fabric.

She seemed to be alone in the room. She listened intently and could only hear the quiet tick of raindrops falling to the ground from the roof, and, under that, the dull susurration of surf.

So she was near the ocean. That in itself was something, a single fact to place herself in the world.

She sat up in the bed.

Someone rose up from the floor in front of her, outlined against the lesser darkness of a window. She stifled a scream and scrambled in a panic off the bed. A voice near the floor, near where the figure's feet should have been, croaked something that sounded like *"Grill arwaaake!"*

Her captor didn't move. She stood across from him, her back against a rough wall, her hands up, her feet apart in a posture the Mind told her body to take. She knew that if she started to attack, the Mind would kill whoever it was that stood before her now.

The figure held both hands above its head, palms out, in the classic Western-movie gesture of "I surrender."

A man's voice said, "I'm not going to hurt you. I promise."

She didn't answer or lower her guard.

"Look, I'm sorry I had to shanghai you like this. I wouldn't have done this way, if anyone had asked me."

"Who are you?"

"That, as they say, depends."

"Depends?"

"On who you are. And who you were looking for, out there in the dark in your skimpies."

She felt herself blush and for an instant was glad that it was dark in the room.

"My name is Song Lan. I work for COSEAR. For the United Nations Council on Space Exploration and Research."

"Yes? Then you don't work for the Company? For Shimizu? You're not a cop?"

"No."

"Well, hell. I thought you were one of their Materials Loss people."

"No. What are Material Loss people?"

He ignored the question. "Who was that with you, earlier, when you were trying to find me?"

"The man at the church didn't tell you?"

"He told me who he claimed to be. What I'm asking you, is who he really is."

"He is who he is. He's Hugh Carney. He used to work for the ISA. He's a doctor."

"Bull."

"What reason do I have to lie to you?"

"I don't know. Most everyone's got a reason, though. What are you doing here?"

"Who are *you*?" she returned, letting a note of irritation enter into her voice.

"Hasn't anyone ever told you that it's rude to answer a question with a question?"

"No," she answered.

"If I promise to move slow, do you think it would be okay if I put on a light? We're a bit behind the times here—I still have to flip a switch."

"Of course," she said. But she didn't let down her guard. He moved over to a wall and pushed at something. The overhead lights came on and she squinted against the sudden relative brightness.

"Who are you?" she asked again. As she spoke, she knew with a quick access of insight exactly who he was.

"Who do you think I am?"

"You're James Harris. You survived the destruction of the colony at 61 Cygni B."

There was silence between them for a long moment.

"I don't know where you get your information, lady, but the Cygni colony's first transmission won't even reach us for another five years. So far as anyone knows, they're doing just fine."

"We both know that that is not true. We both know what happened to the colony. And to you, Mr. Harris."

"Look, I don't know anyone by that name. Check with Shimizu—my name is Daniels."

"I know who you are." She studied his face. "They changed you, how you look, but you're James Harris. I've studied you, I've seen your photos and holos. You're Harris."

He glared at her for a minute, then shrugged. "And if I am, what do you want from me?"

"Help."

"For what?"

"To save the world." As she said it, she knew that that was exactly what she wanted of him. She could only pray that those who had sent her wanted the same thing. Because whatever she wanted, however desperately she might want it, she knew that she would do what she was told.

Even if it meant the end of that same world.

He pulled out a chair from against the wall and sat down facing her. She stayed where she was, still ready to strike. The doubt, almost derision, on his face was obvious.

"I should have known. You're some kind of religious nut."

"No, I—"

"How the hell did you get Carney involved in this? One thing that old bastard isn't is holy. Blackmail? Bribery?"

He came away from the chair, his eyes blazing with anger and . . . something else. She found her own gaze locked into his; she looked into his eyes and was suddenly afraid. She couldn't tell their color in the low, yellow lamplight, but she could see an intensity in them that was startling. They seemed to glow of themselves with an inner fire, and she caught herself wondering why she hadn't seen him earlier, in the dark, just by the light— of insanity? or of something else?—in his eyes. For an instant she was convinced that he was possessed, but then her rational, scientist's mind rejected that for what it must be—a projection of her own fear and guilt.

Flustered, she tried to explain. "I am not a 'nut,' and religion has nothing to do with it. I am a scientist, from Beijing University."

"Yes? You're Chinese?"

"Yes."

"You speak English damned well. Almost no accent."

She shrugged. "Much practice." She could not, of course, tell him about the Mind.

"So what do you want with James Harris?"

"You are Harris?"

"Yes," he sighed. "I'm Harris."

She relaxed a degree, let the Mind retreat beneath the rational surface of her own superego. "What did you hit me with, out in the street?"

Harris grinned suddenly, the expression alleviating somewhat the intensity in his eyes. "I didn't hit you, dear. I just shook you up a little."

He went to a low box on the floor against the wall nearest the door. He ran a finger along the box's seam and it eased slowly open. From it he took what appeared to be a thick rod, about ten or eleven centimeters in diameter. He held it out in her direction and she saw that it was a thin-walled cylinder, inside of which was mounted another cylinder, perhaps three centimeters across. The entire device was a little more than a meter long.

It looked very little like a weapon, and she said so.

"You knocked seven people unconscious with *that*?"

"You bet. And it shook my teeth some as well."

"What is it?"

"Construction equipment. Officially known as a PIM, a Percussive-something-something—I don't remember the entire name. It's a harmonic resonator. Roughnecks call it a vibrator—lots of bad jokes about what lonely ladies could do with one. It's used for loosening construction plates on the platforms, when we need access to wiring or when we're taking something apart to rebuild. You touch a metal plate with this—" He turned the cylinder around and tapped the inner rod, which, she now noted, protruded a few centimeters from the larger cylinder. "—and, bango, presto, the bonding medium underneath turns to dust. Without damaging the plate."

He placed the vibrator back in its box and pushed the lid closed. "Vacuum insulates everything else from it up there. No air, no transmission of sound waves. I'd heard that it could knock a man silly if he were eight or nine meters or less in front of the resonator, if you used the thing in atmosphere. I saw you out there getting ready to wrestle with six young men. Anson—he's the man you met in the *Ti-legliz*—happened to have this baby lying around, so I thought I'd see if it were true. It was. It knocked me down, too, but standing behind it, I got a lot less of the effect than you did."

He looked at her closely, as if the thought had just occurred to him that she had been the brunt of his experiment. "Are you okay?"

"Just a headache. And, as you said, my teeth ache."

He worked his jaw. "Yeah. It does have that effect."

"Why was your friend Anson in possession of a machine for construction in space?"

" 'In possession of?' You do sound like a Shimizu cop. Do you have any idea how much one of these things is worth?"

She shook her head.

"One hell of a lot, to folks who'll restamp its serial numbers and sell it back to Shimizu. He stole it, of course. Or, rather, he was getting ready to fence it for someone who stole it. It's part of the economy here. It's one of the reasons the Company keeps a police force around."

He looked at her hard and pointed to the body stocking.

"That isn't standard issue for Chinese scientists these days, is it?"

She glanced down at the sheer fabric, the gray and black shifting slightly with the movement of her body. "No. It's not."

"And?"

"I—I wanted to be sure to get close to you, to talk to you. I didn't want you to be warned—" That was true enough. "—you've been hiding from us all day."

He nodded. "I thought you were Company cops. My mistake. Call it paranoia. It's not every day I get chased around by old men and pretty Oriental girls."

She felt a strange sensation inside when he said the word "pretty." She felt herself blushing again and suppressed it with a burst of anger. "Where are we, and why did you kidnap me?" she demanded.

"Kidnap? Sweetheart, I saved your ass. There were *six* of those boys, and they knew what they were up to."

She held back the retort that hovered on her tongue. One thing she could not reveal to anyone was what her body and mind were capable of. The odd thought occurred to her then that she, too, was a state secret.

"Where are we?" she asked instead.

"This is Anson's place, the fellow who runs the *Ti-legliz*."

"You said that before. What is a *Ti-legliz*?"

"The chapel you were in. *Ti-legliz* means something like 'little church.' More Haitians worship in them than in the real churches."

"It's not a real church?"

He shook his head. "Uh-uh. Some of the liturgy's Catholic, but mostly it's voodoo. Ghost magic. Benevolent spirits. *Loas*, they're called. Kind of like Catholic saints for the common man, if he's Creole."

"Superstition."

"Maybe."

"You believe in their *loas*?"

Harris shrugged.

She remembered something and looked around the room. "I heard another voice, before, in the dark."

"Say, 'hi,' Bim," Harris commanded.

" 'ello," said a voice from under the bed.

Song jumped and caught her breath.

"Come on out. The lady and I are through wrestling around. It's safe."

In the dimness under the low, steel frame something moved, then edged out into the light. It was furred, relatively small, moving out in a strange, awkward crawl.

It took her a moment to realize that it was a dog, a black-and-white terrier of some sort. It pulled itself free from the confines underneath the bed and rose to all fours, shaking dust off.

"Song Lan, meet Abimdigo, master of all he surveys and my best and only friend."

Song hesitated, then held out a hand. The dog sniffed it and licked her knuckles.

" 'appy to meet," it said, its voice like gargling marbles.

"So am I, Bim. Happy to meet you." She reached to scratch his ears, then looked to Harris.

"Go ahead. He likes it."

She did, and Abimdigo did like it, stretching out flat and moving his head in rhythm with her scratching.

Harris watched her, then seemed suddenly to come to a decision. "Let's go for a walk."

Bim echoed the word, though it sounded more like "auk" than "walk."

"Walk? Where?"

"I want you to see something."

Song felt a moment of apprehension. There was something strange in Harris's voice. But she nodded. "Sure."

"Let's find something to make you decent, first." There was a scarred-up and ancient chest of drawers near the bed. Harris pulled the top drawer out and dug through it. He found a large, baggy shirt and handed it to her.

"That'll keep you from scaring anybody, anyhow." He smiled at her again, and she found that she liked it when he smiled.

She smiled back and pulled the shirt on over her head.

"Auk!" Bim said again, insistent this time.

Harris opened the door and let the dog go first. "Sometimes he's a little hard to understand. Some sounds you just can't make without more in the way of lips than he's got. He does pretty good with vowels. Some consonants give him trouble, *v*s and *w*s, fricatives and explosives."

Song followed Abimdigo out the door. "Your father owns a talker. Two of them, in fact. Rottweilers, he called them."

Harris shut the door, joined them on the steps. "Yes? So? Lots of people own them."

She let the subject drop. These two men are very much alike, she thought. It was an observation at which she suspected Harris would bridle.

A breeze, filled with the smell of salt and fish, blew across her face. She could hear the surf and knew it was close by, but she couldn't see the water in the pitch darkness.

Harris took her elbow and guided her down the steps to the sand. The Mind flinched at the touch, but she controlled it.

As they came out from under the canopy of the trees that surrounded Anson's house, the sky opened up, bright and wide, alive with stars.

She caught her breath and stared. What small part of her life had not been spent underground had been spent in cities. What she knew of stars she knew from charts and pictures, and from the impersonal distance of a radio telescope. She had never seen a sky so black or so filled with the diamond-glitter of stars. It took her breath away.

She stumbled, her gaze locked on the terrifying wonder above in the night sky. Her heart seemed to stop in her chest, her breath refused to come. Her head spun with dizzy vertigo. She started to fall.

Harris was by her side instantly, supporting her. "What's the matter? Are you all right?"

He eased her down to sit on the sandy path. "I guess I shook you up more than you thought."

"No," she said. Her voice was only a gasp.

He followed her gaze up. "It's just the stars."

When she didn't respond, he passed his hand in front of her face. Her eyes focused close onto his palm and she was able to look away from the sickening glory of the night sky. She stared at the ground, her head swimming, fighting back a strong wave of nausea.

"What's the matter?" Harris asked again.

She caught her breath. "Just a minute." Then, "I grew up in the Beijing Catacombs, in the tunnels. I never saw the sky until I was almost seventeen. Sometimes, it's still very hard to take."

"Agoraphobia."

"Yes. Most of the people I grew up among can't leave the tunnels at all. It's just too much, the open space, the sky. It's like . . . you might disappear, as if all the openness could suck you up into itself, body and soul. Everything seems to whirl around and go to pieces. Usually, I can handle it. A lot of forced hypnotherapy."

"Forced hypnotherapy? The stuff they do with sensory deprivation and wires in the brain?"

She closed her eyes, felt the muscles along her jawline jump. "Yes. That's it."

He whistled through his teeth. "Doesn't sound especially pleasant."

"It wasn't."

"If you want to go back . . ."

"No, just give me a minute."

She waited until the heaving, seasickness feeling had completely passed, then she let Harris help her to her feet. When she was standing, she slowly opened her eyes.

"Better?"

"Some. I think I could look up again, in a moment."

"Sure that's a good idea?"

"No. But I want to. I've seen the stars before, at night in Beijing. But not like this; just through the city lights, a few of the bright ones. Not all of the Milky Way like that. And never without all the buildings around." She shuddered. "It was a shock. Kind of terrifying."

She looked at the horizon, realizing she must be looking out to sea, though she still couldn't see the water in the darkness. The stars were low to the horizon there, with nothing in the way to block their light.

She let her eyes wander up again into the vast expanse of darkness peppered with lights. Her head swam again with vertigo, but she fought it back. The stars flickered, sparks against velvet, close enough to touch.

"My god," she whispered.

"Pretty glorious, isn't it."

"Yes. Yes, it is."

"There are few places on Earth, at least on land, where you can see it better."

Enraptured, she didn't answer. Harris seemed to understand. For a long while they simply stood in the path and stared together at the glory.

Eventually, Harris spoke. "Do you know the stars?"

She nodded, then realized his eyes weren't on her. "Yes. I know them. For most of my life I studied them, before I could even see them. When I was a little girl, they represented everything untouchable and out of reach to me. They were dreams."

"Do you know the constellation of the Northern Cross?"

"Yes. It's there." She pointed, drawing the cross. "Between Hercules and Delphinus. Except we called it Cygnus, the Swan— those are his wings." As she said the words, she realized what he was showing her.

"It's dim. You can barely see it." He picked out a single star in the constellation, pointed to it. "That's 61 Cygni. It's a binary, two stars. But you know that."

"Yes."

He was silent for a moment. "That's where I left everything that ever meant anything to me, buried in the snow and ice."

There was nothing she could say. She dragged her eyes away from the blaze of stars.

Harris shook his head as if to clear it. "Let's go. Anson will be finishing up."

"Finishing up what?"

"You'll see." He took her elbow again, and this time even the Mind accepted it, his touch firm and comforting.

He led her into the darkness, away from the sound of the surf. There was no moon; the path was lit only by starlight. She could hear Bim on the trail ahead, rustling through the underbrush that flanked it on both sides.

"We're far from the city?"

"Not far. Over there, no more than a klick or so. Port-de-Paix doesn't have suburbs to speak of. Just kind of peters out into shantytown and second-growth jungle. Used to be more, but since Shimizu enforced population control and started shipping workers out to Japan, a lot of it has gone to ruins or been torn down."

She looked off in the direction he was pointing. There was a very faint glow on the sky above the trees. The city.

She glanced over at Harris. Now that she had a reference point, the Mind oriented her precisely, telling her she was south-southeast of the hotel, maybe five kilometers from the Airpark. If she were to try to take Harris by herself, now would be the time.

But something deep inside her rebelled at the thought. There was something undefinable about Harris that touched her. She had seen it in his eyes: somehow she and he shared an awareness beyond the ken of others. And more than that—again, she had the strange feeling that he was *possessed* by something that had looked out at her through his eyes.

Rationalizations, she told herself. The facts were that there was little chance she could get all the way to Carney's plane without being seen—and even on Haiti, someone would likely want to know why she was carrying an unconscious man over her shoulder.

No. She would wait. Others would come. Probably in the morning, flying in from the East.

"Where are we going?" she asked.

"You're one of those people who can't enjoy a surprise, aren't you?'' He sighed. ''We're going to see Anson. In his *houn-four*.''

''*Hounfour?*''

''His temple.''

''The chapel, you mean? The *Ti-legliz*?''

''No. That is a different place, for different ceremonies. A *hounfour* is a voodoo sanctuary, a *houngan's* temple. Anson is a *houngan*, a priest.''

''A voodoo priest,'' she said doubtfully.

''Right. You never did answer my question.''

''Which question?''

''What you want with me.''

''I told you.''

''I gave up saving worlds. I don't even wear the tights with the letter 'S' on the chest anymore.''

''What?''

''Never mind. Obscure historical reference.'' He pressed her elbow and they stopped walking. ''I would like to know what the hell you're talking about. In clear, unobscure terms, what is it you expect to get from me?''

''The Earth is dying. And I think you caused it.''

''Dying?'' His voice was incredulous. ''Because of me? How so?''

''You wouldn't have noticed it here yet. At least not much. But in China thousands of people a day are already dying. Winter is coming—the *da han*, the Great Cold. In perhaps twelve, thirteen years, most of the world's surface will be in permanent winter. Some crops might be grown, near the equator, but billions will die. The computer extrapolations suggest four-fifths or more of the planet's human population will die. There will be wars for food and for arable land—my country is close to attempting that now. When the struggles are over, few will be left and their survival will be the fiercest sort of struggle. The world will be frozen over, a wasteland of ice and snow.''

She stopped, drew a deep breath. ''All this should sound familiar to you.''

''Yes,'' he answered. His voice was distant, thoughtful. ''It happened on Comfort. The probe—the original Chernetsky-robot survey—made us believe that it was a paradise, warm and fertile. No life more intelligent than a cow. What we found was just as you described. A wasteland. Ice, snow, bitter cold. We set down on the equatorial landmass anyway—where the hell else could we go? Even if the engines could cook up all the zero-point energy we would need to take us fifty times around the galaxy, our ship was built for a one-way trip; there was no way to reactivate the stasis bins, and no way to stock enough provisions in the thing for sixteen years of flight, and no navigational programming for the computers. It killed us, one by one. The cold, the despair—it killed them all."

"Except you," she said quietly. "You came back."

"Yes. I came back."

"You don't remember? What happened, how you were brought back?"

"No. Not everything. Hardly anything, really. What I mostly remember is a *feeling*. Cold. But warm, too. Safe, maybe, protected. Sounds childish, doesn't it? Sunday school fantasies."

"But it's real. You're here."

"I'm here."

"And something brought you. Or, rather, something came here *with you*."

She could see his face, just barely, by the starlight and the wan, yellow glow of the moon just rising above the trees. Comprehension was dawning.

"You're saying I brought the winter with me. What happened on Comfort is happening here." He looked into her eyes. "That's what you're trying to tell me, isn't it?"

"Yes."

He nodded to himself, suddenly distracted. "Maybe I should have known," he whispered.

"Why?" Song asked quietly.

He didn't answer. "What is it you think I can do?"

"I don't know. I guess I was hoping you might have some idea. Do you?"

Before he could answer, there was a sudden, rolling sound in the near distance.

"What?"

"Drums," Harris answered. "Anson's audience will be clearing out soon."

They moved down the path and the drums strengthened, becoming an undertone as insistent as the surf she had heard on awakening, but wilder, quicker, more intense.

"It sounds like a jungle movie."

Harris spoke quietly without looking at her. "I don't think Anson would appreciate the comparison, but I suppose it's accurate enough. That's where the ceremonies originated, in 'darkest Africa.' "

She nodded, then realized that he couldn't see the gesture. "I know a little about this, from an anthropology seminar I attended on primitive ritual. Psychic surgery, healing, zombies and the like. All produced for gullible, paying audiences, usually. Fakery."

As she said the word, she knew it sounded like—probably was—whistling in the dark, but Harris answered her question seriously.

"No, there's no fakery. Anson does give tourist shows from time to time, but he gives them the real thing, in a small dose. They get a taste of the externals of the Mystery. That's all they really want, anyway. Truth—especially someone else's truth— is more than most people care to experience."

"Is that why you've brought me here? To experience truth?"

"Perhaps. My truth, anyway. I stopped believing a long time ago in universal truths."

Shortly she could see a lightening in the darkness ahead that became a bonfire as they cleared the trees. Someone stepped from the darkness beside the path and blocked their way.

"Can I help you folks?"

"*Kouman ou ye,* Jean?"

"James?"

"*Oui.* I've brought a guest. A doubter. Think we can show her the path?"

"Hey, you bet." The man was old, weathered looking. He looked to Song. "I'm happy you've come. This is a good night for the spirits."

"Is there ever a bad night for the spirits?" she asked.

"I've never known of one. Come on in, folks. Anson's clearing out the last of the guests."

They followed him into an empty, fenced courtyard. Near its center a fire burned low, mostly ash and glowing coals.

Anson waited for them near the fire. "Show's over, James. You missed a good one."

"Yeah, I figured. There's something else I'd like you to show Song Lan, though."

Anson looked to Song Lan. She could see the red reflection of the dying fire in his eyes.

"You want to visit the graves."

"Yes."

"You sure you want to do that, Jim?" His voice was solemn.

Harris looked to her. She didn't know what it was he planned, but she felt confident that it was important to him. She returned his gaze.

"Yeah, I'm sure. Let's go take a look."

Anson shrugged, the gesture quick and noncommittal. Then he grinned. "Sure, man. I'll give you the dollar tour. Let me close up."

He went ahead into a low building on the far side of the courtyard. Harris and Song Lan waited outside.

"Graves?" she whispered.

"Yes. You'll see."

His tone said that he didn't intend to explain further. She tried another tack. "This is the *hounfour*, this yard?"

Harris nodded. "This is the center of Anson's power, where he practices his rituals, makes his magic. It's kind of like a hospital for the faithful. They come here when they have problems, and he helps them out."

"With magic."

"With magic, yes. Charms, powders sometimes." He tapped the side of his head with a finger. "There's lots of magic in here. Even a scientist should know that."

"That's not magic. That's imagination, self-delusion. Psychosomatic pain healed through the power of suggestion."

"You're quibbling over terms. Magic is whatever you don't understand. Magic is a mystery. Some mysteries are a little more profound than others."

Anson came back. In his hands was an object that looked vaguely like a golden, metallic rugby ball, rounded and blunt. He handed the object to Harris, who hefted it and held it before Song Lan.

"Do you know what this is?" he asked.

She studied it closely without touching it. Close up, it appeared a burnished, brass color. It was etched with thousands of tiny, dark lines, each the width of a hair. The lines seemed to cut through the golden surface, making the whole appear somehow less substantial, more delicate.

"Take it," Harris commanded.

She complied. When she held it in her hands, it seemed to weigh no more than a child's rubber balloon filled with nothing but breath. But it was undeniably metal of some kind, cool and smooth and very solid in her hands.

Harris took it back and tossed it up. It seemed to hover for an instant before drifting back down into his hands. He then held it high and threw it with considerable force against the wall of the building. It didn't make it. It stopped a few centimeters from the wall as if it had struck an invisible rubber bumper and bounced back into his hands as if it were indeed a gold-colored rugby ball.

"What is it?"

"Damned if I know. Anson thinks it's a talisman, a sign from God."

"And you?"

"I'm not sure I can argue with that. Maybe it is a talisman—" He made his voice unnaturally deep, making his words sound playfully profound. "—an Icon of a Harsh and Jealous God."

"And you believe this?"

Harris was silent for a moment. "No, not really."

Anson grinned, his teeth white in the dimness. "Missy, your friend thinks that thing is a spaceship. For fairies, I suppose."

"A spaceship?" Beneath her incredulity, her heart froze, recalling what she herself had found adrift in space.

"Not a ship, necessarily. It just . . . feels familiar, in an odd way. I *feel* that that is a craft. I don't know how it works. I don't know how anyone would get into it—if that's what you do. Call it intuition. *That* is a craft of some kind. And it has something to do with how I got home—all of this does."

"All of what?"

"You'll see," Anson said. "First, I want to give you something." He handed Song Lan a small bundle, the size of a walnut, wrapped in coarse cloth.

She took it. "What's this? Another spaceship? For fleas?"

Anson chuckled. "No, for luck. Herbs, some bird bones. Nothing too unpleasant. I give them to all my friends. I hope you'll keep it."

"I would be honored." She tried to find a place to put it and finally settled for slipping it under the cloth bodice of the body stocking she wore. It felt bulky and warm against her breast.

Anson looked to Harris, who handed back the golden object. Anson tossed it up, watched it float slowly down, defying everything Song Lan knew about the nature of gravity and the physical universe.

"Let's do it."

Anson put the object away and led them out of the courtyard into the darkness under the trees.

The place Anson took them was nondescript, an empty, weedy field, barren and cold in the moonlight.

In the center of the field were two unmarked graves, side by side, little more than bare rises of dirt.

On the two low mounds were shapes, twists of ribbons, withered flowers, pieces of wood and plastic with circles and crosses of red and black stenciled on them, a colorful scattering of what seemed to be trash. But Song Lan knew better. The bits and pieces had been left as offering or petition.

Two men are buried here," Anson offered. "We don't know who they were. They appeared, as if dropped from the sky, both dead, here, in this field. Not a mark on them. Both of 'em cold as Popsicles. Kids found 'em, both times. Scared 'em to death, just about."

"You didn't report this to the authorities?"

Anson shook his head. "No. Could have been a lot of trouble. Shimizu would've sent their cops and everyone would have grief.

"Besides," he added, gesturing to take in the scattered offerings, "they weren't killed by men. They were killed by a *loa*. It wasn't any of Shimizu's damned business."

"A *loa*?"

"A spirit, missy. A god, maybe. Of sorts. How would *you* explain it?"

"I don't know. But I'm sure there's an explanation to be had. Someone could have dumped them here, during the night."

"No ma'am. Middle of the day. First time, there was a bunch of kids playing out here. They said the air itself went all white and foggy and then he just appeared. Like magic. Sounds like a *loa* to me. Any of your machines can do that?"

She shook her head. "No. There wasn't any identification on them?"

"Just a name, on the first one. It was embossed on his shirt.

Calvin. He was wearing cold-weather gear, soaking wet and nearly frozen through. And in case you haven't noticed, this is the tropics. It gets some cold in the mountains, but down here, never.''

Song Lan stood over the graves and felt an eerie chill go through her. It passed and was replaced by anger and a touch of sorrow. ''You just buried them? You didn't try to find out if they had family?''

Anson was solemn. ''That's right. We keep our mysteries to ourselves. It's our way.''

She turned to Harris. ''What do you have to do with this?''

Harris pursed his lips thoughtfully. ''Anson thinks I brought them here. Just like you think I'm killing the planet. Seems I've a lot to answer for.''

''You brought them? How?''

''The *loa*. It moves through James.''

''Moves through you? What does he mean?''

Harris didn't answer. ''Let's go back to the *hounfour*.''

''You won't tell me.''

''No. I'll do you one better. I'll show you.''

Anson carefully added slim pieces of split wood to the coals in the center of the courtyard.

''Have to be careful with the firewood, these days. Shimizu doesn't allow trees to be cut anymore. Probably a good thing, but it makes the rituals more difficult.'' He leaned in close and blew on the coals. A thin flame flickered up with a crackle among the pieces of new wood.

He sat upright again. ''Luckily, in Haiti you can get almost anything if you're willing to pay enough. James, come and sit by me.''

Harris squatted down beside the fire. Song Lan followed, sitting down in the dirt nearby.

Anson tossed something into the fire that sputtered and smoked, giving off an oily smell.

Song Lan watched doubtfully as the *houngan* drew figures and symbols in the dirt with a twig.

He pointed with the stick to one of the figures he had drawn. It was a simple circle inside of another circle, lopsided and clumsily drawn.

''This is the *veve*—the sign—of James's *loa*.''

"What does it mean?"

"Everything. And nothing. No beginning and no end."

"What does *that* mean?"

Anson shrugged. "I'm not sure. It's strong though. As spirits go, this one is *beaucoup* powerful."

"How do you know about it? How did you come to know its '*veve*'?"

Anson tapped his head with a forefinger, the same gesture Harris had used earlier in speaking of his "Mystery."

"It told me, in here. You'll see." He faced back to the fire. After a moment he began a low moaning that strengthened into a singsong incantation. Some of the words were English or French; others she couldn't identify.

"You're calling a spirit?" she whispered.

Anson shook his head without breaking his chanting. She could see his eyes were closed and his brow furrowed with concentration.

Harris spoke, his voice soft but strained. "It's *my* spirit. I call it. Anson's just doing his own thing. Think of it as atmosphere."

"*Your spirit?* You *call* it?"

He smiled wanly. "Watch."

His eyes closed slowly, a look of concentration coming over his face.

For a long minute nothing happened.

Then everything seemed to happen at once.

The very air between them seemed to become milky and opaque. She found herself rubbing her eyes and realizing that the problem was not her vision. A perceptible chill settled onto the courtyard that was Anson's *hounfour*.

Something touched her mind and she screamed, overwhelmed with images. She flew like a ghost through thin, blue ether, nothing below her but the ravening thinness of air, a deep, wide well that held itself open to swallow her.

Then just as suddenly she was lying breathless on the ground before the fire in the *hounfour*. She felt as if she had been dragged bodily into the air and thrust upward and out into the incredible distance of sky. Amazingly, Harris and Anson looked as if they had not moved; both sat calm and unperturbed, facing the fire.

Harris opened his eyes and grinned at her.

"Enjoy the ride?"

"What was that?" she asked, her voice a hoarse whisper.

"I call it the Angel."

"The *loa*," Anson said quietly. "You rode with it. As I said. Powerful."

"Unbelievable." She could only wonder what the listeners-in-secret who had sent her made of what they had heard.

She hoped it shocked the hell out of them.

It had certainly shocked the hell out of her.

The moon had fully risen when they reached the beach, and it floated above them like a broad, yellow face, familiar and comforting.

They sat together on a blanket Harris had gotten from Anson. Neither of them spoke; silently, they watched the fiery wash of stars displayed across the sky. Bim had walked this far with them, then he had taken off on his own, down the beach.

After a long while, Harris took a deep breath.

"Out there—" He pointed out across the water. "—not very far, is an island named Tortuga. It was a pirates' stronghold a few hundred years ago, a place where they could come to count their money and enjoy their plunder in privacy. It's still a pirate stronghold—different pirates, yen instead of pieces of eight, but still pirates. They weren't all just thieves, you know."

She shook her head. She knew of pirates, but she didn't know where he was leading.

"They were adventurers, first. Men who took chances, pushed the envelope. That's why I had them send me here after they released me from the hospital. For every two weeks I spend down here in drunken reality, I get two weeks up there, walking the razor."

"Sounds a little like adrenaline addiction."

"I suppose that's true enough. You're always a little clinical, aren't you, Song Lan?"

"I'm a scientist," she answered simply.

"Yes. A scientist. Objective, uninvolved."

"Not always."

He gazed up without speaking. Then he brought his eyes down to Song's face. "Even I've got to wonder sometimes if somewhere deep inside I'm not a touch suicidal. Still, I feel alive up there in a way I never can dirtside. I feel . . . connected. Does that sound nuts?"

"No. It sounds lonely."

He nodded. "It is, I suppose. I want that, too, I think. Wanted it."

Song felt his hand touch her wrist, lightly, almost absently.

"I left her there to die. She did die. She's been dead for six years."

"According to what I was told, you didn't leave. You were taken."

He shook his head. "No. That's wrong. I wanted to go. Wanted it more than you would believe. Near the end I prayed . . ."

"And it was answered."

"Yes. It was answered." He was silent for a moment. "Now I'm here. And I wish—at least I think I wish—I was still there." She heard him turn again, felt his breath against her face. "Pretty screwed up, wouldn't you say?"

She reached out into the darkness, felt the roughness of his two-day beard. "Yes. Very screwed up."

"It's still with me. You saw it. Part of it is out there somewhere, where the air is thin and very cold. Cold. It likes the cold." He grinned at her suddenly. "I think that's also one of the reasons I came here, because it doesn't like it here. Too warm. But it's drawn to me—it's here, too, right now. You saw it in the *hounfour*."

"I saw . . . something. I don't understand what happened. What did you do?"

"I didn't *do* anything. I just called. And it came. It came because it's never left me. It's still in here—" He tapped his head. "—like a fly in a bottle."

There was nothing, she realized, that she could say to that. Harris was either entirely insane—which seemed unlikely, given what she had seen—or privy to something she had no way of understanding.

"Why did you show me this? You only met me a few hours ago. You hardly know who I am."

"I don't know," he said slowly. He looked directly into her eyes, and just for a moment she thought she saw in his eyes a flicker of that same strange fire she had seen there earlier, in Anson's house. Then it was gone. "It's strange you should ask— I've been wondered all night what it was I felt about you that kept me from just leaving you out on that street for the cops to pick up. We're alike in some way I can't define. Something told me I could trust you. I went with it.''

"You don't trust many people, do you?''

"No.''

"I am honored.'' It was true; she felt gratitude for his faith. It made the fact that she had no choice but to betray him all the more horrible. But she had to do as she had been told. She *must*; there was no room for hesitation, no leeway for the demands of her own conscience.

A thought occurred to her.

"When do you lift next?''

He hesitated, and her heart clenched like a fist with irrational fear. She knew what he was going to answer.

"In the morning. Just after dawn.''

"So soon?'' she asked, struggling to keep her voice level. She ran through a rapid calculation in her head. They would arrive too late. She felt at once elated and terrified.

She had to struggle to keep herself from touching that spot on her cheekbone. Everything she heard, they heard.

Harris saw her confusion and misinterpreted it.

He kissed her.

She found herself kissing him back.

Without surrendering the embrace, they lay back on the blanket together. Harris touched her and she responded.

Overhead the stars glittered, eternal and uncaring.

After they had made love, they swam in the cool, wine-darkness of the sea. They floated together underneath the stars, and when they kissed, their mouths were salty with brine and the taste of life.

Later, they lay together, the cool breeze blowing across them from off the water.

Song shivered, feeling an edge of chill in the wind. She pressed against Harris's body, feeling the warmth of his bare skin.

She could feel the regular rise and fall of his breath. He was asleep.

She reached with one hand into the body stocking she had discarded. In a tiny pocket beside the control strip in the thigh she found a needle-slim, metallic straw.

With infinite care, she pressed the device against the skin

behind Harris's ear, held it there for a second, then threw it away into the sand.

Under his skin, where he would be very unlikely to find it, was now implanted a microscopically small—less than the width of a strand of hair—transmitter, activated and powered by the electric current in Harris's own cells. It was a much less complex device than the one embedded in her own flesh. It simply sent out a single, repeating signal in the manner of a homing beacon.

Again, she pressed close to him, shivering.

The megalith stood in a flat, nearly empty plain of concrete, four square kilometers of it, broken only occasionally by low buildings of the same gray material. It was a singularly bleak landscape, relieved only by the sharply contrasting structure that dominated it.

The tower was nearly a kilometer tall, a thin, sharply pointed obelisk made of plastisteel sheathed in a rosin concrete and vast panes of clear Plexi. From a distance it looked like an immense, somewhat more tapered version of the Washington Monument.

Up close it looked like something out of a dream, the sliver of sun just dawning above the horizon setting the polished sides afire with light. It seemed to reach up forever, impossibly tall.

The crewboat hissed up out of the water onto the concrete ramp below the tower without appreciably slowing its breakneck pace through the predawn dimness. It slewed past the obelisk and slid into a low hanger, then settled down onto the concrete, its fans wheezing to a stop.

James Harris climbed out of the craft with the rest of his crew, six men and seven women. A few of them talked among themselves, bitching about the crewboat's pilot or about Shimizu's animosity toward unions. The others, like Harris, kept to their own thoughts.

A lift whisked them down to the shuttle level, more than three hundred stories under the surface of Tortuga.

After they were suited up, they filed into the tube breech that held their ''bird''—Shimizu's standard Lift and Reentry Vehicle, called with a typical lack of imagination ''Lurvs'' by the platform roughnecks who were unceremoniously stuffed into the vehicles' cramped passenger bays.

Harris strapped himself into his couch and waited for the quick-count to initial acceleration to begin.

The LRVs were relatively simple in design. Like the old American space shuttles or the Russian *Buran* vehicles, the LRVs were designed to achieve orbit and then glide back down to dirtside for a runway landing. And, like the shuttles, the LRVs used rockets, but only for maneuvering and for initial acceleration.

The ship's engines would fire for a few seconds, sending the LRV down the bore of the acceleration tunnel. Then the bulk of the ship's accretion of velocity would begin, as magnetic pulses literally sucked it along the bore of linear accelerator that was the heart of the tunnel.

As the tunnel led out under the waters of the Caribbean, it angled upward until, a hundred kilometers inland, the LRV would shoot as if out of a gun barrel from the mouth of the tunnel near the peak of one of Haiti's mountains, hurtling upward with enough velocity to throw it into low Earth orbit.

With the perfection of super-conducting magnets and the Chernetsky zero-point generator, the system had been possible for more than fifty years before the Shimizu Company had put it to use. The problem had always been the expense of construction of a mass accelerator dozens of kilometers in length.

One of the companies that Shimizu had acquired early in the process of its monopolizing of the space industry was Barnett Substrate Industries. Barnett's founder, a physicist, had discovered a way, using zero-point energy, the power of gravity itself, to dissolve the molecular bonds in solid rock. This made digging through the stuff easy and cheap; and, as the Shimizu Company was soon to prove, it, combined with the free and limitless power from plasma generators pouring out zero-point energy, finally made the process of lifting mass into orbit economical.

Which was how Harris now found himself strapped into a hollow bullet three-hundred-plus stories beneath the Earth's surface.

He heard the single chime that indicated the beginning of the quick-count to launch and braced himself.

Thirty seconds later the shuttle's engines fired, pressing him back into his couch with the weight of three to four gravities.

The same thought flashed through his mind as always at the moment the pressure of acceleration hit him.

Lord, what a rush!

* * *

Song sat at the edge of the breakwater among the early-morning fishermen and watched Harris's shuttle burn up out of the mountain and lift ever higher into the terrifying height of the sky.

Finally, it winked out into the distance of blue.

When it was gone, she stood and walked slowly back into the city, her mind in turmoil.

For the first time it occurred to her that Hugh Carney would more than likely be waiting at the hotel for her, wondering where she could possibly have gone by herself so early in the morning.

She felt empty and afraid.

And she felt shame.

She would go back to her hotel room, and in some way she would convince Carney to take her off the island. Once back in the United States she could get a flight to North Vietnam—one of the few Asian countries that still had commercial flights to and from the rest of the world—and from there to Beijing.

If they let her, she would go and see Jiang again.

She refused to let herself consider any more of the future than that.

CHAPTER SEVEN

Roughnecks had a word for the process of transferring from the cramped passenger bays of the LRVs to the nonrotating docking carousels of the platforms: "untanking," they called it. Harris thought it captured nicely the sensation as a dozen people simultaneously tried to squeeze themselves through the bottleneck of the single pressure hatch.

From the distance, the docking carousel looked a good deal like a skeletal version of the cylinder in an old-time "six-shooter," a half-dozen or more bays for the LRV shuttles arranged in a circular pattern about a central axis. The carousel's axis was an extension of the platform's own nonrotating axis, an elongated, pressurized tube forming an umbilical between the carousel and the platform.

Harris's crew floated down the hollow axis in single file.

The only member of the crew who didn't untank in a pressure suit was the crew chief, Oyakata, who would direct the crew in their tasks over the next two weeks from the relative comfort of his Company office, in the one-gee level of the platform.

The rest of the crew, carrying their helmets for the moment, would be in vacuum within the hour, working on the construction of a new ring section. The platform was thirty-one rings long—almost a dozen kilometers—at the moment; Shimizu had plans to construct another ten before the platform was finished. The sections that were pressurized were already functional, their farms and laboratories producing specialized medicines and crystals in the low-gee levels and high-yield, gravity-sensitive crops in the higher gee farthest from the axis.

He was already looking forward to his down-shift, four hours ahead. His assigned quarters were in the part of the platform known as Onegee City, and, though he hated to admit it, he had gotten to the point where he preferred normal Earth gravity to free-fall.

Getting older, he thought. Can't take the heat and unhappy about the thought of having to get out of the kitchen.

Life in orbit, at least the part where he wasn't cooped up in a pressure suit, was a pretty pleasant business, he reflected. The Company took a healthy extra piece out of his pay voucher every month so that he could enjoy a good-size room in full gravity in whatever platform his work crew was assigned to, but he could sleep without feeling subconsciously that he might fall at any moment. Tended to give one bad dreams.

And truly he had nothing better to spend his money on, and there was a lot to be said for small comforts.

His first shift outside went by with merciful swiftness. Construction assignments were invariably more bearable than maintenance tours, for the simple reason that the work was constant and rarely tedious.

He shed his suit in the axis lock at the center of the section under construction. The new ring, like the axis, was at present stationary in relation to the completed and pressurized barrel-bulk of the station. When the section was completed, it would be brought to speed around the central axis and then the seals would be welded and the section pressurized.

The first time he had worked on a new ring section for a platform, he had discovered the importance of not watching the rotation of the station as it moved by less than a meter from the bare girders of the construction. Without reference points, that part of his brain that handled things like orientation and balance had been inundated with sensory input from his eyes which said that the section he was *on* was the one that was spinning, while his inner ear told a different story, that he was in fact stationary.

He had come very close to being sick in his helmet, and that could have been damned unpleasant. A pressure suit's helmet could handle liquids, siphoning them away to a catchpocket, but he understood the recirculated smell of your own sickness was more than enough to make you wish you were dead.

Now, as he made his way through the maze of girders to the axis, he kept his eyes automatically averted.

During construction, the crews used a temporary lock installed at the axis. On the pressure side of the lock was a warm-room thoughtfully provided with zero-gee showers—which cost an obscene number of yen per minute, water being a fairly precious commodity in orbit—and personal equipment lockers. He mounted his suit on the rack provided and pulled on the roughneck uniform of shorts and a T-shirt and scooted through the hatch to the axis, pulling himself along by the handgrips set into the curving bulkhead.

A few meters past the hatch was a spin-accelerator set into what was, from his orientation, the ceiling of the axis tunnel. The device looked a good deal like some sort of carnival ride, a steel box inside of which were two wide couches, facing one another. Inside, on the "floor," was a hatch.

Four others were already strapped to the couches. He pushed himself away from the bulkhead into a shallow, gliding dive that brought him into the box's low doorway.

He pulled himself onto one of the couches and the safety belt snaked itself across his shoulder with a mechanical whirr.

Another roughneck pulled herself in. Despite himself, Harris watched with admiration as she settled onto the couch. Low gravity was an unmitigated blessing to connective tissues; nothing drooped in the absence of gravity.

The new passenger smiled and slapped him on the shoulder. "Jimbo!"

It took a long moment for his memory to provide him with a name. Then it came to him. "Patty," he said.

"None other. How's business?"

Harris shrugged. "Just trying to keep the cops off my ass."

Patty's smile became a smirk. "More drunk and disorderlies? I'm surprised Shimizu hasn't already shipped an old sot like you south."

Harris snorted. "Not likely. So long as I'm sober topside, they could give a damn what I do on the dirt. That is, until Company property gets involved. Some foolish fellow with Company security has gotten the idea that I have something to do with missing Company property. Something about all this associating I do with black marketeers, I expect."

"Do tell. Imagine that." The smirk became a grin.

"Yes, imagine." Patty—Patricia Jackson—was, he knew, one of Anson's best sources for the Company goods he smuggled out of Port-de-Paix. Few roughnecks were above the temptation to spirit away loose items of Company property. Patty had made it a steady sideline.

"Got a flop?"

Harris nodded. "I elected for Onegee this tour. I've gotten to enjoy living like God intended, with my feet on the floor."

"Onegee? Rich bastard. Look, how'd you like to do a girl a favor?"

"I'd say that would depend on the favor."

"Do you have any idea what the quarter-gee barracks are like?"

"I'd say I've a fair idea. I spent three tours in 'em before I decided I'd had enough."

"Do you know what it *smells* like up there? Water's so damned steep nobody showers, especially not you goddamned male types. Do you know what I'd do for a real shower? With lots of water? The hot kind? That didn't float up my nose?"

"I'd hesitate to guess."

"Anything you asked. Even the kinky stuff. Hell, especially the kinky stuff."

"And what if I just wanted to get some sleep?"

"Spoilsport."

"I know. It comes from too much clean living. You're welcome to bunk in, however, so long as you don't mind sharing a sack with someone too tired to wrestle."

"Do you snore?"

"Like a shuttle engine."

"I suppose I'll have to grin and bear it. Anything for a real shower."

"That's the spirit."

Another roughneck pulled himself up and the car, sensing it had a full load, began to accelerate smoothly around the circumference of the axis tunnel. Again, Harris made sure to keep his eyes on the floor. When the box had matched the speed of the platform's first level, the hatch in the floor irised open, as did a matching opening in the first level's ceiling.

It was an odd sensation indeed, climbing from a moving vehicle into seeming stillness, though he knew that relative to the platform, it was the *axis* that was moving.

Knowing it didn't keep his stomach from giving a nervous twitch.

"Level One—Gerrytown. Don't step on no old folks," Jackson admonished.

One at a time they climbed down a ladder into the platform. Just beyond the hatchway were a number of lifts, toward which everyone shuffled, being careful not to launch themselves off the tacky surface of the deck in the low gravity.

Harris and Jackson joined two others in an express lift. They slid smoothly down to Onegee, the weight settling on like a heavy blanket.

The lift sighed to a halt and disgorged them into the midst of Onegee City.

All of the Shimizu platforms—nine at last count—had a Onegee City. Onegee wasn't a city at all in the dirtside sense of the term. More like a shopping mall crossed with a Company store and laid out in broad corridors running parallel to the axis.

All of the shops and restaurants were either Company owned or Company leased, and even something as simple as a cup of coffee could cost ten times what it might back on terra firma.

Which meant that more business was done in the narrow connecting passageways than in the corridors themselves. Like the black market in Port-de-Paix, Onegee's black market was tolerated by the Company. Whatever kept the workers contented and the yen flowing.

Jackson's crew had lifted the day before and she knew where to look. They walked spinward from the lift for a way, then she ducked into a small shop that ostensibly operated strictly as a newsstand and came out a minute later with a liter-size liquids bag filled with a clear fluid.

She showed Harris her prize, then stuffed it inside her blouse with a grin.

"One portable party, coming up."

Sometime much later Harris found himself lying on his bunk in his cube. Somewhere nearby someone was snoring. Loudly. He assumed it was Jackson, but his head was spinning and he couldn't gather the initiative to get up and look. Vacuum-still vodka didn't have the skull-splitting potency of Haitian rum, but it still did the job and then some.

Despite the spinning, he felt pretty good. Damned good, he thought.

For a while, he lay thinking about what Song Lan had told

him back in Port-de-Paix. He tried to concentrate on what she had said, but his mind kept returning to other things, the smell of her hair, the strange, barely accented lilt of her voice.

Sometime during his reveries he drifted off to sleep.

October 1 9, 2070

They came for him in the "morning," an hour before the corridor lights came up to full brightness in the platform's version of sunrise.

Harris woke from a twisting, claustrophobic dream to the snake-hiss of burning metal. He struggled to pull himself up, his muscles reluctant to follow the commands of his hung over brain.

He followed the noise to the door. Doors on personal quarters tended toward a brute solidness, a throwback to the days when all doors on orbital platforms were pressure hatches, so they were not easily forced.

Whoever was at the door of his cube wasn't, therefore, trying the brute force approach. The metal around the door's latch glowed red as he watched, then orange, then began to flow in a thin stream down the door's surface to the carpeting, which in turn began to smoke.

He reached around on the floor beside the bunk, found a slipper and threw it at Jackson.

She stirred. "What the hell do you want?" she muttered irritably.

"Somebody's breaking in," Harris hissed at her.

Jackson sat up suddenly, looked at the door. Harris tried not to notice that she'd slept in nothing more than her shorts. Her eyes were bloodshot and she looked a little weathered. She shook her head hard with her eyes closed, then opened them again, wide. "What the hell? What's going on?"

"How should I know?"

Harris made a quick and desperate survey of the room and reaffirmed what he already knew—that there was only one way in and one way out of a platform cubicle. There weren't even air ducts, per se, that he could duck through as they always did in old movies; the entire ceiling was a porous polymer through which air leached, a good deal like the airstones in aquarium tanks.

There was little in the room that could be used as a weapon, either, he reflected. The furniture was all extruded polymer and bolted to the floor. All that could be pulled loose were seat cushions, pillows and bedspreads, and none of that seemed as if it would be particularly intimidating to whoever was burning his way through the door.

"Grab the other end of this."

Harris yanked the coverlet off the bed and tossed one end to Jackson. She scrambled up and grabbed it. Together, they stood beside the door, holding the thin blanket as if it were a tiger net.

"What the hell is going on?"

"I told you, I don't know. It can't be good. Friends knock before they burn holes in your door."

"Christ!" Jackson whispered.

The laser snapped off. Harris tensed, taking a deep breath of air that was heavy with smoke and the acrid smell of scorched metal.

Something heavy hit the door, bowing it. He could see the perforated metal around the lock give and tear.

Once again, the door was struck and this time the lock ripped out of its metal frame and the door burst open. It flew back on its hinges to bang into the wall across from where Harris stood.

A figure stepped through, the flat box of the laser held out like a pistol. Harris nodded and they threw the coverlet over the intruder and then Harris hit it hard with his shoulder, throwing whomever it was off his feet into the room.

Before he could turn something struck him on the back of his head. He fell but did not black out.

A masked form whirled by into the room. Jackson threw a wild punch but her opponent dodged easily and struck her twice in rapid succession, once on the jaw, once in the solar plexus.

She dropped in a heap to the deck.

The man turned back to Harris, took him roughly by the shoulders and lifted him up.

Harris didn't resist. He shook his head, unable for the moment to focus his eyes.

The first man, the one they'd diverted with the sheet, helped the second drag Harris out the door into the corridor.

They pushed him face-first up against the corridor bulkhead in a good imitation of a bum's rush, twisting his arm up into the center of his back and jamming a forearm into his neck.

Harris twisted his head and saw two faces in masks that rippled in shades of gray as they moved. Out of the corner of his eye he saw a blurred glint of light on a sliver of metal.

The first man eased the needle up close to Harris's neck.

With all his strength Harris twisted right. The second man took a step back for leverage and Harris brought his knee up hard into the man's crotch.

The second man grunted in pain and suddenly the forearm was gone from Harris's neck. The first man, needle in hand, backed off a step and Harris tried to dodge around him and down the corridor.

Quicker than he could follow, his assailant danced a graceful step left then spun around, his foot lancing out in a blur to catch Harris on the side of his head.

Harris felt his world explode in a rush of red pain. He fell to the deck and blacked out.

Later, he figured he must have been out for no more than a second, because he came to to find the face in the black-gray mask close to his own. The hypodermic was again against his neck. He felt a cold sting as the needle began to push into his flesh.

Motion caught his eye and he saw the other man was regaining his feet. Just past him he could see Patty Jackson standing in the corridor, her face bloody. In her hands was a PIM resonator.

He remembered thinking *oh, shit* just before the world dissolved into blackness.

When he came to, for the second time, Jackson was dragging him down the narrow corridor outside their room toward the brighter lights of one of the broad mercantile corridors.

He was being dragged backward by the shoulders, and behind him some two dozen meters he could see the two men who had attacked him lying on the corridor deck. Both wore body stockings of the kind he had seen Song Lan wear. Both were stirring.

He struggled against Jackson's grip and tried to get to his feet. Jackson pulled him up.

"Let's *move*, compadre."

"I'm right behind you. Go."

They stumbled out into the larger corridor, started "south," away from the end of the platform that faced the docking carousel for the LRVs.

The corridor was empty, the shops closed.

Where the hell is everyone? he wondered. A few hours before Onegee had been teeming . . . Then he remembered the shadowy dimness in the corridor and realized that it was night in Onegee City. The corridors would be as empty as the streets of any city in the hours before dawn. There might be a cop or a delivery robot around, but the chances for outside help were not good.

"Where to?" he asked Jackson.

"Damned if I know."

Harris looked around, spotted a telephone terminal set into one bulkhead. "We could call the cops?"

"Are you nuts? Those guys were *Company*."

"What makes you think so?"

"Their hands. Yellow skin." Jackson touched the bleeding cut on the side of her face. "I got a pretty good look, close up."

Harris suspected that the two were anything but Shimizu cops rousting them. The odd body stockings they wore preyed on his mind. But he had to agree with Jackson. There was little reason to trust the Company to help, at least not before the situation was a little clearer.

Something occurred to him. "Where did you get the vibrator?"

"I lifted it. Do you know how much one of those things is worth . . . ?"

"What did you do with it?"

"What do you think? I dropped it. I couldn't carry it and you, too. I didn't know how long you'd be out. I barely touched the switch, but all three of you went down pretty quick."

"So now they've got it."

She nodded. "I suppose that's right."

"Damn," Harris said. He thought hard. "Come on."

He picked one of the larger cafes on the same side of the main corridor as their room and ducked in through the open portico. The restaurants never bothered closing off their dining rooms— the fixtures were bolted to the floor and where would you take a plastiform table inside a platform, anyway?

Inside the ceiling was lowered enough to give the place a subterranean feeling, and the paneling was stained dark and textured to suggest wood of some sort. A bar ran obliquely across the left rear of the main room and behind it was a door, closed. Another door stood open across from the bar on the far right side of the room.

He made a quick decision, decided that the open door was probably restrooms and the like, or at best a pool table and dart boards—both games were very popular with dirtsiders visiting Onegee, the platform's spin doing funny things to ball roll and dart trajectory. He sprinted across the room and vaulted the bar, coming up hard against the door.

The door was steel, and, unlike the fellows who had broken into their room, he didn't have anything as handy as a laser to open it.

In desperation, he whispered, "Open," and it slid silently aside.

"Jesus," he said, "they forgot to lock up. No wonder Shimizu loses so much stuff to the black market."

"Will wonders never cease," Jackson offered. She pushed past into the room beyond.

It was tomb-dark inside, ripe with the smell of stored food and beer.

"Leave the lights off," Harris whispered.

He was playing a hunch. He didn't know for sure, but he suspected that though the general rule was one cube, one entrance, platform businesses usually had a bolt hole of some sort to an adjacent corridor. No businessman wants the ash and trash dragged out under the customer's noses.

He bumped into a large machine that he guessed was the food processor and edged his way around it to the right, trying to move quietly. He squeezed past unseen boxes and equipment and found his way to the back wall. He ran his hands along the slightly greasy metal, looking for a door, from where it met the bulkhead to the right to where it met the bulkhead to the left.

He found nothing but bare metal and shelves of foodstuffs. He heard Jackson nearby, searching for the same nonexistent door.

Discouraged, he knelt down and tried to think.

After a minute he stood and worked his way back to the big food-processing machine. He walked around it and felt ahead until he touched the left-hand wall. Again, he started toward the back of the room, letting his hand slide along the smooth metal of the bulkhead.

Three meters before the back wall he found the staircase. He mentally kicked himself for not figuring it out sooner. Of course there would be no back door to a Onegee business, at least not one that led out into the city. Corridor space was too precious in Onegee to waste it on the back-alley business of waste disposal and deliveries.

Obviously the "back door" would be on the next level up, where corridor space was much less dear.

"Jackson!" he hissed. "Over here."

After a moment she joined him.

"You've found something?"

"Yeah. Hold on."

He hesitated before taking the steps, listening. Nothing. Not a sound. He walked up slowly.

At the top, he felt the outline of the door and searched out the release. He punched it and nothing happened.

He almost laughed aloud at the irony of it. Front door open, back door locked.

He pushed at the latch again with no result. He tapped the door's hard surface with a knuckle; it was as solid as a battleship.

Which meant that for better or worse they had two options: to go back out the front of the cafe in the hopes that the pursuit—if, in fact, there had been one—had changed its minds; or, they could stay put and wait for the crowds to return to the shops. A large enough group of people would be effective camouflage, though, he knew, about as much use as so many cattle as witnesses. The larger the crowd, the less they tended to actually see.

He felt a hand on his shoulder and jumped.

"Damn it, Patty."

"What did you find?"

"A locked door."

Jackson made the same examination of the door he had just completed.

"End of the road, then."

"Yeah. Maybe. Look, I think we ought to just wait until people show up to open this place, and sneak out—"

Then the door opened of its own accord. Harris found himself staring in the startled face of a woman still holding an access card in one hand.

He took advantage of her confusion and pushed past her into the hall. Jackson followed close on his heels.

"Hey!" the woman yelled.

"Sorry, got to run!" Harris yelled back. And run he did.

"What now?" Jackson panted. They had stopped to catch their breath, leaning against the blank gray of bulkhead.

Harris shrugged. "I don't know. Maybe you ought to head on in and do your shift outside. Those two jokers were coming after me, not you."

Jackson nodded. "Seemed that way. If they were Company, though, I'd be walking right into their hands."

"If they were Company, there's no damned place you can hide where they're not going to find you eventually. Think it through. You're going to have to use your chit to eat sometime. And where would you go, anyway? They wouldn't let you get aboard any of the LRVs." He paused. "Besides, I'm pretty sure they weren't Company cops."

"Yeah, I was thinking about that. Company cops don't wear hoods."

"And they don't burn your door down. They don't have to. The central computer would override the locks for them."

"Makes sense. So why are we running instead of calling the cops?"

"I'm not sure. I mean, this is plenty strange. How could two goons bent on mayhem get aboard a Company platform—carrying a hand laser no less? I don't know who I can trust."

"Okay. Back to the original question. What now?"

"I think I better take off on my own."

"Hey, wait a minute—"

"No, listen. If they are after just me, why should I let you put yourself in trouble? I don't need the bad karma." He grinned wryly. "Besides, maybe they're after you."

"Now there's a thought. Still, there are two of them—"

"Yeah, but I can hide better by myself. Look, if you want to do me some good, take this"—he handed her his credit chit, a postage stamp–size flake of plastic hung on a key ring—"and go somewhere far away and buy something. Then get the hell out of there. If it's the Company, or if they've access to the computers, that'll get 'em off my trail. And when they get there, they'll be looking for me, not you."

She looked doubtful.

"Do it," Harris said. He pushed himself up away from the

bulkhead. "I'll look you up quick as I get all this business sorted out."

He started down the corridor at a jog. Jackson watched him as he went, shaking her head.

Something very like a plan began to form in Harris's mind as he made his way through the corridors, searching for stairs or for a lift. Each corridor intersection had an alphanumerical designation as well as a normal "street" name—he was making good time down Kurama Corridor at the moment—but the names were so much gibberish to him so far as orienting himself was concerned. He knew a little of the layout of Onegee, but the levels above were a mystery.

And finding oneself in a place where every "street" looked pretty much like every other was something of a nightmarish proposition. There were occasional telephone terminals set in the bulkheads along the corridor, but though any of them could have given him directions, all would have requested him to touch his Company chit to their screens, and Jackson now had his chit.

And he wasn't going to take any chances he didn't have to.

He made do by simply following the same lateral—parallel to the axis—corridor for as long as it took, resisting the temptation to explore likely-looking alleys and side corridors.

People were beginning to appear in the public areas and he slowed his pace; citizens might tend to look with high suspicion at anyone sprinting down a city street in sleepwear, though his baggy pajama bottoms and T-shirt might not get a second glance if he were casual enough, differing as they did only in detail from the light, loose-fitting clothing most roughnecks wore.

And attention was one thing he wanted mightily to avoid. Not only were there persons unknown carrying highly illegal weapons taking undue interest in him, but there was a good chance that the local constabulary would not look kindly on the story the woman who had released them from the storeroom might file with platform security about these fellows wandering around in the storeroom of a Company-owned cafe not yet open for business.

In short order he ran across an escalator and rode it back down to Onegee.

The escalator let him off in a part of the city wholly unfamiliar to him, but what he needed to find in Onegee wouldn't take much in the way of searching to find.

He turned spinward down a transverse corridor. He walked about two hundred meters before coming to the railroad.

Onegee's railroad—or rather *railroads*, as there were a half-dozen "lines," each with a dozen or more "rails"—ran in gentle spirals from one flattened end of the barrel-shaped platform to the other. Anywhere in any of the Onegee cities of the various platforms, you were never more than a few hundred meters from one of the "lines."

Each of the lines was composed of a number of superconductive magnetic rails over which slim, bullet-shaped cars glided. The setup was rather like that of the city subways back on Earth, the trains running through tunnels sunk into the level that insulated Onegee from vacuum.

Harris took the stairs down two at a time to the half level above the tracks where the empty cars waited in their cradles. He settled into one of the single-passenger cars and let the seat strap him in. A display on the dash lighted up and asked him for his ring destination—how far out toward either end of the platform he wanted to go—and asked him for his credit chit.

Credit chit. *Damn.*

He spoke to the car. "Will you take assignment of funds?"

"In what form, sir?" a pleasant, synthesized voice asked.

"Garnishee of wages for one Daniels, James. Employee number alpha-alpha-six-oh-nine."

"One moment."

Harris waited. He could almost hear the condensed-charge electrons zipping along through the computer's acid-etched mind, considering his proposal.

"Voiceprint identification verified. I can accept your assignment, at double the regular fare, Mr. Daniels."

"Do so." So much for Jackson leading the hounds away with his chit.

"Thank you, Mr. Daniels. Destination?"

"Greenbelt."

The railcar sealed itself and flashed a warning across its dash screen. Harris braced himself as the car was nudged out of its cradle into the "arm" that would launch it onto one of the rails as soon as the systems computer decided that there was a sufficient gap in the traffic using the line.

Then, in a motion a good deal like that of a bowler throwing a bowling ball down a lane, the car was simultaneously dropped and slung out along the frictionless rail. The car itself was a ballistic projectile without its own means of propulsion; it would simply glide at an extremely high speed along its rail until it was stopped, either by being "caught"—diverted onto a friction rail and then dropped into a cradle at its programmed destination— or until air friction slowed it down, a process that would require, Harris guessed, a few hundred kilometers more rail than the platform had length.

Harris gripped the arms of his seat as the acceleration jammed him back into the cushions and tried to enjoy the ride. It seemed a bit to him like being shot down the barrel of a cannon.

At five or six kilometers a minute, the train could traverse the platform end to end in under two minutes. Harris guessed his ride could not have taken longer than fifty or sixty seconds, but it seemed even more quickly than that his car was snatched to one side and abruptly stopped. It took another full minute, he was sure, for his stomach to catch up.

The car's door unsealed with a *chuff* of air, and he stepped out and rode the stairs up to Greenbelt.

Greenbelt literally was a belt, girdling the platform around its center for three rings—roughly a kilometer and a half. Its floor occupied the same level as Onegee City, which spread out on either side of it. Its "roof" was six levels higher, and didn't look much like a roof; a series of giant reflectors and filters brought in sunlight and reflected it down on the flora, while scattering prisms made the ceiling the rich and pleasant blue of Earth's own skies.

Sunlight shone refreshingly bright down the length of the last few steps. At the top he looked around at the lush expanse of green around him. It did look a good deal like Earth, the sky blue and seeming much father away than it actually was; it was a little disconcerting that the land curved up spinward and anti-spinward to meet the sky, but he found he could ignore that with a little effort.

He took a deep, satisfying breath of air that seemed different, cleaner and fresher, from what he had been breathing, though if it was, it was only minimally so, as the oxygen produced by Greenbelt's foliage was vented throughout the platform.

He walked out along a path that wound its way through a small copse of trees and out into farmland. Most of the food that the platform grew, either for itself or for export to places like the Lunar and Martian colonies—places where it was immeasurably cheaper to buy food that didn't have to be blasted out of Earth's gravity well—was grown in much smaller hydroponic plots scattered throughout the platform, most of them on levels closer to the axis. Certain crops did better in normal gravity and in real, honest-to-God dirt, and they were grown in Greenbelt.

The trees were maples, small but thick with leaves. Each tree was tapped, a bucket hanging down below the tap to catch the sweet sap. The field beyond was corn: dense, two-meter-tall rows of plants, each row about three-quarters of a meter apart.

The path he was following ended at the edge of the cornfield, and he walked down one of the long rows, enjoying the crowded, whispering secrecy of the empty space between the plants.

He felt safe here, away from the crowds in Onegee. It seemed unlikely anyone would think to search for him in the middle of a cornfield.

The warmth of the sunlight made him drowsy and he stretched out on the clean-smelling dirt and slept.

Something, a sound, awoke him just in time for him to be slapped back down, then flipped roughly onto his stomach. He was held down against the ground, somebody's hand on the back of his head, pushing his face into the dirt. An instant later he felt the sudden wasp-sting of a needle in the back of his neck.

He yelped and tried to break free. The weight on his neck and back was constant, holding him still. The thought, totally irrelevant, that they might not have had quite so easy a job pinning him down if he'd hidden somewhere on one of the low-gravity levels ran through his mind. He could barely breathe, dust and dirt coming into his nose and lungs with every breath.

His assailant waited, pressing him down, two or three minutes. For the drug to take effect, Harris assumed. Then he stood.

Harris breathed more freely, but realized without surprise that he couldn't move. Every muscle in his body seemed numbed. There was sensation—he could feel the ground under him, the sunlight hot on his back—but it seemed filtered, as if someone else were feeling it and he could only empathize.

He felt himself lifted and then he was being carried upside down, across someone's shoulder in a fireman's carry. His vision was blurry and his eyes were dry and scratchy; he tried to blink and discovered he couldn't.

He tried to speak and found he couldn't do that, either; he couldn't control his jaw muscles or move his tongue. All he managed was a drooling gurgle.

His face bounced painfully against the solid back beneath the shirt as his abductor jogged through the cornfield. After a few minutes the sunlight gave way to the relative dimness of artificial light and he knew they were back in the corridors of Onegee.

I can still feel, he realized, and I can still think. I just can't move.

He could still breathe as well, albeit only shallowly, and he could see, though his eyes resisted his attempts to focus. He found he could blink after all, with considerable effort. He concentrated, blocked out the pain in his head and gut, and forced his eyelids shut, then open again. It helped.

The man who carried him darted around a corner and Harris found himself watching the bulkhead to his right going by, his head having swung to the side. He saw a couple of shocked faces passing by, roughnecks wondering what the hell was going on, but the corridor seemed sparsely populated; probably most everyone who wasn't on shift was adding his mass to the breakfast crowds, he thought sourly. The lack of volition was maddening—but at least now his face no longer bounced against his abductor's rather muscular back.

The corridor wall moved by jerkily, gray and featureless. He could see movement out of the corner of his eye, a figure following behind—the second man.

He tried to think. They were carrying him to . . . where? Some secluded place where they could question him? About what? He thought of Song Lan and remembered what she had told him. Still, it seemed improbable; they were expending quite a bit of effort for what would prove to be a slim return.

Of course, he reflected, they could hardly be expected to know that.

Then Harris heard the familiar sound of a lift door opening. His captor stepped forward and was joined by his partner. The door closed behind them.

Harris felt the platform's spin-induced gravity lessen as the lift slid quietly toward the axis hub.

They were headed for the shuttle docks, he realized, his stomach sinking with fear. He was going to be taken off the platform.

A synthesized voice quietly announced, "Level One"— Gerrytown, the level beneath the axis.

Harris forced his eyes closed, gathered his willpower, what control he had, and tried to move his hands. He could almost *imagine* movement, but he couldn't *feel* it, certainly not enough to do anything damaging to his captor.

It was likely there would be little he could do to him even if he were mobile; he and his accomplice had demonstrated strength and reflexes far beyond Harris's own. Drugs? he wondered. Some suprapowerful stimulant?

Such things had existed even before he had left Earth for Comfort, though he understood they had been damned hard on their users. Tended to burn out the central nervous system in fairly short order.

The gravity in Gerrytown was just enough to keep anyone who walked—or rather shuffled—carefully and very slowly actually attached to the corridor floor. Any movement that was a little too enthusiastic could result in broken bones as the person who made the movement rebounded with a force nearly equal to the original impetus off of the hard, steel walls or ceiling of the corridor.

This fact caused the elderly who had paid Shimizu enormous fees to live on the platform's first level—thus the name "Gerrytown"—no inconvenience; few of them were even capable of any sort of sudden and powerful action.

Others had to be careful.

Harris's kidnappers took the corridor in giant leaping strides, as if they were Olympic long jumpers building up momentum for the leap. Inverted and blind, Harris's stomach twisted and knotted with vertigo.

He tried to adjust to the new motion, surrender to it. He swallowed hard and managed not to retch. He caught a glimpse of a shocked and badly wrinkled face peering up at them from a doorway as they flew by.

Why Gerrytown?

Something nagged at the edge of Harris's memory, something about Gerrytown, about the first level down from the axis. There

really wasn't much to El-One. Low-gravity research and production facilities and a few dozen high-rent, two- and three-
room cubes for the tired-of-gravity crowd. Nothing else, not
even the Company dining rooms that served on every other
level—roughnecks preferred to eat out on the lower levels, where
the food tended to stay on the plate.

Then he remembered.

The pods.

The men and women who lived in Gerrytown were of a kind:
most were flatlanders who had spent the balance of their lives
in Earth's cities, all were wealthy—they had to be to afford to
live in orbit—and all were horrified by their own imminent mortality. Gerrytown's low gravity offered them a few extra years
of life; but for flatlanders, an orbital platform seemed a relatively
precarious place to live, floating as it was in a vast sea of empty
vacuum.

Thus the pods. He remembered them from among the thousands of minutiae about the platforms that had droned at him
during the orientation lectures he'd had to attend when he'd first
signed on because they had seemed so singularly ridiculous. He
had had visions of hundreds of geriatric patients, all too frail to
even bear Earth-normal gravity, scrambling into pressure suits
and piloting the tiny, skeletal spacecraft through the atmosphere
and into splashdown in one of Earth's seas.

Unthinkable. Idiotic.

Nevertheless, the pods were there, paid for by men and women
who were too old, too rich, and too paranoid.

Again, he struggled to move his hands. He thought perhaps
he felt some small response in his fingertips.

That might be useful, he thought wryly, if there were some
way to disable two men by tickling them.

They settled to the deck again after one of his captor's long,
finely executed hops. Harris could feel the body under him do
something different than the gather-and-jump that had been taking them in great bounds down the arched length of the corridor—arched because the corridor was transverse to the platform
axis and followed the barrel shape of the platform's sides. He
quick-stepped to slow his momentum and stopped.

There was a new sound in the corridor, a low, mechanical
clatter over the ambient hum of the environmental systems. The
sound wasn't loud but it seemed large, as if the space it was in

were broader and deeper than the corridor down which they had come.

Though he had been able to see little but his captor's back, Harris knew the corridor down which they had been traveling was residential, lined mostly with the doors to individual compartments, like a hall in an apartment complex. This new space, he guessed, since it seemed large and he couldn't hear voices, was one of the structural shafts that ran the longitudinal length of the platform. It would be crowded, he knew, with conduit and pipe, fiber-optic cable and rails for the various autonomous mechanisms that maintained the platforms' internal integrity.

They moved into the larger space, and Harris felt himself being lifted and laid down, face up, into what seemed to be a broad, shallow box. It bounced with the uneasy, suspended feeling of a magnetic railcar.

A railcar in a maintenance shaft? It was a cargo sled, he realized suddenly, used to shuttle gear from one end of the platform to the other. Slow, compared to the passenger rails, but it still would get them to the end of the platform in fairly short order.

He heard a hum of power building and then the rushing sound of a sled accelerating. The sled in which he had been dumped remained stationary, hovering over the rail.

One of his abductors had gone ahead in another sled. Not enough room for them all in one sled, he guessed.

Either that, or he was going ahead to make preparations for their departure.

The one who had stayed behind with Harris climbed into the sled and leaned awkwardly over him to work the controls. The sled accelerated smoothly to twenty or thirty klicks, hovering frictionless above its magnetic rail.

At a conservative twenty klicks per hour, Harris calculated, they would arrive at the end of the shaft—and, literally, at the end of the platform—in five or ten minutes. It was a good guess that that was where they would find the pod bays.

His chances for rescue didn't look particularly promising.

If he were to escape, it would be at his own initiative.

Once again, he closed his eyes and concentrated. He remembered a martial-arts instructor in his basic training, long ago, explaining to the mostly bored class how to gather the body's power into the gut, into the center, how to hold it there until it strained to be released, how to focus that power.

Almost before he realized it, his hand shot out from where it lay beside him. The blow was pathetically weak and uncontrolled.

But it was enough.

His hand struck his abductor on the arm just below the shoulder. He had been leaning forward, off balance. With a startled yelp, he toppled off the side of the sled.

If Harris could have laughed out loud, he would have. As it was, it was enough to move his hand slowly up to his numb face, where he could see it. Fantastic, he thought.

Then he felt the sled settle on its rail and begin to slow.

He fought off a surge of panic. *Why?*

Weight, he realized. The tiny and mostly stupid brain that ran the sled's mechanism had detected the change in the weight of its load. It had decided it had lost cargo and had stopped to wait for human assistance.

Harris lay helpless on his back, staring up at the cables that lined the shaft's ceiling.

After a long minute the now-familiar, masked face loomed above him.

He tried to raise his hand. It was brushed aside and a closed fist slugged him hard in the side of his head, where he had been kicked before.

Pain burst red behind his eyes, then blackness.

He awoke in claustrophobic darkness, unable to move. His arms seemed bound, his legs weighted down. He struggled, panicking, trying to get his arms free.

"No!" he shouted, trying to control himself. The sound was loud in his helmet. *Calm down. Breath slowly.*

He took a deep, shuddering breath and tasted the metallic taste that a hundred years of improvements and research had been unable to take out of the compressed air of a pressure suit.

He searched with his tongue and found the helmet's water nipple and took a long, slow pull of the slightly stale, body-warm water.

A glitter of light caught the corner of his eye and he strained to make out its source. He realized what he saw wasn't one light but thousands in a bright wash through the left side of the pressure suit's visor.

Stars.

He lay partially on one side on a crash couch inside the skeletal framework of an escape pod. He moved his hands and realized that his arms weren't bound; his kidnappers had simply slipped him into a somewhat-oversize pressure suit without bothering to put his arms into the suit's arms, effectively pinning them to his sides.

He tried to turn his head. The effort was painful but rewarding. The bright glare of the Milky Way now burned directly down into his face.

The pod was little more than a heat shield and a steel framework covered with a cheap, transparent polymer. The ride down, he knew, was going to be rough and hot, but survivable, the Kevlar environments of the pressure suits keeping them protected and breathing. The pod itself wasn't pressurized.

He was staring now out one of the craft's transparent sides, watching the stars pinwheel by.

He shifted his gaze, trying to see beyond his chin and the lip of the suit helmet to the fore part of the pod, where his kidnappers would be.

After a few seconds his eyes adjusted to the relative dimness inside the pod and he could make out a pressure-suited form seated on a second crash couch before the bright lights of an instrument panel.

He—or she—seemed to be listening, bent very still over the instruments, though it was hard to tell much of anything about a figure in a pressure suit. Harris thought he could see a mouth moving, talking to someone, through the clear Plexi of the figure's helmet, but he couldn't be sure.

Certainly it was possible he was in radio contact with someone, probably arranging a pickup from whatever ocean or sea he chose to set the pod down in. Harris himself could hear nothing. He assumed that his captors had hooked up his environmental umbilical—he was, after all, breathing—but hadn't bothered to hook up his tap into the pod's communication system. The sort of utility pressure suits that were kept for emergencies, unlike the custom-fitted suits roughnecks wore on the job, were not self-contained. There was no rebreather, no radio circuit.

He tested it anyway, yelling into the microphone built in the helmet's collar ring. "Hey! You! Listen to me. What is this about?"

No answer.

The strain to his neck and shoulders of looking down his own length to the pod's nose became too much and he relaxed back, tried to think.

It seemed clear he had used up any options he might have, at least until splashdown. He was strapped to a crash couch without so much as the use of his hands. He closed his eyes against the harsh glare of the stars. Again, he concentrated on forcing calmness on himself; he chanted a mantra he had learned in basic training, let his muscles go limp.

Something *click*ed against the Plexi in front of his face.

He opened his eyes and stared up into a woman's face, beautiful even through the Plexi, hovering over him like a dark angel. For a moment he thought it was Song Lan, then realized that though she was Oriental, she was a stranger.

"We have new orders, Mr. Harris." Her voice was clear and melodic, though heavily accented. She was touching her helmet to Harris's in order to be heard.

Harris started to speak but was cut off. He could hear honest regret in the woman's voice. "My mission has been canceled. I am sorry. It is probably for the best. They would not have been kind."

"What—" Harris demanded, but she had pulled her helmet away and he swallowed what he had been about to ask.

He felt movement around his ankles, strained to look down and saw for the first time since he had come to the second of his abductors. He—or she—was unbuckling the straps around his lower legs. When she had finished she did the same to the straps that stretched across his chest. Harris tried to sit up and discovered that he couldn't without the use of his arms.

He looked down again, saw her grasp the umbilical to his suit and twist the coupling. There was an audible pop inside Harris's suit when the umbilical separated and sealed itself, and the hiss of the air entering the valve under his chin stopped abruptly.

Harris struggled, tried to twist away and kick but couldn't get purchase. He drifted, weightless, from the couch to one of the clear, polymer bulkheads and hung there, helpless.

Then the bulkhead itself opened up and there was nothing between himself and the brilliance of the stars.

A hand pressed into the middle of his back and shoved him free of the pod.

He floated out, spinning slightly, into the vast, cold emptiness.

CHAPTER EIGHT

The massive granite obelisk of the Monument to the People's Heroes still loomed, after more than a hundred years, over the center of Tienanmen Square, its marble balustrades glistening with ice. Snow drifted down, making the pavements slick and treacherous, and Chiang Se Qi shuffled his feet as he walked head-down through the square.

He stopped for a moment at the monument to read the calligraphy on its north side. The Great Chairman Mao had had inscribed there the words, THE PEOPLE'S HEROES ARE IMMORTAL. He took great comfort in the words; it helped to remember that great deeds were worth the ultimate price they often exacted.

He looked around himself at the bleak landscape of the icy square. To the north he could see the purple facade of Tienanmen Gate. Beneath it flowed, he knew, the *Jin Zui*, the Golden Waters Spring, crusted with ice. Beside it ran Changan Jie, the Avenue of Perpetual Peace. That, too, gave him comfort. It was a reminder that perpetual peace was an ideal, one that often required martyrs.

It was easier to reach his office in the National People's Congress Building through the private entrances on the side farthest from the square, but he enjoyed the walk, even in the hard, winter cold. Especially in the cold, he corrected himself. The frigid weather chased the *shu*, the rats, the people of the Catacombs, underground and left the square nearly empty; it was glorious that way, the gray skies brooding over the mausoleum of the Great Chairman and the memory of the revolution, long past but far from forgotten.

Today he hurried, regretting that he couldn't make the walk

as he usually did, taking his time, enjoying the grandness of the architecture, the palaces in the distance and the walls topped with the brilliant whiteness of snow, the pure feeling of purpose and history the buildings exuded, like an essence. There was no time these days for the leisure he had grown accustomed to. The Central Committee had always before made the important decisions, taken care of the pressures of the state. His responsibilities, so long rather inessential formalities, had suddenly and frighteningly become weighty with an importance he had never known before.

He spoke to the screen beside the door and waited for it to agree that he was who he was—taking an interminably long time at it—and let him into the concourse of the Congress Building. He shook off the snow that had gathered on his shoulders and in the brim of his hat, leaving puddles on the polished marble. He left his coat on and summoned the lift. Even inside it was cold these days; it seemed as if he couldn't remember what it felt like to be truly warm.

The lift opened and he asked for his floor. As it descended he sniffed at the air in the small compartment, smelling something familiar and troubling. He frowned, trying to remember.

Then it came to him. *Tian Shan.*

Underneath the oiled, electric smell of the car was the harsh, lingering odor of the black tobacco that was still smoked only by a few of the oldest members of the Central Committee, men who had spent their youths in the countryside and had come to power during the Great Standoff. Chiang himself had been born in a farming commune; he knew the smell of Tian Shan cigarettes well. He also knew that only one man given to smoking it would have the temerity to smoke in this place.

The thought was fear itself, cold and visceral. If the general knew . . . But of course he knew; there was no other reason for his presence here, in the private offices of the Congress Building. He felt the terror like a pain in his bowels and fought it back.

He stood at the door to the council room, found a kerchief, and wiped the sweat from his face. His coat was suddenly hot and unbearably confining. He pulled it off, then set his face, concentrating on calmness. He thought of his father, killed trying to control the mobs during the food riots of the Shanghai Famine during the Great Standoff. The elder Chiang had died holding his ground against a tidal wave of mindless and desperate people storming the Ministry of Provision. His son could do no less.

He spoke to the lighted panel beside the door. It recognized him and the heavy, bombproof door slid aside. The room beyond was small and dimly lit, the walls paneled in heavy, dark wood, undecorated except for a painting Chiang himself had commissioned, an oil of the great statesman Mao. As he entered four men rose to their feet. Lin Biao, General of the Army of the People's Republic, rose with the others to shake Chiang's hand. The man was much heavier than Chiang remembered, his skin pale, his suit smelling of sweat and cigarette smoke. Chiang smiled and returned the soldier's handshake firmly.

"Chiang Tongzhi" Lin rumbled, "Comrade Chiang. I am pleased you are well."

"Thank you, General Lin," Chiang answered, desperately grateful that his voice was even and calm. "I am always somewhat surprised to find myself in good health, these days. Shall we begin?" He motioned for them to sit.

The general's voice was like the sound of gravel pouring through a tin hopper, Chiang thought. "So many familiar faces! Tell me, Comrade Chiang, what is it you are plotting?"

Chiang knew his face had gone ashen. "Plotting? I serve only the republic, I answer only to the people."

The general nodded. "I do not doubt. It is strange, though, that I see only three members of the Central Committee here, meeting to discuss matters of the greatest importance to the party and to the People's Republic. Forgive me, comrade, but that smacks of conspiracy."

Chiang began to protest indignantly but the general cut him off.

"I am not here to make accusations," he went on. "I am not the fool many of my colleagues—you, for example—take me to be. I am aware that if something important is to be done, it cannot be done by consensus. One man, or a small group of men under one leader, is always best. Subtlety and quickness of decision. You recognized that. I congratulate you for it; self-doubt is for lesser men."

General Lin smiled. When he spoke again, his voice was heavy with irony. "I would leave you alone to solve our great republic's problems on your own, but . . . well, I am a curious man.''

And one who would never miss an opportunity for an advantage, Chiang thought bitterly. He swallowed the sour taste in his mouth. Aloud, he said quietly, ''My friend, I would welcome any assistance you could give us.''

''This is good to hear.''

The struggle had been brief but conclusive. Chiang had, he knew, just handed the reins of power to Lin. It would be the general who, from this moment, held the real strength of command among the men gathered in this room.

Probably just as well, he mused. The responsibility had been hard to bear. Strangely, he felt a fleeting moment of gratitude to the fat, old soldier.

''Zhou,'' he said, addressing his personal aide. He tried to keep the tiredness out of his voice. ''Would you please brief Comrade General Lin on the American treachery?''

Lin listened, his arms crossed, his elbows on the table. When Zhou had finished, the general leaned forward through the cloud of his cigarette smoke.

''So, the Great Cold was given to us by the Americans, then.''

''Just so. Our scientists believe they have used an alien technology to subvert our agricultural production,'' Zhou answered. ''They have done this, of course, in league with the Soviets. Both powers, you will recall, were responsible for the colonizing of the star system 61 Cygni. The spacecraft we have discovered—''

''And the American astronaut? Why, Comrade Chiang, have you gone to so much trouble to retrieve him?''

Chiang made every attempt to appear stunned by the general's question. ''He is the key to everything, General Lin! Obviously, he was the pilot of the alien craft from which the Americans took the technology with which they are subverting our climate.''

''And so?''

''So he would be able to tell us what it is they have done, and how they have done it. He is the only source of information of which we are certain.''

''In that you are wrong, Chiang!'' Chiang noticed he had

dropped the honorifics, and with them all pretense that Chiang was still leader among the members of the Central Committee.

"You are wrong because you make stupid assumptions. Whatever the astronaut Harris knows, he cannot give us what the Americans and the Soviets now possess. He cannot give us what was in that spacecraft. But we do not need him to." The general paused for effect, letting his gaze fall on individuals among the company. Few would meet his eyes.

"We do not need him to because we can take it ourselves. You tell me that the alien ship is still on the path that took it out of our Solar system. That means that no country possesses it. That anyone can claim its technologies through international right of salvage."

He leaned forward again, said each word slowly, with emphasis. "So we go into space and we claim those technologies for the People's Republic."

"That's impossible," Zhou blurted. The general glanced at him coldly before answering. He has ruined any chance he might have had of changing allegiances, Chiang thought to himself. Zhou bowed his head and held his tongue.

"It is true that we do not possess the technology—yet!—for building a Chernetsky starship. But the West does. There is a spaceship in orbit now with a Chernetsky propulsion system."

Chiang felt confusion and tried to think. "A spaceship?"

"A colony starship, I should say, if my information is correct."

Some connection completed itself in Chiang's memory. "The Vega colony. But it is not scheduled to leave Earth's orbit for another year . . . Comrade General, are you proposing that we steal it?"

The general shrugged. "It is empty, is it not? No crew. To me, that makes it a derelict. We salvage that, too."

Chiang nodded slowly. There was a murmur of assent from the rest of the gathering.

"That is where we should concentrate our efforts for the moment. And once we have the alien craft and its weapons, then we will deal with the West and its blatant sabotage of our lands."

Chiang spoke slowly. "General Lin, perhaps you could tell us what we shall do in the meanwhile? A multitude of our people are dying each day of starvation, hundreds here in Beijing alone.

There is no food. The crops do not grow—nothing grows except the *da han*."

"Austerity measures have been implemented. Food has been diverted for the use of essential party members. Those who die are martyrs to the treachery of the West. There are more important matters to be dealt with—do not try to distract me from them, *Chiang Zongli*."

Chiang felt the muscles in his jaw jump at the general's tone, his offhanded use of Chiang's title. *Do not get in my way, Prime Minister Chiang* was his message.

The gall of the man!

Chiang ground his teeth but acceded, nodding slowly.

Lin Biao, General of the People's Army, left the National People's Congress Building with a great sense of satisfaction. His private car, one of only a very few on the streets, slid silently east along the Avenue Changan Jie headed out of the city. For the first time in many years of traveling this route, he looked out on the palaces beyond Tienanmen Gate. Even after the weathering of the centuries and the damages of revolution, they shone with a particular splendor, reminiscent of past glory.

He would spend a few days in his summer house on the coast of the China Sea, he thought. The retreat was his one excess, his one refuge, the one place where he could relax and think. From there he would direct the operation by phone and computer.

He had always had little patience for ineffectual figureheads like Chiang. The motherland had had nearly a century of rule by that sort, given their positions by the mindless bureaucrats of the committees.

Power, he knew, was not something you were given. It was something you took. The prime minister and the babbling puppets of the Central Committee had forgotten that. Or, rather, they had never known it.

His father had been a member of the Central Committee before him, but his father had been weak and unambitious and had accomplished nothing in his life but political mediocrity. Lin felt nothing but distaste for the memory of the old man. When he had died, Lin had only felt gratitude for the fact that his father's ineptitude had remained undiscovered by his colleagues long enough for the son to make his way in the ranks of the party elite, such as they were.

No, he reserved his admiration for his maternal grandfather, a man who had in his youth been one of the last military men to command a great deal of power in the People's Republic. He had been farmed out into a frustrated retirement in the "Gentle Purges" after the Great Standoff with the West. Lin remembered him as a brooding man full of strength and bitterness. He had hated weakness, in himself and in others, ruling his household with an iron fist.

Strength, decisiveness, and ruthlessness were the qualities of a leader.

Chiang and Zhou were weak men. They were incapable of doing what was necessary to defend the state.

Lin had long before developed his own avenues for action. There were others who thought as he thought, who would only need a show of strength to convince them of his worthiness as a leader. Now he had been given the opportunity.

He felt the sudden, heady rush of his own power. He had not even deigned to inform the comrade prime minister that he knew of his ineffectual machinations long before he had chosen to face his Gang of Three when they were busy at their plotting.

He had also disdained to tell them that he had himself canceled the prime minister's operation and recalled his agents.

Let their ignorance continue to be their weakness.

Outside the car the snow had begun to fall in earnest, blanketing the road. The sky was leaden, threatening. He touched a control and the windows opaqued, blotting it out.

CHAPTER NINE

October 19, 2070

He called, the call a prayer of desperation.

It was answered.

From a distance the Angel came, blossoming like a single word, colored white, in his mind.

For a moment he exulted unthinking in its presence. Then he felt confusion, uncertainty. There was a distance in the Angel, an unwillingness that was new and frightening.

He called for it and it refused him. Its frustration flowed over him in an overwhelming wave, the wave generated by a billion separate points of pain and despair that inundated it from the planet below. He wept at its anguish as it beheld the world from above, floating like a vast sheet of protoalgae, its life an energy fed by the sublime fire of the system's single, blazing sun and the soft, rich sea of the photosphere, its mind a simple, powerful empathy tempered only by its own fathomless need.

It heard him and it denied him. He writhed in its pity and its regret. In its way, it had loved him.

Now it abandoned him to his fate.

Harris cartwheeled slowly, end over end.

He was drifting away from the pod, already more than a hundred meters distant.

He knew he had only a few minutes' air in the suit itself, less if he gave in to the hysteria that threatened to overwhelm him. He could feel his entire body shaking in reaction to what the fear was doing to his adrenals.

Again, he struggled to get his arms free and, again, he failed. Pressure suits were not designed for much freedom of move-

ment on the *inside*. The semirigid material gave only enough to
move his arms from the elbows down.

Sweat, pushed along by the pseudogravity of his spin, crawled
into his eyes.

More than fear, he felt a vast aloneness. The silence, the
emptiness were absolute.

Something glittered through his faceplate, a new brightness
in the wash of stars. He blinked and shook his head, trying to
see, maddened that he couldn't rub the burning sweat out of his
eyes.

It drifted out of sight as he spun around and he shouted in
frustration, the sound amazingly loud inside his helmet.

When, after an eternity, it came back into sight, he saw that
it was one of the Company's slender, silver LRVs.

The ship would pass by, he could see, no more than a dozen
kilometers distant—an impossible coincidence. Then he realized that it was in all probability following the same course-
vector as the pod; they were Shimizu police tracking the thieves
who had, in taking the pod, stolen Company property.

They were probably hoping to overtake the pod before it hit
atmosphere.

But there was nothing he could do to signal the ship. Even if
he could have waved his arms, the chance that some member of
the LRV's crew might spot him were infinitesimally small. The
shuttles more or less flew themselves, and whatever guidance a
pilot might give one, it would be by instrument and not by
actually looking out a cockpit window.

Chances were, in fact, the pilot would at this moment be
preoccupied with what his instruments were telling him about
the course from orbit of the stolen pod.

It swung from his sight again and he gasped in frustration and
despair.

Without the drying current of air that usually blew across it,
his faceplate was fogging. As he watched, the tiny droplets crys-
tallized into frost.

It was growing cold in the suit; as efficient an insulator as its
polymer fabric was, without power for the suit's heaters, the
absolute chill of space was leaching away the warmth that kept
him alive.

It would be a race, then, between the numbing cold and suffocation for how he would be killed. The suit's air was already rank and stale.

He closed his eyes and waited to die.

Moments later he felt a tug at one of his legs. He opened his eyes to see a space-suited figure coiling a cable around his ankle. The cable led away to the LRV, now no more than a hundred meters away.

The cable jerked at his leg and he found himself being rapidly reeled in toward the aft lock on the LRV. His rescuer followed more slowly, pulling himself in hand over hand on his own umbilical tether.

Harris watched the process and realized with a certain awe that the man who had rescued him wasn't carrying one of the bulky reaction guns that were used for maneuvering in open space. Which wasn't surprising; there was little need for the devices in platform work, and since they were expensive, there were few of them to be had. It was pretty unlikely one would be among the equipment aboard any given LRV.

Which meant that the man who had rescued him had done so by leaping out away from the hull of the LRV, trusting his own skill and judgement to put him on target. Which took one hell of a lot of coordination—more than Harris knew he himself was capable of.

However it had been done, he was grateful.

It took no more than a minute for the winch to draw him into the open mouth of the lock. Even so, his lungs burned with every shallow breath and his vision had become a red blur. He felt hands grasp him and stand him upright in the lock. He was vaguely conscious of his rescuer joining them and of the lock's outer door irising closed.

Sometime during the lock's cycling, he passed out. He woke to find himself on his back, strapped to an acceleration couch. His helmet was off and he took a deep breath of the sweet, clean air, savored it with his full concentration, and let it out in a dizzy rush.

"Welcome back," a voice said.

He looked to his right and saw the smiling face of Song Lan.

He stared, openmouthed. "How—"

She hushed him. "How do you feel?"

"Like someone hit me with a bat. Twice. What are you doing here?"

"I had to keep them from taking you."

It was all too surreal, too unlikely. "How did you find me?"

"The same way those thugs in the escape pod found you," another voice answered for her. A male face he didn't recognize hovered over him. "I'm a doctor," he said. He held forth a slender, pencil-like tool.

"If you'll permit me?" He pointed to the side of Harris's head.

Harris stared at him for a second, then nodded. "Sure. Go ahead."

The doctor leaned over Harris and braced himself with one hand to keep from floating off as he worked. He touched the side of Harris's head with the tool. He heard a high-pitched hum, like a mosquito's whine, conducted through the bone behind his ear.

"Sonic scalpel," The doctor muttered matter-of-factly. "Just a second. Here it is."

There was twinge of pain as he tugged at something in the flesh. He pressed a bit of cotton wadding against the wound he had just made. "Hold this."

Harris did, pressing a finger against the cotton. The doctor held his hand, palm open, close before Harris's face. In his hand was a tiny, black spiral, a piece of metal that looked vaguely like the broken tip of a microscopic screw.

"What in God's name is that?"

"I don't know, exactly. Some kind of transmitter."

"How did you know?"

"I told him," Song Lan said. Harris turned his head to look at her. She stood, holding herself in place by a strap, against the bulkhead, still in her pressure suit. There was a bandage on her left cheek. She touched it.

"Dr. Carney did the same service for me back in Port-de-Paix that the doctor just did for you."

The doctor nodded. "From what I heard, that one was a little touchier, though. The fellow had to be quick. Damned thing was rigged with an explosive."

Harris shook his head wearily. He looked at Song Lan's face, felt a spark of warmth begin to replace the empty feeling the Angel had left. "I'm afraid I don't understand."

"A very long story. That thing that the doctor took from behind your ear. I put it there." She bowed her head, shame written across her face. "I betrayed you."

Harris made an intuitive leap. "You knew they were coming after me."

"Yes. I knew. And I was ashamed. So I told Dr. Carney that there would be an attempt to kidnap you. Dr. Carney spoke with officials of the Company. They allowed me to come up to the platform. When we discovered that the signal from the device I planted on you was outside of the platform, I thought we were too late."

"That's why you were the one that came out there after me?" He gestured to take in the pressure suit she was wearing.

She looked up, her eyes full of pain. And hope, he thought. "Yes. I made them let me."

"She didn't have to twist anyone's arm very hard," the doctor put in. "That was a pretty hairy jump she made."

"I know. I still don't quite believe it. Or was I hallucinating? You *jumped* from the LRV? I was at least a hundred meters out. If you had judged a degree off—"

She shook her head. "I couldn't have." She hesitated. "It's very hard to explain—"

"And now's not the time," the doctor broke in. "The captain tells me he'll be taking us in for Tortuga in about five minutes. Settle back, son. There'll be plenty of time for explanations later."

"One other thing. The kidnappers—"

"They'll be splashing down somewhere in the China Sea, I'm told. They'll be long gone before we could ever get to them."

"That's it, then. It's over."

Song Lan nodded. "It's over. For now."

Harris settled back on the acceleration couch. The doctor moved over to an adjacent couch and began the process of strapping himself in.

Song Lan pulled herself over to Harris's couch and hovered over him for a moment. He saw that her hands were shaking badly and he remembered abruptly what even looking up into the emptiness of the sky had done to her. That she would brave the ultimate openness of space seemed incredible.

She looked into his eyes and he saw something there he hadn't seen in more than a half-dozen years. And he knew suddenly why she had done what she had done.

She kissed him, quickly, lightly. Then she pushed away and shot across the cabin to her own couch.

Harris watched her go, his heart full and confused. It was all too much to take in at once. He closed his eyes and tried hard not to think about it.

He felt a nudge as the ship maneuvered into its descent. He could see the Earth below in his mind's eye. It seemed to be waiting for him, blue and white and brilliantly beautiful.

And doomed, he thought. Somehow, finally, that fact mattered to him.

3

THE SHIP

CHAPTER TEN

June 6, 2071

His private study was the one place where General Lin Biao of the Army of the People's Republic of China allowed himself to relax. It was a stark room by Western standards—a large hardwood desk into which was set the black square of a computer's screen, a broad, intricately woven antique carpet on the floor, some few books on a shelf behind his chair.

In one corner near the ceiling a machine was mounted, a simple, black box sixty centimeters on a side; it was an adaptation of a device used for entertainment in the West, but it would be put to a different use today, a way its inventors would never condone because they were weak and had been made soft by their own decadence.

Soon, he would, through it, actually live the glory of a battle he had sent other men to fight.

There were a few framed photographs of himself as a younger man hung on the walls, with his first command, an aerial gunship, and, later, standing a missile watch during the terror of the Great Standoff with the Western powers.

Those same powers now threatened the homeland again. This time the outcome would be different. There would be no treaty, no loss of face. If he had his way—and he would!—the Americans and the Soviets and the handful of nations that were their obedient toadies would go down in fiery ruins before the might of the People's Army.

He took one of the Tian Shan cigarettes that he favored from the mahogany box on his desk and lit it. He savored the first lungful of the harsh smoke. The rough-cut black tobacco smelled to him of farmland, of simpler times.

It had not been easy. There had been much resistance. Those he couldn't convince he had eliminated. But his agenda—the republic's agenda!—was now in place.

He sat comfortably in the leather chair before the desk and contemplated the prospect of victory.

A chime sounded, musical and startling. He touched a control on his desk and the screen embedded there filled with the face of Zhou Li, his aide-de-camp.

"The assault force has disembarked the orbital vehicle."

Lin Biao smiled.

It had started.

"And the other matter?"

"Has been taken care of. The traitor to the republic will be in our possession very soon."

"Good." He touched the control again and Zhou Li's image faded.

He took from the center drawer of the desk a black tab the size of a thumbnail. It was tacky on one side, and he pressed it to his right temple.

He said the word that would activate the machine then closed his eyes and waited for the battle to begin.

It all seemed to happen very fast.

James Harris found himself one fine, summer day on a commercial LRV—Shimizu's, of course—lifting for a platform in high orbit, from which he and two other members of the crew of the newly commissioned Chernetsky starship *Phoenix* would be transferred to Kennedy Pressure, on the moon.

The project was ostensibly sponsored by the United Nations, but few of the member countries had any knowledge of it—only Japan, the United States, the Soviet Union, and the United Arab Republics. Which was why it was being staged from an American base on the moon—and why the mixed-nationality crew was taken up piecemeal, each man or woman in the guise of a platform roughneck.

The gee force pressed him back into the couch as the LRV shuttle blasted down the ringed length of the accelerator. Seconds later it eased off as the shuttle cleared the open muzzle of the tunnel and rocketed out of the mountain and into the open blue sky. He felt again as if he could breathe.

One day after the *Phoenix* project had been initiated, Harris had accepted the UN's offer to join the crew as an advisor.

It was a decision he had made with some reservation. Foremost in his mind was his suspicion that Hugh Carney had had a good deal to do with the offer. And it was bitter medicine indeed to take anything from Carney. There was still too much unresolved between them.

And then there was Song Lan.

She had made the best of it, making herself cheerful around him, keeping out of his way when he was moody and withdrawn. But he could see the wistfulness in her eyes.

They had spoken of it only once, when he had first learned of the expedition. She had cried then, and hadn't spoken of it since.

As much as it might trouble him, though, he didn't see that he had ever had any choice. He had been selected, as surely as the hand of God had chosen Moses—or, more appropriately, he thought, Job—when the Angel had descended to the frozen surface of Comfort to take him up.

He had tried to explain that to Song. It had seemed to have little effect.

He had given up and had tried to live with the quietness and the tragic glances. Without her having said it, he knew she didn't think he'd be coming back.

He had to wonder himself.

On the surface, the entire endeavor seemed pretty improbable and not a little suicidal. Whatever the Angel was, he could no longer call it to him, and without contact there was no avenue for entreaty. It became obvious to all—even to the rather slow-witted politicians who controlled the Japanese, American and Soviet space programs—that the ship that had brought him back was the only possible source of help.

Thus the *Phoenix* project.

And what ate at Song Lan the most, he knew, was the fact that the project had been her own idea.

She had been interrogated for three days by the security agencies of the major powers of the UN. In those three days, she had told them all of what she had withheld before from Carney. She had told them about the dangerous desperation of China's ruling clique—something they already knew from their own sources— and she told them about the spacecraft she had discovered.

Somewhere, moving through space at twenty-thousand-plus

kilometers per second on a vector out of the Solar system—
having somehow obviated the effect of planetary gravity—was
an alien spacecraft. On that spacecraft was the possibility of
salvation for them all. There, in a solid, tangible form, was hope
for a clue.

If they could get to it.

It had been Song who had suggested going after it, using the
Chernetsky starship that had been intended for the colonization
of the fifth planet of Vega. With the ship accelerating at one
gravity, they could catch up with the alien ship in a matter of a
few weeks.

For the second time in his life he would board a starship that
would take him far from Earth into the empty void between
stars. It was not a prospect he especially relished.

The Cygni expedition had been the first of Earth's attempts
to colonize the stars. The Vega colony was to have been the
fourth. Whether the two ships that had been sent out in the
interim had had more luck than his own wouldn't be known for
more than twenty years.

When the Chernetsky zero-point drive had first become a
practical source of propulsion, the old fires of empire, which
had burned low in the twenty-first century, had been rekindled,
not in individual countries but in the world as a whole.

With the colonization of the moon and Mars, Earth's frontiers
had seemed finally to have disappeared. When a team of scientists at America's Jet Propulsion Laboratory demonstrated that
an infinite source of power was to be had out of the forces
inherent in the very vacuum of space, it was as if another Co-
lumbus had announced the opening of a New World to the west.

Automated probes were built, one at a time, at great expense,
and launched toward a half-dozen systems that radio telescopy
had identified as having likely Earth-like planets within their
heliospheres. Every industrial country on the planet contributed—with the notable exception of the People's Republic of
China, a land too torn by inner strife to give its attention to the
stars.

Then the laser message from the probe that had been sent to
61 Cygni had been received by the lunar observatories.

In computer code, it had sent them pictures of paradise.

A colony ship had been built, and when it left Earth's orbit,
he had been aboard it. And when the ship's computers had awak-

ened him, he had been one of the first to see the icy hell they had traveled so far to find.

In another five years the message they had sent then would reach Earth after traveling across billions of kilometers of space at the slow speed of light. It would be the first the Earth would hear of a disaster that had lived in his memory for more than six years.

The Vega ship he would soon board was part of the reason he had been tucked away and forgotten by the world. Too much had been invested already in a dream that could be soured by the failure he represented. By the time the message from Cygni reached Earth, three more colonies to the stars would be on their way, the colonists secure in their metal coffins, in the dreamless near-death of the stasis fields.

Maybe the bureaucrats had been right, Harris thought, though for all the wrong reasons. Maybe it was better his tragedy be kept from the world so that the world would continue to finance the construction of starships whose purpose was to seed the galaxy with humankind.

Because it was beginning to look as if the world they had left behind was in grave danger. Without the Earth's support, the moon colony and the orbital platforms could continue on for a few years, perhaps even a decade or more. But eventually mankind itself would be buried in the ice that was beginning to creep across the face of his world.

Then, only the star colonies would be left of all the billions that had been the race of man.

The Vega colony's ship waited for them now in orbit, a bright, tenuous bit of hope.

It wouldn't have much longer to wait.

And when its engines flared into life, James Harris would be aboard.

He felt the gentle bump-and-push of the shuttle's attitude jets as it moved to match orbits with the platform. The sensation was a welcome change from the monotony of free-fall. Not for the first time he felt a twinge of jealously for the LRV pilots, who could actually see what was going on. Shimizu had been too cheap—too efficient, they would argue—to bother with viewports or even monitor screens in the passenger bays.

After an interminable wait as the pilot eased his craft into the docking carousel, the hatch irised itself open and they untanked one at a time.

Waiting in the passageway of the carousel umbilical was a heavyset, bulky figure in a pressure suit.

"Bulgakov!" Harris said, surprised, recognizing the man as one of the Soviet members of the *Phoenix*'s crew, a Rasputin-like giant whose mind was as encompassing as his huge body.

"James," Bulgakov acknowledged, grinning. "It is good to see you again."

"Likewise. I thought you were waiting for us with the others, on Luna."

"The situation has changed." He jerked his head toward a nearby pressure lock. "Perhaps we should go outside for a min-ute, to enjoy the stars."

Harris nodded, again surprised. "Sure, Mickey." He turned to Harper and Matsura, the two crew members who had lifted with him. "You two move on down to the spinner. I'll be along. Seems the mighty Russian wants to talk."

He pulled himself along the bulkhead to where Bulgakov waited. The others sailed down the axis toward the spin-accelerator that would let them into the platform proper.

"What's up, comrade?" Harris whispered.

Bulgakov grinned and shook his head. "Outside."

A rack of air tanks was attached to the bulkhead beside the lock. He grabbed the handles to either side of a set of tanks and eased backward against them until he felt them click into place. Bulgakov followed suit. Harris donned his helmet and sealed it, then murmured the word "air" in the humming undertone that the suit's computer listened for, and a cool draft began to blow gently against his faceplate.

He knew why Bulgakov wanted to meet him outside, in vac-uum. The platforms were notorious for being functioning em-bodiments of the old axiom about walls having ears. Shimizu's execs liked to know what the workers had on their minds and were not above listening in to private conversations.

Outside, there was little to fear. Vacuum doesn't carry sound. He squeezed in beside Bulgakov in the tiny utility lock and together they waited in the claustrophobic closeness while it cycled.

The rhythmic thud of the pumps faded into the silence of airlessness. Bulgakov waited until the lighted panel to the right of the outer door flashed green before leaning close and touching the faceplate of his helmet to Harris's.

"We will not be going to the moon," Bulgakov announced.

Harris wasn't surprised—he had assumed as much when he had seen Bulgakov—but he was curious. "Is there something going on?"

Bulgakov shook his head slightly, his face so close to Harris's own that his blocky features seemed exaggerated and over-done—a caricature of the much-feared Ivan of the Cold War years of the last century.

"I do not know. Perhaps. All they have told me is that the GRU has advised that the launch of the *Phoenix* be moved to today. I believe they intend to begin the expedition as soon as we arrive."

"What does Soviet military intelligence have to do with the *Phoenix* project?"

Bulgakov shrugged, a gesture that lost much of its force in a pressure suit.

"Is the *Phoenix* ready to fly, even?"

Another shrug. "It seems it will fly today whether it is ready or not. The rest of the crew is in transit as we speak. You and the others are the last."

"When?"

"As soon as possible. We have commandeered a Shimizu orbital shuttle. Matsura will pilot."

Harris started to object, then nodded. " 'In an advisory ca-pacity'—that's what they said when they hired me."

Bulgakov nodded. "I understand. You were a pilot, before."

"Yes. A long time ago. Now, I consult. I should be grateful—I could have been left behind."

Bulgakov shook his head gravely. "No, my friend. I for one am happy to have you with us. You have faced this beast in its lair and lived. To me, that means you are fated to live long, and I am gratified to have a lucky man as a companion. Even in an 'advisory capacity.' "

He slapped Harris hard on the shoulder and whispered to the black square under his chin. The green light on the bulkhead flickered to yellow and the lock began to pressurize.

Matsura mumbled a subvocal string of coded instructions and the transfer shuttle's maneuvering jets *ping*ed and eased the un-gainly craft out of its cradle.

The shuttle was roomy compared to the LRVs. There were no size or weight constraints and no need to worry about aerodynamics in its design. Where the LRVs were slender needles with retracting delta wings, the transfer shuttle was a blocky maze of girders designed to secure pressurized storage containers for transfer between orbital stations. At one end was a large control cabin.

Harris sat strapped to one of the seats arranged directly behind the pilot and copilot positions. While the gee force of the initial burn pushed him into the seat, he tried to relax and enjoy the view. In direct contrast to the claustrophobically enclosed LRVs, the cockpit of the transfer shuttle offered a wide expanse of Plexi through which he could see a thin sliver of mottled, dusky blue—the Earth herself—against the deep velvet of space.

Matsura muttered another command and the attitude jets fired, pushing the crescent of blue from the Plexi. A brilliant wash of stars pushed forth from the darkness as the ambient glare of the Earth shifted out of view.

"We're on the wire," Harper reported from the copilot's position.

Harris touched the buckle on his harness and the straps pulled away. He drifted forward to look over Matsura's shoulder. After a moment Bulgakov floated up beside him.

The shuttle's "instruments" were a mixture of the familiar and the arcane to Harris. Voice control had been a novelty but not unknown in his day—he flinched inside the smallest amount at the phrase; the sound of it made him feel ancient—but the graphic, heads-up navigational displays he had known had been replaced by a floating whirl of numbers and symbols suspended in the air between the pilot and copilot.

As he watched symbols and objects—each outlined in a seemingly random array of colors and accompanied by a string of numbers—appeared and disappeared as they entered or left the space—thousands of square kilometers of it, Harris guessed—encompassed symbolically by the boundaries of the holograph.

As the transfer shuttle adjusted its position relative to the objects represented in the holo, the contents of the holo shifted relative to the craft's orientation. It was all too much for Harris to follow; it frankly made him more than a little dizzy.

Bulgakov pulled himself forward and poked a finger into the display. He pointed at a narrow cylinder within which was suspended the letters *PH* and the inevitable string of numbers and symbols.

"This is the starship?"

"That's it," Harper answered. "We're still a few hundred kilometers out."

"This is a lunar lifter?" He indicated a fine line abutting the cylinder.

"Yeah. Lunar registry. Small one. Few thousand tons cargo, half-dozen passengers and crew."

"And this?" His finger hovered before a blunt trapezoid. It was no more meaningful to Harris than any other figure in the display, but he could see that it was different in one aspect. No numbers accompanied it.

Harper shrugged. "Beats me. Matsura?"

The pilot shook her head. "I don't know. One second." She whispered to the ship's computer. After a moment, "No registry, lunar or Terran. It's a bogie."

"A bogie?" Bulgakov asked.

"A unidentified flying—or orbital—object," Harris explained. "Roughneck talk. Means the computer doesn't know what the hell it is."

"Is that possible?"

"Shouldn't be," Harper said. "Could be a research craft of some kind, I suppose. I hear there've been some shots out of Tyuratam for the asteroid belt in the last year."

"No, it's not Soviet," Matsura said. "It's the wrong configuration. Wrong heading as well. If I am not mistaken, its pilot intends to match orbit with the *Phoenix*."

"You are sure of that?" Bulgakov demanded.

"No. I will be in a few minutes, though. I would wager a month's pay on it now."

"That's good enough. Raise the *Phoenix*. Tell them they are threatened. Find out if they have seen it themselves."

Harper nodded. "Roger. Whoops, just a moment; message coming in *from* the *Phoenix*." He tilted his head to listen to a barely audible buzz coming from the headrest of his seat. "Say again, *Phoenix*? Roger. I understand. ETA six minutes, give or take."

"What's going on?" Harris asked.

"You wouldn't believe it."

"Try us," Bulgakov rumbled.

-"Somebody just started a war."

There was silence for a long moment.

"What the hell is that supposed to mean?" Harris asked finally.

"Somebody just blew up a Soviet low-orbit military platform. Nuked it."

"Manned?"

"No. But there'll still be hell to pay."

Bulgakov grunted. "He is right. The presidium and the Ministry of Defense will not be understanding. Who is the culprit?"

"Unknown."

"The Chinese," Harris said.

"Probably," Matsura agreed. "But what would they have to gain?"

"Siberia."

Harper twisted around to stare at Bulgakov. "What the hell would the Chinese want with *Siberia*?"

"They have made punitive claim to it since their revolution. Parts of it were ceded to the czar in the nineteenth century. It has always been a point of contention between our nations."

"It's possible," Matsura offered. "From the intelligence I have seen, the crises they face with feeding their people have put insurmountable pressure on their ruling clique. Acquisition of arable land would be a priority for them, I would think."

"Siberia is not an especially arable land, my friend," Bulgakov observed.

"No, it isn't," Harris said. "Would the Soviets necessarily respond to a provocation like this with strategic weapons?"

"No. There would be much talk, first. Threats. Troop movements. They might attempt to invade their communication and computer networks, subvert their systems."

"Brinksmanship," Harper ventured.

"Yes. Like the Great Standoff. Or the Cuban Missile Crisis in the last century."

"Again, to what purpose?" Matsura asked.

"A diversion, maybe. Would anyone notice a shot out of, say, that launch facility the Chinese built on the Nanshan plateau in inner Mongolia back in the fifties?"

"No. I wouldn't think so," Harper answered, "not with all the excitement. The satellites and defense platforms would be looking for reentry vehicles, for ICBMs. They probably wouldn't pay any attention to a launch into high orbit. Not right away, anyway. But, Christ, the Chinese haven't launched an orbiter in, what, ten or fifteen years. Their technology stinks. And they've got bigger problems than the conquest of space."

Matsura spoke quietly. "I see where you are leading, Mr. Harris. But what an incredible chance to take!"

"Desperate times make for desperate men."

"What the hell are you boys talking about?" Harper demanded. Harris remembered that Harper was also from Texas; stress had put back a little of the drawl in his voice that years away from home had blunted. "Are the goddamned Chinese starting a war, or not?"

"Not, I'd say."

"There is another one," Bulgakov announced suddenly. He pointed out another tiny trapezoid entering the lower left-hand border of the holographic projection.

"What the hell are they?"

"Warships," Harris answered. "They are going to steal the *Phoenix*."

"Or they are going to destroy it." This from Matsura.

"Why?"

"To keep us from having it. To keep our countries from making an alliance with an alien intelligence."

"That's insane," Harper declared angrily.

"No, my friend," Bulgakov said softly, "it is politics. It is desperate old men afraid of losing their power. Or longing to achieve it. It has happened more times than you would believe in the history of our world."

"In my country as well," Matsura agreed. "The question before us now is not historical, however. Our problem is what can be done about it."

"The *Phoenix* is aware of the approach?" Bulgakov asked. Harper nodded wordlessly.

"Could they move the *Phoenix* out of danger?" Harris asked.

"No. Not without killing us. This shuttle isn't shielded. The engines on that ship create a massive stress on the fabric of space—enough stress to open a rift into an alternate reality. That's where all that sudden thrust comes from, the interface of the Chernetsky generators with a tachyon reality. The wave of hard radiation produced would be deadly this close up.''

Harris swallowed. ''It strikes me that the lives of four crew members would be relatively unimportant. There are many others aboard the *Phoenix*. And if the Chinese take it—''

''The *Phoenix* is aware of that possibility,'' Matsura interrupted. ''They indicate they still will not fire the drive.''

''What now, then?''

''I would tell them to prepare for an assault,'' Bulgakov said quietly.

''More than an assault. Tell them that the Chinese are going to take the *Phoenix* from them.'' Harris shook his head at the useless irony of it. ''And tell them there isn't a damned thing they can do about it.''

Matsura whispered to her instruments and new lines of letters and symbols appeared floating in the air. ''The first of the bogies is about ten minutes behind us. Should we abort and return to Shimizu Six?''

''What the hell else can we do?'' Harper demanded. ''This bus isn't armed. If we keep going we'll probably get blasted.''

''We can assume the Chinese vehicle is armed?''

''Without a doubt. Heavy lasers at the least, I'd say.'' Harris answered. ''An LRV would have some protection because its surface is reflective. This heap could be cut into pieces pretty quickly.''

Bulgakov spoke up. ''Consider this, though. What will the Chinese boarders aboard those ships do with the crew already aboard the *Phoenix*?''

''What could they do?'' Matsura returned. ''They would transfer them to the two lifters and return them to the planet.''

''Do you think that is likely?''

''Not damned very. They'll space 'em, sure as hell,'' Harper said.

''Probably,'' Harris agreed. ''Transferring the crew would take more time than they're likely willing to spend. For them, this is a combat mission. It might be a regrettable necessity, but I don't think they'd consider that they had a choice in the matter. They would space the crew.''

Bulgakov nodded. ''Precisely. Their commanders will be military men. The two vehicles will be provided with scuttling charges. They will destroy them when their objective has been taken. The crews of both of the attacking ships will have to be accommodated aboard the *Phoenix*. There will be no room for the present crew."

"And what exactly do you propose we do about that?" Harper asked.

"I propose that we rescue them."

"We do have ten minutes' head start," Harris offered.

"Ten minutes is nothing to a laser. I doubt that the commander of the Chinese vehicle realizes yet that we intend to rendezvous with the same target as he. When he does, it will take little enough effort to destroy us." Matsura's voice was frank and businesslike. Harris appreciated her calm and wished he could share it.

He put his hand into the projection the way Bulgakov had done earlier. "This is the *Phoenix*?"

Matsura nodded.

"So these two are the Chinese ships, here and here." He touched the two tiny, green trapezoids, then moved his hand to the miniature cube in the center of the display. "And this is us?"

Again Matsura nodded.

"What if you adjust your course-vector like this—" He moved his hand in a gentle arc north and west relative to the display until it was between the *Phoenix* and the unidentified ships. "—would that be possible?"

Matsura whispered. After a moment, she answered, "Yes, though not as directly or as quickly as we might like. What would be the purpose, though? They would simply destroy us and move on. As a shield, we would be a particularly vulnerable one."

"Only if they fire at us."

"I see!" Bulgakov announced, excitement in his voice. "You think that the Chinese might hesitate to fire on us for fear of damaging the *Phoenix*."

"Yes. At least until they were close enough to be assured that the laser wouldn't go around or through us. As a shield we aren't much, true. But as a target, we're even less. It would be like shooting at a wire window screen unless they were lucky enough to target the control cabin."

"That's one hell of a big 'unless,' " Harper said. "A gigawatt laser could turn this box into ash, and us with it, in a fraction of a second.''

Harris shrugged. ''At least we'd never feel it.''

''There's a comfort,'' Harper said wryly. ''And if we do get to the *Phoenix* without getting fried, what then? Do you think they'll just let us leave? Or will they burn us and the people we've just rescued as soon as we move away from the starship?''

''I don't know. I say we take that chance.''

''Gentlemen, I'll need a decision very soon if we are to do as Mr. Harris suggests.''

''Do it,'' Bulgakov ordered.

Harper hesitated, then shrugged. ''What the hell. I've always wanted to be a hero.''

''Brace yourselves then, gentlemen.'' Matsura mumbled to the ship's computer. ''Burn in three, two, one—''

Harris felt the sudden weight of the transfer shuttle's acceleration push him back into his seat.

He felt afraid, but he also felt more alive at this moment than he had since he had returned.

He watched the stars pinwheel by as the shuttle changed its orientation and was suddenly glad he had been given this chance.

He whispered a prayer of gratitude.

When they were within a half-dozen kilometers of the *Phoenix*, the trailing Chinese ship changed its course.

Matsura pointed out the change, following its new course with a finger that plowed through the cloud of holographic symbols.

''Why the hell are they doing that?'' Harper asked. ''They'll have to correct course to bring them back in. It'll cost them ten, fifteen minutes of maneuvering, easy.''

''Parallax,'' Harris answered. ''They're angling for a shot. At us. When they reach an angle from which they can get a clear shot without endangering the *Phoenix*, they'll burn us up.''

''What can we do about it?''

''Nothing. Not until we've gotten the *Phoenix* crew on board. Then maybe we can maneuver some, try to evade their lasers.''

''Evade? This thing maneuvers like a wounded whale. And you're talking about lasers—the speed of light, you know. We'll be sitting ducks.''

''Sitting ducks?'' Bulgakov asked.

"Easy targets," Harris translated.

Bulgakov grunted. "Again, we will simply have to hope that our Chinese comrades will be so distracted by obtaining the *Phoenix* that they will allow us to escape unscathed."

"How likely is that?"

Bulgakov shrugged. "We have come this far."

"And what of the *Phoenix* herself?" Matsura asked. "What are the implications if they are allowed to take possession of the starship?"

Harris answered slowly. "Maybe everything. Maybe nothing. As melodramatic as it sounds, it really could mean the end of mankind, in the long run. That's assuming that there's something aboard that alien ship that could stop the cold. At the very least, the Chinese will have first crack at whatever's aboard the ship. Weapons, maybe."

"Again," Bulgakov said, "there is nothing we can do to stop them. Perhaps it is better—who knows? Perhaps they will travel to meet this alien and it will turn *them* into ash."

"Wishful thinking," Harper said.

"Gentlemen," Matsura announced, "rendezvous in five minutes. I would suggest we suit up."

They spent the five minutes it took for the shuttle's computer to bring them the last few, careful kilometers helping each other into the backpacks and checking the suits' readouts. Then it was simply a matter of waiting. When the shuttle had matched orbit with the *Phoenix* they would set up a crew ladder between the air locks of each craft and begin transferring the crew.

After what seemed an eternity, Matsura's voice sounded in Harris's ear. "We're stationary relative. Go get them."

Harris and Bulgakov moved into the air lock and cycled through, leaving Matsura and Harper in the cockpit, monitoring the approach of the Chinese spacecraft.

Harris pulled himself along by the handholds set into the cabin's exterior bulkheads into the maze of girders that made up the greater part of the transfer shuttle's length. Bulgakov followed and hovered from a crossmember over Harris's shoulder as he began to extend the "ladder" that would connect the shuttle to the *Phoenix*.

Harris read off the proper combination of numbers in the requisite monotone whisper and the ladder began to extend itself, a series of jointed, polymer triangles through which the crew members would pull themselves over to the shuttle.

He whispered an adjustment in the ladder's course across the gap between the shuttle and the slender, elongated cylinder that was the *Phoenix*'s life-system. In the distance, to the cylinder's "north," he could see the concave disc of the Chernetsky generators and the steel/polymer matrix cables that tethered it to the life-section. Each cable terminated in a steel knuckle that seemed small relative to the life-system, but that he knew weighed tons and was as large as one of the smaller hovercars he had dodged in Port-de-Paix's streets.

He looked over his shoulder to Bulgakov. As he did so, the oblong oval of the shuttle's cabin seemed to dissolve in a burst of intense, green light, collapsing in upon itself like a crumpled wad of paper in a camp fire. His faceplate's filters adjusted instantly and automatically, but he was still nearly blinded, the afterimage glowing hellishly green on his retinas.

Then for a second there was nothing. No light, only the glowing tendrils of superheated metal where the cabin had been. Then the beams of coherent light—six of them, he saw now— moved toward him, beginning to consume the rest of the shuttle piecemeal, and the green glare of the reflected light flared again. So intense was the heat he could feel it like a sudden flush across his skin through the insulated fabric of his pressure suit. Drops of molten metal began to spatter against the girders around him.

A single word echoed loud in his helmet. *Jump*.

All he could see of the *Phoenix* through the afterimage from the laser's flash was a teary blur. He crouched and thrust out hard toward it.

Then he was floating through the emptiness of space. For one panicky moment he was convinced that he had jumped wrong, that it hadn't been the *Phoenix* at all he had seen but the still fading afterimage of the destruction of the shuttle's cabin.

Then he struck the hull, shoulder first, hard enough to drive the breath from his lungs. The force of the impact sent him skidding along the smooth, metal surface of the hull. Something caught at his elbow—a projection, probably a handgrip—and flipped him onto his back, but he continued to slide and bump across the *Phoenix*'s plating, rolling, helplessly thrashing his arms, trying to find a handhold.

Something brushed across his palm and he grabbed at it con-

vulsively. His momentum swung him around in a flat arc and
then he was jerked to a halt, the metal rung hard and secure in
his hand.

He reached for the rung with his other hand and held it tight
in both hands, breathing hard.

After a long moment he looked up. The transfer shuttle was
a twisted glowing mass a hundred meters away. Beyond it he
could see the blunt shadow that was the first of the Chinese
ships.

He drew himself close to the rung and reached ahead for the
next one.

He had moved no more than a dozen meters across the curve
of the *Phoenix*'s hull when a voice spoke in his ear.

"James?"

"Mickey!" He felt a rush of relief at the sound of Bulgakov's
voice. It seemed comfortingly near, though he knew that that
wasn't necessarily the case.

"Where are you?" he asked. There was no response. Then
he remembered and keyed his radio with his chin. "Mickey!
Where are you, old son?"

"James! I am glad to hear from you! I am beside the *Phoenix*'s
primary cargo air lock. I was about to cycle through. I had
assumed you, too, were dead."

"Not yet. Not by a long shot. I'm headed for the air lock
now."

"I would hurry. The Chinese have deployed their troops. We
do not have much time."

Harris glanced up and saw that it was true. The ambient light
from the planet below reflected white off of a cloud of spots that
seemed to halo the darker bulk of the Chinese lifter. Each spot,
he knew, would be a soldier, using backpack jets to propel him
toward the *Phoenix*. In a few minutes at most, the *Phoenix* would
be boarded like a merchantman beset by pirates in the Spanish
Main of the seventeenth century.

And like those pirates, they would be unlikely to take prisoners.

Harris pulled himself along from rung to rung as quickly as
he was able. Shortly the lock and the suited form of the big
Russian loomed into sight.

Bulgakov gestured and he put on an extra burst of speed. The outside door of the huge air lock was open and he pulled himself inside. Bulgakov followed and worked the manual controls that would close the outside door and begin the process of pressurizing the considerable volume of the compartment.

As the outside door began slowly to iris shut Harris saw the halo of dots around the Chinese ship blossom with dozens of pinpricks of green light. Metal boiled out from the bulkhead a meter away and level with his helmet as laser light melted and vaporized it, stitching an uneven, charred line a half-meter long between Bulgakov and himself.

"They've seen us! They're firing!"

"Yes," Bulgakov answered simply.

The door closed off the remaining opening with excruciating slowness. The lock was the largest on the *Phoenix* and was meant for cargo transfer; it was not built for speed. Harris gritted his teeth, his skin crawling, and waited for one of the invisible beams of light to burn through the fabric of his suit and into his flesh.

By the time the door had completely closed, he was mildly amazed to find himself whole and alive.

The inner door began its slow process of irising open and he grabbed a handhold and tugged himself through the narrow but widening opening in its center.

Inside was chaos. The staging area just inside the lock was cluttered with crates and boxes of supplies, strapped haphazardly to the deck—or what would be the deck under acceleration—walls and ceiling. Some smaller boxes and debris were floating loose. All had obviously been loaded aboard in a hurry.

A woman's face peered at them from around one of the crates fastened to a bulkhead. She held an American military-issue Beretta pistol at arm's length. Her aim wavered from Harris to Bulgakov and back again. Finally she decided that Bulgakov was the greater threat and held the gun on him.

As well as he could in zero gravity, Harris held up his hands. Bulgakov followed suit.

She stared through their faceplates for a long moment. Then she lowered the pistol.

He whispered to the suit's microprocessor and the helmet's locking ring whirred open. He twisted and lifted it away.

"We're friendly."

"You're not Chinese. That's all I needed to know. We have to get forward, quick."

"Sure. Why?" As he asked, it occurred to him that the woman who hovered before him now, holding herself in place by a cargo strap with one hand, a weapon in her other, was not one of the ship's complement. She was younger than anyone who had been assigned to the crew—twenty or twenty-one, he guessed—and she was a stranger to him.

Which left the question of who she was and what she was doing aboard the *Phoenix*.

He started to ask.

She made an impatient gesture with the pistol. "No time to explain. We've got to get strapped in. We're going to light the torch."

They took the broad, longitudinal passage in Tarzan fashion, hurtling breakneck from handhold to handhold along the textured surface of the bulkhead, the woman in the lead, Harris close behind.

"The *Phoenix* is ready for launch?" Harris shouted at the girl as she pushed off from a handgrip set into the bulkhead to glide smoothly away down the passage.

"No," she shouted back. "We're launching anyway."

"Launching anyway?"

Bulgakov drew abreast of Harris and then passed him, thrusting away from a handhold into a long, gliding swoop, like some sort of oversize bird.

Harris followed, confused, but willing to forgo answers for the moment. The image of the cloud of space-suited soldiers haloing the Chinese ship, heading for the *Phoenix*, was still vivid in his mind.

He could see the end of the passage ahead. The hatch at its end was open and the girl and Bulgakov darted into the room beyond. Harris followed close behind.

The control center for the *Phoenix* was the top "floor" of the cylindrical, half-kilometer-long life-section. It was a large, circular room filled with viewscreens and instrumentation. There were eight acceleration couches, four of them adjusted to serve as seats, holding their occupants upright before instrument consoles.

Harris, Bulgakov, and the girl came through the "floor" of

the room, popping through and catching themselves on hand-holds. The girl pulled herself to one of the couches.

The four seats were occupied; on the screen before one of the posts was the same image he had seen minutes before, from a slightly different perspective: the Chinese ship and its threatening halo. The dots seemed considerably larger. Whether it was because the soldiers were that much closer or because the camera that fed the screen magnified the picture, he could now make out detail, the rounded shapes of helmets, the suggestions of arms and legs.

Before another post, rising from a horizontal console, was a holographic display much like the one in the transfer shuttle. It swirled with a myriad of moving, colored figures. In the upper right-hand quadrant of the display was a large trapezoid. He realized suddenly that the scale was much larger than in the one he had watched in the shuttle.

The tiny figures suspended in the holo, each with its attendant stream of numbers giving course-vector and relative speed, were men, the same soldiers he saw on the video screen as a halo of growing dots around the Chinese ship.

The seat before the holograph swung around. In it sat a gray-haired, heavyset man.

Hugh Carney smiled at his son. "Hello, James," he said quietly.

It took Harris a long moment to recover. It took control to keep from staring, slack-jawed, like an idiot at the old man.

When he spoke, he was surprised to hear anger in his own voice. "What in bloody hell are *you* doing here?" he demanded.

"Trying to keep the bad guys from taking this ship away from us. You want to settle into one of those couches, so I can get back to work?"

"Answer me first."

One of the others seated before the instruments broke in. "Listen, we don't have time—"

"Answer me," Harris said again, his eyes never leaving Carney.

"Gentlemen!" The voice, Harris realized, was that of Bill Gorton, the expedition commander. "I realize the both of you are civilians, but I'd sure as hell appreciate it if you'd save the pleasantries for later.''

Harris said nothing. He knew he was being an ass, and he knew the timing was lousy, but he felt compelled. He stared at Carney without moving.

Carney sighed and looked to Bulgakov as if for intercession. The big Russian remained silent. ''All right. I was on Luna, working for COSEAR. They hired me on as a consultant—''

''Why wasn't I told?''

''Need to know, I imagine. What would you have done if you had known?''

Harris ignored the question. ''That doesn't explain why you're here, aboard the *Phoenix*.'' He knew he sounded petulant but couldn't help himself. Carney was the last person he had expected—or wanted—to see.

''You gentlemen want to can this discussion? We've got a couple hundred armed boarders coming down our throats—''

Carney, too, ignored Gorton, who cursed and turned back to his display.

''Look, I heard some things. Satellites had shown some activity at China's Mongolian launch facility. I followed a hunch and talked my way into a ride up with a cargo lifter. The same lifter that the Chinese blasted about five minutes after they finished with your ship. Andrea—the nice lady with the pistol there—was the lifter's pilot—'' He stopped speaking and his eyes narrowed. ''Where are Matsura and Harper?''

''Dead. They were still aboard the transfer shuttle when the Chinese burned it.''

''Damn. I'm sorry to hear that.''

''What of the rest of the crew?'' Bulgakov asked.

''Most of them made it up. Maybe a dozen are still on Luna, but the key people are here. We've got most of the launch crew, a few of the military people.'' He grinned suddenly. ''Most of the politicos got left behind on Luna. Damned shame, that.''

''You're still going to fire the drive?''

''We are, if you'll please take a seat. The initial acceleration should be somewhere in the neighborhood of five gees. I imagine you'd be more comfortable if you weren't smeared against a bulkhead.''

Harris felt frustrated and confused. Things were moving too quickly. He stood without speaking for a long moment. Then he pushed over to one of the empty couches and pulled himself down into it, letting it mold itself around him.

The woman who had met them at the cargo lock shifted to the couch beside Carney and began to mutter to the ship's computers.

He waited for the sudden breath-stealing weight of high acceleration. When it came it came abruptly, without warning. He wondered in a detached way about the hundreds of men who were watching at that very moment through the faceplates of their pressure suits as the drive blazed to life.

He wondered what they saw. In a way, he envied them.

General Lin Biao watched in wonder the sights seen by another man's eyes. He could see the elongated bulk of the starship in the near distance, set against a background dense with the glitter of stars.

The arrangement he now enjoyed, the grandstand view of the assault on the Westerners aboard the starship, had taken a good deal of effort to arrange. The technicians and surgeons under his command had been reluctant to perform the manipulation that had been necessary because it had involved a loyal member of the People's Army.

He had insisted; it had been done.

A low-ranking officer had been selected. A large portion of his cerebrum had been excised to make room for the device that now relayed the visual data that was being fed into his mind.

The soldier had lost some functions—speech, some higher-order thought processes. Sacrifices were necessary: war demanded them, the reaffirmation of the Glorious Revolution that Lin Biao had undertaken demanded them.

"Turn your head right," he ordered. After a moment's lapse the soldier through whose eyes he now saw complied.

His field of vision shifted to take in a score of others who moved in tandem with him toward the objective ahead. Each wore a pressure suit of brilliant white. Each was followed by his own condensation trail from the carbon-dioxide jets mounted to his backpack. Each helmet was marked with the red star of the republic in bright relief. Each soldier carried a weapon: some few held stubby rocket launchers; most carried laser rifles, sleek black forms of plastic and metal.

Glorious.

As he watched several of the soldiers fired, the muzzles of their weapons sparkling brilliant emerald-green for the briefest of instants.

He commanded his eyes to look down at the weapon in his own hands. He had the soldier aim and push the tab that would fire it. The weapon flashed.

He peered at the starship, searching for some effect.

A hint of movement ahead caught his eye. The soldier looked up without his command, distracted by a sudden brightness. A stream of light, incredibly bright, burning like a hundred-kilometer-long electric arc, flashed from the edges of the dish that was the starship's drive.

Lin Biao gasped in awe.

Then he cried out in pain and fear, real if only secondhand. It felt as if a live wire had been thrust through his eyes into his brain.

Then the universe seemed to dissolve into a blizzard of mono-chromatic snow. Somehow, impossibly, he thought he heard a man scream; it was piercing, agonized.

He tore the wafer from his temple.

Stunned, he sat unbelieving in his chair, staring at the black box mounted in the ceiling across from his desk.

After a time, slowly, he lowered his face into his hands as they lay on his desk. Deep inside, in a place he had never known existed, he felt the sudden need to weep. But he could not; he did not know how.

When he closed his eyes he could see the same empty rush of snow, as if the pattern were burned forever into his mind. It seemed endless: insubstantial, distant, icy cold.

CHAPTER ELEVEN

June 6, 2071

"It's getting pretty cold out here. Don't you think you ought to come inside?"

The woman was tall and muscular—*hard* was perhaps the best word to describe her—but Song Lan saw pity and concern in her eyes as she leaned over her where she sat in a deck chair, looking out across the midnight beach.

Song Lan shook her head. "No. I'll stay here for a while. I want to be alone."

The woman shrugged then and withdrew. The women who were assigned to watch over her—this one was named Sarah, she believed—were always attentive and painfully careful to be unobtrusive. But after a few days with her they inevitably began to feel the need to do something for her, to comfort her.

She couldn't help her misery any more than they could help their empathy. But she wanted nothing more from them than to be left alone, and a flicker of anger colored the sickness and longing in her heart when they insisted on intruding into her pain.

She stared silently out across into the darkness beyond the breakers. After a time the woman went back inside the house.

The day before, she had sat on the beach, alone except for the watchers from the house. The morning had been clear and cold, the breeze, smelling of fish and salt, blowing into her face from off the water.

The beach had been mostly empty, the weather too unseasonably cool for any but the die-hard surfers in their heated wet suits and a very few older people walking slowly along near the water where the sand was firm enough to make the walking easier.

A pair of sea gulls had settled onto the sand near her, looking for a handout, the cold wind ruffling their feathers and making them look vagabondish. They had reminded her of what she learned about her new homeland in the months since abandoning her old.

One of the many facts kept from her—from all Chinese—was that mankind had nearly killed itself, years before she was born, not with his much feared weapons, but like yeast in a wine vat with his own waste. They—*we*, she thought with a touch of amazement—came to the very brink before pulling back, before stopping the outrages of industry, the madness to *consume*. The Earth had healed herself, slowly, painfully.

She listened to the soothing susurration of the waves and remembered that even the great oceans, mortally wounded, had thrown off the chemical insults of a hundred years in less than two dozen with the help of bacteria engineered to consume the poisons. And the animals had come back, a few species, like the gulls, spontaneously; most, like the dolphins, cloned from frozen tissue. Some—the great whales: the blue, the sperm and the others too large to successfully clone—were gone forever.

Even now, the very word *disposable* seemed mildly obscene to the Western ear. If it couldn't be recycled or reused, it wasn't made.

Now the Earth was once again very nearly an Eden. It was clean, population and hunger were coming under control, and most—though not quite all—of its people lived reasonably well and usually happily.

Except in her own country, where men and women still lived in ignorance, fear, and hunger, where industry still bled poison upon the land.

It was all threatened now, she knew. The ugly as well as the good.

An old, thin man among the handful that walked the beach had caught her eye. He had left the wet sand near the water to venture into the hard going of the dry, loose sand nearby. He had walked toward the low dunes and back to the water three times as she watched. It had puzzled her until she noticed that his mouth was moving with each step and realized that he was counting.

The third time he came up the beach, when he reached what seemed to Song Lan to be an arbitrary distance from the surf, he turned and stared out to sea, shaking his head in seeming disbelief.

For a long time he had simply stood there, looking, she thought, for something in the water.

A kind of curiosity she hadn't felt in a very long time had taken hold of her. She had stood from the sand and walked toward him, not knowing what she would say.

He had turned to her before she was close enough to speak and eyed her critically; he seemed annoyed and she very nearly turned away. But wanting to know was the stronger need and she held out her hand in greeting. The thought passed through her mind—and was as quickly ignored—that the watchers in the beach house would at this moment be in a panic of nervous worry over who the old man might be. She only hoped they would have sense enough to keep their distance.

The old man took her hand and smiled reassuringly.

"You don't know me . . ." she started.

"But you want to know what the hell I'm up to, walking up and down out here in the cold," he said flatly, his voice gruff but not unpleasant. "I saw you watching."

"Well, yes." She was embarrassed, regretting her rashness.

"What's your name?"

"Song Lan. Song Lan Harris."

"A strange name!" he had said. "Jaime Palacios. Glad to know you. You're Chinese?"

She had nodded. "Yes."

"That's okay," he said. "My parents were from Cuba. They hated the Communists, but that was a long time ago. Hate does nobody no good."

He had pointed out across the cool green-blue of the Atlantic.

"The ocean's going away."

She held her breath. She was sure she knew exactly what he meant, and it frightened her. Still, she asked, "What do you mean?"

"It's *going*. Leaving. Going *away*." She noticed a tremor in his hand and the sharp, burnt smell of the sand. The world seemed to narrow itself to this moment, as if condensing the essence of its truth into this one place and time.

The old man had lowered his hand to his side and looked at

her. "I've been walking this beach for the better part of sixty years. High tide used to come up to here, a year ago—" He pointed at the sand near their feet. "—and that's high tide there, now." He gestured to the water, twenty yards away.

"Tides vary . . ." she had protested.

The old man shook his head. "Not this much. I was a fisherman, once, with my father. I know the tides. This time of year in this place, it comes so far up this beach. The ocean's going, and it ain't gonna stop. I know it." His eyes shone with conviction. "It ain't gonna stop till it's gone."

His words rang in her ears with the sound of revelation. It was not going to stop. The oceans were becoming ice, locked into the glaciers, into the snow that no longer melted.

The old man had shrugged and turned his back to her and started back toward the surf. He had stopped about halfway to the wet sand and turned back to her for a moment.

"I ain't crazy. And when it's gone, we're all gonna be gone, too." He shook his head regretfully. "Gone for good. Gone like the dinosaurs."

Song Lan spoke to the house and asked it to turn out the floodlights that illuminated the beach between the deck where she sat and the water. She sat alone, listening to the rush and sough of the surf.

As she watched, the darkness that brooded over the emptiness of the sea began to soften almost imperceptibly. A spectrum of colors—increasingly brilliant, many hued, beautiful—rippled in gentle waves across the sky and reflected back from the water below in a building intensity of light.

Song Lan sat up and stared, wonder and awe filling her heart. She knew what it was; she had seen the tapes, heard the descriptions of the launches.

Bim stirred from where he lay near her feet and whined. She put her hand on his head and comforted him without taking her eyes from the waves of shifting color that flowed and shifted across the sky.

As quickly as it came the aurora faded.

When it was completely gone she sat for a while looking out into the empty sky. Then, eventually, she went inside and made her way to the room that had been hers since James had left and she had been brought to Miami by the Americans so that they could watch over her.

She lay down and waited for sleep. She felt strangely relaxed, as if she had been given a signal to quiet her fears. When sleep came, it was deep and peaceful.

She woke suddenly, unsure whether the sound she had heard were real or only the residue of some dream.

She heard a growl near the foot of the bed and realized that that had been what had awakened her: Bim growling.

She sat up in the bed and saw in the scattered moonlight that streamed through the window that the dog was standing with his muzzle against the crack under the door.

He growled again, then whined, scratching against the floor-boards near the bottom of the door.

"What is it?" she whispered.

"Noisssess," he sputtered.

"Where?"

"Out."

"Far away?"

"Clossse. Coming."

Glass shattered suddenly in another room.

She sprang up out of the bed. Bim barked nervously and she shushed him.

A voice called out and there was the sound of a struggle. Then she heard the sizzle-hiss of a laser burning into something solid. She went to the one window in the room and eased it open. She stepped through and Bim followed, jumping through onto the deck outside.

Bim snarled and she turned to see a shadow ripple and move quickly toward her across the deck, the camouflage it wore shift-ing with the dappled pattern of the moonlight against the side of the house.

She whirled to face the threat and the Mind took over. Her body crouched low and slashed out with a vicious upward kick. She was startled to see her adversary dance nimbly back, mov-ing so fast she could barely make out the movement, the hard blade of her instep missing his head by centimeters.

He has been changed, too, she thought. And then, *they were sent after me, to bring me back.*

In the corner of her eye she saw another movement, in the window through which she had just come.

The Mind understood the threat in an instant. In one movement she recovered from the kick and leapt over the deck's railing, falling three meters to the sand below.

She rolled with the impact and came to her feet running. As she ran she ducked and weaved, making random movements to foil the aim of anyone who might be sniping at her. She didn't look back.

The moonlight made the beach dangerously bright. She ran back among the dunes, trying to stay within the shadows and high grass and sea oats.

If there was pursuit, she couldn't hear them.

She ran for another minute, then scrambled up into a place where two dunes ran together to form a pocket between them. She lay there, close against the sand, trying to control her breathing despite the demands of her burning lungs, listening. The solid bulk of the dunes blunted the sound of the surf, though the persistent rush and return could still conceal the sound of footsteps.

For the moment she felt safe, at least long enough to think through what she should do next.

There had been three agents of the American CIA in the beach house. She assumed that they were dead. As well armed and well trained as they might be, she knew—better than anyone else could—that they would have been no match for the *changed* agents her government had sent to take her.

Which left her to her own not-inconsiderable devices. Hand to hand, she was sure she was the equal of one of them. But there had been at least two, and together they could subdue her easily.

She could expect no help, at least none that could come quickly enough to do any good.

Which meant she must hide and wait. Bide her time until the opportunity presented itself to contact—

A rustling in the grass a few meters behind her interrupted her train of thought. She tensed but didn't move. The Mind wouldn't let her; it knew like the instincts of some primeval animal that sudden movement was a betrayal.

Slowly, almost imperceptibly, she turned her head. She could see nothing. She heard the sound again, a body moving low through the weeds.

Bim stepped out onto the stretch of open sand between herself and the grass. He had been hurt, she saw; his head was bloody and he limped as he came to her.

She felt a surge of rage so intense it nauseated her. Despite the Mind, she moved toward the injured dog.

A piece of the shadow below the dunes tore itself loose and leapt at her. She twisted around to defend herself and as she did Bim snarled and launched himself at her assailant, teeth bared.

As she watched, the fur on his chest sparkled green for an instant, the green disappearing into a growing, burning blackness. The dog collapsed soundlessly into a smoldering heap.

Her rage and the Mind became one. She struck while the shadow figure was still distracted by Bim's death. She slapped the flat box of the laser from its hand and in a continuation of the same blow she jabbed the stiffened fingers of her right hand into its throat.

It was over in the mindless fraction of an instant. The figure dropped, dying as he fell, strangling on his own crushed larynx.

And then something hard struck her from behind and the world seemed to shatter into shards of light. She wasn't aware of falling, of being rolled over, but she found herself staring up into the brown, almond-shaped eyes of a woman.

A needle shone for a second in the moonlight before it slipped into the flesh of Song Lan's neck.

Then the world spiraled away into darkness.

CHAPTER TWELVE

June 27, 2071

Life aboard a spaceship was not in itself demanding. But the initial excitement of launch quickly faded into the ennui of routine, and boredom settled in like a cloud.

Harris found himself avoiding the other members of the *Phoenix*'s crew as the days wore on into weeks. There was no communication with Earth; the radiation from the drive would have made a mess of any microwave transmission and the communications computers were not up to the demands of focusing a laser at velocities near .3 c. He occasionally played chess with Bulgakov or took a meal with one of the others, but more and more he kept to himself.

The ship's computers provided some diversion, games, experience programs, and "tactical simulations"—Harris tried a few of these and found them addictingly real. The device itself was simple: a wafer of conductive material placed against his temple. Then he closed his eyes and asked the machine for the situation he desired; the sensory input was entirely visual, the device stimulating the nerve pathways that fed in the neural cortex. But it *seemed* much more than that. Somewhere, somehow the brain supplied suggestions of the missing sensations: touch, smell, taste.

Most of the programs were military—not surprising, since the system had originally been designed for the military and the condensed-charge memories of the ship's computers were military hardware. But there were a good number of other scenarios. In exploring the computer's collection he even ran across a few fairly explicit sexual programs—doubtlessly squirreled away there by some technician. He played one of those just long enough to realize what it was about; voyeurism, even with an element of participation thrown in, was not to his taste.

He found himself spending long hours in his cube letting these visions play through his head. He climbed mountains, drove ancient motorcars down tracks of asphalt, fought battles with swords and with lasers. He tended to favor the programs that featured individual combat; he could lose himself wholly in the intensity of fighting to stay alive—and even if the experience wasn't real, the adrenaline was, and that was enough.

On this "morning"—morning because the computer had brought the corridor lights up an hour before—he closed his eyes to find himself in a place of thick jungle and deep shadows. There were other men with him, all clothed in loose-fitting, camouflaged uniforms. Each carried a weapon at the ready. There were two men ahead of him, walking carefully down a narrow trail. He sensed that there were others behind him, comrades; he didn't know how many.

Sunlight dappled through the dense overgrowth. He thought he could feel a pervading dampness, smell the dankness of mold and decaying vegetation. Everything about the place seemed too close, threatening; he had the sudden, overwhelming feeling that unseen things lurked just off of the trail, hidden in tangled undergrowth.

The soldier who led them stopped suddenly, crouching. He held up one hand, closed into a fist. For a long, tense minute they all waited, watching, listening.

He found himself staring at the hand. He could see a streak of dirt across the man's knuckles. Anticipation made his mouth dry, his throat tight.

The hand opened suddenly, the fingers spread. *Scatter*. He found himself dodging into the dense undergrowth, crouching behind a thick matting of leaves, his rifle at the ready.

Another man had taken up position beside him. He looked into the soldier's face and saw fear there: the man's eyes darted forward and back along the length of the trail they had just left, looking for something that terrified him.

There was movement along the trail. He crouched just a little lower, his elbows deep in the muddy grass. He slowly brought the muzzle of his rifle to bear.

An Oriental woman, dressed in loose, black clothing, appeared on the trail. She was armed, but for an instant she seemed to be alone and his rifle wavered a centimeter.

Then, as she approached, he could see others behind her. Men, a half dozen or more, all dressed in olive uniforms, all carrying rifles. The muzzle of his rifle steadied.

Something inside Harris rebelled at the scenario. He knew that in a moment the entire squad would open fire. The woman would die, her companions would die. It was real, he knew; ambuscade was a part of war.

He heard the first stutter of fire to his right. The woman jerked and twisted around. He found himself staring at her as her knees folded and she collapsed slowly, her face twisted into a grimace of agony.

He tried to close his eyes and remembered the eyes through which he saw now were not his own.

"Off," he said. The vision faded. He opened his eyes and pulled the wafer from his temple.

There was a sound in the room that, for just an instant, he thought had somehow carried over from the waking dream of the program.

Then he recognized it as the tone that announced a visitor at his door.

"Come," he said quietly. The door opened soundlessly. A figure stood there, outlined by the brighter lights of the corridor.

A woman's voice spoke. "I was beginning to wonder if you'd ever decide to come out of it."

"Lights," he commanded, and the strips recessed into the top of the room's walls glowed into life.

Andrea Coles stood by the door of his cube, watching him.

Harris's first reaction was irritation. He started to snap at her to get out, then caught himself. She was smiling at him.

"What do you want?"

"We're going into turnover in about an hour. We'll be back to zero gee for a while. The captain wants everyone aware of the change," she answered. Her voice seemed loud to him, harsh. He felt somehow hung over.

"Is that it?"

"No. I wanted to talk to you."

"So talk."

"I was wondering how a dream junkie managed to insinuate himself into something as sensitive as the *Phoenix* project."

"Dream junkie?"

She pointed to the wafer he held in his hand. "You're wired. Have been since launch."

He looked at the wafer, set it down on the chair's arm. "You've got a point to make?"

She shrugged. "No. Just curious. I know why everyone else is here. I'm an accident, a shanghaied lunar-shuttle pilot. You, on the other hand, don't seem to have a reason to be. Not here. Call it nosiness."

"What if I tell you it's none of your goddamned business?"

She shrugged again. "I'll leave. You can stick your wire back onto your head and disappear into never-never land. Nothing lost, nothing gained."

He sat up and the chair followed him, molding itself against his back. "And what do I get out of this exchange?"

"Is that a proposition?"

He smiled. "No. Just a weak attempt at humor."

"Too bad."

He looked up at her and she met his gaze. "I'm the fellow who started all of this. Or so they tell me."

She looked doubtful. "What do you mean, you started all this?"

"Do you know what's going on? All of it? Where we're going and why?"

"I think so. As much as Carney and the others cared to tell, anyway. We're paying a visit to a genuine ETI."

Harris nodded. "An extraterrestrial intelligence. It brought me home, that intelligence, all the way from 61 Cygni Beta Two. All the way from Comfort."

"Say that again?"

"I was part of the Cygni expedition. Launched about the time you were born, I'd expect."

She looked more doubtful. "You're joking."

"No, I'm not."

"Then you've been using that thing for far longer than you should have." She gestured to the wafer. "You can't distinguish reality from dream anymore."

"Maybe so. That'd be a relief, everything a dream. Once, a while back, I thought it might be. Now I know better. Besides, if I'm dreaming, you don't really exist and the whole damned discussion's moot."

"You want me to show you the holes in *that* logic?"

"No. You asked me, I told you. It's true. I was brought back. Like a ghost from the past."

"How come I didn't hear about it?"

"Nobody heard about it. It was hushed up. They gave me a new name and touched up my face. Like nothing happened. That's how governments handle things they don't understand. They bury them. Cover them over and pretend they don't exist."

"You sound bitter."

He shook his head. "No. I was more than happy to disappear. Then this thing showed up." He gestured vaguely at the bulkhead to take in the space beyond and the alien ship somewhere ahead in its distance.

She sat down on his bunk. "If you're telling me the truth . . . my God. No wonder you're a wirehead. I would be, too."

"Dream junkie? Wirehead? You think I'm some kind of addict?"

"You're not? We're only three weeks out, and you've spent twenty days of that dead to the world. Sounds like addictive behavior to me."

Harris picked up the wafer. He touched a drawer set into the wall beside the chair and it slid open. He placed the wafer inside and pushed the drawer shut. It closed with a metallic click.

"You're right. It does." He blew out his breath in a loud sigh. "I've hidden inside my head for a good long while. Even I'm starting to get tired of it." He looked up at her again and again she met his gaze.

"Curiosity satisfied?" he asked.

She stood. "To an extent. Turnover in an hour. You'll want to secure your personals."

"Tell me something."

She shrugged. "Ask."

"How well do you know Carney?"

She looked at him, considering. "Not well. I was just his pilot. I know he's your father."

Carney nodded. "He planned this, you know."

She shook her head. "No, I don't. How could he have arranged for what happened?"

"He didn't. But he put himself in the right place at the right time. He's wanted this his whole life. He's the reason I ended up as one of the Cygni colonists."

"I don't believe that."

"What do you mean?"

"I mean you don't strike me as the kind to do anything against your will. The apple doesn't fall far from the tree, they say. How hard did you struggle against going?"

He stared at her. "Not hard, I suppose."

"I'd say you both got what you wanted, then." She turned to the door and it opened for her.

"Are you a shuttle pilot or a shrink?"

"I'm just an objective third party, Mr. Harris. And a woman. Sometimes that's all it takes."

She stepped out into the hall and the door slid closed behind her.

For a long while he did nothing. The wafer in the drawer tempted him for an instant, but he realized he didn't want the dreams anymore. It was the same thing he'd done when he was dirtside in Port-de-Paix with his week-long drunks.

It was hiding, and hiding from reality was the act of a coward. Song Lan had taught him that—and she had done it the hard way, by example.

He pulled himself up from the chair and strode up to the door and out into the corridor.

He had been up to the *Phoenix*'s bridge twice since her hurried launch. Both times he had been tired of the artificial dreams and had been seeking diversion. He had found very little of that there. After the initial sequences had been initiated by her pilots and navigators—a group that now included Andrea Coles—the computers took over.

Both times he had been back to the bridge, a lone member of the crew had been keeping watch, presiding over displays that told Harris little about the ship's functions. The experience had only emphasized for him his own essential ignorance as a man out of time and out of place.

As the *Phoenix* was under acceleration, and had been, at one gravity, for three weeks now, the "corridor" down which he, Coles, and Bulgakov had rushed in the moments before launch was now a long, vertical shaft. Set into the walls of the shaft were rungs—the same ones he had used to push himself along in weightlessness.

He had seen Bulgakov take the entire length of the shaft—

almost two hundred meters—in a full-speed rush up the rungs. The Russian disdained the mechanical methods provided for reaching the top of the twenty-story building the *Phoenix* had become under acceleration.

Harris felt a bit too old for that, though he knew he was no older than the Russian, at least not physically. He was out of condition, and frankly had little ambition toward regaining the agility and strength he had possessed fifteen years before.

Set into the wall next to the rungs was a webbed seat, designed to be folded into a recess at the bottom of the shaft when the *Phoenix* wasn't under acceleration. A short, temporary bridge followed the wall from the corridor that held his cube, suspended a dozen stories from the shaft's end, to the left.

Harris called up the lift-seat, and when it reached his level, he strapped himself into it and let it take him up to the "top" of the *Phoenix*.

Almost all of the couches were occupied, adjusted up into seats before the instrument displays. There were a half-dozen people on the bridge, all too busy to notice his entrance.

Carney, Harris noted, was one of them. The old man was engrossed in conversation with the computers.

Bill Gorton—"Captain," most of the crew called him—was at one of the stations, giving a string of encoded instructions to the processor that controlled a holograph patterned in the air before him.

He finished and saw Harris standing nearby.

"Well, if it isn't the lost consultant. Come up to watch the hoopla?"

Harris nodded. "Anything I can do?"

"Afraid not. There's not really much any of us actually *have* to do. Most of what we're doing now is running diagnostics, making sure the computers know what the hell they're doing."

"Do they?"

"We better hope so. So far everything seems nominal. We've been into the countdown for about six hours now."

Harris pointed to the holographic display. In it a skeletal *Phoenix* floated. Different sections were outlined in colored relief. Numbers and symbols floated around in an indecipherable —to him—alphabet soup.

"Us?" he asked.

"Us, indeed. Making sure everything's secured before the

drive is shut down. Computer's keeping track; I'm just helping it out a bit. A couple of the others are doing a shipwide tour to make sure everything's battened down.''

Harris nodded. ''Andrea was by my quarters.''

''Good. I'll tell you, I'm glad we ended up hijacking her. She's one hell of a pilot. Flew for Shimizu for a year, moved over to the lunar fleet a few months back. She knows what she's up to. We'll need her when we rendezvous.''

Harris didn't comment. He was glad she was aboard, too, but for other reasons. He had always needed someone to kick him in the ass to set him right, he reflected. She had made him realize the cowardice of his dependency. He wouldn't let it happen again.

''How long to turnover?''

''About forty minutes. We'll be in transition for maybe an hour. Then back to one gravity for a few weeks, peeling off the velocity we've built up. When we've matched the speed of the target, hopefully we'll be within maneuvering proximity. *If*, of course, the thing continued on the same vector it was following when it blew by Luna and *if* it hasn't changed its velocity to any appreciable degree. Like it or not, it's all up to the hardware.'' He tapped the console under the holograph with a knuckle.

''And what will we do if it isn't there when we get there?''

The captain shrugged. ''We go home.''

Harris was silent. He was thinking, We'll go home—but will there still be a home to go to? Or only a rugged hell of cold and ice?

CHAPTER THIRTEEN

August 4, 2071

For weeks she had known only darkness, alone.

At first, she had thought it was punishment, or that they had hoped to elicit something she had managed to hide from them through the subtle torture of isolation.

Now she knew better.

They had forgotten her.

Only their functionaries remembered, providing her an occasional meal, water to drink—what was necessary to keep her alive.

They had questioned her, painfully. And she had told them everything she knew, secure that nothing she could tell would be of any use to them.

And then they had dropped her into the dark heart of an oubliette and had forgotten her.

Now she waited.

Two things kept her sane: memory and—irony!—the Mind. She had spent her first few days of captivity feeling her way around the room in which she was kept, searching with the help of the Mind for a flaw, a means of escape.

She had found none. Food and water came into the room by means of a tiny dumbwaiter, the infrequent sigh of its hydraulics the only sound she ever heard.

That sound and the t'ai chi exercises Jiang had taught her when she was a child became the center of her existence. She worked through the complex forms almost constantly, the Mind guiding and refining the movements into an exquisite, time-absorbing ballet.

177

More and more she lived inside herself, remembering. Less often, she wept.

Once, when she was a child, she had been lost in the lower reaches of the Catacombs. She had wandered, helpless and hungry in the blackness, for uncounted dozens of kilometers. She had been saved by the sound of someone singing. She had followed the melodic rise and fall of that single voice, panicking when it hesitated or grew quiet, ecstatic when it seemed to grow closer.

The voice—a female worker tending crops—had finally led her to one of the enormous caverns devoted to farming fungus, and from there to the salvation of a stairwell.

Someone singing! What she would now give for the sound of a human voice!

There came a time in the darkness when she began to doubt her own reality. She shouted into the blackness but the voice seemed to echo inside of her head, detached, insubstantial. The sensations of her body seemed suddenly meaningless, not her own.

In desperation she struck her fist hard against the concrete of the wall. Pain! But it was her own, it was real, and for that it was welcome.

She sat alone in the darkness and wept in thankfulness for the simple fact that she could still *feel*.

And when she had wept herself out, there was still only the darkness and the silence.

CHAPTER FOURTEEN

August 16, 2071

Hugh Carney was wakened from an uneasy sleep by something brushing across his face. He sat up in a panic and found himself propelled out of his bunk by the sudden motion. He drifted for an endless second or two before coming up with a bump against the cube's "ceiling."

"God*dammit*! Lights!" The strips glowed to life. The room was alive with objects floating in a slow circle, rebounding softly from the walls, propelled, he guessed, by residual inertia.

He was weightless for the second time since the *Phoenix* had left Earth orbit. Which meant the drive had been shut down.

Which meant they had arrived.

He struggled clumsily to pull himself down to the door, cursing under his breath at the arthritic stiffness of his joints. For years he'd had trouble for the first few hours of the morning, and weightlessness didn't make the ache any easier to take.

Gorton was going to get an earful for not sending around a general warning.

God, he felt old!

He pushed out through the door into the corridor, headed for the bridge.

Bill Gorton was seated before a proximity display. Andrea Coles floated over his head, holding herself in place with one hand against the bulkhead above. Carney pulled himself over to the station.

The holo before them was dominated by a single, ovoid shape sketched out in the skeletal lines of a diagram. Near the narrow end was a shallow, concave dip in the surface, as if someone had scooped a sample out of its hull with a spoon.

As Carney watched, the sketchy outline filled in with color, a bright, flat white.

It looked like a dented, hard-boiled egg.

He forgot his irritation. "Do you have any interior detail?" he asked, speaking loud enough to be heard over the noise. Most of the crew was on the bridge; he heard both excitement and fear in their voices.

Gorton looked up. "Good to see you, Doctor," he said. "You're the last of the crew to poke his head in. We've been looking it over for about an hour now, and no, we don't have any idea about its innards yet."

"Why not?"

"Think it through, Doctor. Whoever's in that thing over there has the power to travel considerably faster than light, a trick our physicists still insist is impossible, not to mention they've managed to change an entire planet's weather patterns. They might not like us throwing radiation hard enough to penetrate a spaceship's hull at them."

"I see your point. Have you tried radio contact?"

"Sure. Everything from ELF to microwave. No response. Which frankly, I don't find all that disappointing, Doctor. This whole business scares the crap out of me."

"You and me both, Captain."

"We've matched velocity with him. He's still doing the same clip as he was when Lunar Eye picked him up six years ago. There's been no reaction to us that I could discern, though I'm damned if I know what we should be looking for."

"Did you think there'd be a blinking neon sign: WELCOME MEN FROM EARTH?"

Gorton smiled wryly. "Not likely. This thing's a blank slate, though. No power signature. Hell, no thermal radiation of any kind, at least none my instruments pick up. Highly reflective . . ." He clicked his tongue thoughtfully against the roof of his mouth. "What do you think, Doctor? Should we try to board it?"

"You're the military man, Captain. You tell me. I do wonder what'll happen if those folks happen to *resent* you boarding that thing." He reached into the heart of the hologram and outlined the shape with his hand. "Christ, it does look like a flying ovum."

"If you say so, Doctor. We'll try a few more things before we actually go over. Visual displays. Low-wattage communications laser. Smoke signals, if nothing else works."

"I wish you luck, my friend."

"Wish us all luck, Doctor. I don't have a good feeling about this business. You know the old saying about bearding a lion in his own den?"

"I do. And I wonder how wise it is to let the lion know you're coming."

Gorton shrugged. "Probably an academic question. Somehow, I think if we can see him, he can see us. And he doesn't seem to want to talk."

"Maybe he can't."

"Come again?" Gorton said, his voice shaded with just a touch of incredulity. "Take another look at that spacecraft. Do you think we could build anything like it? Its technology is certainly more advanced than ours. I'd think it could talk circles around us."

"It might not be a technological problem. More likely, it's a physical or conceptual difference that's keeping 'em quiet. Despite what the idiots who've been claiming off and on to have been contacted or abducted by aliens in the last two centuries have said, it's damned unlikely whatever's in that lopsided henfruit out there is going to look like you or me with some minor modifications—an eggplant head or forty-foot tentacles. More likely, it's an intelligent bacteria who does its living in a fine mist of ammonia and hydrofluoric acid. Or maybe all it *is* is a fine mist of ammonia and hydrofluoric acid. Who the hell knows?"

"That, Doctor, doesn't make me feel any better."

"Or me, either, Hugh," Coles said from above. "If I understand you right, just shaking hands with this thing could be fatal to one of us."

"Damned right it could. Hell, I don't *want* either of you to feel better. I want you scared enough to wet your pants. Maybe that way you'll be marginally better prepared for what we might meet over there. I want you to be *careful*; I'm depending on you to get my poor, cranky old carcass back home intact."

"I'll do my damnedest," Gorton said. "But I'm not making any promises."

"I'm not asking you to," Carney said. As he spoke, two more

of the crew floated onto the already crowded bridge from the access corridor. Bulgakov nodded to Carney. Harris ignored him.

Carney, as he had been doing for weeks, let the slight pass. There was a problem there that wasn't going to get better by itself, but he didn't quite know how to approach it.

His style had always been head-on, damn the consequences. But he sensed he was going to have to leave any overtures to the boy—*to the man!* he reminded himself. That was a mistake in perception that could prove costly.

Harris settled himself into one of the couches proximate to the console and ordered it into position before the tablelike projector. He muttered instructions and the same figure that hovered before Gorton drew itself in an instant in the air before him.

Carney watched him study it and wondered what was going on in his head. After all, so far as they knew, the object projected before him was the means by which he had been snatched up and brought back to Earth.

Carney tried to imagine the emotion his son must feel and failed. As old and as world-weary as he felt, there was nothing in his own experience to compare it to.

Harris, for his part, was as unsure about his own emotions as the old man was. When the image first appeared, there had been a flicker of recognition, almost a déjà vu. But it was as quickly gone.

It was obviously artificial, though it looked very little like a spacecraft. It was brilliantly white, without much in the way of surface features. No obvious locks or ports. No discernible means of propulsion.

"What makes it go?" he asked Bill Gorton. He pointedly ignored Carney where he hovered near Gorton's shoulder.

"Good question. I'll be damned if I can answer it. *Nothing* makes it go, from what I can see. The computers concur."

"As do I," Bulgakov murmured.

"You were the next expert I was going to consult. What do you think of her design, Mr. Bulgakov?"

"Very strange. Very strong, though. She was built to take much pressure, much stress."

Gorton raised an eyebrow. "Yes? How can you tell?"

"The teardrop shape is not only aerodynamic, it is also naturally sturdy. Like an egg."

"Dr. Carney called it an egg a minute ago. I thought eggs were fragile."

"It's like the party game," Coles said. Everyone craned their necks to look up to her where she floated near the ceiling. "The material itself, the egg's shell, is fragile, but the structure keeps it from shattering. Have you ever tried that old party trick of trying to break an egg in your palm by squeezing it?"

Gorton thought for a moment, then nodded. "Yes, come to think of it. When I was a kid. Wouldn't break. I remember being shocked about it. I was under the illusion that I had a hell of a grip."

"Same principle. Nature has always been the best engineer, you know. The shape itself tends to distribute stress outward around its circumference, but the internal structure of the shell is carefully designed, too. The material of the egg's shell is actually made up of individual cells held in place by a bonding agent. The cells are vaguely pyramidal in shape, the base toward the inner surface of the shell. Pressure flexes the shell in such a way that the force is redirected sideways to adjacent cells. It's why you can't break one by squeezing it in your hand, even though the material itself is actually very brittle."

"Interesting," Gorton said. "Why would they need that much structural stability? That thing obviously wasn't designed for atmosphere."

She shrugged and he looked to Bulgakov. Bulgakov echoed the gesture.

"Who can know?"

Another crewman joined the crowd around the station. Harris recognized him as one of Gorton's men, a member of the American military's intelligence service. His name, Harris remembered, was Rainey. The man smiled and nodded and pulled himself close to Gorton's seat without saying anything.

"Do you know what's inside?" Harris asked Gorton.

"Not yet. As I was telling the doctor, I don't think we want to throw anything at our friend that he might take as a provocation—"

"It's a derelict," Harris said suddenly.

Gorton swiveled in his seat to stare at Harris. "What do you mean, derelict?"

"I mean there's no one aboard. No life. It's dead."

"How the hell do you know that?" Carney demanded.

Harris looked at the old man, but his attention was elsewhere. *How do I know that?*

He searched his memory, but all that was there was the subtle sensation of déjà vu he had felt on first seeing the alien spacecraft.

But he knew with absolute certainty that nothing aboard the ship was alive. He was equally certain that at one time there was a life-form aboard, one that lived and breathed as he did.

"I don't know," he said slowly. He could hear the wonder and confusion in his own voice. "But it is. No one over there will care if you use your penetration radar or your magnetic resonators."

Gorton shook his head in disbelief. "I'd like to believe you . . ."

"Believe it," Harris said. "Whoever or whatever built and flew that ship is dead. They have been for millennia."

The shocked silence lasted for only a moment.

Then, Carney asked quietly, "Have you remembered something? From before?"

Harris squeezed his eyes shut. His head was beginning to ache. "I don't know. It just came to me. A feeling . . . *no*, more than that. A *certainty* that there were beings there, on that ship. And now they're gone. Dead."

"These beings were there when you were there?" Bulgakov asked.

"No. They are thousands of years gone. I'm certain of that. That ship out there is *old*."

"And you just *know* this," Gorton said. There was clear doubt in his voice. He stared at Harris.

Harris returned the gaze. "Yes."

Gorton looked at Carney, raising an eyebrow. He was asking, Harris knew, whether Harris's sanity could be trusted.

He expected Carney to simply shrug and avoid comment. He was surprised to see the old man shake his head. "I believe him, Bill. It's not all that unusual for trauma to cause memory lapse. Sometimes a *feeling* is simply a memory trying to make it to surface. He's been there—at least we think he has. That gives him credence enough in my book."

Then came the shrug that Harris had expected. "Of course, what you believe is your own damned business."

"I think he's right," Coles said suddenly. "If something were alive over there, there would have been a change of some kind. Maybe not communication, but certainly *reaction* of some sort. But there's nothing. And there's no drive! It's just a projectile, like a Mariner probe."

"That is no projectile," Bulgakov said. "A projectile would have been affected by planetary gravity on its way through the Solar system. But you are right. I am suspicious that there has been no sign or signal from it."

"That's all good and fine," Gorton said. "But I'm still not going to risk my ship or the mission on a feeling, or even a conviction without some empirical evidence to go along with it. We're going to take this slowly—very slowly. If we can't elicit a response from the beings in that ship, then and only then will we consider an invasive overture."

He stopped and took a deep breath. "Even then, I think we ought to be careful about radiation. There might be other things on board that ship that could be damaged."

Harris saw Gorton catch the eye of the intelligence man, Rainey. He saw something in the look that passed between them that bothered him.

"What, specifically, are the 'things' you're so worried about damaging, Captain?" Harris asked.

Gorton seemed to size up Harris for a moment before answering. "Records, for one thing. If they use—or used, as the case may be—magnetic recording media, we might well destroy whatever information it might contain."

"So it's just software you're worried about?"

"What's your point?"

"You don't have your eye on the military uses of whatever technology we might find over there?"

Gorton shrugged. "That's far from being my only priority. But, yes, we should be careful not to damage anything that might be of value to the countries involved in this project. And if there are weapons over there, or recorded data and specifications for weapons, I'd as soon keep them intact. You do remember that little party the Chinese were trying to throw for us as we left, don't you, Mr. Harris?"

Harris nodded. "I remember. I also remember the Great

Standoff and what you military types did with nothing fancier than thermonuclear warheads. More than five million people died before that 'limited exchange' was brought under control.''

''You're saying you don't trust me,'' Gorton said. He smiled without showing his teeth.

''You might say that.''

''Well, Mr. Harris, I guess I'll just have to live with that. You're only a consultant on this mission. You've been consulted. That's as far as your responsibilities or your input in the decision-making process goes. We will do what we have to do, whether you like it or not.''

''I never had a doubt about it.''

''I'm glad to hear it.'' There was an icy edge to his voice. ''Now, if you folks don't mind, I'd like all nonessential personnel to clear my bridge. We've got work to do.''

''Now hold on, Bill—'' Carney began.

''That includes you, too, Doctor. Coles, we'll be needing you in a few hours. The rest of you ought to return to your quarters.''

''Is that an order?'' Harris asked.

''It is a sincere request, gentlemen. One that I would appreciate you complying with.'' He turned to Rainey. ''Mr. Rainey, would you please help clear this bridge?''

Rainey moved to comply.

Harris was tempted to resist. He had just learned something new about Bill Gorton that he decidedly didn't like. But Bulgakov and Carney moved away from the station and pulled themselves over to the railed hole in the ''floor'' that led to the access corridor.

After a moment's hesitation, he followed them.

CHAPTER FIFTEEN

August 17, 2071

"I hate to admit it, Doctor, but I need your help."

Gorton held himself in place with the chair rather than sitting in it, a fact that told Carney that the captain was indeed uncomfortable having to ask favors.

Carney tapped a finger against the side of the word processor he had been using when the door of his cube had signaled Gorton's desire to see him. On the face of the thin, twenty-five-centimeter-square screen were the last few words he had entered into his journal. Now he quietly told the machine to save the text and shut itself off.

"Well, Captain, I'm gratified I can be of use."

Gorton took a deep breath. He was fatigued, Carney saw; much of the confidence of the day before had drained away from him.

"We tried to get inside the ship. No go. There don't seem to be any breaks in the hull's surface. No pressure locks, no instrument pods or antennas. Nothing."

Carney folded his hands across his chest and pursed his lips. "I don't see how I can help."

"We've since tried every method at our disposal to determine the inner structure of that craft. Nothing works. The thing seems impervious to radiation, despite the fact that the instruments on Lunar Farside had no problem getting an internal reflection. We finally tried sounding it with explosive charges—"

"Christ!"

"Don't worry; we didn't damage it. I don't think we *could* damage it. That's some bloody egg! For all we know at this point, the damned thing could be solid through."

"So you've reached an impasse."

"That's about the size of it."

"And you want me to . . . ?"

"Talk to Harris. See if he can tell us anything. I thought if we could take him over there—"

"You can't ask him yourself?"

Gorton grimaced. "I already have. He turned me down flat."

"What makes you think he won't give me the same answer?"

Gorton seemed surprised. "You're his father!"

"Pretty much in name only. His mother raised him. Until the Cygni expedition, I hadn't seen him since he was six." Carney shook his head. "He resents me far too much to listen to me."

"Damn it, Doctor. If we can't find a way into that thing, or a way to get its occupants to communicate with us, we will have to resort to methods that are considerably less passive than we've been using."

"Meaning?"

"Meaning lasers. High explosives. Whatever it takes to crack that thing open."

Carney feigned surprise. "You're that certain now that there are no life-forms aboard?"

Gorton shook his head tiredly. "No. I'm no more certain of that now than when Harris made his grand revelation."

"And you'd still make an attempt to rupture the hull of that spaceship?"

"Not because I want to, Doctor. You know the stakes here as well as I do."

"I suppose I do, at that." He made a decision, pressed the buckle of the belt that kept him in his chair, and floated upright. "I'll talk to him."

Before he made his way to Harris's cube, he called Andrea Coles and asked her to meet him there.

It was a kind of cowardice, he knew, insinuating a third party into what could be a volatile confrontation; but there were good reasons for her presence there, the least of which would be to distract Harris from his dislike of his father. He knew Harris trusted her.

Coles was waiting for him outside the cube's door. As he approached she raised a questioning eyebrow.

Carney brought his mouth close to her ear and whispered,

"I'll tell you both at the same time and save myself some breath."

She shrugged acquiescence and he placed his palm against the door's surface. Inside the room a chime sounded.

The door sighed open and they entered. Harris was waiting, floating in a lotus position in the center of the room.

"Remember this, old man? Or was TM as de rigueur in your military training as it was in mine?" Harris spoke without opening his eyes.

"They taught it to *me*," Coles declared. "I guess they still think mellowness will help keep you from losing it on those close approaches."

Harris opened his eyes.

"Andrea!" He turned his gaze onto Carney. Carney felt more than a little withered by it. "Well, old man. Felt you needed reinforcements!"

"Do you blame me?"

"Not for that."

Carney let the jab pass. He decided on the most direct approach. "Do you know how to get inside of that ship?"

"What if I do? What we came out here to find isn't there."

"You don't know?"

"No."

"What is it *you* think we came out here to find?"

Harris looked to Coles before answering, and Carney wondered at the meaning of that glance. What was Harris thinking?

"Salvation," Harris said.

"And you don't think that we can find that on board that vessel out there?"

"No. I do not."

"Would you care to explain?"

"No, I would not."

Smug bastard! Carney felt a rise of resentment that he quelled with difficulty. This was not the time for this! he reminded himself. Soon, maybe, he could allow what was between them to come to a head, but not now.

Coles came to his rescue. "I don't understand," she said quietly.

Harris turned his attention to her. "What don't you understand?"

"Any of this. What's going on, to start with."

"He's refused to help Gorton open up the Egg," Carney said. "We're here to find out why."

"Why is easy. There's nothing alive aboard that ship," Harris said.

"There might be technology that could—"

Harris interrupted. "There's nothing on that ship that's going to save us."

"You know this for a fact?"

"Yes."

"How?"

"I don't know how! I just know it's true. Whatever technology or knowledge is aboard that ship, it won't help. The race that built that thing had nothing to do with what's happening to the Earth. It isn't a *machine* that's killing us, it's a *being*, and that being is back where we started—it's back on Earth."

There was a long silence. Coles seemed confused. Carney was deeply shocked.

"Let me understand you. You knew *before we left* that whatever caused all this wasn't aboard that ship?"

"Yes."

"Then for God's sake why? You could have said something—"

"Would you have believed me?" Harris pushed against the cube's ceiling and drifted down to face Carney and Coles where they hung against the wall by the door.

"Who can say if you would have been believed? And what does it matter? You had an obligation—"

"To whom? Certainly not to you."

"Of course not! To everyone! To Song Lan!"

Harris was silent, staring at the older man. His hands were clenched into fists.

"Why did you come out here?" Coles asked suddenly.

"Because I thought, maybe . . . I thought it might be out here, too. With the ship."

"It?" Carney asked.

"The alien. I call it the Angel. It's what brought me back from Comfort. I don't know what it is, but part of it is here, in my head. I can feel it even now. Sometimes I see it in my dreams: it's nebulous, bright, *immense*. Part of it is back on Earth. I don't know where. Just *there*. I thought that that ship might reveal it to me—to *us*. I thought we could find out what it was.''

"And now you think differently?" Carney asked.

"Yes. When I saw the ship, I knew. It isn't there. Nothing is there—it's a derelict, an empty hulk. It used the ship, somehow, but that's all. There aren't any answers there, for you or for me."

"Why didn't you tell anyone about this Angel? Does Song Lan know?"

Harris bit his lip. Carney could see that he was calm now, no longer angry. "She knows. But she knew it was something I didn't want anyone else to know. For a while, when I first began to become conscious of it, I kept quiet because I thought I was going insane. I thought I had gone mad, because of Sarah, because of what happened. Then I just thought it wasn't anyone else's goddamned business. It came for *me*, it cared for *me*."

Carney heard a strange note of petulance in Harris's voice. As he continued to speak, it modulated into something very close to bitterness.

"Then it left me. I called it and it wouldn't come. When I called it again, it wouldn't even answer. It deserted me, left me to die."

"You thought it had come back to this ship?"

"I don't know. Maybe. Or that part of it had never left the ship. An essence. But I was wrong."

"You're certain of that."

"Yes. I would know if it were there. It's not."

"Which means it's still on Earth, somewhere."

Harris shrugged. "More than likely."

"What is it doing to the Earth's climate?"

Harris frowned, thinking. "I don't know that, either. It had never occurred to me that the Angel could have caused what happened on Comfort." He shuddered visibly. "How could I believe that it could kill everything and then save me? It brought me home!"

"Why?"

"I don't know, damn it!" Harris snapped. He grasped the back of a chair. Carney could see his knuckles turn white where he gripped it.

"And you don't know how to stop it?"

"No!" Carney saw him look at Coles again and knew what was going through Harris's mind.

It was why he had brought her.

Coles seemed suddenly to realize she had been used; she glared at Carney, anger in her eyes. But she stayed silent.

Carney spoke then with a confidence he did not feel. "Your Angel is a disease. Not for a body, but for a planet. You brought a virus back with you. Or, rather, it brought you."

Harris squinted as if in pain, rubbed a hand across his eyes. "A virus?"

"Think it through. Why would your 'Angel' turn two separate worlds into ice palaces? Just for the practice? Because it could do it?"

"Why?"

"Same reason kings build castles. Or gophers dig holes. By instinct, to make things as amenable as possible to one's survival. The same reason a virus kills its host—sustenance, growth. And because that's how it's made, what it's programmed to do."

Harris shook his head. When he spoke there was a note of desperation in his voice. "I can't believe that. It saved me. It brought me back. I thought it was . . . a *loa*."

"A *loa*?"

"A spirit. Like a ghost." He hesitated. Carney heard something strange, plaintive in his voice. "I thought it was sent by God."

Carney snorted, projecting a derision he did not feel. There was something here, close under the surface! If he reached it, what might he find?

"What kind of God destroys his own children?" he asked.

Harris's eyes blazed. "Hasn't that always been the way of it? Isn't that what religion is about? Grace and retribution? Sacrifice and salvation?"

He stopped then, his face suddenly ashen with understanding. Revelation! Carney thought.

Harris spoke slowly, carefully. "It came to me when I was freezing to death in that hole on Comfort because *I prayed to be saved*. All that was in my mind was to *come home*. So it brought me home."

He looked up at Carney, pain in his eyes. "I brought it here. There was a price for my salvation. A sacrifice. That's why it left me. It had done for me what I asked once. It found what it needed on Earth as it did on Comfort. The books were balanced."

Carney shook his head. "No. It's not a god, it's a thing, satisfying its own needs. Somehow, it's feeding, and that process is bringing on the cold." He stared at the ceiling, letting the idea work itself out in his mind. "That's what most gods are. Human constructs. Analogs for our own aspirations and needs. That was always the flaw of religion: the idea that God needed us. Our worship, our sacrifice. *Things,* animals like you and me, demand sacrifices and feel the need to give them. Gods, I think, are beyond that."

Harris nodded slowly. "Yes. Not a god. An Angel. Intangible but real. I remember . . . I remember an image: a vast sea, fire, intense fire. But nurturing. Like bathing in ambrosia, in the very stuff of life. An abiding *hunger*. Physical hunger."

"Gods don't feel hunger, do they? Or need spaceships, for that matter."

Harris shook his head as if trying to clear it. He took a deep breath. "Even if it isn't God, it's beyond anything we can do to it."

"Maybe. Then again, perhaps there is something in that ship that can give us a clue."

Harris nodded again. "Okay. Tell Gorton I'll go over there with his people. I don't know how to get into that thing. But maybe something will come to me."

"That's about all we can ask."

"Yeah." Harris was still pale. He looked drained, exhausted.

Carney turned to Coles. She still hung against the bulkhead without speaking. She still glared at him.

"We'll go now. Maybe you can get some sleep."

"Sure," Harris said.

As the door slid shut behind them, Coles stopped before moving away down the corridor. She looked at Carney. "I'm not so sure that was a good thing you did in there."

Carney sighed and rubbed his forehead with the palm of one hand. "No, probably not."

He watched her pull herself away along the corridor. Again, it occurred to him that he felt terribly old.

He grasped one of the rings set into the bulkhead and followed her.

CHAPTER SIXTEEN

August 18, 2071

To Harris, the oblong hatch of the ORRV's access tunnel looked uncomfortably like a metallic rictus, a mouth into which Andrea Coles dived, headfirst, followed by Bulgakov and two of Gorton's men, a Japanese soldier named Miyazawa and another soldier, Russian, whose name Harris couldn't recall.

Miyazawa and his companion cradled laser rifles against their chests as they drew themselves one-handed through the hatch.

Harris went in last, squirming and pulling his way through into the cramped interior of the Orbital Repair and Recovery Vehicle that the *Phoenix* used as a launch. The ORRV was one of the small, standardized craft used by orbital stations and defense platforms for maintenance and repair: they looked from the outside a good deal like the small submarines used for the exploration of the deepest canyons of Earth's seas; there were thick, bug-eyed observation portholes around their perimeters and each bristled like a fat insect with antennas and manipulator arms and claws.

Harris had been aboard them dozens of times, but for some reason this one seemed particularly cramped and crowded. As he emerged inside of the cabin he had to suppress a panicky surge of claustrophobia.

"Welcome aboard," Coles said. "Find a hammock and secure yourself. We'll be under way shortly."

He nodded, but she didn't see the gesture. Her attention was already on her preflight routines. The pilot's station at which she was seated was surrounded on three sides and overhead by instruments and readouts. Three separate holographic displays floated before her; in the central one were the two ships suspended in miniature.

He pushed his way to the rear of the vehicle and settled into the cupped webbing of one of the hammock-seats by which the ORRV accommodated passengers. Bulgakov slapped him on the shoulder, reaching through the restraints of his own hammock.

"Harris, my friend! If you cannot coax this egg open, maybe I could give it a rap or two, like making breakfast!"

"Maybe you could. It would certainly make our friend Gorton happy."

"Sealed," Coles announced quietly. "Separating . . . *now*."

There was a small surge of pressure as the ORRV moved away from where it had nested against the side of the *Phoenix*. Harris peered out one of the small portholes and watched the gray hull recede. After a moment, a wedge of black filled with stars began to push into the gray and move across the Plexiglas as the ORRV drew farther away from the bulk of its mother ship.

The launch spun slowly around on its axis and the bright bulk of the Egg came gradually into view, pinned against a black background by the *Phoenix*'s spotlights. It looked much as it did in the holos: organic, solid, and nearly featureless.

"She is beautiful, in a strange way," Bulgakov observed.

"Yes, she is," Harris said.

Miyazawa leaned forward and peered past Harris at the ship, then shrugged.

"You went over with the first team?" Harris asked.

"Yes," Miyazawa said. "We spent many hours studying the hull. There is no way in. It is sealed, like a real egg."

Bulgakov nodded. "I have studied all the tapes, and there are indeed hours of them. Every centimeter of that hull was covered, visually at first, then by other means, both passive and invasive. Nothing. Not a hole, not a crack. And not a sound, either. They have placed listening devices on the hull. They hear only silence, like the grave."

"That's what I told Gorton. It's dead. You don't need a door on a mausoleum."

"It cannot be a mausoleum."

"Why not?"

"For many reasons. You, for one. If you were brought back to Earth inside of that *egg*, then it is a spacecraft, and there is some way inside of it."

"I agree. *If* I were brought back inside of that thing. But what if I weren't. What if it were just a coincidence—"

"Some coincidence!"

"But if it were, this entire project would have been one monumental waste of time and effort."

Bulgakov shook his head slowly. "No. The coincidence is too great. That the first artifact from another civilization that has ever been found should be found at this moment, when our own civilization is imperiled by a force we do not understand. It is too much to believe that one is not connected to the other."

"Maybe it isn't an artifact at all. Maybe it *is* an egg, something organic in a way we can't understand. A seed."

"That would make no difference. That it should be discovered now makes it relevant to what happened. It was first observed, you will remember, at almost the moment you were translated back to your home world. The universe is not so fickle, I think."

"You have more faith in the universe than I do, then. This seems exactly the sort of joke it would play. Like plucking a man from the peace of his grave and telling him to live again. Only to begin slowly to kill him again. That sounds more like the universe I've come to know."

Bulgakov shrugged. "Perhaps so. Then perhaps the physicists and philosophers are correct when they say that the universe is at the heart only random. Maybe events occur simply because they occur."

"That would be a hell of a note, don't you think?"

"We're about there, boys," Coles said over her shoulder. "There's virtually no spin, so I can line us up manually. I'll come in to within about three meters, and we'll cruise around till somebody says stop."

"Okay," Harris replied. He glanced over at Miyazawa; the soldier was watching him noncommittally.

Watching and listening, in order to report to Gorton. Our great leader doesn't trust us. Which is just fine; I don't trust him, either.

"Okay," Coles said, "come up and take a look."

He unstrapped himself and leaned forward from the hammock. He spilled out of it and tugged himself forward.

Coles, as small as she was, filled most of the available space before the cramped pilot's console. Harris pushed his head in close over her shoulder.

The central display directly before her was a projection of the hull of the alien ship as it passed by beneath them. It appeared to be motionless relative to the launch; only the changing shadow along one side of the display betrayed that the launch was moving slowly along, parallel to the Egg's axis.

"Not much in the way of surface features," Harris commented.

"Nothing at all. Just the dimple on the nether end. And nothing there either, except a concave indentation, about a hundred meters in diameter and three deep in the center. We couldn't even get a sample of the hull material, the stuff's so dense. I imagine we could burn a chunk out, but I don't think Gorton's quite that desperate yet."

"Don't bet on it. If we don't find a way to get in, he'll cut it open, sure as hell."

"Then he's going to cut it, because there's no way into this thing. Trust me, we looked. We looked a *lot*."

"I believe you."

"We'll be over the dimple in a second. There."

The shadows in the display changed and Harris realized that the hull beneath them had changed shape and was angling away from them.

Coles murmured to her controls. "Adjusting elevation. We'll follow the curve down to the center."

"Could you hover there, over the center?"

"Sure. Why?"

"I don't know. A hunch." More than a hunch, though he didn't say so. He suddenly felt a strange awareness, again a feeling like déjà vu, though not of having experienced something before, but having *known* some fact or process that he had forgotten so completely that only the sensation of vague familiarity was left.

Coles murmured again to her controls. "Okay. On station. We're over the center. What now?"

"I don't know. Sit here for a minute."

"Whatever you say, boss."

Harris studied the display. The hull at this point seemed much as it had outside of the dimple, flat and featureless.

"No difference in the hull material here?" he asked.

Coles shook her head. "None that my instruments can detect."

"I don't know. I think this feels right."

Coles peered up at him. "Feels right?"

"Yeah. Maybe. Can you get closer?"

"I can snuggle in to about a meter. Hold on." She whispered and the shadows in the display shifted and grew larger.

Harris stared at it, wondering what to do next.

"This thing's equipped with a mating collar, isn't it?" he asked suddenly.

"Sure. But there's nothing you can find out in the collar we can't pick up by instrument."

"Maybe, maybe not. Is there any reason why you couldn't seal it against this hull?"

Coles raised an eyebrow. "No, it'd be easy enough to do. The thing's as smooth as a baby's butt. But why go to the trouble?"

"I want to touch it, I think."

For the first time Coles turned completely away from her instruments and swiveled in her seat to face him. "You mean with your bare hand?"

"Yes."

"No, cowboy, you don't want to touch it. I thought you were a platform roughneck. Do you know how *cold* the metal of that hull is? I can seal the collar against it and pressurize, but it would take more time than we have air to get the surface warm enough so that you could touch it without getting your hand flash frozen."

"Call it another hunch."

"I call it insane stupidity."

"Will you do it?"

"Hell, no."

Harris hesitated. "What if I suit up? Use gloves?"

She squinted at him as if she couldn't quite make out the expression on his face. "In that case, I suppose so. Do you mind if I ask what you think you might accomplish?"

"I have no earthly idea."

Coles sighed. "All right. Hold on to something for a minute. I've got to maneuver around a bit."

She whispered to the controls and the ORRV spun slowly on its axis, bringing the hatch around to face the Egg's hull. Then the shadows on the display, unaffected by the spin, began to change again as the launch moved away from the hull to accommodate the collar.

The ORRV's mating collar had been designed for versatility; it was used primarily to make repairs easier on the outer hulls of orbital stations. The collar's walls were semirigid, made of the same material as pressure suits.

The skirt at the collar's bottom—the part of it that actually made contact with a hull—was what polymer engineers called an "animate material": it "sensed" the surface underneath it and molded itself to its contours to form a seal so that the collar could be pressurized. Once the collar was pressurized, the hull underneath could be breached without endangering vacuum-sensitive areas underneath.

The first time Harris had worked inside a collar, he'd poked at the skirt with a tool's handle out of curiosity. It had resisted, then it had slowly given way. A little experimentation showed that the stuff was as hard as a rock if you poked at it quickly, but was as soft and malleable as bread dough if you pushed slowly down into it. At a command from the ORRV's operator, the material of the skirt would contract like an anemone, withdrawing into a thin bead along the lower edge of the collar.

Coles whispered, watching her displays.

"Okay. It's deployed," she announced a few moments later. "Pressurizing."

Harris moved to the overhead lockers and pulled down a pressure suit. He left the helmet in the clips that held it in place.

As he began to don the suit, Bulgakov and the two soldiers struggled free of their hammocks.

Both Bulgakov and Miyazawa pulled suits down from the lockers. Harris sealed his suit and eyed the two men critically.

"Just how much room do you two think there is inside the collar?"

Miyazawa hesitated. Bulgakov kept on, pulling the suit clumsily up over his ample frame.

"I will go," Bulgakov announced. "There will be room for two."

Miyazawa started to protest. Coles spoke up over her shoulder. "You can watch what's going on from up here, Lieutenant. It's a pretty good view. Sound and everything."

Miyazawa scowled. He obviously did not care for the idea of letting them go into the collar unescorted. He also, Harris guessed, had orders to cooperate to the best of his ability. After a moment, he began to repack the pressure suit he had taken from the locker.

"I will watch, then." He turned and pulled himself back to where his companion was still waiting among the hammocks. They spoke together for a time, then Miyazawa announced, "Alexi will observe from the hatch."

The Russian soldier cradled his rifle and checked its charge.

"Pressurized," Coles said. "And warming. You won't need your helmets, but it's still damned cold in there."

"Okay," Harris said. He pulled himself next to the hatch and subvocalized the three-number sequence printed beside it. The hatch opened with a pneumatic *chuff* and swung slowly outward.

Icy air puffed through the opening. Harris pulled himself through into the space beyond.

The collar was no more than three meters in diameter, two high. Lights burned brightly around the underside of the hatch, illuminating the space inside. A few bright stars glittered through the clear polymer of the collar's walls, the ones bright enough to make it through the ambient glare of the lights. He drifted down against the gleaming white surface of the alien ship's hull.

Bulgakov followed, his pressure-suited bulk making the drumlike space inside the collar seem suddenly very cramped.

Harris tapped at the hull with his gloved fingertips. The sound was metallic, solid. Color moved across its surface as he turned his head and he was startled to see his own reflection staring back at him from the polished, pearlescent whiteness of the hull.

Bulgakov settled beside him. "Do you see something?"

Harris shook his head and ran the fingertips of his glove across the surface. "No. It's beautiful, though, isn't it? Like mother-of-pearl. Seems metallic. Solid. And slick as glass."

"It is beautiful. A lovely enigma." He tapped the hull with a gloved knuckle. "But how do we get inside of it?"

"Beats me." He spoke into the pickup inside the mating ring of his helmetless pressure suit. "You hearing us okay, Andrea?"

"Just fine." The amplified voice echoed oddly in the space inside the collar. "Good picture, too. Wave to us, boys."

Harris waved a hand obligingly. He glanced up at the un-smiling face of Miyazawa's Russian companion, staring down from the mouth of the hatch.

"What's the surface temperature in here?"

There was a moment's hesitation. "About a hundred degrees

absolute and warming slowly,'' Coles answered. ''Still considerably frosty. I'd avoid touching it with any bare skin. Or at least not any you want to keep.''

''I read you. No touching.''

''That's a roger.''

Bulgakov had anchored himself by his suit's tether to the wall of the collar. Harris held out a hand, and Bulgakov towed him in close to the wall. There was one problem with working inside of a pressure collar, and that was the difficulty inherent to weightlessness of maintaining position over whatever you were working on. The slightest pressure against a surface would send you drifting off to bump against a hull or wall: without the dampening effect of gravity, simple action and reaction became annoying.

On the outer skin of an orbital station, it was rarely a difficulty; inevitably there was a nearby surface feature to anchor oneself to. Not so here.

Harris had come prepared, though. He uncoiled a length of cord and tied one end to one of the eye-rings mounted in the collar's wall about half a meter above the sealing skirt.

Then he shoved away from the wall and drifted slowly across the three meters of open space to the far side of the collar. There he tied the loose end of the cord.

He pulled himself out across the resultant bridge until he was positioned over the direct center of the area encompassed by the collar. He reached out a hand and placed it palm-down against the hull. He could feel the chill even through the insulation of the glove.

''Andrea?''

''Yeah, boss.''

''This is the exact center of the dimple?''

''Where your hand is?''

''Yes.''

''Pretty much. Maybe a few centimeters aft of the place you're touching.''

''Here?''

''Yes. I think so. As close as I can estimate, anyway.''

He pressed on the spot, gently at first, then with more pressure. The cord-bridge bowed out from the hull where he held it with his other hand.

Nothing happened. He felt strangely disappointed. Why had

he even thought that something might happen? He didn't know; but the feeling that something should have happened lingered.

"What are you doing?" Bulgakov asked.

"I was about to ask the same thing," Coles's voice said.

He let off the pressure and let the bowed cord press him back down close to the bright, reflecting whiteness of the alien ship's hull.

He watched his own dim, blurred reflection for a long moment, not moving, a certainty forming in his mind.

His first instinct had been to touch the hull, and not with the dead material of a glove. With his hand. With his own bare flesh.

He tucked the cord under one arm and manipulated the seal that encircled his right wrist. It opened and he pulled the glove free from the pressure suit's sleeve.

"James!" Bulgakov bellowed.

He dropped the glove and it floated slowly down toward the hull. He held the bare palm close above the hull's smooth surface. He could feel the harsh bite of the radiated cold completely through the hand.

He reached down the remaining few centimeters.

Coles shouted *"No!"* It reverberated with surprising intensity inside the collar. Out of the corner of his eye he saw Bulgakov swarm out onto the cord, pulling himself hand over hand toward Harris.

He pressed his palm against the hull.

It was solid, ungiving. There was no sensation of cold; the hull felt slick and hard and faintly warm.

He shoved downward, pressing with all the strength in his arm and shoulder. The cord bowed out until his arm was completely extended, reaching out above his head.

The hull under his palm softened suddenly, the way the material of the mating collar's skirt did when you pushed against it slowly. He felt his hand sink into it, as if into warm, opalescent taffy.

The tension in the cord launched him forward, shoving him in one sudden thrust through the material of the hull, like an arrow shot in slow motion from a bow.

The cord was jerked from his grip. Before he could scream he was engulfed in darkness. Above him a pinprick of light glowed bright for a instant and then was swallowed.

He fell.

One incredulous thought flashed through his mind. *Falling?*

Then something struck him hard in the middle of his back and he stopped caring.

Bulgakov snatched at Harris's booted ankle as it slipped through the suddenly liquid material of the hull. He missed and the boot was gone with the rest of Harris, absorbed like a hot needle into a ball of wax.

The momentum that drove Harris into the hull thrust Bulgakov down against the hull as well. He didn't sink into the hard whiteness—he bounced, striking the hull hard with his shoulder and then rebounding slowly up against the wall of the collar. He slid up toward the open mouth of the hatch, grappling for a handhold. He caught the knurled edge of the hatch and jerked to a stop.

Coles's face joined that of the soldier Miyazawa had called Alexi, framed by the hatch above him.

"I saw it in the holo. What in God's name happened?"

"I don't know." He pushed away from the hatch back toward the hull—too hard. He struck the hull, bounced again, catching the line Harris had stretched as he floated up.

When he had steadied himself he pressed his gloved palm against the spot in the hull through which Harris had disappeared. It was hard, unyielding. He could feel the intense cold through the insulation of his glove.

He stared at the shifting opalescence. After a moment, he reached with his left hand to undo the seal on his right glove.

A hand grabbed his wrist and jerked it away. He growled and jerked it back, twisting to stare into Coles's face. She held tight to the fabric of his suit sleeve.

"No! Not yet!"

"James is in there! He has no helmet! No pressure!"

"Damn it, if there's no atmosphere in this thing he can breathe, he's dead by now anyway!"

Bulgakov ground his teeth and slammed a fist against the blank whiteness of the hull.

"We cannot just leave him there," he hissed out from between his teeth.

"We have to. For now. Let me contact the *Phoenix*. Make a few tests."

"Tests!"

"Yes. And then we'll see."

Bulgakov slammed his gloved hand against the hull again, not so hard as before. Coles could see the muscles jump in his jaw.

"All right," he said.

He was out, he was sure, for no more than a few seconds.

The darkness around him was absolute. He took a deep breath. The air smelled strange and musty, but was breathable. He groped around himself with his hands, one bare and one gloved, and felt only a smooth, flat surface.

He moved to rise and was rewarded with a sharp, shooting pain in his side. A rib, he guessed, broken or badly bruised. He explored the place gingerly with his fingertips, but could tell little. Other than that, he seemed to have escaped serious injury despite the force of the fall.

Fall?

He pushed himself up onto his knees, realizing with a sudden shock that he shouldn't have been able to accomplish that simple act. When he had pressed himself up from the surface underneath him, he should have drifted out away from it, weightless.

But he wasn't weightless. He pushed gingerly up onto his toes, feeling the familiar sensation of gravity, not appreciably heavier or lighter than Earth normal.

He stood unsteadily, peering into the darkness, straining to see. Then he remembered the light-strip set into the shoulder of the pressure suit he wore. He touched it with his gloved left hand and it came alight.

The glow revealed a vast, vaulted room. Amorphous shapes crowded around him and he ducked defensively, crouching down. The shapes seemed to move in the shifting light from the glowing strip attached to his shoulder.

It took him a second to realize that the shapes were not moving. He reached to touch one, a flat, tapering slab two-and-a-half meters tall, a meter wide. He touched its left-hand edge and found that it was impossibly thin—no more than a few millimeters. He tapped at it. It was as solid as rock. He pushed at it with both hands; there was no more give than if he were shoving at a mountainside. A thick layer of dust brushed away underneath his hands.

It was vaguely warm in the same way as the hull material had been, but it did not soften under the pressure of his fingertips.

Instead, as he pressed against it, he felt the beginnings of a tingling, crawling sensation, as if ants were slowly making their way up his arm from his hand. He took his hand away and the sensation stopped.

He detached the light-strip from his suit and held it close to the object's surface. It shone with the same off-white luster as the hull, but there seemed to be movement inside of it, a current of twisting, sinuous shapes flowing up from the deck to the top of the slab, where they simply . . . disappeared? He walked around it. The far side was the same, the lines and vague shapes flowed upward like ripples in a current.

He stared at it for a long while, then turned away. Whatever the slabs were, they were obviously as far beyond his understanding as a condensed-charge circuit would be to a Galileo or a da Vinci—though even as that comparison came to him, he realized he could be giving himself a good deal too much credit even then.

He turned slowly, trying to take everything in. The room was littered, seemingly at random, with the strange, regular forms. So far as he could tell, they were extensions of the material that composed the deck and hull, flowing up to form identical trapezoids, none of which seemed to have a discernible purpose.

There was nothing that looked recognizably like furniture or instruments. It looked more like a gathering of abstract sculptures; they lacked a representative familiarity, but there was something vaguely pleasing about the flowing movement inside the shapes.

A thick layer of fine dust covered everything; it rose with an unnatural sluggishness under his feet as he turned, as if it were denser than ordinary dust. Watching it, he decided the gravity must be somewhat lower than Earth normal, the difference no more than one might experience descending in a relatively slow elevator back on Earth.

Above his head the hull arched across, unbroken, from one side of the "room" to the other. At either end of the room were vertical bulkheads, closing it off from the rest of the ship. He could see nothing that reminded him of doors or hatches in either of them.

Then again, he thought, there had been no door through the hull either. Until he had made one. He studied the section of curving hull directly above his head but could find no difference between it and the rest.

He spoke into the pressure suit's microphone. "Coles?" There was no answer. It only made sense that if the hull stopped radiation from the *Phoenix*'s instruments it would block radio transmissions as well.

He took another deep breath, tried to identify the smells in the room. Dust. A tinge of something acrid, spiced, familiar: it came to him suddenly—cloves. The air in the ship carried the bitter smell of cloves.

He closed his eyes and made an effort to open himself to whatever might be here, to whatever feeling or inspiration might come. His overall impression was vague: he felt *age*—the ship, he was convinced, was very old, unutterably ancient—but little else.

It struck him as strange that he didn't feel afraid. When he thought about it, it seemed he should be terrified. He was alone, inside of an alien ship. Despite his conviction that the ship was deserted, there was no objective proof that that was actually the case.

He took another breath, marveling that the ship was pressurized and had an atmosphere that he could breathe. Was that intentional? he wondered. And was it a condition he could rely upon continuing? Or would another section of the hull soften and open itself to the vacuum of space?

Suddenly he found himself regretting that he had left the helmet of his pressure suit aboard the launch.

There was no sound, no motion. He felt a minute drift of warm air against the skin of his face, but couldn't spot its source.

What now? he wondered. He flexed his knees, testing his weight again. Gravity! How in the name of all that was reasonable could there be gravity?

He looked up again to where he knew Bulgakov was, and probably Coles and Miyazawa by now, all trying to figure out how he had come to disappear through the now-intact surface of the ship's hull.

He looked at his hand, flexed it. It felt none the worse for wear for having been pressed against a surface that Coles's instruments had registered as being intolerably cold. Was what happened a characteristic of the hull, or something the craft or its inhabitants had arranged especially for him?

If someone else were to press his bare palm to the Egg's shell, would he slip through as Harris had done, or would the flesh of his hand freeze instantly to the bitterly cold metal of the hull?

Many questions. No answers. If he were weightless, it would be a simple matter to leap across to the hull and try to push his way back through the hull. But he wasn't weightless.

He walked across to the nearest bulkhead, dust puffing up under his feet at each step. It was as featureless as the broad expanse of the hull overhead. He stood before what he judged to be the center of the bulkhead and pressed his palm against its surface.

The material resisted, then softened and gave way. It felt liquid between his fingers, a slightly warm, thickly viscous fluid. He pushed again and his hand slid in to the wrist. The stuff on the wall resisted the cuff of his pressure suit as he pressed his hand farther in, but then yielded to it slowly. It took considerable pressure to force the cuff in.

His fingertips broke through into an open space, and he started to jerk his hand back, then realized that whatever was beyond, it wasn't the freezing vacuum of space.

He pushed his arm through up to the elbow. The sensation was odd, even through the material of the pressure suit's sleeve. The bulkhead seemed to grip his arm as it yielded, holding him like some sort of living sphincter; it was nearly impossible to move his arm up or down or to either side. He could only move *through*.

He opened and closed his hand. So far as he could tell, there was nothing but open space on the far side—pressurized, obviously, and warmed, much as the room he was in was warmed.

He drew his arm back. The hole he had made sealed itself soundlessly as he withdrew his hand; as he watched, a single, barely discernible ripple started out from his fingertips as the wall's material closed behind them.

It spread as he watched, flowing out to the deck and hull. There was no reflected return ripple. The deck and hull seemed to absorb it.

It was as if he stood before a vertical wall of water, held in place by some force he couldn't begin to understand. No, not water. Only one ripple, disappearing instead of reflecting, and only when he withdrew his hand, not when he had put it in. Something else, not acting or reacting to physical rules he had known as indisputable fact, as gospel of the highest order. Something unbelievable.

He touched the bulkhead with his gloved hand. It resisted, as hard and solid as the bulkheads in the *Phoenix*.

He pushed a bare finger in. Withdrew it. A tiny, almost invisible ripple ran out, disappeared into the hull.

Incredible.

He turned and surveyed the room again. Except for the strange figures, it was empty. He let his gaze drift across the strange, twisting shapes; they were intriguing but . . . empty. For no reason he could rationally explain, he was suddenly certain that there was nothing he could learn in this part of the ship.

He turned back to the wall. Beyond it was . . . what? No way to know except to look.

He hesitated, then took a deep breath and placed his forehead against the bulkhead. The material softened beneath his skin, causing a curious, tickling sensation.

He braced himself, took another deep breath, and pushed. His head slid in with frightening ease. He kept his eyes shut and tried hard to ignore the claustrophobic sensation of being *engulfed*.

The collar of his pressure suit butted against the wall and it became much harder to push himself into the material. He felt the top of his head break through as his shoulders touched.

He pushed against the growing resistance and felt his head come through the wall to the level of his eyebrows. His lungs began to burn with his held breath.

A sudden surge of panic overwhelmed him and he struggled back against the grip of the wall's substance. It let go of him and he flew backward like a cork yanked with sudden force from a bottle. He fell hard against the deck, yelping at the pain that shot through his injured side.

He pressed a hand against the pain and glared ruefully at the wall. There was something about bare flesh that made it give way. Once it was opened, inanimate material—the substance of his suit—could be introduced, but there was resistance.

He had come through the hull easily enough, but the force built up in the taut line had driven him partway through in that instance, and the gravity inside the ship had done the rest, the sudden access of weight pulling him through. Gravity wouldn't help him in this situation, at least not so long as its force was directed down toward the deck.

Momentum wasn't the answer; if he simply backed up a few steps and ran at it, it would be, he suspected, a good deal like barreling full tilt into a brick wall. Until it was "opened," the wall's material seemed to act like the skirt on the ORRV's mating collar—it gave way to slow pressure, but was hard as rock to quick jabs at its surface.

He could probably push his head completely through to the far side, but then would he be able to keep the pressure up to get his body through? And would there be something to grasp on the far side so that he could drag his legs and feet through? He glanced at the bulky boots of the suit and was sure they would not be easy to force through the material of the wall.

Common sense said that if resistance was the problem, remove the resistance.

He pressed against the seals that attached his right boot to the suit's leg and pulled the thing off. In a few minutes he had the pressure suit and the jumpsuit he had worn underneath it off.

He needed light. He tugged at the light-strip and the static seal that held it to the suit resisted, then gave way. He held it in his left hand, pressed against his wrist. He rose to his feet, wondering for a moment if his bare soles would sink through the deck beneath him. But the deck held firm, warm but hard under his feet.

He stood naked before the wall and pressed both hands into it. Then he touched his forehead once more against the surface and felt it go liquid beneath his skin.

He pushed until he felt the wall flow past his chin and close around his neck and then he shoved forward with all the strength in his legs.

It was like diving into a pool and then back out again through a surface somehow dizzyingly misplaced. He slid through, slick as a fish, and crashed to the deck on the far side.

He pulled himself quickly up, favoring his much-abused side. He was in a room even larger than the first, but otherwise much like it.

He held the light-strip out and turned slowly around. As the space around him revealed itself, he again felt a curious, growing sense of déjà vu. The conviction arose in him that he had seen this room before.

No, not seen. Something different. *Felt?* No. Just *knew.* He *knew* this room. The shape felt a part of him in some deep, subliminal way, as if something inside of him had been molded to it.

He tried to identify the source of the feeling, looking inside himself. As quickly as the feeling had come, it faded. The room seemed as alien and unfamiliar as the first.

The room was empty except for two of the trapezoidal slabs, rising up from the deck in the center, facing one another about twenty-five centimeters apart. They looked much like the ones in the first room: tall, regular, fluid.

These were subtly different, though. He came close, held the light-strip near the surface of one and peered at the movement within. It seemed more rapid, a roiling flow right at the surface.

He walked slowly around the two figures, marveling again at how thin they were. Gravity, he thought. The same generated forces that held him to the floor must hold the material of the slabs so solidly erect.

Gravity? Mankind had solved the problems of gravity—or so he thought—at the same time he had harnessed the zero-point energy that was responsible for it in order to power his space-ships and his industries. But planetary gravity was a result of a planet's mass shielding objects near it from the zero-point energy with which the vacuum of space itself was infused. The vacuum fluctuations on the far side of an object actually pushed an object toward a larger mass because the larger mass blocked the energy that would push it away with equal force. Thus the effect physicists through the centuries had described as *gravity*.

So how could gravity be *generated*? It would be making a *presence* out of an *absence*. Something out of nothing.

At the moment, though, he was ready to believe almost anything was possible.

He passed a hand through the space between the two shapes and felt the crawly-ant sensation, like a strong static current crackling across his skin.

He faced one of the slabs and reached to touch it with a fingertip, brushing away dust. The lines inside the slab rippled and swam, like a river in whose depths waited . . . what? Revelation?

He pressed the palm of his hand against it, expecting crawly

ants. His hand seemed to sink into the surface and dissolve
and . . .

Chaos.

The milky stream seemed to engulf him; his eyes, his mind
were filled with it. A scene flashed through his mind, as clearly
as if he saw it with his own eyes. Fire and ice. A single flame a
galaxy long, the raw, burning sensation of absolute cold.

He jerked his hand away and leapt back as if he'd been
shocked. He stared at it, wondering.

He reached to touch it again.

Then he heard a voice and stopped. It sounded human, but
distant and blurred. He listened intently, then recognized it.
Bulgakov. It was the big Russian, shouting, somewhere on the
ship.

He faced the wall through which he had come. He heard the
shout again, through the bulkhead. He touched the material,
again surprised: impervious to radiation, yet it conducted sound!

He took a deep breath and dived through.

He landed with considerably more grace this time, taking the
force of the fall the way he had been taught during his basic
training, so many years ago. He came through headfirst, already
tucking his head in so that his shoulder would hit first. As he
struck the deck, he rolled into a shock-absorbing judo break-
fall.

The softer landing didn't keep his side from wrenching him
around into a fetal curl with a sudden jolt of pain.

He groaned and pushed himself up, looking for Bulgakov. He
held up the glowstrip, making the shadows dance eerily in the
room. Nothing. Only the queer, identical shapes rising from the
deck that he had seen before, buried in their thick coating of
dust.

Movement overhead caught his eye. He craned his head, staring up. As he watched a hand broke through the underside of
the hull in the same spot he himself had come through.

It was followed by another hand, then the rest of the arms,
then a head, bulging out the plastic material of the hull.

Bulgakov's blocky face emerged, hanging head down. His
bare chest broke through, then his movement through the hull
stopped. He seemed lodged there, halfway through.

He blinked, staring down at Harris.

Harris waved. "Good of you to drop in." His voice sounded startlingly loud against the dead silence of the room.

Bulgakov grinned. "You have looked prettier, my friend."

Harris looked down at his own nude body, mottled with splotches of the gray dust.

"Are you all right?" Harris asked.

"I think so, though it is not an experience I would recommend. It is a bit too much, I think, like a birthing, and I am grateful to have no memory of the one experience at that I have already had. This is the second time I have come through. The first time was very difficult, with the pressure suit. The gravity! It is incredible. What is causing it?"

"I don't know. What's holding you up? Are you stuck?"

"No. Miyazawa and his friend are holding me by my ankles so that I do not slip through as you did. Are you hurt?"

"No. A little shaken. Maybe a cracked rib."

"Where were you when I came through before?"

Harris waved toward the wall. "There's another space, beyond the bulkhead."

"Is there anyone aboard?"

"No. That is, I haven't seen anything to suggest a crew. I haven't gone outside of the two rooms." It felt odd, his head tilted back, talking to someone who hung suspended upside down, his body seemingly cut off at the waist.

"I am going to kick, so that they will draw me back up. I will return."

Harris nodded. "I understand. I'll be here when you get back."

"I expect so." Bulgakov said. A second later he disappeared, drawn back up through the deceptive solidity of the alien ship's hull.

Harris found his jumpsuit and pulled it on, then sat down in the dust to wait.

"James?" Bulgakov's head reappeared, emerging through the hull as before. This time he came completely through, dangling from a line tied to his bare ankles. He wore nothing but boxer shorts. He was lowered slowly down until Harris could take his shoulders and ease him to the deck.

Another head poked through the hull above. Miyazawa pulled himself through, then swarmed down the line. His laser rifle was strapped close against his bare back. As he reached the deck, he unlimbered the rifle, peering at the misshapen figures that surrounded the open space in the center of the room.

"The ship is empty?" he asked.

Harris nodded. "So far as I can tell. Except for those things." He pointed to the figures scattered about the central empty space into which they had descended.

"What are they?"

Harris shook his head. "You've got me. I haven't the first idea—"

"They could be statues," Bulgakov ventured, "representations of the life-forms that built the Egg."

Miyazawa tapped one of the forms with a fingertip. "Perhaps. If so, I do not think we would be able to communicate with them. That the form would be so different would suggest that the sensory apparatus would be very different as well."

"Maybe it's art," Harris offered.

Miyazawa scowled. "For art, it is very ugly."

"When was the last time you saw a Picasso or a Von Geit? The last thing art has to be is beautiful."

"Whatever they are, they do not seem to be threatening," Miyazawa said. He moved to the same wall Harris had tested earlier. He pressed a finger to it, watched it sink in, withdrew it.

He turned to Bulgakov. "How much of the ship's volume is contained in this one space?"

Bulgakov surveyed the room thoughtfully for a long moment, considering. "No more than a tenth, I would estimate. It is only an estimate, though. It could be less or more. Probably less. It is a very large egg."

Miyazawa stamped one bare foot against the deck, sending up a puff of dust. "What is causing the gravity?"

Bulgakov shrugged. "No way to know, until we look. The physicists would say, I think, that it is impossible to generate gravity without mass. But it is here, which I think is evidence enough. After this amazing thing—" He gestured to take in the hull and bulkheads. "—I can believe in many things."

Miyazawa nodded slowly. "Many things do not bear much thought."

Bulgakov snorted. "That is not what I said. The military mind! If you do not understand it, you ignore it."

Miyazawa spread his hands in a gesture meant not to placate so much as to indicate his indifference. "For a soldier, understanding is not as important as survival."

"And following orders."

"Yes. And following orders."

" 'Into the jaws of death . . .' "

"If necessary."

Harris broke in. "Do we explore the ship?"

Miyazawa stared at him for a moment before answering. "No. We do not. I have spoken to Captain Gorton. A team will be sent over after we return to the *Phoenix*. They will be better prepared—"

"Better armed!" Bulgakov growled.

"—Better prepared for what might be encountered in the remaining sections of the ship."

Harris was tempted for a second to tell them about the figure in the adjacent room, but for reasons he hadn't quite thought through yet, he held his tongue. He needed time to think.

"We should leave," Miyazawa said.

Bulgakov seemed ready to argue, but Harris nodded in agreement. He was deeply tired. There would be time to return later; then, perhaps, he could spend a little time alone with the figure in the adjacent room.

Bulgakov scowled, but acquiesced. "I will go first, then, to help Alexi pull you up."

He took the line in his right hand and jerked it once, testing. Then, grunting at the effort, he towed himself up, hand over hand. When he neared the hull, he reached out a bare hand. After a moment, it sunk slowly into the pearlescent material. He took a deep, audible breath, then pulled himself up into it.

He struggled, his feet kicking, and then was through it. Harris shivered inwardly at the thought of having to emulate that claustrophobic, wriggling crawl through the viscous stuff of the hull. It was bad enough to simply dive through it.

He began shucking his jumpsuit.

It turned out not to be as bad as he had feared. When he reached the hull, he pushed his arm through nearly to the shoulder, sliding his hand along the line where it pierced the hull.

He felt his hand reemerge into the pressurized atmosphere of the collar. Then someone grasped him by the wrist and yanked him through before he even had time to take a last deep breath of the alien ship's clove-scented air.

He popped through into the collar with only a moment's struggle against the panic of being engulfed by the hull. Bulgakov grinned down at him, still holding his wrist, from the vantage of a framework of metal bars crisscrossing like a tic-tac-toe game from one side of the collar to the other. Through the transparent walls of the collar he could see the welcome glimmer of the stars.

Bulgakov guided him close to one of the bars and he pulled himself up onto the framework. The air in the collar was bracingly cold compared to that in the ship, and his teeth began to chatter.

Someone laughed and he looked up to see Coles grinning down at him from the hatch.

"My, my. I haven't seen this much gooseflesh in years. Come on up, Mr. Harris. I don't have champagne, but I do have reconstituted orange drink and some blankets."

She offered him her hand. He took it and she pulled him up into the warm safety of the ORRV.

CHAPTER SEVENTEEN

Harris shot along the corridor from the control deck, grabbing angrily at the handholds as they came into reach and shoving himself at breakneck speed down the length of the passage.

Gorton had his goddamned nerve.

But as the old saying went, there were more ways than one to skin a cat. And he was going to do his damnedest to skin this one, Gorton be damned.

He came even with the side corridor he wanted and jerked himself to a stop. His momentum brought his feet around in a wide arc, and he yanked himself savagely back into line with the side passage and pulled himself into it.

At the end of the short side passage was the same cargo room and lock into which he and Bulgakov had escaped a few short weeks before from the swarms of Chinese soldiers. Coles was there, directing the loading of a cargo container that would be lashed to one of *Phoenix*'s two ORRVs and towed over to the Egg. Cargo handlers growled and rumbled, loading equipment into the hovercar-size container.

Harris drifted up behind her and tapped her on the shoulder. She turned and said, "Hi! Just a second," then finished tapping a series of numbers into a memory card. She then pitched the device—into which she had been recording the container's cargo, he guessed—in the general direction of a clay-grip mounted against one bulkhead. The clay-grip was a flat square of malleable polymer-putty that would stick to anything pressed—or tossed with enough force—against it. It was the perfect solution to free-fall clutter in a workspace; this one held an assortment of tools and electronic parts.

She twisted around, using a crate that had been lashed to the deck for leverage.

"What can I do for you, chief?"

"A lot, I hope."

She frowned. "What did you have in mind?"

"You know Gorton won't let me go over to the ship."

"Yes, I'd heard. You or Carney. I've got orders to stay aboard the ORRV, myself, while we're over there."

"Yes? I didn't know that. What the hell does he think he's doing?"

She shrugged. "What he thinks he has to, I guess. He's under a lot of pressure, here. And it's a responsibility he didn't exactly ask for."

"No?"

"No. You don't know about Gorton, do you?"

He shook his head. "They didn't tell me very much before flying me up here. Especially not about personnel. I'm only a 'consultant,' remember."

"I remember. He was a famous man, for a while, a few years back."

Harris smiled wryly. "I've been in seclusion for a long while. I dove into a bottle and only recently came up."

She nodded. He knew she had expected as much. "Among other things, Gorton used to be one of the top officers in the UN security forces."

"Yes? So?"

"He made rather a mess of it, from what I understand. Or, at least, a mess was made and he was in the middle of it. There was some trouble in Argentina, with what was left of the Ricos government, and you know the UN has tended to be a little militant since China dropped out and tried to start World War Three. He sent in some troops, a few people got killed, some children at a school. Nothing major, compared to the sort of horror that has been going on down there for forty years now. It stank a lot though, politically. He lost his appointment. I think it weighs on his mind."

"What you're saying is that he's worried about his career."

"Something like that."

"Does that son of a bitch have any idea what's at stake here?"

She shrugged. "Sure. But he's a politician. That's a pretty single-minded breed."

"And now he's in control of this expedition."

"Yeah. Go figure."

"I was hoping you might know what's going on over there. All of Gorton's people are being pretty tight-lipped."

"I know. It's like a police state around here. Gorton's scared, I think. He's in over his head with this. I do know the technicians don't have to get naked to get through the hull anymore."

"Oh, yes? How did they crack it?"

"Low-voltage DC current."

"Electricity?"

"Yeah. You got through because of the galvanic current in your skin. It turns the stuff the hull's made of into what the technical people are calling a 'field-secured liquid.' "

"Which is?"

"I don't know exactly. And I don't think they do, either. Bulgakov could tell you more—"

"I don't see very much of the great Russian anymore. And when I do, he glowers. I think Gorton's riding him pretty hard. Sees him as another weak link, I guess. Almost as unreliable as I am."

"Ask him anyway, if you get a chance. He thinks that the same energy that makes the gravity on board the Egg keeps the hull—and everything else over there, for that matter—intact and in place. It's probably what makes it go, as well—hence that kinky hull shape, to withstand the pressure. They still don't know what generates it."

"I've a feeling they never will. I don't think we've got what it takes to understand that ship."

She cocked an eyebrow at him curiously. "You don't think us human types are bright enough?"

"It isn't that. I don't think we're . . . *right*. Our perspective is not the same. We look at our universe differently than they did, I think. And so the universe they looked at was different, acted according to different rules. That ship over there is impossible for us to understand because it would be impossible for us to conceive of it—if someone else hadn't already made it and put it out here for us to find."

"That's a little hard to swallow. A little frightening, too."

"It should be. I think Gorton and his people are screwing around with things that could land them in a world of trouble." He was thinking of the figure in the second room, the scene he had witnessed for the briefest of instants when he had placed his hand against the shifting surface. A vision? Something more? Questions.

"I need you to take me over there," he said abruptly.

Coles said nothing for a long moment, simply watching him. "I can't do that."

"Why not?"

"You know why. Gorton doesn't want you over there. You're not part of his team. For the moment, I am."

"You're proud of that?"

"I couldn't give a tinker's damn about it. It is my job, however."

"You sound as bad as Miyazawa. Duty above all."

"Something like that." There was a hard edge of anger in her voice, but she was controlling it. He pushed a little harder.

"Where does your duty lie, Andrea? With Gorton? He's just a martinet who's worried about his job. The whole goddamned world? That's an abstraction. It's too easy to ignore. Don't you have family, someone you don't care to see frozen or starved to death? Gorton's not going to find anything over there. Nothing important. *I can.*"

"What makes you so damned sure?"

"*I don't know.* But I can. I know it."

"You know, it's funny, you seem to know a lot of things you just don't know."

"The ship is deserted, like I said it was."

"Yes, it is," she admitted grudgingly.

"I have to go over there. That much I'm certain about. I do."

"You said before that there was nothing there that could help us. That's what you told Gorton."

"I was wrong."

"How do you know you're not wrong now?"

"I *don't*, damn it. But I do know that Gorton and his crew aren't going to find it."

"It?"

"Yes, it! Are you a pilot or a psychiatrist? It! Whatever is over there."

"What makes you think Bulgakov or one of the others won't find this 'it'?"

He spoke slowly, trying to sound reasonable, patient. "Because they haven't found it yet. Or anything else. There's something over there I found before that I couldn't tell you about—"

"You found something! And you didn't report it?"

"No. Not to that jackass Gorton. I needed time to think about it. Now I've thought about it; now I need to go see it again."

"It! What *it*?"

"Take me over there. I'll show you."

"Christ. You're just determined to get me fired, aren't you?"

"You can't save the world while you're covering your ass. That's Gorton's problem. Don't make the same mistake he's making."

" 'Save the world.' You make it sound like some kind of corny Buck Rogers thing." She bit her lip, grimaced. "Shit. All right. I'll take you."

"Good!"

Suddenly she grinned. "You might not think it's so good, once you find out how you'll be traveling." She jerked a thumb in the direction of the cargo container.

"You're kidding."

She shook her head. "Uh-uh. It's that or nothing. I can't take you aboard the ORRV. One of the military people is always aboard."

"Will it be pressurized?"

"No. I'd wear a suit, were I you."

"I'll do that. How do I get out of there?"

"Shouldn't be too hard. They've set up air locks in the hull. I edge this sucker up against the larger one, cut her loose, then dock the ORRV against the smaller one. No one will screw with the container until I give the word. I'll hold off for a couple of minutes, and you can cycle through."

"Into the first chamber we found?"

"No. Forward of there; I guess it's forward, anyway. Toward the smaller end. Another room, almost as large, without the crazy statuary."

"How do I find my way back to the first chamber?"

"Get lucky, I guess. You'd better be damned careful, though. There probably won't be anyone in the room with the cargo lock, at least not till I report the container as docked, 'cause there's nothing interesting in there for them to play with. Gorton's got at least a dozen people over there, though, and they're scattered throughout the ship."

"They haven't found anything?"

"Not that I know of. But that's not really saying very much. I'm not exactly in the loop. But Gorton's just as tight-assed as ever, so I'd guess he hasn't found anything too significant. He's not the sort to hide a success. And, hell, they don't even know what it is they're looking for. Gorton was pretty ticked not to find live aliens aboard."

"They've found dead aliens?"

"Yes, sort of. The exobiologist—Davis?—thinks that's what all the dust in there is. It tests organic. Dead alien. Very dead, for a very long time."

Harris nodded. "I'm not surprised."

"I'll bet you're not."

He gestured toward the container. "When do you take this over?"

"In about two hours. You're sure you want to do this?"

"I'm sure."

"Then be back here in an hour, suited up. We'll get you over there."

"I appreciate this."

"You'd better. Now make yourself scarce. The less you're around here in the next hour, the better."

He took her hand and squeezed it. Then, on impulse, he pulled her close and kissed her solidly, once, on the cheek.

She blushed and drifted back from him. "Do you always get what you want, Mr. Harris?"

He grinned. "Only when it counts, Ms. Coles. And then only when I'm feeling lucky."

"Well, I hope you keep feeling that way, at least for a few more hours."

"Count on it."

He wedged himself between a pair of crates lashed to the deck across from the container's pressure hatch and watched as the hatch irised shut.

When it was completely closed, he tapped the light-strip in his suit's shoulder and, by its illumination, surveyed his accommodations. The container was small and packed almost full; his field of vision was limited to a space about two meters square.

He whispered to his suit's controls and it dialed his helmet radio into the general communication frequency that the ORRV used. The signal was scratchy because of the container's walls, but he could listen in.

Then he turned off the light-strip and sat in darkness, waiting.

An interminable time later he heard Coles log in with the *Phoenix* and announce her departure. He felt a jolt as the cargo bay's loading machinery shifted the container into the lock. A few minutes later there was another jolt as it was delivered out of the lock to the ORRV launch waiting outside.

There was more waiting as Coles attached the container to her ship. There was a bump, then the sudden weight of acceleration. He braced himself with the lashings that held the container's cargo in place.

Then the weight was gone, and he relaxed for the ten minutes of drift before Coles would begin the close maneuvering near the Egg. He listened absently to the radio chatter between Coles and the *Phoenix*, his mind on what waited aboard the alien ship.

What did wait there? That was the prize-winning question, wasn't it? He saw the two trapezoidal plates in his mind, standing close against one another, that strange, staticlike energy flowing between them. He felt an odd shiver of fear run along his spine. Was there something there he should be afraid of? Somehow, now, alone in the cramped interior of the cargo container, he felt that there was.

He forced himself to look at that fear—was he afraid for his physical well-being, of death? No, he decided. It was something else. What he might learn? Maybe. He had the sudden craving for a drink of the Haitian rum he'd kept himself sodden and oblivious with for so long. What did that say about his fears?

He knew one thing. He no longer wanted to be here. He wanted to be home. He could picture in his mind Port-de-Paix, the warm feeling of belonging, men and women easy together, in no hurry to *do* or to *achieve*. Song Lan had fallen into that rhythm with him; together they had made it home, a place of intimacy and unhurried security. To lose that again! He felt a sudden longing deep in his gut that was so intense it bordered on passion. Home!

Then something in what was being said on the general radio freak caught his ear and dragged him back to reality.

"Say again, *Phoenix*," Coles was demanding. He could hear a strange, tense urgency in her voice.

"Bogie. I said bogie, at your forward nine. Mother of God! The son of a bitch came out of nowhere!"

"Nine—? I see it. Good Lord, it's *huge*!"

"It just *winked*—"

Another voice broke in; after the first few words, he realized it was Gorton. "Can the chatter, *now*! Russo, get off this freak. Coles!"

"Yes, Captain?"

"What do you see?"

"It's enormous. Ten or a dozen times the volume of the *Phoenix*. And it's . . . hold on a second."

There was dead air for a few long moments. Harris felt a surge of passionate frustration; something out there—another ship?—had amazed and frightened Coles and he was literally blind to it, locked away inside a windowless cargo box. He had no choice but to quelch his frustration and wait, listening for Coles to continue.

"It's full of *holes*," she said finally.

"Say that again."

"Holes. Big ones, little ones. Some are pretty ragged, probably meteoroid hits. The thing's punched through like Swiss cheese."

"We can see some of it on the holos. How extensive is the damage?"

"Very extensive. But it *is* a ship. Looks one hell of a lot more like one than the Egg does. Exterior is clearly metallic. It's maybe a kilometer and a half long—Christ, is that possible? *Phoenix*, can you confirm?"

A different voice came in. "That's confirmed. One thousand seven hundred meters. We've got a clear read on the interior as well: it's mostly hollow and sectioned into decks. Not too different from a lunar lifter, but about fifty times as big."

"Any signs of life?" Gorton again.

"Nothing I can see," Coles answered. "It really looks dead. Not in the way the Egg does; this thing looks *destroyed*. It looks like space junk. *Huge* space junk."

"Any markings?"

"None I can see."

"Where did it come from? Why didn't anyone spot this thing's approach?"

The first voice answered. "There was no approach. It came

out of nowhere. It just appeared. The screens were clear, then
suddenly it was just there.''

Two people tried to speak at once and Gorton roared at them
again to clear the frequency.

"Nothing just appears out of nowhere!" Gorton shouted, after catching his breath.

The thought crossed Harris's mind that Gorton had forgotten
at least one thing that *had* appeared out of nowhere: Harris
himself. But he had left the Angel behind, back on Earth. Or
had he? Who could know what that entity was capable of?

"It's matched velocity?"

"That's confirmed."

"How?" Coles asked. "That thing is *dead.* I'm not kidding.
I can see clear through one of the bigger holes near what looks
like the stern. I'm going to make a close transit, get a better
look."

"Negative, ORRV One. Bring the launch back to the *Phoenix*, Coles. Now."

There was silence for another moment. "Acknowledged. In-
itiating the program now," Coles said finally.

James Harris sat in the darkness of the cargo container and
wondered. Another ship!

Curiouser and curiouser. He settled in to wait.

The captain was not a man of indecision, Harris decided. By
the time Coles had made her way back to the cargo bay to set
him free, Gorton had already ordered a boarding party. Bulgakov and Miyazawa, Coles informed him, were already suiting
up even as he struggled out of his own pressure suit.

He freed himself from it quickly and hurried to the ORRV
staging area.

He arrived just as Bulgakov was preparing to board. The big
Russian held his helmet in one hand and dug into his ready bag.
He pulled for a small, tarnished, silver flask and offered it to
Harris.

"You must drink to me, James! It is my turn to be first inside."

"What is it?"

Bulgakov clucked his tongue. "What a question! It is vodka,
of course."

"Of course." Harris took the flask, took a tentative sip from the nipple attached to the flask's neck, then a swallow. The alcohol burned in his throat and made a warm place in his stomach.

He handed the flask back to Bulgakov, who tipped it back and swallowed deeply, then sighed in appreciation. He turned the flask in his hand, studying it.

"This was taken from the palace of the last czar by my three times great-grandfather. I had the bladder put into it and the nipple, so that I could use it here, with no weight. Something like this, you use. A drink from it is a drink of memory."

He held it suddenly out to Harris. "Keep this for me, until I get back. It doesn't fit so good, inside the suit."

Harris hesitated, then took it. "Sure."

Miyazawa came into the staging area, suited up, carrying a laser rifle. He nodded to Bulgakov and Harris, then slipped through the access tunnel into the ORRV. Coles, Harris knew, was already aboard; she had only left the craft long enough to get her instructions from Gorton and to let Harris out of the cargo container.

Bulgakov slapped him on the shoulder, then followed Miyazawa into the vehicle.

When he was gone, Harris made his way up to the control deck.

The room was crowded, which was fortunate. Gorton, he suspected, would probably have him off the *Phoenix*'s bridge if there weren't so many faces there that he could make himself inconspicuous.

It was predictable enough to not even be particularly annoying that the captain, after having stooped to begging his help, would loathe the sight of him.

There was a tension in the room that had been lacking when they had found the Egg; as strange as it had been, it had been expected, was what they had come to find. This was something else; he smelled fear on the bridge.

Nobody liked a surprise: not one this big, not this far from the warm safety of home.

Gorton had made a fortuitous—for Harris—concession to the crowd of onlookers. In the center of the circular space encompassed by the bridge, a holograph projector had been set up; displayed at twice the image-size of the projections at the command stations was the new arrival.

It was awesome, even rendered secondhand.

Coles's description had been accurate enough, but she had been unable to convey the sheer scope of the thing she was describing. It was *huge*.

It was also riddled with ragged gouges and holes—he counted more than two dozen, and there were doubtless hundreds more that the holo's resolution was too coarse to pick up. Despite the ancientness of the Egg—and he was certain that it was immensely ancient—it showed little sign of the passage of the eons.

Not so this ship. It was a battered relic of another time, certainly millennia gone. Space was a big place; for the alien craft to have suffered so many random meteoroid hits, it had been adrift for a far longer time than he cared to contemplate.

That was assuming of course, that the myriad punctures in the alien ship's hull were made by meteoroids. One of the things Coles had told him after releasing him from the cargo container had been that Gorton and his people had come to the conclusion that the damage was natural in its origin; they reasoned that a race capable of interstellar flight would not use—or be vulnerable to—primitive projectile weapons of the sort that might be capable of making the punctures that dotted the craft's surface like acne scars.

A comforting conclusion, if true. Other than small personal lasers, the only weapon the *Phoenix* carried was a heavy-duty communications laser—and the Chernetsky drive itself, of course. He remembered the Chinese lifters they had left behind in Earth orbit: Gorton had explained in a briefing shortly after what had in all probability happened to the ships and to the soldiers in space around the *Phoenix* as she lit her drive. It would not have been pretty to see.

But for that particular defense to work, the intended target would have to be fairly close by when the drive was turned on. Which would give them, whoever they might be, plenty of time to saunter slowly up and punch the same sorts of holes in the *Phoenix* as riddled the hull of the newcomer.

Coles's voice boomed through the bridge. Someone murmured to the computer, turning the volume down.

"This is ORRV One," she said, pronouncing it the way roughnecks would, "Oh-rev One." "One hundred meters, closing at one meter per second." Her voice was calm and professional, but he thought he could hear an edge of tension in it.

A new shape appeared in the hologram, an elongated cube, and moved to obscure one of the larger punctures in the ship's hull, just below the polyhedron shape that capped the cylinder structure.

Coles said, "Fifty meters. Reducing to one-half meter per second. No signs of activity, no signals. Adjusting attitude."

Then, "On station. Proximity is three-oh meters. We're lined up. Waiting for your go, *Phoenix*."

Gorton's voice came on. He sat at a control station not fifty feet from where Harris watched, and his voice echoed in an odd stereo effect. "You have clearance," he said shortly. "Board her."

A few moments passed, then Coles said, "Boarding party away."

Harris moved over to the station occupied by Gorton, being careful to stay out of the captain's line of sight. Three others—Carney among them—hovered near, watching a flat virtual image projected there. The view was from a camera mounted near the ORRV's air lock.

It showed the interior of the breach in the alien ship's hull, illuminated by the ORRV's floodlights. The hole was oblong—whatever had struck it had done so at a slight angle—and very ragged at the edges, and the material of the hull around it was striated and showed signs of having endured incredible stresses.

In the deeper darkness inside the ship, where the launch's floods did not penetrate, he could see two pinpoint flickers of light: the hand torches carried by Bulgakov and Miyazawa.

Miyazawa's voice sounded, made muffled and breathy by his helmet. "We are approaching the ship's axis. No signs of life. Very little discernible detail. Three decks have been breached horizontally; very little of the interior structure at this location has survived. Deck separation is comparable to the *Phoenix*, about two-and-one-half meters."

Gorton muttered to the computer. The ORRV's view of the puncture from the outside was replaced by an image that moved with an odd, jerky randomness. Light flashed across jagged, torn metal, reflecting back and creating confusing, shifting shadows. It took Harris a moment to figure out that the new image was being transmitted from a camera mounted in the helmet of one of the boarding team.

A figure swam into view, startlingly white in the harsh glare of the torches. Harris recognized Miyazawa. It was Bulgakov's camera, then.

For a long moment there was only the gentle susurration of an empty frequency, then, "There is a vertical passageway through the axis, about three meters in diameter."

Harris stared at the display, trying to make out detail in the low-contrast dimness; he could see a deeper darkness in the shadows, a circular opening half-obscured by debris.

The image expanded. Bulgakov moved closer to the opening and began shifting floating pieces of metal.

Coles's voice broke in. "Does that passage lead aft or forward?" she asked.

Miyazawa answered, "This particular opening, forward. There is another aft. I suspect the passage runs the length of the cylindrical portion of the ship. I assume the decahedral structure contains the bridge if one exists."

Decahedral! Harris thought. Leave it to Miyazawa to take the time to count the sides.

"You are probably right," Coles said. "Aft would be a bad idea anyway. I'm picking up a good deal of radiation from that end of the vessel. I'm guessing this thing was fusion powered. Might not be a really good idea to waltz into a breached reactor core."

"Affirmative," Miyazawa said.

On the screen, Bulgakov was pulling away a meter-long shard of jagged metal. Harris felt the mother-hennish impulse to tell him to be careful, that the sharp edges could easily hole a suit, but he squelched it.

Then the way was clear and Bulgakov shone his light into the passage. There was nothing so far as the light reached but smooth walls broken only by two shallow grooves that ran precisely opposite one another, arrow straight, into the shadowy distance.

"We are proceeding into the shaft," Miyazawa announced.

Harris watched as Miyazawa's white-suited form pushed into the view of Bulgakov's camera and floated into the tunnel's breach. Bulgakov followed, the camera alternately showing the blank wall of the shaft as he pushed himself along and Miyazawa's booted feet, stark against the darkness ahead.

More silence as they moved up the passage. Then the lights picked up something in the near distance that reflected back into the camera. Harris realized he was holding his breath; the entire bridge was quiet, anticipating.

Miyazawa and Bulgakov came up to a blank, featureless wall. The shaft was plugged. There was no evidence of a release or dogging wheel if it were a hatch. Only a thin, dark seam around the circumference of the plug.

Miyazawa pushed against the plug, but had no leverage and very little traction against the smooth walls of the shaft. He slipped away from the plug as he shoved, and drifted slowly back out of the view of Bulgakov's camera.

"Permission to burn through?" Miyazawa asked.

"Granted," Gorton answered.

"Now hold on a second," Carney broke in. "Don't you want to try some other options before you start cutting holes in things with a laser?"

"No," Gorton said shortly. To Miyazawa, he said, "Go ahead. Burn through. Start with a minimal setting."

"Acknowledged."

"Damn it. You don't know what's on the other side of that thing!"

"He's got a point, Captain," Harris said, despite his fear Gorton might order him off the bridge. "There might be pressure behind the plug. Somebody's air."

Gorton looked up, saw Harris and scowled. "It's a chance I'm willing to take."

"Even if it means killing whatever might be aboard that ship?"

"That's correct."

Miyazawa's laser flared, filling the screen with reflected green light. Bulgakov stood off several meters, widening the camera's view.

"Relatively high melting point," Miyazawa reported. "Ah! I've broken through."

A thin fog puffed past Miyazawa into the tunnel.

"Atmosphere!" Carney said.

"Continue cutting," Gorton ordered.

The laser flared again. It took several minutes for Miyazawa to burn out a section of the plug large enough to pass through. More fog bled into the tunnel.

"Atmosphere, but not much pressure."

"No," Carney agreed. "But who's to say they needed as much as we do?"

Gorton didn't answer. The green glare of the laser ended abruptly, the cut-away disc of metal floating out into the tunnel on a last puff of opaque fog. Bulgakov moved aside and let it drift past.

The edges of the opening Miyazawa had made glowed a dull red. Miyazawa played his light into the cavity beyond, and Bulgakov pulled himself closer, giving the watchers on the *Phoenix* a view of what Miyazawa was seeing.

Chaos. Nightmare.

Bodies floated toward the camera's eye, propelled by the still-escaping atmosphere toward the hole, dozens of them, clearly humanoid, but just as clearly *wrong*. Proportions were skewed, arms too long, legs too short, the torsos thin, warped reeds.

A body bumped into the hole, one of its queasily distorted arms tearing loose as pressure tried to push it through.

Harris heard himself gasp. Bulgakov jerked back from the hole, widening the view. Harris caught a glimpse of a mis-shapen, mummified face, the empty sockets of two round eyes, placed as a human's would be, staring out at him across the distance of centuries.

Harris's mind rebelled. He felt himself trying to scramble away from the screen, backpedaling ineffectually against empty air.

And then the screen was suddenly washed clean with a rush of bright static. The display cleared itself, empty air replacing the bright rush of white.

"Oh, my God, *no!*" Coles's voice burst out over the loud-speaker. It sounded thin and terrified.

"What's happening?" Gorton demanded. He whispered to the computer, and when nothing reappeared in the display, he pounded a fist against the console and cursed. Coles was silent. Harris thought he heard her sob.

"Mother of God!" a voice cried out from behind them. They all turned, Gorton struggling up from the chair.

In the big display in the center of the bridge, the fist-size shape of the ORRV floated alone.

The alien ship was gone.

CHAPTER EIGHTEEN

"Confirm!" Gorton shouted. People moved, orders were muttered to the computer.

"Status confirmed," someone said. "It's gone. It just winked out, the way it winked in."

"Coles!" No answer.

"Coles!" Gorton shouted again. "ORRV One, acknowledge!"

There was a crackle, then Coles spoke, her voice toneless with shock. "Oh-rev One, here."

"What's the situation? What do you see?"

"It's gone," she said, her voice breaking. "They're gone."

"Bulgakov and Miyazawa—they didn't get out?"

"Get out?" Coles demanded. Anger replaced the shock in her voice. "Of course they didn't get out! How the hell could they have gotten out?" she raged.

"Stow that!" Gorton said, his face reddening. He looked around the room. Everyone was silent now, looking to him. He looked back to the empty air where the display from Bulgakov's helmet camera had been.

He swallowed, and the high color drained from his face. He suddenly looked frightened. "What do we do, now?" he said, almost as if he were talking to himself.

"That's your decision," Carney answered. He was holding himself in place by the back of a seat before an empty station. Harris could see the whiteness of his knuckles where he gripped the seat's back.

More silence. Then Gorton turned back to the station. He

murmured to the computer. The black space filled with a holographic display of the Egg.

"It's still there," Gorton said. Relief was obvious in his voice. He pushed himself up from his seat, his eyes never leaving the display.

"Recall everyone from the Egg," he said abruptly.

"Now wait a minute," Carney began.

"No," Gorton said. "I want it done now." He looked around the room at the people, his people, who watched him in silence. "I gave an order."

"Yes, sir," someone said. Everyone except Carney and Harris began to move at once, settling in at command stations or leaving the bridge to take up their posts on other parts of the ship.

"ORRV One," Gorton said. "Return and dock with the *Phoenix*. Now. Then seal her up for flight."

"Aye," Coles answered. "Program running." Harris could tell she had regained some of her composure, but she still sounded angry. She's compensating, Harris thought. She can't deal with the shock and the sudden grief and is substituting anger.

And what are you doing? he asked himself. What did he feel? Numbness. Thinking to avoid feeling. He searched his own emotions and found no anger, not even at Gorton, only a sudden, wrenching sense of loss. He reached down a hand to touch the flask Bulgakov had given him, feeling the cool shape beneath the cloth of the thigh pocket of his jumpsuit.

He felt a tightness in his throat. He shuddered suddenly, shock and sorrow blowing across him like a cold wind. It was not the time! Not the place! He pushed the grief back, locking it away. He knew he would have to face it, sometime. But later. There were things he had to do.

Carney had pulled himself over to Gorton. They both hovered, face to face. "You're being too goddamned arbitrary, Bill!" Carney was saying.

Gorton's face was imperturbable, set like stone. He had made his decision, Harris could see, and there was nothing anyone could say that would change his mind.

"We've done all we can do. There's nothing further to be gained by this." He raised a hand to his eyes, seemed to falter for a second.

Then he said, "Get off my bridge, Doctor."

"Not until you listen to me. What if that ship comes back? Bulgakov, Miyazawa. They're inside that thing, damn it. We can't leave now!"

"They have four hours. After that, their air will be gone and we will leave. All we have accomplished here is the discovery of two useless derelicts and the loss of two members of my crew. We've done enough."

"Enough! There are ten billion people back home who wouldn't see it that way! Remember your mission, Captain!"

Gorton's eyes blazed. "Get out," he said coldly, "or I will have you dragged out."

For a long moment, they stared at each other in silence. Then Carney turned without saying a word, found a handhold, and pushed himself to the railing around the access shaft and out of the control room.

Gorton turned his attention to Harris.

"Do I have to get someone to take you off my bridge?"

"No, Captain," Harris answered. "I can manage on my own."

He brooded, alone with his thoughts, until the four hours were up.

Then he came to a decision.

He found Coles in her cube. She didn't answer the door's hail, so he tried a little trick Anson had taught him long ago to get past the secured doors of Shimizu storage facilities.

Electronically sealed doors usually operated on voice-pattern recognition; you asked a door to open and if it was programmed to recognize you, it would. But all the doors had a malfunction override that accepted a magnetic-code key—a skeleton key of sorts. But you had to have the right skeleton key.

Unless you knew Anson's patented jimmy. It worked, he understood, about a third of the time, though he'd only actually tried it himself once before. He took the magnetically coded chip Anson had given him from his wallet. The code-key contained the standard, patterned sequence that all doors recognized, but the special identity sequence that made one key distinct from another was missing, blank.

He braced himself with the handhold beside the door, pushed

the chip quickly into the slot in the door's jamb, then yanked it instantly out again.

At the same moment, pitching his voice high in the hope it might help, he said sharply, "Open."

There was a buzz. The door hesitated, opened a crack and closed again, then slid completely open.

He stepped inside. Andrea was in her bunk, still in her jumpsuit, one of the bunk's retaining straps wrapped around one wrist. She was sitting upright, her knees drawn up, her arms around them, her face tucked into the hollow.

"Andrea," he said gently. He pulled himself down to sit on the edge of the bed beside her and put his hand on her shoulder.

After a time, she said, very quietly, "I'm so sorry."

"It wasn't your fault."

"I know that."

"There was nothing anyone could do. It was over so quickly. They never knew what hit them."

She looked up at him, shuddered. "What if they're still alive? Alone, in that ship, with those . . ." She broke off, took a deep breath.

"I know, I know," he said. He heard a tremor in his own voice and shook his head hard as if to throw off the emotion that made an apple-hard knot of tightness in his throat. Bulgakov. There had been so much hurt, so much loss. He thought of Sarah, so long dead, so very far away.

So much loss.

"Andrea," he said. "You have to take me over there. To the Egg."

She stared at him blankly, as if she didn't understand.

He shook her gently. "You have to take me to the Egg, Andrea."

"Why?" she asked finally.

"There's something over there I have to find. What we talked about before. There's a message, I think. For me."

"Message?" Her voice was hoarse and she had closed her eyes. But she was listening.

"Yes. Sort of." He told her about the vision, the sweep of flame and cold that had touched his mind for that brief instant.

"But what does it mean?" He had her full attention now.

He shrugged. "If I knew, I probably wouldn't have to go back over there."

"You can't. *We* can't. They're evacuating the Egg, and they'll be using both ORRVs to do it."

"Who's piloting?"

"No one. The computer can make the run on its own, now that I've programmed it. All they have to tell it is when. Come to think of it, *you* could fly it. What do you need me for?"

"To watch my back. Besides, what the hell do I know about flying an ORRV? I'd touch the wrong button, vocalize the wrong instruction . . . then where would I be?"

"Probably ramming the *Phoenix*'s life-system," she said grimly. "I guess I see your point."

"What about after, when they've finished pulling out?"

"What after? Gorton's going to have us out of here as quick as he's able." She shook her head slowly. "I think he was more shaken up by losing Miyazawa and Bulgakov than I was."

"It will take a while to secure from free-fall. A lot of instrumentation has to be prepped for gravity."

"That's only a couple of hours. Do you realize what could happen, if they finish up before we get back?"

"You're afraid they might leave us?"

"You're damned right I am."

"Could that happen? Wouldn't they miss the launch?"

"Hell, I don't know. There are fail-safes—a ton of bells and whistles ought to sound off the moment I separate her from the hull, but everyone's in such a bloody rush. You saw Gorton. He might leave even if he did know we weren't aboard. Hell, the way he feels about you, it might be an incentive."

"So you won't do it?"

"Do what? Steal UN property? Go creeping around an alien ship with you on a hunch, when only a few hours ago another ship disappeared God knows where with two of our crew aboard? Is that what you're asking me to do?"

"Yes."

"You're crazier than Gorton."

"Maybe so. But Bulgakov was your friend, too."

Her eyes narrowed. "What is that supposed to mean?"

"If we don't go, he will have died for nothing. You will have kept me from giving his death some meaning."

"You don't even know for certain that he's dead!"

"Time," he murmured to the room. A digital representation

of the hour appeared, hovering in the middle of the room. Tenths and hundredths of seconds flashed by dizzily.

Coles stared at the numbers until they disappeared.

"Their air gave out twenty minutes ago," he said softly.

"Oh, God."

"Will you take me?"

She put her face in her hands and sighed. "Yes."

CHAPTER NINETEEN

August 22, 2071

When they entered into the darkened foyer of the staging area, a voice asked calmly, "Going somewhere?"

Harris pulled up short, grabbing at the handgrip beside the entrance, Coles piling into him from behind.

"What the hell?" he blurted.

"Lights," the voice murmured, then louder, "I asked you if you were going somewhere."

The lights blinked and came on. Hugh Carney hovered before the access tunnel to the ORRV. He was smoking a cigar, the smoke forming a cloudy nimbus around him where he floated, upside down to their orientation.

"I had an idea the two of you might end up down here," he said.

"How—?"

"Intuition, maybe. I didn't think you'd sit still for Gorton just abandoning the Egg. You know something about that thing you haven't told. I feel it. Spill."

"What in God's name is that *stink*?" Coles demanded. She pushed past Harris into the staging area.

"That, my dear, is a cigar, and a damned fine one. Tobacco's a little hard to find these days—one of the many vices mankind has more or less given up, to its detriment. They still grow it in a few places, though—Honduras, the Dominican Republic—and I know a fellow down in San Marcos, back in Texas, who still keeps a humidor. Rob. Big guy, looks like a bear. He manages to get a few boxes in every once in a while—"

"That's not the point," she sputtered, "nobody *smokes* aboard a spacecraft. The air handlers—"

Carney blew out a ring of smoke, adding to the pall around him. "I could give a bloody blue damn about the air handlers! Are you planning on stealing one of the good captain's launches or not?"

"Yes," Harris said. "We are."

"Then, by God, let's do it."

"Why are you here? What does this have to do with you?"

"Not a damned thing. But I'm going with you. I'm not about to lose the only chance I'll ever get to set foot aboard an alien spaceship. I've waited more years than you can know . . . Besides, I might be of some help. Andrea should stay aboard the ORRV, just in case the *Phoenix* shows some sign of going someplace—"

"—Hey, wait a minute—"

"—and, you never know, you might need someone in there, just to watch your back."

"Damn it, I said wait a minute—"

"He's right, Andrea. You'll need to stay up top. I don't see," he said to Carney, "why I need you, though."

"Need me or not, you've got me. I'm coming."

"Gentlemen," Coles said, "would you care to table this discussion? We don't have a lot of time."

Harris bit his lip. "All right. Let's go. I'll fill you in during the transit."

Carney grinned suddenly and stubbed his cigar against the deck.

"That's all I wanted to hear."

The launch separated from the *Phoenix*'s hull with a gasp and a bump. Coles fired the attitude jets, pushing it off toward the Egg.

Almost immediately a voice squawked over the launch's radio, demanding to know what the hell Coles thought she was doing. When she didn't reply, Gorton's voice came on.

"ORRV One, you are to return to the *Phoenix* immediately. Coles, dock that craft or it will be the last flight you ever make. Answer me, Coles. ORRV One—"

Coles spoke to the computer. Gorton's voice was abruptly silenced. " 'You'll never work in this town again,' " she said ruefully.

"He means it."

"I know he does. He might even be able to do it. The UN has a lot of pull with Lunar Lines."

"You could take us back."

"No. It's too late. I'm not going to back out now."

"Glad to hear it."

Carney spoke from where he lay in one of the acceleration hammocks. "Something just occurred to me, folks. What about the other launch? Couldn't they come after us?"

Harris was startled. "I never thought of that!"

"I did," Coles said grimly. "I disabled ORRV Two. Nothing serious—I just erased the core memory in its computers. It should take them a few hours to reprogram. Hopefully, we'll be back all on our own by then." She glanced over to Harris. "Won't we?"

"I surely hope so."

Harris stepped through the metal frame that had been installed into the bulkhead between the two rooms he had visited before. It hummed faintly, generating the current that kept the stuff of the bulkhead from closing down on it.

Carney followed gingerly behind, flexing his knees against the gravity. "Plays hob on the joints. But screw 'em. There's no dignity in bobbing around like some kind of goddamned parade float. A man needs to walk upright."

Harris stood a meter back from the shifting face of the nearer of the two trapezoids and stared into the roiling vertical flow.

"What is it?"

"I'm not sure. Touch it."

Carney did, then drew his hand back. "Odd sensation. I wonder what Gorton's boys and girls thought of these."

Harris shook his head, shrugged. "Nobody was talking. But I suspect if they'd discovered anything they understood, we would have heard about it."

"Probably." Carney touched the surface again, pushed his palm flat against it. Harris tensed, more than half expecting Carney's hand to suddenly dissolve into the surface. Nothing happened. Carney pulled his hand away and dusted his palm on the thigh of his jumpsuit. "Well, what now?" he asked.

Harris didn't answer. He placed his palm on the smooth face of the plane. The crawling sensation began. He held his palm there as the sensation moved up his arm. Nothing more.

Carney looked at him, puzzled. "What is it?"

A river flowing, fathomless depths. That's what he had been thinking before, when the slab had . . . spoken to him. He looked into the shifting, ripple-patterned current.

Depths.

The crawling across the skin of his palm intensified. His hand seemed to dissolve into the held stream of the slab, the current flowing through and around it. He stepped forward.

Fire expanded like a blazing blossom in his mind.

He screamed and tried to jerk away but the flames were all around him, burning . . . but not burning. He was not consumed, not even hurt: there was no pain, only the intense, compacted glare of the fire. The thought came to him that he was experiencing something akin to the virtual reality programs he had become addicted to on the Phoenix.

But this was more. He was part of it, he realized, and growing, expanding outward, becoming conscious of himself, mind and understanding dilating out in flaring, concentric rings of awareness.

I am aware, he thought, *I have been aware. But the thought itself seemed apart from the process, irrelevant. He felt awareness grow and tear free from the now-distant spark of the furnace. He felt himself expand, following the light that had come from nothingness as it expanded outward in a white-hot sphere of gas and fluid matter.*

The universe flowed outward from its beginning at the speed of light and he followed it, aware, alive, feeding on the blinding stuff of creation. Images, thoughts flared across his burgeoning consciousness, a consciousness composed of a billion individual cells of awareness, each integrating into a whole. I am becoming. I am.

And then he floated alone, different, helpless in a warm, muffled, amniotic blindness. The world, all of it he knew, convulsed in upon him and he was squeezed and forced down, struggling. Again, and light flared, blinding in its intensity. He emerged, took a first burning breath and screamed, born . . .

Light! He rode the remotest currents of air on a thousand nameless worlds. He watched stars flare and die, and with the ease of a thought he flickered, dissolved and moved on . . .

Pain. He stood in a darkened doorway and watched his mother weep. She cried as if her heart were breaking, great, wracking sobs that left him helpless and trembling, wondering where his father had gone . . .

A voice. An anguish that bleeds into his understanding like a wisp of dark smoke. He listens, touches another mind and feels the cold whip of empathy: its pain becomes his pain, its need, his need.

Home.

It—he, they—expands its—their—consciousness into the ether, finds in the intersteller spaces the held volume of atmosphere that is necessary. He—it—understands the word ship. *With a sense that is not quite human, he hears the name of a race eons dead, a race that existed parasitically with other forms who paid it for passage among the stars in the currency of access to their more corporeal forms . . . a race whose own form was like to the condensed-charge, zero-point energy that drove human starships, whose name was not a word but a sibilant exhalation of modulated energies . . .*

James Harris dreams. In his dream he stares out into a light that is blackness, that is the absence of light, into emptiness coalesced into form, into the open face of the deep.

Death. He had died. Then something—someone—had grown, embryonic, inside his cooling body, branching out through his neural pathways . . . Resurrection.

He opens his eyes onto a landscape of brilliant white. There is no demarcation between land and sky; light reflects, becomes an ambient, blinding glare. He stumbles, falls, rises again. The cold is omnipresent but almost unfelt. In the middle distance he sees buildings, aircraft. He stumbles again, falls. Before he loses consciousness he hears a voice . . .

Like a fly in a bottle, a bottle around a fly.

Angel.

James Harris dreams, but it is not a dream. He is aware of himself—of them-self—as a vastness spread like a film across a warm sea of atmosphere. He is intensely aware of his own chemistry, in the strings of life-infused hydrocarbons that are his physical form when he chooses to manifest it, ethereal and transparent. Hungry. Energy soaked, imbibing the life-stuff of a proximate star.

He is alone but not alone, self but not-self. Alive. Alive. Changed . . .

Release. He burst through the rushing surface and into air, gasped for breath. He tumbled down onto the deck.

Before him the pearlescence of the vertical river flowed on. He knew it now: its stream was indeed the stuff of revelation. Of memory. Of Self.

There were hands on his shoulders. He turned his head to look up into the face of his father.

Father.

Sadness and loss overwhelmed him. He felt the tears well in his eyes and run across his cheeks.

"What happened?" Carney was asking. "What did you see?"

Harris tried to speak but couldn't. He swallowed hard. "Myself," he whispered.

Carney shook his head, not understanding.

"We have to go back," Harris said.

"Why?"

"I can't explain," he said. He felt immensely alone, immensely sad. "But if I don't, the Earth will die." He looked up into Carney's eyes. "Everything will die."

Inside him, awareness flowed like the held river inside the slab, filling him with a harsh consciousness of inevitability.

Circles within circles; no beginning, no end.

Eternity.

Within him lived a splinter, a seed of the beginnings of all things.

He must return to it. He must become once more a part of the whole.

Even if it meant he himself must die.

CHAPTER TWENTY

August 23, 2071

Song Lan heard the sound of voices, the roar of a multitude, muffled and distant but unmistakable, and thought, *I have finally gone mad.*

Regardless, she crouched on the floor of her cell and listened. She could feel it now through her fingertips—a vibration through the stone.

It surged and receded, a rumbling susurrus like the sound of surf. She listened in awed fascination.

A deeper tone sounded. After a moment she recognized it as the throaty pounding of explosives. Artillery? She felt a mixture of exhilaration and frustration. Something new! Relief from the unending silence and ennui! She burned with an intense desire to *know.*

The pounding seemed louder, seemed to reverberate through the stone with a growing strength. Underneath it was the faintest suggestion of a wail, a sorrowful, lost sound. Air-raid sirens? She reveled in the smorgasbord of sensory stimulation. *If I could only see!*

That she could hear what she was hearing, in the basement hole into which they had dropped her, spoke of unimaginable events. *Had the West finally invaded as the party rulers had claimed they would do all these many years? Had the final war begun?*

She could believe that, having seen her own country, the horror and the contradictions, from the outside.

Something very like thunder roared suddenly nearby. Pieces of the room's ceiling gave way, rattling to the floor. She could smell dust shaken from the floor and walls. Then the whole room shuddered and threw her down flat on her stomach, as if a giant hand had picked the building up and were shaking it to see what might fall out.

She pulled herself to her knees, trembling.

The room shuddered again, throwing her back against a wall. She tried to catch her breath, trepidation becoming real fear.

Once more the floor pitched out from under her. One corner of the room crumbled away. Light, blinding in its sudden intensity, poured into the room. The muffled complaint of the siren became a banshee wail, deafeningly loud. She heard screams and the shouting voices of thousands. She rubbed fiercely at her eyes, blinking back tears, trying desperately to see.

One corner of the room, from halfway up the wall to the ceiling, was gone, had fallen inward to form a rough slope of rubble. Tentatively, still half-blind, she crawled to the ramp it made and began to climb up. Broken chunks of concrete rolled under her bare hands and feet and she had to fight sudden vertigo to keep from falling back down into the room. *So much light!*

And so much space! She looked out through the hole in the broken wall down from perhaps one story above the street level of Tienanmen Square. She had not been dumped into the bowels of the secret police's dungeons after all! *They made me think they had buried me to intensify my despair.*

The day, she realized, was badly overcast despite what seemed to her oversensitized eyes to be the unbearable brightness of the light. A slow, heavy snow was falling. Tienanmen, she saw, was filled to brimming with the living and the dead.

A mass of people—soldiers, the *shu* of the Catacombs—milled chaotically around the central monument. Bodies lay in random heaps around the square. Before the tomb of Chairman Mao a bunker of sandbags had been constructed. Above the bunker the red-starred flag of the republic flew from a pole. She saw a stuttering green flash from the bunker and heard the sound of automatic weapons being fired in response.

They were firing a laser weapon into the crowd, she realized. She watched in horror as a dozen people were burned down. Many of the soldiers in the crowd were firing back.

At the far end of the square two tanks squatted like awkward green tortoises. Both of their turret guns, she realized, were trained on the very building from which she watched.

There, then, was the source of the tremors that had rocked

her prison. As she watched, one of the turrets swiveled down and away to point toward the makeshift bunker beyond. For a long second it simply sat there, as if contemplating the blank, brown face of the sandbags.

Then its gun roared fire and smoke and a gaping hole blew out of the front of the bunker. The laser's flickering light died abruptly.

Song Lan watched in horror and amazement. Soldiers killing soldiers! Hundreds, possibly thousands, dead in the square.

With the bunker's laser gone, a mass of people, soldier and civilian alike, swarmed into the hole the tank had blown in its structure. The sounds of shooting intensified.

Then the world shook again, pitching her from her perch down into the square. She fell hard onto the stones, chunks of masonry raining down on her back and shoulders. She heard the report from the tank's cannon a moment later.

The Mind forced her to her feet, though pain shouted at her from her forearms and from her back. She knew her flesh was torn and abraded, but the Mind poured endorphins and adrenaline into her bloodstream, constricted certain blood vessels, dilated others. The pain was suddenly gone and she found herself running, crouched low, across Tienanmen Square.

The crowd had thinned somewhat, many of the *shu* retreating back to the Catacombs. The pavements were littered with bodies. She dodged and leapt, hurtling them like so many inanimate obstacles. The Mind thrust her ahead, past faces that stared at her in wonder. A man reached to touch her and she slapped him back.

She saw the open mouth of the central entrance to the Catacombs. It was barricaded with debris, broken office furnishings, a battered groundcar. The Mind was taking her there, to the sanctuary of the endless depths, the thousands of kilometers of tunnels.

No.

She forced herself to stop. The Mind gave in reluctantly to her will. She stood, trembling from the terror and the adrenaline, and looked around herself.

The body of a woman lay at her feet, the eyes open and staring up. Others, some alive, some dead, lay or crouched on the pavements. Most of the mob had either returned to the Catacombs or were among the thousands that were storming the bunker.

She heard the tanks' cannons and turned back toward the building from which she had come. Its facade was pockmarked with shell holes and a fire was burning in the top floors. As she watched another shell impacted and the top floor of the People's Congress Building collapsed in upon itself, belching flame and masonry into the square.

The breathless wail of the air-raid sirens stopped. The noise of the crowd around the bunker intensified accordingly. Small arms popped sporadically. The tanks held their fire, waiting for a new target.

Song Lan started toward the milling mass of people who now surrounded Mao's tomb. She moved into the shoulder-to-shoulder mob, shoving and pushing her way through. People resisted, shouting, screaming, mad with the fever of revolution. A man turned to her, his face red with his own blood, his eyes fevered and insane. He grappled with her and she allowed the Mind to take her body for an instant, applying subtle leverage to the man's shoulder as she twisted and threw him aside.

She pushed and shoved, fighting her way to the front. At the cavity the tank's shell had made in the bunker were more dead, some burned by lasers, some riddled with bullet holes. The air stank savagely of death and burnt flesh.

Here there was a break in the crowd, the ones outside reluctant to continue in despite their fervor, the ones inside already deep within the structure. She clambered over the bodies into the dimness beyond. Passages led left and right from the breach in the outer wall of the bunker. Ahead, beyond, was a single room that had contained communication equipment. Two uniformed bodies lay in the room.

She chose the left-hand passage and started down it.

The passage followed the outside wall of the bunker, curving around until it came to the facade of Mao's tomb. She moved as quickly as she dared along its length, struggling with her own sudden distaste for the dark confinement of the tunnel and with the fear-inspired surges of adrenaline that threatened to turn her own will back to the programmed survival imperative of the Mind.

The passage came to an abrupt end at the polished stone of the outside wall of the tomb. There the pavement had been taken up and a hollow beneath revealed.

Three bodies lay at the lip of the opening, two civilians and a soldier, all three badly burned by laser fire. The sandbags that made up the walls around her were scorched and streaked. The smell of death, of blood and burnt flesh, was hellish, but Song Lan brushed by the carnage and started down the metal steps that led beneath Mao's tomb.

The steps led into a narrow tunnel. She followed it for perhaps a dozen meters. It ended in what had once been a formidable iron door; its battered remains now hung from one twisted hinge. It had been pushed aside to reveal a dimly lit room beyond.

The carnage in the room was almost more than she could bear. Dozens of bodies filled the room, burnt, torn, dismembered. The floor was thick with blood. The entire scene was given a ghastly unreality by the one strip of lights still working in the room, which flickered from dim to bright every few seconds, throwing moving shadows across the wanton butchery that had been committed there.

The Mind intruded for a second, identifying the smells of cordite and ozone in the thick stink that filled the room. The computer equipment that lay smashed among the corpses was the source of the ozone; the cordite was from the rifles of the soldiers who had joined the mob in assaulting the bunker.

Two more doors—both sundered by explosives—led from the room at opposite sides. She gave the Mind a little more free rein, let the map-and-compass element integrated into her own brain cells take possession for an instant. The Mind oriented her with a dizzying suddenness; she was ten meters below the ground's surface, it told her, directly beneath the center of Mao's tomb. The passageway to her left led to the Catacombs. The other led back toward the building from which the tanks had liberated her.

Without hesitation, she chose the passage to the right. The ones she wanted to find would be there.

And when I find them, I shall kill them. My path has been chosen for me, but I shall follow it nonetheless.

She picked her way through the bodies and debris and entered into the lightless black maw of the tunnel.

As little as she liked it, she was forced to open herself further to the Mind's influence. It guided her through the pitch darkness, telling her of movement ahead in the distance. She found herself crouched low, moving fluidly along one wall. She felt the cold smoothness of its stone at a distance, as an abstraction.

The Mind possessed her wholly—but it carried her forward, bending to her resolve.

Light. An illumination flickered across the darkness ahead. She heard a scream, abrupt and shockingly loud. She moved closer and saw figures crouched against the tunnel wall. The Mind identified weapons, uniforms—but among the soldiers were civilians. Rebels, then. Revolutionaries.

Beyond the figures, the tunnel debouched into what seemed to be a wood-paneled hall. The paneling was scorched, embers glowing and smoldering in the gouges made by laser fire. There were other figures in the hall itself, sprawled loosely across the carpeting.

As she watched, one of the uniformed figures in the tunnel lobbed something—a grenade of some kind, she realized—into the hall and then pressed back against the wall of the tunnel.

Then, as if some sort of trick of the eyes, the grenade flew suddenly back into the tunnel's mouth. It struck the wall and bounced in between two of the people crouched there. Instantly, the Mind threw her flat against the tunnel's floor, her arms over her head.

She was still more than twenty meters away; the concussion was deafening, reverberating in the enclosed space of the tunnel. Shrapnel rattled against the walls around her. Something hot stung one of her forearms. She ignored it.

When she looked up one of the people—a woman, her face torn and bloody—stood, swaying, in the tunnel's mouth. The others lay on the tunnel's floor, dead or unconscious. The woman took a step, stumbled into the hall. Instantly, laser fire flashed from two or more sources. The woman collapsed into a burnt and smoking heap.

The Mind told her the laser fire had come too quickly for human reflexes—for human reflexes other than her own, or those of others like her. Quicker than thought, she leapt past the rebels into the open hall. She saw the dazzling green flare of a laser and the Mind snapped her body in a forward roll.

She came to her feet and dodged again, slamming flat against a wall. A pinpoint of searing fire flared in her shoulder; the Mind blocked away the sudden surge of pain.

She spun, struck out with a heel at a figure crouched in the center of the hall. More fire burned into her side. Her heel made contact and she felt the thin bone under her opponent's temple shatter.

The Mind threw her down, rolling as another laser beam searched for her, stitching a burning line in the carpet beside her. She pitched forward, slamming into the knees of another opponent. Something struck her hard between the shoulder blades, driving the breath from her lungs.

She punched at the specter of a face and it moved to one side so fast it blurred in her vision. Another blow struck her on the shoulder that had been burned and despite the Mind's control she screamed. *Agony!*

In pure reaction to the pain, she lashed out with a fist and felt it contact flesh.

Her attacker fell back, sprawling onto the carpet. In an instant, she was on him. She drove two stiffened fingers into the shallow pocket of his larynx, felt the cartilage crush in under her fingertips.

He rolled away, choking, struggling to breathe through the wreckage she had made of his airway. Carefully, before he could rise to his feet, she struck the back of his neck with the blade of her right hand, putting all of her strength and the surgical expertise of the Mind into the blow, severing the spine just below the skull.

She whirled away from the body, searching for another opponent.

There was none. The hall was empty of life.

For the space of a dozen heartbeats she simply stood there, letting her breathing slow, letting the surging of the adrenaline abate. Pain throbbed at her shoulder and side through the barrier the Mind had erected against it.

One end of the hall ended in a lift. Its doors were welded shut. The other end was an impressively massive armored door. Between them was the tunnel's mouth—the paneling around it was broken and gouged, suggesting that the tunnel had been recently dug.

Song Lan moved to the door. It was thick steel, impervious to anything even she could muster against it. Beside it was a panel, behind which was the door's voice circuitry.

She went back to the bodies of two men she had killed. She retrieved one of the hand lasers and burned away the fastenings that held the panel shut. The Mind told her what needed to be done; she pried open the outer casting of the hand laser and then smashed the inner workings against the sharp edge of the panel.

She took from the laser a thin sliver of broken crystal. With it, she made a careful, tiny scratch, the Mind guiding the movement of her hand, between two of the minuscule electronic condensed-charge paths on the ceramic wafer that was the door's memory. The door slid open.

Three men waited in the small room beyond. All three wore the uniforms of officers of the People's Army. Two held handguns.

The Mind reacted. Before they could move their fingers the two or three millimeters necessary to fire their weapons, she killed the two armed men. Their deaths were almost perfunctory, a momentary distraction; in a instant she had jammed the heel of her palm upward into the face of one, driving the bridge of his nose into his brain, then pirouetted away and crushed the throat of the other.

The third man did not move. His hands were in the pockets of his coat. The Mind's accelerated perceptions fell away and Song Lan stood across from him, waiting for the move that would let her kill him.

He did not make it. He simply stood, watching her.

"You," he said. His voice was tired, but not frightened. "I did not expect you."

She said nothing.

"Do you know who I am?"

"No," she found herself answering. She studied him, trying to remember his face. He was an old man, wearing the uniform of a General of the Army. His features were lined, but still hard; it was a cruel face, she thought.

"I do know you, however. I had them bring you home."

"You had them bring me . . . home," she said flatly. She felt slow witted, uncertain. The effort to control the pain of her wounds had drained her. She felt punch-drunk on adrenaline and endorphins.

"Home. To the country you betrayed."

"I betrayed nothing," she flared.

"Then protect me! So far as I know, I am the only surviving member of the legitimate government of your country. *Your* country. *Your* people. You have the ability to save them by saving me. You can stave off a hundred—a thousand!—of those . . . *revolutionaries*.'' He gestured to the hall.

She looked out into the hall, at the bodies there. She touched her cheek, the spot where the listening device had been, buried in her flesh like an electronic tick, before Hugh Carney had taken it out. ''Those revolutionaries *are* my people. You have starved them and killed them. All of you old men.'' She felt her resolve return, and with it some modicum of her strength. ''I should kill you,'' she said.

He shrugged. ''All I have done, I have done for the people.''

'' 'The People's Heroes are Immortal,' '' she quoted.

''Just so.''

''I should kill you,'' she said again.

''Perhaps.'' She saw a sudden change in his eyes, a narrowing. She threw herself to one side just as a hole burned through the pocket of his coat and green fire blossomed forth. She rolled underneath the laser beam. As it followed her down, she whipped her right foot forward, catching him at the ankles.

He fell heavily, the laser beam arcing up across the room to score the ceiling, then flickering back down to the floor.

Song Lan leapt to her feet, ready to slash out with all the power and speed the Mind could give her. But the general lay without moving, the laser gripped in his hand still burning through the smoking wound that began under his chin and drove through his face and the top of his skull to scorch the dark wall paneling beyond.

Then his fingers gave up their spasmodic grip on the hand laser and it dropped away, clattering to the floor.

She stood and stared at the general's destroyed face, her sense of resolve and purpose draining away. The pain from her wounds began to flood through the wall of chemical control the Mind had built against it.

She looked down at the wound in her side. It bled in fitful trickles from the charred gash midway between her hip and her ribs. The sight made her suddenly light-headed and she swayed, then stumbled to the door and into the hall. The bodies there were as she had left them; there was no movement or sign of life in the dark mouth of the tunnel.

She started for that opening. She took two steps before the darkness overwhelmed her and she fell.

* * *

Light flickered.

Awareness avoided her like something alive. She groped for it, struggling to remember, to see . . .

Someone was holding one of her eyelids open, shining a small flashlight across her retina. She tried to speak and heard the unintelligible croak of her own voice.

"Be calm," someone said. "We have come to help."

The glaring light was taken away and she was staring up into faces, three of them, looking down at her.

One of the faces was Jiang's. She looked up into the wrinkled, weathered face of the old woman and felt the tears well in her eyes, tears of relief and of infinite sadness.

"Mother," she whispered.

"Yes," Jiang-a-yi answered. "I am here. Do not talk."

"The revolution . . ."

"Is spreading. It is in Beijing and Shanghai, in some of the other cities. Do not talk now. We will take you to a safe place. You will be all right."

" 'The People's Heroes are Immortal,' " Song Lan whispered.

"Yes," Jiang said. "Yes."

4

REUNION

CHAPTER TWENTY-ONE

Gorton had been waiting for them. He would have been pacing if that had been possible in free-fall; instead they found him blocking the hatchway that led from the ORRV staging area, bobbing slowly up and down, pushing himself off the bulkhead with his hands and then his toes.

Hugh Carney noted with a certain clinical detachment that the captain was well on his way to hypertension, if the man couldn't find a way to deal less explosively with his frustration and anger. As they pulled themselves through the hatch from the launch, he grabbed a handhold and faced them, his face a florid red.

"You had no authorization. None. If you weren't civilians, I'd have you in a military prison the moment we touched down. As it is, I'm going to do my damnedest to see you prosecuted under UN civil statutes—"

Carney tuned the voice out. Gorton's ire was no longer important. If he was to believe his son—and the evidence of his own eyes—they had found what they had come so far to find.

Only, he had no earthly idea what it was James Harris had found.

He had watched Harris *soak* into the coruscating flux of the slab, absorbed like a shadow into a space much too small to contain his mass. He had tried to follow Harris into the thing, but where it had yielded to the son, it had offered only impervious solidity to the father.

He had stood for nearly ten minutes, watching the rippling movement inside the thing, feeling the electric crawling move up his arms to his shoulders and chest. It had made it hard to breathe, as if his lungs had become congested with thousands of fluttering moths.

Then it had moved into his head, up to his eyes. Suddenly he was blind, his vision replaced by a darkness pierced only by the same expanding, molten swathes of color he remembered from so long ago, when he and his brother would sit together in the darkness and press their thumbs against their eyelids, trying to share the colors that played across their retinas.

Still, he had stood there, his palms pressed flat against the warm surface, while strange colors and flaring light played across the darkness of his inner eye. It had been like the undulating brightness of an aurora, spread in long, flaming waves across the blackness. In it, for an instant, he thought he had seen the unsteady movement of figures moving across a star field so full of lights it was like the rushing blizzard of an empty holo channel.

It had been ghostly and unreal, and for a moment he had felt a part of it.

Then he had heard the sound of a body falling to the deck. He had snatched his hands away and instantly his sight had returned. James Harris lay on the far side of the figure formed by the two planes. He had come out of the thing through the other of the two slabs.

And then he had half carried Harris back to the ladder. Together they had climbed into the launch. Harris had been withdrawn and unresponsive on the trip back; Carney had let him be, giving him time.

And now they waited together in the *Phoenix*'s ready room, being inundated by Gorton's bad temper. Carney decided he had heard enough.

"If you'll excuse us, Captain—"

"Like hell!" Gorton snapped. He blocked the exit with his own mass. To one side of him was one of the soldiers, Soviet from his insignia. It was clear neither of them intended to let Carney or the others past, at least not until Gorton had finished his diatribe.

Carney pushed himself away from the bulkhead directly at Gorton. The Russian soldier moved to intercept him, but Carney straight-armed him, shoving hard against the man's chest. The soldier floated helplessly back, his own momentum transferred to Carney.

Carney barreled toward the captain like an overweight missile. The captain held his ground until the last instant and then yanked himself aside. Carney flew through the hatch and into the corridor beyond, Gorton's shouted curses dogging his heels.

Coles followed close behind, one hand on Harris's arm, guiding him along.

They made it to the corridor that ran parallel to the ship's axis, the bridge at one end, the bulk of the ship at the other, and turned away from the bridge. Carney kept a weather eye out for pursuit from Gorton and his friend, but none seemed forthcoming.

There wasn't, Carney reasoned, too damned much more the man could do to them—at least for now—than curse and shout, perhaps confine them to quarters. There was no brig aboard the *Phoenix*, and there were no real putative actions he could take.

Though, Carney though wryly, if floggings were still an option, he was sure the captain wouldn't hesitate to administer them all a dose. For now, he'd just have to swallow his ire. When they were again Earthside, that situation, as Gorton himself had indicated, could change dramatically.

He'd burn that bridge when he came to it. For now, he wanted to get Harris to a safe, quiet place, and, when the boy felt like it, talk over what had happened aboard the Egg. Coles too, he knew, must be near bursting with curiosity—but she had kept her peace, sensing, he guessed, that something disturbing had happened to her passengers.

He led the way down to his own quarters. When the door had closed behind them, he settled into his chair, letting it cradle him close while it began to knead and massage his back. He let himself go oblivious for a few seconds as the chair worked his aged and abused muscles. It would be all too easy to withdraw, to let the lethargy that suddenly seemed to drain away every erg of his strength take him.

For the first time in many months the specter of his own mortality passed through his mind. What would it be like to die? To *cease*. Peaceful, maybe. Serene. But there were things that must be done first.

When he opened his eyes again, he saw that Coles had guided Harris into one of the two hammock-chairs in the room. She had strapped herself into the other. She was watching Harris, who was watching nothing. His eyes were unfocused and distant, his face haggard and drawn.

He suddenly looked at Carney.

"What did you see, over there?" he asked.

"Not much. After you . . . disappeared, I touched the thing, and I saw . . . lights, images. Nothing very definite." He hesitated. "Except, at one point I thought I saw stars, millions of 'em. One right on top of the other. Like at the center of the galaxy."

"Yes," Harris said, "then what?"

"Then nothing. You came out and I picked you up."

"What exactly happened in there?" Coles broke in. "You two haven't so much as breathed a word."

Harris shook his head slowly. "I don't even know if I can explain."

"He went inside one of the plate structures."

"What plate structures? I've never been inside the goddamned thing because that tight-ass Gorton—"

"They're trapezoidal plates, maybe two-and-a-half meters tall, a few millimeters thick. They're solid, though there's some kind of movement inside, all in one direction. He stepped inside one of 'em, then popped out of another one a few minutes later."

"Stepped inside of something a few millimeters thick?"

"Yes."

"How?"

"How in the hell should I know?"

"I didn't go inside it," Harris said. "I went through it, to someplace else. Or maybe sometime else. Or both."

"Like through a door."

"Yes. Sort of. Or through the surface of a river, down into its depths. And its depths were memory. And time."

"What did you see?" Coles demanded, her voice impatient and excited.

"Myself."

"You said that before," Carney said. "What does it mean?"

Harris hesitated, rubbed the palm of one hand across his forehead. "I told you, I'm not sure whether I can explain this. I'm not sure if I know the words. I saw . . . *creation:* The beginning. I was there."

"Creation? Of what?"

"Of *everything*. Of the physical universe." The hand he had pressed against his forehead moved to his temple. "*My* memories. My *self*."

Carney looked to Coles, saw her frown in confusion. "I don't understand."

"I know. I didn't understand, either. I don't think I really wanted to understand. Gorton, the others, don't want or need to understand. Man is an intensely anthropocentric creature, did you know that?"

"No," Carney said. The glazed abstraction had returned to Harris's eyes; he saw distances there, a queer doubleness of vision. It occurred to him that while Harris might again be with them after returning from the wonderlandish looking glass of the *place* into which he had disappeared, he might not still be entirely *of* them.

Was the man who had come out the same one—in any but the obvious details of appearance—who had gone in?

"The Christian Bible says that man was made in the image of God. Do you believe that?"

The Christian Bible? Carney wondered. Aloud, he said, "I don't know. Who can really say?"

"*I* can say! It's wishful thinking! We're not only anthropocentric, we're anthropomorphic. We want the creator to look like us because we are too narrow-minded and insecure to think it could be otherwise. Does God have breasts? Testicles? Do aliens? We came out here looking for an alien, or at least that's what we thought we were looking for. But we were really looking for ourselves."

Carney was silent, listening.

"We have always looked for ourselves, like a debutante who loves her own reflection in the mirror! All the thousands upon thousands of eyewitness stories about aliens coming to visit us over the last two centuries and always the aliens looked like us, kidnapped us and dissected us the way *we* confiscate and take apart things we don't understand. Those weren't aliens! They were reflections of our own needs. Hell, look at the 'alien dust' Gorton's biologists found in the Egg. The aliens who made that ship were about as much like you or me as a lightning bolt. The organic matter they found over there was *cargo*—maybe intelligent beings, but more likely cattle, or what passed for it, being ferried somewhere to some other race—"

Harris's voice trailed off. For a long moment, he seemed totally lost in his own thoughts, staring out somewhere beyond the wall of Carney's cubicle.

"And . . . ?" Coles finally prompted.

Harris blinked and looked at her. When he spoke, his voice was very quiet, very tired. "We have met the enemy, and he is us. Or, rather, he is me."

"What—?"

Harris put his head in his hands and spoke that way, his voice muffled. "I killed them."

"Killed who?"

"Bulgakov. Miyazawa. At least. Maybe the whole god-damned world, as well."

"You're talking nonsense, boy. The shock of—" Carney began.

"No! Don't patronize me! I know . . . more than you could ever guess. I brought the derelict here, the one Bulgakov and Miyazawa were aboard. I also made it go away."

"How?" Carney knew the disbelief was heavy in his voice—but what Harris was saying!

"I'm not entirely sure. The Angel . . ." He took his hands from his face and looked at Carney. His eyes were wide with pain and remorse. One of his hands wavered in the air before him, then sunk down to his lap. "I don't think it saved me. I think this is not . . . me, or not all me. I think I might have died on Comfort."

Carney fought his way free of the chair's grip, not waiting for its servomotors to cycle back and release him. He was too agitated to stay still in the machine's comforting grasp.

He shoved himself up to the hammock-chair Harris occupied and stopped himself by one of its supporting straps. He hovered before the younger man, staring incredulously into his face.

"*Died?*"

"Or worse. Died a little. Just enough so that the Angel had to fill in the blanks, replace the damaged parts."

"Replaced? With what?"

"With itself."

"Itself? *Itself?* What the hell are you talking about?" Carney swung around to face Coles, who was sitting quietly in her hammock-chair, her eyes moving from Carney to Harris. "Do you hear this?"

She nodded. He turned back to Harris. "Do you know how incredibly . . . insane what you're saying sounds?"

"Nevertheless, it's true. It's one of the things I learned . . . in the other place. The plates are . . . gates, of a sort. Where you go is . . . inside. You get sort of folded in upon yourself, physically and mentally. It's how the aliens who built the Egg got paid their freight fees . . . you become the same sort of essence they were, but with your memories, your experiences, intact. You exposed yourself—your true self—to them. And to yourself. They were beneficial parasites, like your own intestinal flora—they gave and they took. What they gave was passage, what they took was memory."

"Where are they?"

"Gone. Dead. For eons."

"And the Angel?"

"I don't know if I can explain it—"

Coles broke in. "What about Bulgakov and Miyazawa?"

"What do you mean—?"

"You said you made it go away."

"I did. When it appeared, I was thinking of home, of going back. The Angel found me a ship. *I* found a ship. Somewhere, out in the void, and I brought it here."

"The two you had weren't enough?"

"It's not like that. I'm not talking about doing something consciously. There's no *logic* to it. The part of me that is *not me* sensed the need I felt and did what it could to fulfill it. It knew that I needed a *ship*. It found me one. That's all I know about it. The Angel is capable of things you could never understand."

"You sent the derelict away? Where?" Coles demanded. Her tone was accusatory. She had freed herself from her hammock-chair and was hovering before it, facing Harris.

"I don't know. When I saw those . . . bodies, I just reacted. I never made any conscious decision—before I could think, it was just *gone*. I don't know where. Light-years away, probably."

"Why didn't you bring it back? Once you knew—"

"I couldn't. It's not like that. It's . . . beyond me now, somehow. I feel like I could . . . do something, begin *something*. But there's more to it." He shook his head. "I can't explain . . . I have to want it, passionately, without reservation, not just here—'' He tapped the side of his head with a finger. ''—but here.'' With the same finger he tapped against his chest.

Coles just stared at him. He continued, ''And I can't. They're dead. Their air is long gone. If the ship came back, someone—you, maybe—would have to go after the bodies. I can't want that. Not with what happened.''

''It's emotion,'' Carney said suddenly.

For the first time, Harris smiled, just for an instant. ''Yes. You understand.'' Again, Carney sensed that queer doubleness, the feeling that when his son spoke, something else was revealed.

''Maybe. Your 'Angel,' where did it come from?''

''Genesis. The real beginning, for this universe at least. I think it is a part of the flux from which everything was created. I was there, in memory, in that fraction of an instant when *nothing* became *everything*. We became . . . *aware* together. Its essence is pure energy, pure encompassing awareness. It lives by manifesting itself as matter—long strings of hydrocarbons, I think, and pockets of reactive gasses—and spreading that matter like a thin sheet of algae over the atmospheric ocean of a planet like ours, one close to a star but not too close, with liquid water available to it.

''It has existed this way from the beginning, soaking in a star's radiated energy until the star moves out of the main sequence. Then it moves on. It has done that thousands of times, with no thought to the consequences its life might have on other beings. How could it know that by changing the temperature on a planet's surface by a few lousy degrees it could wipe out a race? In all its time, moving outward from galaxy to galaxy, from star to star, out from the core, into our own galaxy, it had never had direct contact with intelligent, feeling beings forced on it—we must be an exceedingly rare kind of beast, or perhaps it is rare for intelligence to develop on planets as relatively undemanding as ours has been. I think perhaps sentience demands more adversity, usually, than we've endured . . .

''Regardless, one fine day a few years before the colony ship settled into orbit around 61 Cygni Beta Two with me aboard, sleeping like a baby, the Angel found itself on that selfsame planet. Then, sometime later, it found me. Dying. Or dead, buried in a snowdrift. It was emotion, as you said. Empathy. I drew it to myself—the essence of it, apart from the physical, consuming part still afloat in the stratosphere—by the intensity of my need. Emotion, severe, wrenching emotion. It's drawn to it like a moth to a light, so long as there's cold. It *feels* our pain, but it needs the cold, cold nearly as intense as that at the edge of space, to manifest itself, to take human flesh into itself. Those bodies the children found in the field outside of Port-de-Paix, they were nearly frozen through . . ."

He shuddered. "How's your Dante, Father? Do you remember what kind of sinners were cast into the ninth circle of hell?"

"Yes, I do. They were the traitors. To kindred and country in the first two rings, to guests and benefactors in the third and fourth. Judas Iscariot was there, in the fourth."

"Just so. Dante's lowest hell was a giant lake of ice into which the lowest of the damned were frozen like leaves in a skating pond. Traitors to country and king and brother and guest. I've just begun to realize what I am, and the first thing is that I am a self-damned traitor to the whole world and to every living soul on its ice-rimed face."

"But—"

Harris cut him off. "The Angel came to me like that, frozen into the heart of the ice, and took me up. It tempted me with my own life. It saved me and took me into itself because at that moment I cared for nothing so much as my own poor self. What was left of that self, anyway. For, Father, I am a construct. A Frankenstein's monster, made of human flesh cemented together with the stuff of creation. The stuff of the Angel. My own flesh and mind are strange to me. Haunted."

Carney shook his head slowly, emotion making an apple-hard fist in his throat. "You can't . . . I didn't know."

"You couldn't. I couldn't. Until it was shown to me. God! Can you believe the irony? That of all the random possibilities, it found the Egg to stow me in while it . . . brought, *translated* it and me back to Earth. And the Egg is probably the one place in the universe where I could have found the truth . . ."

He stopped, shook his head. "No, that isn't true. If I hadn't buried my head in rum and self-pity for all these years, I think I might have discovered this inside myself, all on my own, given time and enough desire. And enough courage."

Carney whispered, " 'Sometimes even to live is an act of courage.' Seneca wrote that down two millennia ago. It's still true."

"Yes," Harris said. Tears began to well in his eyes; he brushed them slowly back. He looked up at Carney. "I have learned so much, come to understand so much. Even you, old man." His voice cracked. "My father. So many years . . . so much loss."

Carney gripped his son's shoulder. He could feel Harris shaking under his hand. Slowly, almost reluctantly, he pulled his son close and held him in his arms.

Yes, too many years. He felt his own age, deep in his bones. And in his arms he held something—a sorrow—infinitely older, something that touched the very essence of infinity, hidden inside this man he could still remember as a little boy. But his son, now, was even more than a stranger—he was alien, separate.

"We're going home," he said, very quietly.

CHAPTER TWENTY-TWO

August 23, 2071

Captain William Gorton, of the United Nations Spaceship *Phoenix*, was not a patient man. He had been raised by a man even less patient than himself, and those first years of harsh discipline had made him intolerant and hard.

He had never blamed his father for the harshness or for the affection even now he felt he had been denied. It had given him an inner strength, a resilient core of self-reliance onto which he could fall back at need, and for that he was grateful.

Over the years there had been many tests of that fortitude, at the military school in Perth when he was a teen, later at the United Nations Aerospace Command Academy, and since in his various commands. He had weathered them all; he would weather this one. But he would not brook any more of the sort of willful insubordination he had had to endure on this mission. It was bad enough that he had failed—politically, the fact that the failure and the loss of Bulgakov and Miyazawa were not his fault would matter little. They were still his responsibility.

He lay in his hammock and glowered at the thick darkness that gathered in the corners of his room. In the "morning," after he had gotten some shut-eye and put the disturbing events of the last twenty hours behind him, he would give the order for the drive to be fired. He wanted to enjoy one last night of weightless sleep before the pseudogravity of acceleration made it again difficult for him to sleep.

The confined spaces on board spaceships made him slightly claustrophobic; the lack of gravity alleviated the feeling somewhat. It was a weakness in himself that he would never have admitted to anyone else.

He heard a noise at his door and sat suddenly upright. The door's announcer remained silent, but a voice said loudly, "Open."

His door slid open. As quickly as he could move he tore with one hand at the static closures on the straps that held him inside his hammock.

With the other hand, he reached for the K-bar survival knife held by a clay-grip on the bulkhead near the head of his bed.

Something—a body—flashed across the strip of light provided by the open door and swarmed over him where he lay. His hand was slapped away from the knife.

Years of martial drill made his reaction instinctive. His fist shot out into the darkness and struck flesh. The blow threw his attacker up toward the ceiling of the room and he used the reaction of pushing that much mass away from himself to roll hard to the left, tearing free from the hammock's restraints.

Once free, he shoved himself up to the ceiling and grabbed at whatever part of his opponent he could lay his hands on. This turned out to be a leg. He grasped the knee in both hands as it kicked at him and jerked the knee's owner down to face level; then he snaked his forearm across the attacker's throat as he struggled to break free.

Without loosening his choke hold, he pushed himself away from the ceiling with his feet and shot back to the hammock, dragging his captive down with him. He came up hard against the bulkhead, using his shoulder to take the shock. His captive squirmed and clawed at his arm. He pulled his right forearm tighter against the throat, and with his left hand snatched the knife from the clay-grip.

"Lights!" he shouted, and placed the point of the blade at his attacker's throat.

Hugh Carney and James Harris hovered just inside the door, their hands open and out to their sides. He glanced rapidly from one to the other, held his gaze on Harris for a long second, then lowered it.

He looked down at his captive. Coles's face was congested with blood and he could tell that she was near to losing consciousness. He let her go and pushed her away from him; she sucked in a desperate lungful of air, her hands at her bruised throat, as she cartwheeled across the room. She came up against the far bulkhead and hung there upside down, eyes closed, gasping for breath.

"What the hell are you doing in my quarters?" he demanded.

Carney spoke, his hands still spread wide. "Well, Captain, somehow we didn't think you'd talk to us if we just called you up and asked. This seemed a little more direct."

"What it seems, mister, is breaking and entering and aggravated assault. I'll add that on top of the other felonies you've committed when we prosecute you in front of a UN magistrate."

"Your privilege, Captain. But why don't you hear us out first?"

"Hear you out. Why? After you've attacked me in my own bed—?"

"I didn't attack him," Coles croaked. Her eyes were open, but she still kept her hands at her throat. "I saw him trying to reach something. That knife."

"She thought she was defending herself, Bill," Carney said.

"Doctor, to you I'm Captain Gorton, and I doubt that claim will carry much water in a courtroom." He spoke to the room, "Give me an open freak. Bridge!"

After a moment, a male voice answered, "Bridge, aye."

"Send a security team to the captain's quarters, on the double."

To Carney, he said, "I expect that gives you somewhere in the neighborhood of two minutes to say your piece, Doctor."

Carney pursed her lips. "Time enough, I think." She nodded to James Harris. "Tell him."

Harris began to speak.

By the time the three soldiers of Gorton's security team had arrived, he had lost interest in having Carney and the others arrested. He dismissed the security team and let Harris finish what he had to say.

When Harris had finished talking, he pulled himself into a hammock-chair and sat there cross-legged, trying to think through what he had just heard.

"Why should I believe any of this?" he asked finally.

"I find it pretty hard to take, too. But I have no choice but to believe it. It's part of me, like some sort of organ transplant. I can feel it, inside of me, as we speak."

Gorton shook his head. "Damn it, if what you say is true—"

"It is."

"—then I have a moral obligation to help you." He bit his lip, shook his head again. "The bitch of it is, I do believe you. After what I've seen out here . . . The problem is, I don't think the boys at the UN Security Council will be so open-minded. They expected us to come back with gadgets—or alien prisoners, at the least." As he spoke, he found himself staring at Harris. If it were true!

Harris looked up to meet his gaze. There was a quality to the man's eyes that bothered Gorton in a sudden, inexplicable way. He had seen something like it in the eyes of a very old man when he had been a foot soldier, many years before in Nepal, when his UN battalion had participated in the liberation of the country from the Chinese. They were the eyes of a mystic, fathomless, knowing. Harris had changed; he felt the last vestiges of his distaste for the man drain from him.

He looked away from Harris's eyes, for some unexplainable reason ashamed.

Then Harris closed those disturbing eyes. His forehead furrowed with concentration.

The harsh bray of a Klaxon sounded and Gorton jumped. *Damn.* This whole business had him as tense as a wire.

"Open freak! Bridge, what the hell is going on?"

The reply was terse and frightened. "Another ship, sir."

"Where?"

"Twelve o'clock level at one-point-oh-six klicks."

"Life?"

There was a hesitant pause. "Uncertain, sir. There are lights but no movement. The thing is about forty meters long, but, sir—it's only a meter through at the widest, and it's twisted around like some kind of crazy DNA strand—Shit!"

"What's that? Bridge! What the bloody hell—"

"It's gone, sir. Disappeared, like the last one. No change, no last heading, just . . . nothing."

He had been staring up at the ceiling, concentrating on what he was hearing. Now he glanced down to Harris . . . and nearly jumped out of his skin. A thick, white mist, like damp, cold smoke, now enveloped the man. And the mist *moved*, writhing around Harris as if alive.

Coles and Carney were staring wide-eyed at the apparition as well, and for the first time since he had known the old man, Gorton saw fear in Carney's expression. Trepidation settled like ice to the bottom of his own stomach and he felt the sudden urge to cross himself, though he hadn't so much as entered a chapel in thirty years.

Harris opened his eyes. Through the fog, Gorton could see that sweat was pouring down his face. His eyes were livid with . . . grief? Anger? Violent emotion, whatever its source. The mist swirled and gathered, then faded and was gone.

"What did you do?" Gorton whispered.

"I brought it here. For you."

"The ship?"

"The Angel. A small piece of it. I know it now. It can't refuse me anymore."

"How—?"

"I thought about what would happen to everything I love if I can't convince you I'm telling the truth. Pain and fear. That's all it took."

"Where did it go?"

"The ship? Away. I don't know where."

"I don't understand—"

Harris smiled a strange, wry smile. "I've been hearing that a lot lately."

"You have some kind of power? Magic—?"

"Yes. I guess you could call it that. Mystery. Whatever we can't understand is a kind of magic."

Magic. When he was young, it was a thing he had had no trouble believing in. His own father was half Australian aborigine, and that race's blood was seeped in nature mysticism and ritual. Even his father had believed in the mysteries of luck and fortune. But it was harder now; he was older; he had lived through the harshest kinds of reality in places where good fortune was itself a myth.

But he had seen the alien ships. He had watched one of them disappear, and just now he had watched as James Harris willed another of them into existence. It was too much even for his hardened skepticism.

"I'll do what I can. I can make some of the arrangements now over the communications laser, and the rest when we establish orbit. When this all comes out, they'll retire me, probably without pension." He grinned then, feeling suddenly almost lighthearted. "But then, screw 'em if they can't take a joke. Some things you do because you have to."

"Aye, Captain, that's true," Carney said. "And some things you do just because they're right."

Captain William Gorton, of the United Nations Spaceship *Phoenix*, blew out his breath in a long sigh and then nodded. "Too right. I'll give the orders. We'll be under way in an hour."

CHAPTER TWENTY-THREE

November 19, 2071

Despite the powerful Western curatives they had given her—liberated from the private clinics of the overthrown traitors—Song Lan was still very weak when the Revolutionary Council summoned her.

Despite Jiang's insistence she be taken before them on a litter, she was determined to stand before the council under her own power. It seemed only right; the council was comprised of democratically elected heroes of the Second People's Revolution. She felt she should stand before them as an equal in the new order.

Still, it was very hard. Jiang-a-yi supported her as they crossed Tienanmen from the entrance to the Catacombs. They had to walk carefully through the rubble and the shell craters filled with snow, the bitter-cold wind doing its best to blow them off their feet. Song was amazed at the amount of destruction that had been accomplished since she had last seen the square, in the moments before she had descended into the tunnels beneath Mao's Tomb.

The tomb itself had weathered the storm well, though many of the older structures flanking the square—particularly the state offices—had not, thanks to the protection of the bunker the traitors had built before it. The Monument to the People's Heroes had not been so fortunate; where it had stood there was now only a jumbled pile of snow-dusted rubble.

Just as well, she thought. She remembered a book that her husband had given her in those precious few weeks they had had together, by an American woman named Maya Angelou. Angelou had written of her own people, oppressed for centuries, that they needed no monuments to their poets and heroes—slavery had cured them of that weakness.

It was true. For a people freed from suffering under the hand of an oppressor, no construction of marble or metal could embody the joyous thing in their hearts.

Jiang steered her toward the ruins of the People's Congress Building. Something inside of Song Lan flinched at returning to the place in which she had been imprisoned for so long—how long, exactly, she still was not sure. But she refused to let doubt and fear sway her; she continued on.

The top floors of the Congress Building were gone, destroyed by the shelling and fire. They had been additions to the original building, though, and most of the older structure was still intact, pocked with a half-dozen shell holes. It had been pure luck that a shell from the tanks firing on the building had struck in just the right place to make it possible for her to escape from her cell. Luck or, perhaps, fate. She had the odd feeling that what had happened had been long destined to happen, that she had only played a role for which she had been fated.

Superstition. Chance had made her a hero of the People's Revolution. She suspected that was usually the way of it. Being in the wrong place at the right time.

They entered through the large opening where the building's central doors had been. The inside stank of smoke, but the walls broke the tearing force of the wind and she was grateful for that.

Jiang led her to the room where the Revolutionary Council waited for her. When they approached the door, Song gently put aside the older woman's hand and entered by herself, walking stiffly but upright.

Eight people awaited her, five men and three women. All were standing; all seemed weary and haggard, and for a moment she felt an irrational moment of fear. Then one of the women, a gray-haired matron, smiled and gestured for her to sit, and she felt suddenly at ease. They knew who she was and what she had done. She was among those who had suffered, too.

For more than hour, she poured out her story to them. They listened without comment, and she found herself worrying that they might not believe her.

When she had finished, one of the council members, a young man dressed as a student, said quietly, "Then despite all we have gained the people of China are condemned to die."

"I do not know if that is true," she answered. "It is possible that we might communicate with the creature my husband called the Angel."

"And how is this to be done?" the student asked.

She bit her lip before she answered, thinking hard about the things that had so occupied her mind in the many days of her convalescence. "This Angel manifested itself once before to me, as I told you, when I was on the island of Hispaniola—" She continued on quickly, not wanting to dwell on the reasons behind her presence in Haiti—the shame was still very strong. "—but I do not believe that it would manifest itself there again. It came because James Harris called it. My husband is no longer on this planet. But I believe there is still one chance . . . one opportunity for us to contact it. There was something my husband said, about the cold . . ."

She explained her plan to them, watching their faces for their response to what she proposed. She saw doubt in some faces, a reluctant acceptance in others. When she had finished, they whispered among themselves, and when they had come to an agreement, they turned back to her.

"It will be done. We have reestablished diplomatic communications with the United Nations. I believe they will help us."

Song felt the slow stir of conflicting emotions: elation and hope, but also the sour acid of fear.

For soon she would walk into the belly of the beast and ask it its name. And if it did not answer, they all would die in the deprivation and desperate violence to come.

She bowed to the council and, with as much dignity as she could muster, walked slowly, painfully from the room.

CHAPTER TWENTY-FOUR

December 19, 2071

A lunar shuttle met the *Phoenix* three hours after the starship achieved Earth orbit. Most of the *Phoenix*'s crew stayed aboard her to shut down her systems and prepare her for another long wait in mothballs. Her captain and three of her civilian passengers were aboard the shuttle when it separated from the starship and made a highly irregular rendezvous with a United Nations military platform.

Only one—Andrea Coles—was still aboard when it resumed its scheduled course and headed back for the moon. By the time she had set foot on lunar soil, a message of gratitude and a lavish commendation had been communicated from the captain of the *Phoenix* to her employer, Lunar Lines.

The captain and the two remaining passengers took the regular supply shuttle from the platform. When it landed at Kennedy Air Force Base, Florida, an American military jet helicopter was waiting for them, its engines idling, its blades already turning slowly in the blowing snow. The captain of the *Phoenix* had called in a good many IOUs.

Ten minutes after their arrival, James Harris and his father were in the air again, bound for Amundsen-Scott Station, Antarctica.

Captain William Gorton watched the copter lift from the pad and felt a strange, uncharacteristic sorrow. The last conversation he had had with James Harris played itself over again in his mind.

He had wished Harris luck and had shaken the man's hand. Harris had thanked him.

Then, enigmatically, Harris had smiled and when he spoke,

the words filled the captain with a sudden, unbidden grief. Even now, Gorton felt the weight of it, lingering like a taste—something bittersweet and exotic—remembered from childhood.

"I'm going home," he had said.

CHAPTER TWENTY-FIVE

December 20, 2071

Song Lan had been in Antarctica for more than three weeks when news of the *Phoenix*'s return came. The joy she had felt had overcome—almost—the despair of her own failure.

From Beijing, she had been taken by one of the few aircraft that had not been destroyed during the week of the revolution to Taiwan, and from Taiwan a UN jet transport had brought her directly to the tiny research station. From the air as they had approached, it had looked like a single mote of ash against an eye-achingly bright expanse of pure white stretching from horizon to horizon.

Closer in, the mote had resolved itself into a compound of several buildings bounded on two sides by runway complexes. On the runways were a dozen or more planes of various sizes. Most of Admundsen-Scott Station, she understood, was down below, under the ice.

For obvious reasons, she had had no real trouble adjusting to life in the tunnels. For three days, severe weather had kept her below, huddled in the damp living spaces with the station's crew.

On the fourth day the weather had cleared and she had ventured out onto the ice. She had no specific idea about what she had to do; all she really had was the story—rumor at first, and later confirmed by a memory-card dossier given her by Taiwan's ambassador to the UN—about James Harris's inexplicable arrival eight years before on the antarctic ice somewhere near Amundsen-Scott.

The one thing she did have was that momentary connection to the Angel that James had given her in Anson's *hounfour*. She

had gone out onto the ice and called to it, hoping it might somehow know her and answer.

It had not. Day after day she had found herself alone in the
empty, white vastness, bone chilled and exhausted from the
strain of concentrating on that image she had seen when the
Angel had visited her, startling blue skies, an endless, bottomless sea of air and in it . . . life, intelligence. The Angel.

She wandered aimlessly across the featureless face of the frozen desert, waiting for a sign. Three times, she was rescued by
helicopters from the base, twice when her wandering had taken
her too far out into the emptiness to make it back before dark.
The third time she had left the radio, the electronic compass,
the signaling beacon attached to her parka—all things that
seemed to her tainted by civilization—behind, in the vague hope
that that sacrifice might help lure the recalcitrant spirit to her.

Nothing had worked. She had admitted her failure.

But now, even that seemed to matter little. James Harris was
back! The sooner she was in his arms, the sooner she would
know a modicum of peace.

And he had been the one to tell her of the Angel's affection
for the cold; he had been the one it had brought to this place.
Where it had refused her, perhaps it would answer him. Time
would tell, and for that she was willing to wait.

She had the station's communications officer send a message
to the *Phoenix*, telling her husband to contact her. She could
only hope that it had reached him before he left the ship.

The copter settled very gently onto the helipad, throwing up
a dense cloud of ice crystals. James Harris and Hugh Carney
ducked out of the craft's amidships door and dashed blindly
through the stinging swirl of ice.

A door opened for them in a nearby building and suddenly
they were inside, in the calm, warm quiet. They shed the borrowed parkas they were wearing and allowed themselves to be
led down a flight of steps into the heart of the station.

James Harris found himself walking carefully down the steps,
as if he carried something fragile inside he was afraid he might
destroy. The thought had occupied his mind for all the weeks it
had taken to return, *If I die before it is done, the whole world
dies with me.*

As they reached the foot of the stairway, a woman—blond,

muscular, her face florid from the cold—rushed up the hall to meet them. She came up to James Harris, her eyes bright with excitement.

"Are you James Harris?" she demanded.

Harris nodded. "I am."

She took his arm and pulled him along down the hallway. "Buster," she said, "have I got a surprise for you!"

Harris allowed himself to be towed down the hall and through a door marked READY ROOM. Inside the room, a half-dozen people sat at tables drinking coffee or watching a recorded movie flickering slightly out of focus over a holograph projector.

At one of the tables was Song Lan. She stood as he came into the room, her expression a mixture of joy and shock.

"James!" she cried out, and ran to him.

He held her in his arms as the woman who had dragged him in explained loudly to Carney, "I only saw the flight manifest two minutes before you landed—but when I saw his name, I knew—" Harris lost interest in the voice, his entire attention—as divided as it might now be—upon the woman who now pressed, crying, against him.

For several precious minutes nothing existed for him but Song Lan.

Then there was a hand on his shoulder that refused to be shrugged off. Finally, reluctantly, he let the world again intrude.

It was the florid-faced woman. "My quarters are all yours," she was saying, "for as long as you need them. It's quiet there, private."

He nodded gratefully. What had to be done could wait, at least a few more hours.

CHAPTER TWENTY-SIX

December 21, 2071

He awoke with the same strange feeling of peacefulness he had felt on awakening every morning since he had come face to face with the thing inside himself. The nightmares of all the years since he had returned from 61 Cygni were only a bad memory, especially now that he saw them for what they were—the pleadings of a guilty conscience.

Because for all those years he had sublimated the truth, walling it off from himself with grief and anger and alcohol. Facing that truth—or rather, he thought wryly, having his face rubbed wholesale in the stink of that truth—had brought him far more than peace of mind. It had brought him a resolute courage, had reopened for him the potentials inside himself that had made him part of a star-colonizing expedition in the first place.

For the first time in a long while, he felt like a man, in both the generic and gender senses of the word.

Song Lan slept peacefully beside him. He buried his face in the long, black forgetfulness of her hair and felt her stir.

He held himself very still, felt her slip back into sleep. For a few minutes he watched her sleep, studied the lines of her face, the brow, even now, in sleep, furrowed with worry. His heart filled with love and a terrible feeling of impending loss—to find so much and then to walk away from it again!—and finally he had to look away to keep from losing the strength of his resolve.

Then, very carefully, he rose from the bed. He took his clothing out into the hall with him and dressed there, getting one odd look from a crewman who passed by.

Then he retraced the steps they had taken in getting to Major Jensen's—he had discovered in passing that the florid-faced woman was the station's commander—quarters. It wasn't easy; his attention had not been on where they were going earlier.

Still, the station's layout was simple enough, and before long he found the flight of steps that he and Carney had taken the day before. He climbed them quickly, intent on the objective he had set for himself . . .

Hugh Carney sat in a straight-backed chair at the top of the stairs. He had leaned the chair back against the wall and put his feet up on a desk. He was alone in the room, which contained only cold-weather gear scattered among a few desks and sealed crates.

Carney blew out a puff of smoke and studied the cigar he held in his hand. "The major gave me this," he said. "It's good to find a kindred soul this far out in the wilderness. Hell, it's a pretty good cigar, too. Mexican, she tells me. There's been an embargo on their agricultural products for ten years, but a UN friend of hers got a couple of boxes out past their customs people in a diplomatic pouch—"

"You were waiting for me."

Carney nodded slowly. He put the cigar in his mouth, drew on it, then put it down on a plate he had been using for an ashtray, letting the smoke trickle slowly from the corner of his mouth. The plate was cluttered with the ash and butts of several cigars. "Yeah, I was."

"You're pretty good at this. This makes twice now you've caught me on the way out."

"What can I say? I'm your father. Half of your genes are mine. I had a feeling you wouldn't wait too long on this, even with Song to distract you." He waved to a chair next to the desk at which he was seated. "Sit down for a minute, son. I want to talk."

"Nothing really to talk about, old man," Harris said. But he took the seat Carney offered.

"You never did explain just exactly what it was you plan to do. It was enough for Gorton that you knew the nature of the threat and that you thought you could do something about it. I think he just assumed you were going to talk the thing out of it. There's more to it than that, though, isn't there? Don't lie to me. You owe me that much."

Harris shook his head, shrugged. "I don't really know."

"You're not coming back, are you?"

Harris turned away and stared at the floor for a long moment before answering. "I don't know that, either, not for certain." He didn't look up, didn't meet Carney's eyes, when he answered. He didn't want his father to see how much the lie was costing him.

Carney tilted his chair forward, let it settle to the floor. "Have you told Song?"

"No."

"What's going to happen out there?"

"I don't know."

"Damn it, boy!" Carney shouted. "I'm your *father*!"

Harris looked up then and saw tears in the old man's eyes. It wrenched at him somewhere deep, in the part of him that was still his own soul. "I don't know," he repeated, very softly. "All I can tell you is it has to be done. For all of us."

"Can I at least go with you?"

"No."

"Why?"

"Because it's something I have to do by myself. For myself." He hesitated. ". . . And I don't know what might happen to you, if you were there."

"What should I tell her?"

"Tell her . . . tell her I will miss her. Tell her I love her."

"You don't think she knows that already?"

"Tell her anyway."

Carney nodded. "All right."

"Do you remember . . . ," Harris said suddenly, ". . . do you remember just before you left my mother? I was six, maybe seven."

"Six. Yes, I remember."

"Do you remember a song she used to sing then, something about, 'I once was lost, but now I'm found, was blind, but now I see . . .'?"

" 'Amazing Grace.' It was her favorite hymn."

"It's something like that for me, now. I was blind. Now I understand so much more than I ever did before. I understand why you left us."

"Yes?" It was Carney's turn to stare at the floor.

"It was something inside you that wouldn't let you stay. A restlessness. Two people so strong-willed they might have canceled each other out. She was miserable when you left her, but even she knew it was for the best, I think.''

"Believe it or not, you were a strong-headed little bastard, yourself. Genetics. You couldn't help it. Your mother and I were a mistake. Sure, we loved each other. But we shouldn't have been together. We were both just too damned bad tempered. Then you came along, and that made things worse.''

"You do what you have to do.''

"Yeah, I guess that's how it is.'' Carney picked up the cigar, drew on it and found it dead. He placed it back carefully on the plate. "You're going now?''

"Yes.'' Harris took the borrowed parka he had worn in from a hook, pulled it on.

"I'll never see you again, will I?''

Harris didn't answer. He leaned close to his father and, on sudden impulse, kissed the old man on the forehead.

He turned to the door and told it to open, then walked out into the blowing snow.

Song Lan woke with a start. She sat up quickly, searching the small room for her husband, then she rolled out of the bed and began dressing in a panicked frenzy.

She knew where James Harris had gone; she had been certain of what he intended from the moment she had seen the vague doubleness that lived in his eyes. But she did not think he would go so soon and without a word to her. Foolishness, she knew now. Wishful thinking. What drove Harris was larger and more profound than simple love for her.

She was weeping furiously as she drew her boots on.

She ran down the hall from the major's quarters, found the nearest staircase topside, and rushed up it. The room at the top of the stairs, a waiting area of sorts for personnel arriving and departing on the regular service flights, was crowded with desks and chairs and cold-weather gear. And Hugh Carney.

Carney stood as she came into the room. She passed him and snatched down a parka and gloves. When she turned from pulling them on, he stood in front of the doorway, blocking it.

"I can't let you go.''

"Hugh—Father—I don't have any choice. He is my husband. I must be with him.''

"If you go out there, you might not come back.''

"I don't care," she said. She stepped up to face him and he reached for her. The Mind responded and she suppressed it fiercely—she would not hurt him! She relaxed her hold just enough for it to guide her hand to a pressure point under the old man's arm. His legs gave way underneath him and he collapsed down onto the hard, plastic matting of the floor.

He still grappled at her but she pushed his hands away. As she stepped through the door he lay there in a heap, helpless and weeping.

The door closed behind her, shutting off the sound of the old man's grief.

The ice sheet beyond the station was nearly featureless. She ran out beyond the flight line of the western runway and scanned the horizon for as far as she could see. The line between earth and sky was blurred white, the sky a milky overcast of clouds and blowing snow.

Whiteout. That was what the station's pilots called it; they had told her that over the hundred-plus years of the station's existence, more than thirty planes had gone down in the Antarctic because the clear demarcation between sky and land tended to disappear as light diffused by wind-borne ice crystals bounced between the permanent ice pack and the low-hanging clouds. One pilot had described for her the eerie disorientation, as if the plane had flown into a limbo of eternal whiteness.

A spirit-place, she thought, a place for ghosts.

For the first time since she had become a berserker in the tunnels under Tienanmen, she gave the Mind free rein, let it take over her body and senses completely. It studied the terrain around her through her eyes, noted details, unevennesses in the distribution of the wind blown ice crystals beneath her feet, patterns inside the natural patterns.

She set out at a jog trot across the frozen wasteland.

James Harris squatted beside a sharp-edged ridge of ice and watched the whiteout settle in around him like a brilliantly bright fog. Even with his eyes closed, he could still see the misty glow, as if he were trapped inside a fluorescent bulb.

Everything he did now was by intuition, by some vague instinctive sense for what was necessary. He *knew* he would have to come back to the pole. He knew as well that the moment was close when he would have to call the Angel back to him, when the whiteout was complete. He listened to the howl of the wind, muffled by his parka's insulated hood and thought he could almost hear distant voices, thin and indistinct.

The ridge above him was not a natural feature. Five kilometers below the ice, wells had been drilled into the bedrock to get at the oil riches hidden beneath the continent; the ridge was a surface pipeline that had acted over the years like a drift fence, gathering the blowing crystals of ice into a formidable ten-meter-tall ridge of packed snow and ice.

When the time was right he began to climb it.

He had climbed only three meters up the rough slope when he heard the voice again. This time it was closer and clearly human.

He jammed his gloved hand into a crack for support and turned clumsily around to look out across the ice plain. The glare of the ambient light reflected from the ground and sky made his eyes ache, but he could make out a figure in the middle distance, trudging toward him.

A moment later he could make out what the voice was saying. "James," it was shouting. "James!"

Song.

He sighed to himself in exasperation and started back down the slope. As he reached the bottom Song Lan ran up and threw her arms around him. Her face was obscured by the fur edging of her parka's hood, but he could still see the dark anguish in her eyes.

She held him close, trembling.

After a time, she said, "I will not ask you why. I only ask that you come back with me."

"I can't. I can do some good here, now. I *have* to."

"Why must you be the hero?"

"I don't know. I was chosen I guess. Fate, luck. Bad timing. I don't know."

He saw her grimace, as if the words were all too familiar to her. "What will you do?"

He looked up toward the top of the ridge, some ten or perhaps eleven meters over his head. "I need to get up there. After that . . . we'll see."

"James, please . . . I will go with you."

"No."

"Why?"

"No!"

"Tell me why!" she cried. She was beating her fists against him then in a fury of grief and frustration. He weathered the blows, unresisting, until she stopped and fell weeping back into his arms.

"James!" she moaned, the anguish in her voice tearing at his heart.

"I know," he said, "I know."

In the end, she followed him up despite anything he said to her. There was nothing he could do; if he tried to restrain her by tying her up or knocking her unconscious, she might die before someone searching for them might find her. It was a chance he would not take.

And the time was very close.

So he pulled himself up the slope toward the ragged top, acutely aware of her climbing up below him. She was slower than he was, clumsier because of the stiffness of her nearly healed wounds. Her heard her slip once and jerked around, almost losing his own grip on the ice. She had caught herself by one hand, the fingers of her glove bent around a narrow shelf. She stared up at him as he looked back, her face set in an expression of grim determination. Then she pulled herself back up.

He turned back to his own climbing, hurrying to get ahead of her. Five minutes later, he made the top of the ice ridge, then worked his way a few meters farther along to a relatively flat spot on the ridge's crest.

He stood there for a long moment, looking out across the vast emptiness. It was eerie, the reflected brightness, the horizon indiscernible in the blanketing white haze.

Then, quickly, he began to strip off his outer clothing, parka, insulated jumpsuit, and boots. The wind raked across his bare skin like knives and he knew that unprotected he would die in minutes. Already his entire body burned fiercely with the cold. It was summer in the Antarctic, but the difference in degree of coldness mattered little to his naked body.

He cleared his mind, pushed back the physical pain and concentrated on the image that he had been given by the Egg, the searing, expanding fire flaring out from the black face of the void, and *called*.

Almost immediately the white haze of snow and light around him seemed to coalesce into something more tangible. He reached out a hand already numb and unfeeling and groped at it as if trying to tear a piece loose. His mind didn't seem to be working right. He blinked and was suddenly, intimately conscious of the lids sliding slowly across the surface of his eyes.

He felt something touch his hip and he looked down, moving his head with infinite care as if it might shatter if he moved it too suddenly. Song Lan was on her hands and knees beside him, reaching up . . .

He felt the spirit enter him then, and before he could speak or even think of speaking, it possessed him utterly; that part of him that had been *replaced* flowed outward, was *inhaled* into the essence that was the Angel.

The breath of life was drawn out of him and like Elijah he was taken up by the whirlwind.

As she reached up to touch his face she saw it grow suddenly pale and transparent, as if the substance of it were leaching away into the blinding whiteness that surrounded them.

She tried to scream at him, get him to look away from *it*, from whatever possessed him. She gasped in horror as she felt her hand sink into his flesh as if into cotton candy.

Then . . . vertigo.

It was as if she had fallen into a bottomless well of blackness. A ravening depth of air opened up beneath her and she was falling . . . Some part of her mind, a residue of the passive objectivity forced on her as part of her scientific discipline, recognized the experience. Once again, she flew with the Angel.

The belly of the beast. She wondered abstractly if she, too, had dissolved into it or if as before her body remained below and only her mind had been taken up.

The blackness was divided before her in a rush of burning light and color. She felt sundered from herself, lost. Her mind spun with delirium and she wondered for an instant if she were falling forever into madness.

Then she felt a comforting warmness flow through her like a drug. She felt wrapped in a current of something and recognized it as emotion—but tangible, like a blood-warm river in which she floated, held, safe. Loved.

She thought the word *James* and felt him respond. He caressed her in a coruscating flood of warm sparks, as if the river that held her were gentle fire somehow made liquid and calm.

Then came the taste of regret and sorrow. She heard a word, slow and sonorous, as if shouted, echoing, across a great chasm of time and space.

Good-bye, it said.

She opened her eyes on a blank, flat whiteness and the cold wind howled, suddenly loud, in her ears.

She was back. And she was alone.

She squatted on the small patch of flat ice on the crest of the ridge. The sky was clearing; the horizon had reappeared and patches of vivid blue showed through the cloud cover. She started to shake uncontrollably. A feverish delirium took hold of her and she swooned.

Somewhere far away, but growing closer she heard a sound above the whistle of the antarctic wind.

Slap, slap, slap, slap. It boomed across her, suddenly close, and she cringed from it.

She rolled onto her back and stared up into the hard blue of the sky. A helicopter, black and red and impossibly real, soared into her field of vision.

Inside it, though the clear Plexi of its bubble, she saw a man in a white crash helmet wave to her. The helicopter steadied, hovering over her, the blast from its blades whipping loose crystals of ice into a biting whirlwind.

They had come for her. To take her home.

CHAPTER
TWENTY-SEVEN

James Harris dreamed and the dream was a desire that wound its way like a thread through the thing he had called *soul*.

He searched for the limits of his awareness and found none; for a time—minutes? hours? millennia?—infinity occupied his consciousness. He moved, whole unto himself, through the vastness of the cosmos, driven by the single imperative that he had brought with him into this . . . union? Symbiosis? *Existence*. No more or no less than that. Completeness.

He understood, as if from some ancient, fading memory the *word* for what moved him now into the cosmic ether.

The word held within itself the meaning of the place; it was cold, still, distant. It was where he belonged. He would return there, the part of him that was James Harris and the part of him that was not. He would incarnate himself as he had always done, becoming that film of life that rode the thin currents far above, drinking in the golden streams of light—the stuff of his own violent genesis. And when the fusion fires of that sun cooled he would move on.

But never again to that place where pain lived in the multitudinous pinpoints of awareness scattered like stars far below.

He would return to the place of his death and of his resurrection.

The word was *Comfort*. The word was *home*.

ABOUT THE AUTHOR

JOHN M. BLAIR was born in St. Petersburg, Florida, in 1961. He received a Ph.D. in English from Tulane University in 1989 and now teaches at Southwest Texas State University in San Marcos, Texas. He has published articles and poetry in various literary journals and magazines and has been an avid reader of science fiction for over twenty years. *Bright Angel* is his second novel.